Lady of the Play

You have showed a tender fatherly regard
To wish me wed to one half lunatic,
A mad-cap ruffian and a swearing Jack...
—The Taming of the Shrew, Act 2, Scene 1

July 1577
Rocester, Staffordshire

"I shall not, I will not!" Ely stomped into the room she shared with her sisters. "The thought of being in the same room with that detestable man, let alone sharing his bed, was beyond belief." Ely flung herself on the bed next to Kate, her face flushed with fury. "Father called me a disobedient shrew."

"Where is he now?" Dorothy looked toward the door as if expecting their father to come storming in.

"I don't know. He ordered me to my room to think upon the proposal." Ely turned herself over and stared at the ceiling.

What They Are Saying About

Lady of the Play

"A thoroughly enjoyable read and lovely book! I was almost sorry to edit the last page. I was particularly impressed with the literary references and the amount of research that has gone into writing it.

Essentially two storylines in one book, the author has woven them together beautifully. The plot unfolds perfectly, the characters are easily imaginable and well described (and well researched in the historical chapters). The descriptions of clothing, environs and society of the time in the historical chapters were also beautifully crafted, evocative and clearly well-researched.

Generally speaking, this book ticks all the boxes of 'great reads.' I may be biased somewhat as I, too, am an avid Shakespeare fan (I have acted many Shakespearean roles as well) and for sure, other 'Bardolators' (apparently this is now a word for fans of Shakespeare) will love this! Indeed, readers fond of historical or semi-historical novels will enjoy it, too. Please write some more!"

—Ingrid Delle Jacobson, Editor

Lady of the Play

Deena Lindstedt

A Wings ePress, Inc.
Historical Fiction Novel

Wings ePress, Inc.

Edited by: Jeanne Smith
Copy Edited by: Heather O'Connor
Executive Editor: Jeanne Smith
Cover Artist: Trisha FitzGerald-Jung
Woman image by cottonbro from Pexels
Stage image by Mary Bettini Blank from Pixabay

Wings ePress Books
www.wingsepress.com

Copyright © 2021 by: Deena Lindstedt
ISBN 978-1-61309-511-9

Published In the United States Of America

Wings ePress Inc.
3000 N. Rock Road
Newton, KS 67114

Dedication

To: Meg Roland, my Shakespeare professor at Marylhurst University in Portland, Oregon. She was the inspiration for me to begin my research journey into the life of Elizabeth Trentham.

To: Mandy Ellis, of Rocester, Staffordshire. I met Mandy while she was taking flowers into St. Michael Church in Rocester when I was conducting research into Countess Elizabeth Trentham Vere's life. Mandy was kind enough to take me on a tour, telling me the history of the church, the town, and abbey. Several months later, and without being asked, she mailed me articles of the Trentham family written by Roy Burnett, taken from the Uttoxeteradvertiser.CO.UK, as well as copies of Staffordshire Parish Register Society.

To: Dr. Daniel Wright, a professor at Concordia University, who invited me to deliver my paper, "Shakespeare, Perhaps a Woman," at the 11th Annual Shakespeare Authorship Studies Conference. Through networking at the conference, I was able to learn of the shake-spear clue in KJV of Psalms 46 and Elizabeth Trentham's will in which she bequeathed money to her "dumb" man.

These are the events which led me to begin writing my novel, Lady of the Play.

***

Prologue

Coincidence is a word we all use to explain the inexplicable, a happenstance event you soon forget as you go on with your life. But when coincidences start piling up, you come to believe that something more is happening—indeed, you begin to believe you're receiving guidance from 'out there.' Perhaps coincidence is too commonplace to explain what happened. Was it a predestined chain of events put into place over four hundred years ago?

One

It was nearly six when I let myself into the house. Tossing my raincoat and purse onto the sofa, I flipped through the mail. An envelope with a Hot Springs, Arkansas return address, and tiny blue roses decorated along one edge caught my eye. Thinking it was a bereavement letter from someone my mother knew, I ran my fingernail under the flap, pulled it open and slid out a letter edged with the same blue rose stationery. The handwriting was a bit wobbly.

Dear Ms. Parsons,

I am writing this letter to ask for your help in a research project I hope to begin shortly. It concerns an article you wrote in Marylhurst University's literary review several years ago titled "Shakespeare, Perhaps a Woman."

I have found something I know would be of interest to you concerning the same subject. I hesitate to tell you too much in this letter, but it is important you call me so I may explain. You will be both surprised and delighted. My phone number is 501-554-1332.

This is a matter of much urgency. I am more than willing to pay for your time and travel expenses to Hot Springs.

My nephew Clayton Darnell is a Portland attorney. His secretary, Jenna Brooks, helped me locate you. Feel free to call either of them to vouch for me. Please call as soon as possible.

Yours Sincerely,
Sudie McFadden

Stunned, I reread the letter. What in the world could she have found? And to contact me based on an essay I wrote when I was still in college? I considered calling the attorney, but looking at my watch I saw it was after office hours. Okay, nothing ventured, nothing gained. I retrieved my mobile phone from my purse and keyed in the phone number. While the phone was ringing, I sat and looked around my mother's home. Cardboard boxes cluttered the living room, ready for the moving van next week.

"McFadden residence."

"May I speak to Sudie McFadden, please?"

"It's for you, Aunt Sudie. Sounds like a Yankee." The woman's voice had a heavy Southern accent.

"Hello?"

"Ms. McFadden, this is Cynthia Parsons. I just received your letter and—"

"Oh, Miss Parsons. I've been waiting on pins and needles until you called. Would you mind holding? I have guests and they were just leaving. I'll be right back."

I could hear voices, then a door closing. "Thanks for holding. I didn't want to talk with others listening in."

"No problem. You certainly have raised my curiosity. What did you find?"

"I'm not really sure, but I think—no, I'm positive it is an original page from Shakespeare's *A Midsummer Night's Dream*."

"What?" She must be mistaken... "I hate to disappoint you, but are you aware no original Shakespeare writings have ever been found?"

"I know that—but you need to see this. It looks like a draft of the play. It mentions Lysander and Helena. Are you familiar?"

"Yes, I'm a big fan."

"It's a passage that takes place in the woods. Puck, the fairy, has put drops in Lysander's eyes and..."

"Yes, yes. I remember how the couples get mixed up and..."

"That's right. The page is so fragile, it nearly broke off in my hand. I have it enclosed in plastic now."

"That's absolutely amazing. But to know for sure, you'll need it tested to see if it dates back to the sixteenth century, unless you've already had that done."

"I know, and I will. But it's something I want my nephew to arrange. I mentioned him in the letter. He's a Portland attorney."

"Have you told him of the page?"

"I considered calling him right away, but decided to wait a bit." She cleared her throat. "I think he'd want to make it public, and I don't want to—not yet." That would be logical, I thought, but before I said so, she continued. "Anyway, he's very busy now with a big trial. I've given this a lot of thought, and have decided I'd like you to help me prove a woman could have written the page."

"What makes you think it was written by a woman?"

"Because it was inside the cover of a book of prayers that belonged to an ancestor of mine, Lady Katharine Stanhope."

Thinking that didn't mean it was written by her, I asked, "Where and when did you find it?"

"About two weeks ago. I was in my attic looking through an old steamer trunk for a picture. I picked up an *Anglican Book of Prayers* that's been in my family for generations. The leather binding had become so flimsy, a piece of paper covered in handwriting fell out. It had been sandwiched in the cover."

"Then what did you do?"

"Well, I had trouble deciphering it. The writing is very dim in places and it was written in the old style of English—what we'd consider misspelling now."

"Yes, Early Modern English came about in the 1500s. Writing of that period could be a mix of Middle English with New Modern. You have the right era." I paused for a few seconds. "I would very much like to see what you've found. If it is an original writing of Shakespeare's, it could make you famous, and rich, too."

"The last thing I want is publicity, and the money is not important. And please keep this confidential. I'm fearful this could leak out to the press before I'm ready to release it."

"Yes, I agree. You must be careful." I switched the phone to my other ear.

"You mentioned a project. What did you have in mind?"

"As I said, the book had Lady Katherine Stanhope's signature. I believe she was a great, great, many times over, grandmother of mine. If she hid the page in the cover of her book, she may have actually written the play. It makes sense she would want to leave evidence that she was the author. It's something I would do, anyway."

I grinned, happy that she couldn't see my skepticism. "Did you happen to Google her name?"

"If you mean on the internet, then no. I have a computer, but I mainly use it to check my email."

"Don't worry about it. I'll do it." I pulled a small tablet from my purse and scribbled her name. "Just so you know, finding anything about her will be a difficult undertaking. When I was researching my article, I tried to find a woman of the sixteenth century with the right qualifications to write plays. I gave up, since so little was written by, or of women four-hundred years ago. You probably already know girls of that era were not allowed to attend school."

"Yes, I know. However, it would bring me a great deal of pleasure to prove a long-ago grandmother of mine could have been Shakespeare—anyway, I'd like to try. I also know I need help from a historian."

I'm a history teacher, not a historian, but didn't correct her. "Let me ask what you have in mind with your project. Do you want to prove Lady Stanhope wrote this play, or that she was in fact Shakespeare?"

"Both actually, but I'd settle for just the play."

"Wow." I looked around the room, thinking how difficult it would be to leave right now. "Would it be possible for you to come to Oregon instead of me flying to Arkansas?"

"I'd love to, since I'm originally from Oregon, and my nephew lives in Portland," she said, "but my doctor has forbidden me to travel. I'm eighty-eight, with a bad heart. Like I mentioned, I'm more than willing to pay you..."

"I appreciate the offer, but I don't feel right about that. After I see what you have found, we can discuss how we go forward. But my leaving for Arkansas right now is a problem. My mother recently passed away and I've been handling the sale of her house here in St. Helens. The movers are due to arrive next week." Thinking about my cousin who still lived in St. Helens, I continued, "Maybe I can work something out."

"That would be so wonderful," she said.

"Tell you what. I'll make a couple of phone calls and call you back tomorrow, if that's okay."

After I hung up, I called my cousin and asked if she'd mind supervising the movers next Tuesday. Not wanting to give her the reason for a trip to Arkansas, I padded the truth by simply saying I had a research job offer. "The mover is bringing a portable container. for me to keep Mom's furnishings in storage until I find a permanent home in Portland." She offered to come on Saturday to help me finish packing, too. I happily accepted.

I then called my realtor, gave her the same story and asked if she would arrange for someone to clean the house after the movers were finished. "Also, when I return, I'll need a temporary place to stay while looking for a condo to buy. Can you recommend somewhere nice?"

"Yes, I think I can. When will you return?"

"I'll be gone at least a week. I'll call and give you an exact date."

"You still need to close with escrow, but I can set that up after you return." With that done, I decided I could make reservations to fly out on Sunday.

That night, I couldn't get my mind off my conversation with Sudie. To prove her long-ago grandmother was the playwright would be a colossal undertaking. That thought really set my mind whirling, thinking about the whimsical play. I wonder if the play could have been based on a dream?

Two

There sleeps Titania sometime of the night,
Lulled in these flowers with dances and delight.
And there the snake throws her enameled skin,
Weed wide enough to wrap a fairy in.
—*A Midsummer Night's Dream*, Act 2, Scene 1

June 21, 1570
Rocester, Staffordshire, England

The Trentham girls had been in the fields for most of the afternoon, searching for the five plants their mother wanted to hang on their doors. Ten-year-old Elizabeth's basket contained wild roses, St. John's wort, trefoil, and vervain, but they still hadn't found the yellow rue that grew close to the ground. Mounds of cut hay lay baking in the fields with a few scattered cows grazing among the lush grass. The sun felt warm on Elizabeth's back as she plowed through the reeds that grew along the banks of the River Dove. Spotting the elusive blossoms, Elizabeth called back to her sisters.

"I found the rue!" The girls ran to the riverside to join her as she cut several stems from the low-growing plant and put them in her basket. "Here, let me put a sprig in your hair. It will ward off the pixies," she told her six-year-old sister, Katherine.

"But what would they do if I didn't have it?" she asked as she fiddled with the blossoms in her hair.

"They would surely lead you astray—perchance you would never return to our home." Katherine looked wide-eyed at her big sister.

"Master Anton told me there are no such things as pixies," Dorothy, now eight, said as she pushed one of the sprigs into her own pocket. "Only fairies, I think."

"If that were true, why would Mother be having us search for plants to ward off evil spirits?" Elizabeth took Katherine's hand when the little girl tripped over a rock. They chattered on their walk back to the manor, looking forward to the Midsummer Eve festival on the hill tonight. Food had been prepared over the past two days for the feast on the morrow.

Elizabeth took special note of a thicket of ferns as they walked across a small circular clearing surrounded by beech and oak trees. She remembered their nanny Mary's story of how to see the fairies. Looking around the clearing, she thought perchance this circle of trees could be just as magical as the circle of huge stones that stood on the faraway hillside. An evergreen tree with a wide, gnarled trunk stood apart from the other trees. She identified it as an ancient yew, known to have mysterious properties. Thinking she should cut off a bough to add to her basket, her stomach emitted a large growl that changed her mind. It was nearly time for their meal.

~ * ~

That evening, after the bonfires were lit, the women and children sat together on a grassy hillside and watched as nimble men jumped through the fires, a ritual used to assure crops would grow as tall as the men could jump. The marching watch-folk wore garlands around their necks and carried lanterns atop poles as they wandered from fire to fire.

The girls' mother, Jane Trentham, told of her childhood in Chester where she had seen Morris dancers dressed as dragons and unicorns. "Did you know the fires will cause snakes to roll themselves into a hissing ball in order to create the serpent's egg?" she said. "And anyone who finds the glass bubble will achieve magical powers." The women in the group regaled each other with their own stories of the wonders that could happen on a night such as this.

Long after the women and girls had returned to the manor, Elizabeth lay in bed with her two sisters, telling them a fairy story. When she was sure they were asleep, she crept out of bed. Still in her nightdress, she slipped on her shoes and tiptoed down the stairs. She took a sprig of rue from the arrangement hanging on the door, poked it into her thick hair, and left the manor.

The full moon was high in the sky, allowing her to see where she was going. She looked back to make sure all the candles were out at the manor. An owl hooted, causing her heart to beat faster. She walked across the meadow toward the circle of trees. Entering the wood, she saw the thicket of ferns in the center of the clearing. She lay down in the grass and straightened the long gown over her slim body.

She thought of the circle of huge upright stones on the faraway hillside. She had always desired to visit the stones on Midsummer's Eve, because it was said whoever slept in the center of the stones and was awake at sunrise would become a bard. She loved reading King David's Psalms in the Bible, which gave her a love for poetry. She so wished to have his same talent when she grew up, but she was far too fearful and not brave enough to venture into the mysterious stones, especially after dark.

Please dear God, have this circle of trees be as blessed as the stones on the hill and give me the talent to write as you did for King David. She thought about praying she'd see the fairies too, but then thought perhaps she would be asking God for too much. She would take her chances.

When the moon was directly overhead, she turned on her side and, as Mary had instructed, pulled a fern toward her, scraping the black spores from its underside with her fingernail and into the palm of her hand. She closed her eyes and rubbed the spores onto her eyelids. Believing she needed to wait a few minutes to have the best effect, she breathed in deeply. A bullfrog's croaking, along with the buzzing of insects, lured her to sleep.

Hearing voices, she turned onto her stomach and cupped her chin into her hands. She peeked through the grass and saw two fairies flutter over a bush and land on a large boulder nearby. In their wake, several other fairies scattered about the clearing. The fairies were not tiny, as she had imagined—they were nearly as tall as her baby brother Tommy, but much slighter. Their tiny, double wings were delicate, almost transparent.

She listened intently to the conversation of the two on the rock. Crowns on their heads twinkled in the moonlight. They were arguing.

"Am I not thy lord?" the king said. "You are disobedient to my wishes. I order you to rid yourself of the changeling."

"Aye, thou art my lord," the queen answered. "Nevertheless, thou know'st the mother has died, leaving the boy in my care. He is mine and will serve me well."

"You will be rid of him, as I command." The king raised his wings in agitation and flew off toward a tree in the distance. The queen seemed to dissolve before Elizabeth's eyes.

Laughter came from a small fairy sitting on a branch of a tree. Elizabeth knew he must be mischievous because he had the same face as their cook's son. His name was Robin, but everyone called him Puck.

Her dream began to show her terrifying sights of pixies digging a grave and three witches stirring a cauldron. She patted her head, relieved to find the sprig of rue was still in her hair. She silently prayed the magical properties of the plant would ward off their evil intent. The witches and pixies vanished when a white unicorn with a flowing silver mane and tail trotted into the clearing. Puck darted from the tree and onto the animal's back. The unicorn reared and began to gallop toward the river with Puck giggling his enjoyment and bouncing upon its back.

For several more minutes, Elizabeth watched the festival of the fairies as they played their games. She wanted to join them as they fluttered between each bush. Try as she might to rise, she instead fell back into a dreamless sleep.

Something brushed her cheek. Opening her eyes, she saw it was Puck. He held a feather in his hand. "Wake up, mistress, 'tis nearly sunrise." Sitting up quickly, she rubbed her eyes. Squirming around, she searched for him, but he had vanished.

The sunshine flickering through the ancient yew and onto each dew-soaked needle set the tree ablaze with thousands of tiny lights. Anyone watching would have seen her red-gold hair aglow as if it were on fire. She sat in awe, beholding the crystalline yew and knowing the circle of trees was more sacred than the circle of stones on the distant hill, and she had been awake to see the sunrise.

"I have had a vision most rare," she said, "surely the most magical of all midsummer nights."

Three

Next morning, I woke up early, happy it was my last day to substitute teach at a local high school. I quickly showered, put on my brown plaid wool skirt and ivory top. Brown boots on, then a wool jacket, as the temperature had dropped into the high thirties. While I drank my first cup of coffee for the day and munched on raisin toast, my cell phone rang its familiar Beatles' tune. "Hi, Josie."

"Good morning, Cynthia. Did I call at a bad time?"

"No, just finishing breakfast. What's going on?"

"Nothing, really. Frank's going to be out tonight and I thought I'd try to talk you into having dinner with me this evening."

"Wow, Josie. I'd love to, but not sure... I'm leaving town on Sunday and there's still a lot to do before I leave."

"Where are you going?"

"Hot Springs, Arkansas."

"You're kidding. What's in Arkansas?"

"You won't believe it. I got this letter from an elderly woman..." I went on to tell her about the letter and briefly of my conversation. I looked at my watch and realized I needed to leave. "Tell you what, I'll drive to your place after school and tell you all about it."

On the drive to the school, I thought of my relationship with Josephine Jenson. Having finished my undergraduate work at Marylhurst University, I'd been taking graduate courses at Portland State University during my first year as a teacher at Lincoln High School. Josie was about eleven years younger than I and an assistant librarian at the university. Notwithstanding the age difference, we became good friends. Twelve years later, she's thirty-six and the head librarian. Josie has a live-in partner, Frank Hacker, who is a chemistry professor. He's a terrible flirt and I don't care for the man, or even like to be around him. Since he wouldn't be there, it was easy to accept her invitation.

I managed to make flight and hotel reservations during my lunch break, and then called Sudie and told her of my plans. She wanted me to stay with her, but I declined. I wouldn't feel comfortable staying with someone I hadn't yet met.

It was just after six when I pulled into Josie's driveway. The light from the porch reflected on an overgrown rhododendron bush near the wide steps that led into her two-story house. The house was familiar to me, since I had rented a room from her before moving back to St. Helens to care for my mom. That was about a year ago, when my mother was fighting a losing battle with colon cancer. Frank moved in right after I left. Josie opened the door before I could ring the bell.

"Come on in. Thanks for driving on such a miserable night."

"No problem." We stood in a small foyer as she helped me shrug out of my damp raincoat. She hung it on a coatrack as I entered the living room. The room was the same, except for the wide-screen television in the corner. A fire blazed in a white fireplace now stained yellow with age. Besides a matching sofa and chair, a bookcase overflowed with hardbound books.

"Where's Frank?"

"He's in Vancouver. He goes there every Friday to play poker."

"A friend's house?"

"No. It's a bar with a back room. High stakes game—hope he's lucky for a change."

She offered me a glass of wine, but I declined, opting to wait until we ate. I sat on her super-soft sofa, with Josie in a wingback chair. After she read Sudie's letter, I gave her the details of my conversation.

"This is unreal. My God. Wait till Frank hears about this."

"Hold on. She said no publicity. It would be tragic if this leaked out before she was ready."

"But he's my partner."

"Let me think about it." I struggled to stand. I held out my hand and she pulled me up. "Thanks." I put my arm about her shoulders and gave them a quick squeeze. At five-eight, I felt like a giant standing next to her, since she's barely over five foot. "I'm suddenly starved."

"It's ready," she said.

We walked through her dining room and into the large kitchen. Her blonde hair had been pulled into a ponytail and she had changed from her professional clothes to gray jeans with an oversized pink shirt. I still had on the same clothes from this morning.

Ceramic soup bowls, plates and wineglasses were set on a small table underneath a window. A plastic-wrapped plate of sandwiches was on the counter next to a slow cooker filled with chicken tortilla soup. The wonderful aroma made my mouth water.

"Sit down, Cynthia. I bet you're anxious to see the page."

"Absolutely." I unwrapped the plastic from the sandwiches. They were chicken salad with dried cranberries and slivered almonds. "Yum." I put the plate on the table. She retrieved an open bottle of rosé wine from the refrigerator and filled our glasses.

"Let's toast Sudie and Shakespeare."

"Hear, hear!" We clinked our glasses. "What a weird and wonderful coincidence she remembered reading my article."

"Isn't that the truth? I'd love to read it, too. Your theory that

Shakespeare could be a woman is a fascinating subject." Josie stirred the soup.

"It's in storage now, but I'll try to remember to give it to you." I helped myself to one of the chicken salad sandwiches. "It'll be a nice break to go somewhere different." My mouth was full after taking a healthy bite.

"You've decided to go, then?" she asked.

"By all means! My funds are limited, though. I won't close on the house until I get back."

"She did offer to pay your way." Josie ladled soup into our bowls.

"I didn't feel right about accepting money for something I could benefit from, too...that is, if it truly is an original..."

"I understand." She passed me a bowl of corn chips and I sprinkled a few on my soup. "So, what do you think she wants from you?"

"To help her prove her ancestor wrote *A Midsummer Night's Dream*."

"To do that, you'd have to prove she was Shakespeare, don't you think?"

"I mentioned that to her." We stopped talking while we ate. I wiped my mouth and looked at her. "We're thinking the same thing, aren't we?"

"Yeah, I guess so." She laughed. "What an undertaking. Can you imagine the research that would need to be done? You'd be required to search archives in England to find proof of her grandmother's existence, let alone find out if she was smart...or educated enough to write like Shakespeare."

"You're a better researcher than me, Josie. I mean, you're a college librarian and have access to so much..." I helped myself to another sandwich.

"Cynthia! I was hoping you'd ask. I know the UK has been downloading some of their archives on the internet. We can at least start with Lady Katherine Stanhope."

"We'll need Katherine's husband's first name, and if he was a knight, or royalty maybe. Also, her maiden name."

"This is going to be so much fun. I'll start researching tomorrow," she said. We continued to eat, both of us deep in thought.

I finished and took another sip of wine. "I've been thinking about the *Midsummer* play. Have you ever seen the 1930s movie? Mickey Rooney played Puck. He was wonderful, and only a little boy at the time. Some say it's the best movie of *Midsummer Night's Dream* ever made."

"I don't remember if I ever saw it. I'll have to check it out," she said.

Josie and I were sharing cleanup duties when we heard the front door open and close.

"That's Frank. Don't mention anything about where he was tonight. He's sensitive about anyone knowing he gambles," Josie whispered.

"Hello, Cynthia. I didn't know you were coming or I would've stayed home." I could see why Josie would be attracted to him. He had the swarthy good looks of an aging rock star—longish salt and pepper hair, a closely cut beard and mustache. His build was husky, but he was not much taller than me. He wore black slacks, a light blue shirt open at the collar, and a herringbone gray blazer.

"It was kind of spur of the moment," I said, looking toward Josie.

"I was sorry to hear about your mom," Frank said.

"Thanks. I should be heading home. I still have so much to do since her death."

"We just finished eating. Are you hungry? Lots of soup left," Josie said, giving Frank a hug.

"Had dinner at the club." He removed Josie's arms from around his waist. "Maybe later." He picked up the half-bottle of wine. "Don't be in a hurry to leave. It's early yet." He looked at the label. "You two drinking this camel piss? Why didn't you serve her decent wine?"

"Because she knows it's my favorite," I snapped back. It wasn't, but that was no reason to criticize her. He proceeded to take a bottle of liquor from a cupboard, filled a cocktail glass, and dropped in some ice cubes from the freezer.

"This is my favorite. Johnnie Walker Black." He held it up before taking a sip. He leaned against the refrigerator, acting like the lord of the manor.

"Yes, stay a bit longer. It's only eight." Josie seemed almost panicky, and I wondered if she was afraid of the man. She gazed at me intently, trying to send a silent message, but I couldn't read her. She shifted her gaze toward Frank. "You'll never guess what happened to Cynthia. She…"

"Hold on, Josie," I said. "I thought we agreed to keep this between us."

"No, we didn't…did we?" It was obvious she wanted Frank to know, and was going to tell him after I left anyway, so I just as well could tell him myself.

"You two are typical females. Why not just blurt it out? I'm interested in…whatever concerns you, Cynthia."

There's that look again. I bet he thinks his smile is seductive. Well, it isn't. It's disgusting. He's supposed to be in love with Josie. Why can't she figure him out? Then I knew; it's called being thirty-something with few prospects. I'm forty-seven, divorced for twenty years and never have found another man.

"Before I tell you anything, you both must promise you won't say a word about this to anyone. Agreed?"

"Absolutely," Josie said, looking at Frank.

"Of course we agree." He smiled and took another drink of scotch. "Tell me."

"Well, okay then. I received an odd letter from an elderly woman in Arkansas. She found a page she thinks was written by Shakespeare."

"I doubt that," Frank said.

"She believes it…we do too, don't we, Cynthia?" Josie grabbed Frank's arm. "She actually found an original handwritten page from *A Midsummer Night's Dream!*"

He jerked away. "You're stupid. No one has ever…"

"No, she isn't stupid. Josie is the most brilliant woman I know, and I don't appreciate your saying otherwise." Damn, he makes me mad.

He seemed a bit shocked at my outburst, then put his arm around Josie's shoulders. "I'm sorry, Josie. I shouldn't have said that. What makes her think it's an original?" Frank sat down and she joined him at the table.

"I'll explain," Josie said. She then gave him the details on how and where Sudie found the page. "Sudie said the original owner of the book of prayers was Lady Katherine Stanhope, and it was she who probably hid the page in the cover of the book. I'm going to research her name. She wants Cynthia to help her find proof she is..."

Frank started to interrupt, but I waved him off. "Right after she found the page, she remembered reading an essay I wrote when I was still an undergraduate. It was about my theory that Shakespeare could have been a woman. My professor had it published in Marylhurst's literary review."

He didn't seem to be listening to me when he said, "An original Shakespeare writing? Such a discovery would be invaluable; if true... it could be worth a fortune." Frank's face became animated. "The page will need to be tested to make sure it's four hundred years old. I can use the lab at the university, both on the paper and ink." He said it like it was a foregone conclusion. I needed to stem his tide of enthusiasm.

"Wait just a minute. First, the page does not belong to me. Second, Sudie may have already arranged for testing." I knew differently, but sure didn't want him to know. "She was adamant her find must be kept secret until we finish our work. I was trying to do that." I looked at Josie and she did appear shamefaced, but there was no reaction from Frank. "If this should leak to the press prematurely, it would be devastating for that poor woman." I turned toward Frank. "Promise me you won't say a word to anyone."

"I've already agreed to keep it quiet, but you must keep us in the loop. And if there is anything I can do to help, let me know at once."

"I'm thrilled to help with the research," Josie said. "What if Sudie's grandmother really was Shakespeare?"

"Hold on, you two. She wants you to prove a woman wrote the page?" He scoffed. "That's impossible. Everyone knows girls four hundred years ago couldn't even attend school, let alone have the intellect to be Shakespeare. The page was probably written by the man himself. Why it was hidden is anyone's guess. At any rate, she should just make it public." He stood and confronted me directly. "You'll be barking up the wrong tree, Cynthia, trying to find proof a woman...! What a waste of time. It's just feminist wishful thinking."

"It isn't a waste of time. I learned girls in wealthy families were often tutored along with their brothers. Besides, we won't know till we try. Isn't that right, Josie?" She nodded vigorously. "I really need to leave now." I headed toward the living room with them following on my heels. Josie was telling Frank about the research she planned to do. I shrugged into my coat and turned around.

"Just remember, I'm counting on you to keep this, whatever it is, between us," I said, trying to ignore Frank and his huge smile. "I'll be really angry if this should leak out to anyone. Is that understood, Frank?"

"Yeah, yeah, sure. Don't worry." He tried to hug me, but I pushed him off and opened the door.

On the drive home, I thought of Josie, and her relationship with Frank. *It's obvious he is only using her—and him living in her house like it was his own. I bet he doesn't even pay rent. And why wouldn't he want it known he plays poker? That's no big deal, unless...Maybe he's in deep. I'll have to have a serious talk with Josie when I get back.*

Four

Our remedies oft in ourselves do lie...
      —*All's Well That Ends Well*, Act 1, Scene 1

June 1572
Rocester, Staffordshire

"Wake up," Dorothy said, shaking her sister's shoulder.

"Go away." Elizabeth rolled over in bed.

"Mother said to get up. She is having us take classes with Master Anton today. She said she cannot abide having us underfoot."

Elizabeth stretched and shielded her eyes from the sun that streamed through the only window in the room. It was another beautiful midsummer day, two years after the momentous morning when she had witnessed the sunrise through the crystal tree. Dorothy's perpetual whining grated on her nerves.

"Mother said to get up—now!" Dorothy pulled on the covers.

Elizabeth, having celebrated her twelfth birthday a fortnight ago, and welcoming the body changes that came with it, felt too mature to be told what to do, especially by her younger sister. She flopped over in bed.

"I am certain Mother would not expect me to take schooling."

"Yes, she does. She told me." Dorothy stamped her foot.

"Oh, fie." Elizabeth sat up and rubbed her eyes. "Did the guests from Chester arrive?"

"Yes, and they are all talking about the performance today."

"The festival? Oh, I had nearly forgotten." Elizabeth sat up in the bed she shared with her sisters. Their father had arranged for a traveling troupe of acrobats and actors to perform to help celebrate Midsummer's Day in Rocester. The players had arrived three days earlier, much to the excitement of all the village folk. No one in Rocester had ever seen a stage performance, and they didn't know quite what to expect when they saw workmen nail a platform together for a stage. A poster had been tacked to the tavern door for those who could read: *The Play of the Wether, a New and Mery Interlude of All Maner of Wethers*. The play was still popular forty years after its publication, when the playwright and poet, John Heywood, had presented it before King Henry VIII.

"Grandfather Sneyd, Great-aunt Dorothy Sneyd, and Uncle Ralph are all here," Dorothy said. "The men are breaking fast with Father, but we are being sent to our tutor this morning." Dorothy's pouty face put Elizabeth in mind of their brother Francis' bulldog.

After a quick breakfast of porridge, the oldest Trentham children—Elizabeth, Francis, Dorothy, and Katherine—tromped up the stone steps to the tower room. Three-year-old Tommy was confined to the nursery under the capable watch of his nanny.

Anton Regiers looked up from his tall desk as the children clomped into the tower room. "I know you do not relish the thought of school on a holiday. Instead, we shall discuss the background of what you will see in the play today." After the children were seated, he described how the play had been based on a myth wherein chaos and confusion resulted when Jupiter tried to please everyone with the weather they desired. He held them spellbound for the first twenty minutes, until they began to squirm. Elizabeth raised her hand.

"Master Anton, pray may I be excused to finish the assignment you gave me yesterday?" Elizabeth had been given the task of translating a passage from the second book of Sir Thomas More's *Utopia* from Latin to French, an assignment he usually gave to students as a punishment. Elizabeth, however, relished any assignment that gave her an opportunity to learn a new language. Regiers was impressed with her scholastic development. He called her his Bethlehem Star because she was brighter than any student he had ever taught. She could not only speak Latin fluently, but had also nearly mastered Greek and French, Regiers' native tongue. She wanted to learn Spanish and Italian, too. Mayhap someday.

"Surely, Mistress Elizabeth, you will want to hear the rest of the play and how it relates to both Greek and Roman mythology?"

"Yes, sir."

Regiers continued his lecture for several more minutes, until Dorothy interrupted.

"Prithee, Master Anton, when may we take our leave? I am certain any minute the players will begin." Dorothy squirmed on her stool, her face and pinafore stained with dirt and strawberry juice from raiding her mother's private garden before breakfast.

Francis boxed her ears. "Be quiet, you scurvy pig! Do not speak without permission." Since returning from Chester, he boasted the superior attitude of being his father's privileged heir. He had been rooming at his grandfather's home while he attended grammar school.

"Do not speak to your sister in such a manner. You are not Lord of the Manor yet." Redheaded and with a temper to match, Elizabeth stood a foot taller than her brother. She pushed him with such force that he toppled from the bench they shared. He stood, grabbed her by the hair, and pulled her to the floor. Adding to the melee, Dorothy jumped on Francis and began to pummel his back. Katherine, not to be outdone, joined the fray by setting her teeth solidly into Francis' leg. He screamed, turning his wrath on his little sister.

Anton Regiers was small but wiry. "Halt!" He grabbed Francis by the shirt and pulled him upright. "Elizabeth, comport yourself like a lady." Her petticoats and pantaloons flew into view as she kicked her legs, struggling to right herself. "If you cannot behave yourselves, no one will see the play." Francis forgot about his throbbing leg and quickly sat on the bench. Elizabeth joined him post-haste.

"We beg your pardon, Master Anton," Elizabeth said. "Francis must learn to respect his sisters." She tugged at a sleeve that had become undone in the struggle.

"You may leave to repair your garment." Knowing he had lost all semblance of control, and anxious to see the play himself, he walked to the window of the tower, where he had a commanding view of the countryside. "It appears the crowd around the well grows larger. You may all take your leave, but wait for your mother to grant you..." He looked back and found himself talking to an empty room as the children noisily raced down the stairway.

Elizabeth hauled herself up short when she saw her great-aunt, Dorothy Sneyd, near the library door. "Elizabeth, please, come here. I want to wish you a belated happy birthday and give you a gift."

"Thank you, Aunt." Elizabeth followed her into the room, excited at the prospect. "I must tend to this," she said as she held up the sleeve that had slid down to her elbow.

"Let me see." Her aunt pulled at the sleeve. "'Tis only untied." She tied it more securely. "There. You are put back together." She patted Elizabeth's back.

"Thank you, Aunt."

"This is from your godmother." She handed her a leather penner. Elizabeth gasped with pleasure when she opened the lid. Inside were sheaves of paper, two fine goose quills, ink and pounce pots, wax for sealing, and a penknife to sharpen the quills.

"How wonderful!" She picked up a quill and rubbed the feather against her cheek. Putting it back in the box, she removed the pounce pot and shook out a tiny bit of drying powder into her hand. "I shall always treasure it. But why, Aunt? The queen has never sent me a gift. I thought she would have forgotten she is my godmother."

"The queen has not forgotten you." She put her arm around Elizabeth's shoulders. "Were you ever told I was a lady-in-waiting to Catherine Parr when she was married to King Henry the Eighth?"

"Now I remember. You knew Queen Elizabeth when she was a girl."

"Yes, I knew her well. I loved her as you love your younger sisters." Her aunt took the penner from Elizabeth's hands and put it on a small table. "However, that is not the reason the queen agreed to be your godmother."

"Yes, I would like to know for sure. I am but a country squire's daughter."

Dorothy looked into Elizabeth's eyes, and it seemed Elizabeth was finally to have the answer that had perplexed her since she was a small child. Why her?

"Did your mother tell you the story?"

"She told me Grandfather Sneyd paid a ransom so his first grandchild could have the honor of being one of the queen's goddaughters. Is that not true?"

Worry lines appeared between her aunt's eyes. "You must not ever doubt your mother." The disappointment in Dorothy's eyes was not unnoticed by Elizabeth. Then she smiled and added, "I did write to the queen and told her of your scholastic achievement and your passion for writing verse. I am certain that is the reason she selected this gift."

Elizabeth was wise enough not to question her aunt further, hoping someday she would have a complete explanation. "I must write and give her my thanks."

"That would be appropriate. I am sure she would be pleased to receive a letter from you." Dorothy sat in a chair. "Perhaps you would want to serve the queen as a lady-in-waiting when you are older."

"Lady-in-waiting?" Elizabeth walked to the fireplace and turned around. "I have never thought on the matter. Would she accept me?"

"I have no doubt she would, providing your father approves. However, methinks he would prefer to see you settled in a good marriage." The older woman looked down and brushed at a small wrinkle in her skirt. "You are still too young to discuss such matters." The conversation was interrupted with the noise of the children. Someone knocked at the door.

"Enter," Dorothy said.

"Elizabeth, we are to leave. Come." Katherine stood first on one foot, then the other in her excitement to get underway.

"You run ahead," she said. "I will walk with Great-aunt Dorothy."

~ * ~

After the play ended, the children sauntered down the dusty path toward home. They passed St. Michael's church and went across the field to the reconstructed abbey, now the manor house. Francis cavorted ahead, re-enacting the jumping maneuvers of the fool in the play. The girls laughed uproariously with the memory of the bewildered players when it had "rained," soaking their costumes from a water contrivance behind the stage.

"Such a pity Diana's beautiful long hair became snarled and wet," Dorothy said, turning to her older sister. "When my hair is longer, I will sit upon it."

"It was a wig, you airling," Francis said, re-joining his sisters. "'Twas a lad who played the part."

"Certainly not!" cried Dorothy.

"Now who's the airling?" Elizabeth piped up. "Surely a mistress."

"Father!" Francis ran back to their father, who was strolling with his father-in-law, Sir William Sneyd, and William's son, Ralph Sneyd. "Pray tell these proud mistresses that the players were all men."

Elizabeth, Dorothy, and Katherine waited for the men to catch up. They were dressed similarly in dark clothing, white ruffled collars, worsted doublets with puffed sleeves, black cotton leggings, and ankle boots.

"Yes, 'tis true. Only men or boys perform on stage."

"But why, sir? It would be amazing to be an actor," Elizabeth said. "And the stories I could spin for them—they would surely cast a spell on all who chanced to see them!"

During the summer months when Elizabeth was not at her studies, one could find her near the riverside, the tall grass and wildflowers providing a nest while she composed music on her lute or created stories. The family's evening entertainment often centered on Elizabeth when she read one of her new poems, played a tune she had composed, or acted out all the parts of a play. Her wit was sharp, her humor keen, and her ear in tune to the variations of language. She was much in demand by her family and friends to tell stories, using visiting travelers and townsfolk as characters for her dramas.

Her father drew next to his eldest, his voice firm. "Mistress Elizabeth, it is one thing to perform for your family and quite another to do so for strangers. Learn this and learn it well. Your mother has told you repeatedly it is unseemly for a woman to bring attention to herself or value it overmuch. You are fortunate to have a tutor. I will hear no more of it. Hasten to your mother and tell her you have not learned her wise teaching." Francis' smug look infuriated Elizabeth as he took on the same arrogant posture as his father.

"Why cannot a girl ever be the equal to her brothers?" Elizabeth whispered to her sisters as they hurried back down the path looking for their mother. Jane was walking with Tommy and the other women. "By my faith, I will slip away and join a traveling troupe of players, even if I have to disguise myself as a boy."

"You darest not!" piped up Dorothy.

"You most of all know what I dare." Elizabeth kicked at a clump of dirt; it disintegrated, blowing dust back at their feet. "If only boys are to receive honor, perchance I shall become a boy and in so doing will be treated as such. From now on, you are to call me Ely and give me the same honor as Francis. Do you understand?" Dorothy and Katherine stopped to stare open-mouthed at their determined sister.

"But we don't honor Francis," Dorothy said. "He is only a brother."

"Someday, when he is a man, and inherits all this," Elizabeth said, swinging her arms wide, "and if you want to continue to live here, you would be little more than a servant." Her face turned rosy in her agitation. "That is why women want to get married."

"I do not want you to be a boy," cried little Katherine. "I love my sister Elizabeth. I don't want you the same as Francis."

Elizabeth lifted her sister in her strong arms and kissed her dusty cheek. "Never fear, my sweet Katherine. I will always be your sister, but you must call me Ely, and I shall call you Kate. Have we a bargain?"

Five

It was Sunday afternoon when I landed in Little Rock. I picked up my rental car and drove the fifty-five miles to Hot Springs. When I entered the small city, I drove down a tree-lined avenue my guidebook said was Bathhouse Row. I passed a public fountain where a man and a woman were filling plastic bottles with water. Perhaps the claims were true about the benefits of the therapeutic waters. It was interesting to learn the city was located inside a national park, and I looked forward to exploring.

I found my hotel without too much effort. When I entered the lobby and registered, I felt transported back to an earlier era. The afternoon sun shone through a glassed-in terrace where a few elderly people sat reading or chatting with each other.

I called Sudie to let her know I'd arrived. She said she'd come right over and meet me on the veranda.

I took a quick shower, applied light makeup, and put on my new navy-blue sheath I hoped Sudie wouldn't think too short. Twenty-five minutes later, I reentered the lobby and walked past several potted plants into the terrace room. A white-haired woman signaled to me and stood with the help of a cane. A middle-aged black man held her elbow. Sudie was short in stature, maybe five-two, and the man with her wasn't much taller. She wore a tweed skirt, a white blouse and floral cardigan, and sensible brown shoes. The sun shining on her sparse white hair seemed to cast a halo around her welcoming face.

"Cynthia?"

I clasped Sudie's warm, bony hand in both of mine. "It's so good to finally meet you," I said. Her thin lips broke into a smile so warm and inviting that I impulsively kissed her gently on the cheek. The wrinkles on her face had been artistically minimized with makeup and she smelled of old-fashioned face powder.

Sudie's escort broke in. "If y'all don't need me, Miss Sudie, I'd be leaving. What time you want me back?"

Sudie turned to face him. "Oh Luther, I'm so sorry. Cynthia, may I present my good friend, Luther Bigalow. This is Miss Cynthia Parsons, come from Oregon to visit."

He lowered his head after our eyes met and I turned to Sudie. "I rented a car. I'll be happy to take you home."

"That's very kind of you." Luther raised his arm as if to object, but Sudie touched him gently. "You don't have to bother with me anymore today."

He bowed his head and left. I saw him replace his cap as he walked through the lobby toward the front entrance.

"I ordered tea," Sudie said as we seated ourselves in wide-armed wicker chairs. A white-coated waiter brought in a silver tray with a flowered china teapot, cups, and saucers. *Petit fours* were arranged on a plate with a lace doily. He placed the tray on a small round table that separated our chairs.

"Would you pour, please? With my arthritis, I'd have most of it on the tray." Tea seemed perfect for the afternoon and the charming setting. I poured each of us a cup. I felt pleased she had made the effort—not to mention that the pretty little pastries made my mouth water.

Sudie asked about my flight and we compared the weather in the Northwest to the South. I told her I was happy the tornado season had passed. She assured me tornadoes bypass Hot Springs because of their mountain. I looked out the window to where she pointed toward a high hill, which was decidedly not a mountain by my standards. After our cups were empty, with just a few crumbs left on the pastry plate, I brought up the subject that had brought me here.

"I'm anxious to see the page you think may be from *A Midsummer Night's Dream*. When can I—?"

"All in good time, my dear." Her pale blue eyes seemed to darken as she held up a bony hand. "First, I'd like us to get acquainted." Perhaps noticing my confusion, she added, "It's not that I don't trust you, but I must make certain you're the person that is meant to learn what I feel must be true." She gazed at me as though she were trying to look deep into my soul. I wasn't certain how I could telegraph my trustworthiness, so I straightened my spine and tried to assume an intelligent expression.

"You're very pretty." She cocked her head to one side. "You put me in mind of a friend of mine from years ago. Lucinda was tall and slender too, and she had your same peaches-and-cream complexion, same dark hair and eyes. Are you Spanish?" I appreciated her compliment; my looks didn't exactly stop traffic, though I didn't consider myself homely either.

"No, not that I know of. My mother's family was from England and my father's mother, too. My dad died when I was still a teenager. My brother was already grown and married. He married a Canadian girl and they live in Montreal. They have two grown children, plus a grandson." I went on to tell her about my mother's illness and death.

"I understand you have a son, you're divorced, and never remarried." My suspicion she'd had me investigated was confirmed. Her face flushed with embarrassment. "My nephew's secretary found your address—and only the basics. I hope you don't mind. I just didn't know how to go about finding you. I didn't mean to pry. I hope you understand."

Sudie's genuine look of concern won me over, and I could have forgiven her for just about anything. I patted her hand. "Of course I don't mind. I'm flattered you went to all the trouble; otherwise, how else would we have met?" We smiled at each other, and I felt an invisible bond begin to form between us. "You're right, I'm divorced. My son, Mark, is in the Air Force—he's a helicopter pilot. He graduated from the academy and is stationed in Germany. I saw him...and my brother, too, in September. They came home for my mother's funeral. It was great to have them with me for a few days."

Sudie smiled, and I went on to tell her of my life.

"I'm forty-seven, and a history teacher. I went to work at a bank right out of high school and a year later married my boyfriend. He was a sophomore at Oregon University at the time. Our son was born seven months later."

I must have blushed, because she said, "That's okay. Many marriages start out that way."

"It's pretty common in a small town where there's very little for teenagers to do." I took another sip of tea. "Anyway, we moved to Eugene so Alan could finish school. His family was well off—father owned a hardware store in St. Helens. They supported us until after Mark was born, then I went back to work until Al graduated. Our marriage wasn't very happy—we were both so young. After Alan graduated, he got a good job working in human resources for a large corporation. He had an affair...with a co-worker. He married her right after our divorce was final. His company transferred him to San Francisco. I pretty much raised Mark alone—with my mother's help."

"Your Mark must have been a good student to be accepted into the Air Force Academy."

"Yes, he was. I'm very proud of him," I said. "He's engaged now—to a German girl. That means I'll probably see even less of him...darn."

"You must have gone to college yourself."

"It wasn't easy. I enrolled in Marylhurst University because they offered online, night and weekend courses. My mother didn't have the money to help me, but she did babysit while I worked at a bank in St. Helens, and took mostly night classes. Now, I'm debt free from student loans, which is a relief. I was thirty when Lincoln High School in Portland hired me to be one of their history teachers. I continued my education by taking courses at Portland State to get my master's degree. I love teaching, but had to quit a couple of years ago to take care of my mom. That brings you pretty much up to date. Your turn. I know you went to Marylhurst, too. How else would you have had access to their literary review of twenty years ago?"

Sudie laughed. "You're right. I entered the convent at Marylhurst in 1948." Her eyes twinkled. "It didn't take me long to discover I wasn't cut out to be a nun. I left the convent, but continued with my education there." She picked up her teacup with shaky fingers and took a sip. "It was shortly after the Korean War began when I met my future husband at a dance. Paul was an army officer from Arkansas. We fell in love." A slight flush came to her face as she looked off into the distance. "We discussed getting married before he went to Korea, but I had my heart set on a church wedding. We agreed it would be best to wait until after the war."

She paused to take a deep breath. "I graduated in 1953 and we were married the next year, two weeks after Paul returned from Korea. In the college chapel." She closed her eyes for a few seconds and I knew she needed to go home, but she continued on.

"We moved to Hot Springs right after the wedding, because Paul was anxious to get back to his law practice. I taught first and second grade at a Catholic school for years, but when Paul became involved in politics, I stopped teaching to support his career. He became an appellate judge in Little Rock, but twelve years later, he had a stroke and had to retire. He was never the same. He died ten years ago."

I murmured a few words of sympathy. She patted my hand and smiled. "Don't worry, my dear. I've adjusted beautifully. We had a wonderful life together, and I've been happy living here. My only regret is having no children of my own."

The waiter returned to remove the tea service.

"You talked over the phone about your nephew."

"Yes, he's my only living relative. My brother's son. I'm very fond of him. My Paul was a big influence on Clay. That's why Clay's an attorney now." She cocked her head to one side, looking at me. "He's a widower, a bit older than you. Turned fifty this year. You live so near each other, it would be nice if you could meet."

I couldn't help but smile at her matchmaking.

"Clay has a stepdaughter, Colleen. She's an art student in Paris. Clay comes to Hot Springs quite often to check on me. There's another nephew—my husband's sister's grandson. He lives here, but to tell you the truth..." She leaned closer to me and lowered her voice. "I have difficulty with them, especially his wife, Patricia. In fact, it was she who answered the phone when you called. She and Tom never quite forgave Paul for marrying a Yankee."

I smiled, remembering that was what she had called me, too. "They're good to me now, but I suspect it's because they think they're inheriting my house." Before I could respond to this tidbit, Sudie seemed to wilt into her chair, and her eyes closed.

"Sudie, are you all right?"

"I am a bit tired," she admitted, opening her eyes. "I should call it a day."

"You stay here while I pull my car out front." I stood. "Will you be okay?"

"I'm fine. I'm sorry I'm fading out on you. This heart of mine never lets me forget I'm eighty-eight." With a trembling hand, she thumped her chest in frustration.

When I returned, Sudie stood, leaning heavily on her cane. I rushed to support her, realizing the effort it had taken for her to meet me at the hotel.

"I don't want you to worry about me. I have these spells often."

After I helped her into the car and fastened her seat belt, she spoke through dry lips to give me directions.

"Do you have someone to take care of you?"

"Nolah's there. She's been my housekeeper and friend for over thirty years."

We had only driven about six blocks when she pointed to a house on the opposite side of the street. It had three stories, and was white with green trim. Two gables extended out over a steep roof. A flight of steps led to a wide porch that spanned the front of the house. The lawn was brown from what appeared had been a hot summer. The branches of a huge magnolia tree hung over the driveway, ending at a two-car garage. I pulled up and parked.

Before I opened the car door, Sudie leaned toward me and startled me with a question. "Do you believe in psychic experiences?"

"Do I what?" Sudie's clear blue eyes stared into mine, her face very pale. I could tell this was not a frivolous question. "Do you mean paranormal...?"

"Yes." She reached for my arm.

"I don't know." Her eyes searched mine. This was obviously not the answer she wanted to hear. "I guess there could be some truth to..."

"Good." She squeezed my arm. I continued to stare at her, trying to figure out what had prompted the question. "Maybe we should go into the house," she said.

As I helped her up the wide steps, the door opened and a large black woman rushed to meet us.

"Miss Sudie! You shouldn't have tried to go out. Where is that no-good man? I told him not to leave you." She shot me a stern look over the top of Sudie's white hair.

"Don't fuss, Nolah. I'm fine. Just tired."

The doorway was wide enough for the three of us to enter abreast into a foyer tiled in gray slate, polished to a high gloss. On the left, an open doorway led into a dining room. A crystal chandelier hung over a table covered with a lace tablecloth. Straight ahead, an open stairway curved up and around, coming to an end at a landing at the top. On the right, an arched entryway let into an old-fashioned parlor. The furnishings reminded me of my father's grandmother; she'd also had a penchant for crocheted doilies, which decorated the back of a flowered sofa and the side tables. Lacy sheers covered three wide windows while heavy brocade drapes hung at the sides. A closed door led off this room. We helped Sudie settle into an overstuffed chair near a Tiffany-style floor lamp.

"Please sit down, Cynthia. I'll rest here for a bit."

"Miss Sudie, you know you should lie down," Nolah said.

"I will in a few minutes. Would you bring me the bottle of sherry? I believe it's in the buffet in the dining room." Nolah pushed a footstool under Sudie's feet. "Get a glass for yourself and Cynthia, too."

"There, that's better," Sudie said, relaxing deep into the chair. "Dr. Gingrich said a bit of wine was good for me. That's the only part of having a bad heart that's fun." She looked exhausted, and her lips were so white they seemed to disappear into her pale face.

"I'd better leave so you can rest," I said.

"Yes, I will, but first we need to make plans. There's so much I need to tell you. How long can you stay in Hot Springs?"

"I have a return flight in a week."

"Oh, my. That might not be enough time."

Nolah returned with a wine decanter and three crystal cordial glasses on a silver tray. She set it on a table near Sudie's chair.

"Thank you, Nolah. I want you to meet Cynthia Parsons. She met Luther at the hotel." I smiled when I realized Nolah was married to the diminutive man, thinking the woman must top her husband by a good six inches and at least a hundred pounds. She was attractive, with large dark eyes and long curly eyelashes. Her black hair had been straightened and brushed into a pageboy style.

"Don't you tell Luther I've been drinking this time of day." She poured the wine. "Pleased to meet you," she said, looking toward me.

"Do you and your husband live here?"

"No. We've a place on the other side of town." She handed me a glass. "I sure am glad Miss Sudie finally has a companion."

Companion? Does Sudie expect me to be her companion?

"Nolah, she's not the one I plan to interview." She turned toward me. "I have an appointment with a practical nurse tomorrow morning." I struggled to hide my relief. "But I did invite Miss Cynthia to stay with me while she's here. Right now, she's staying at the Arlington."

"All's I got to say is it's about time someone here was lookin' after you full time. Even Mr. Clay's been wantin' you to do that—or go into a retirement home."

"Nolah, you know perfectly well I have no intention of leaving my home. I have you and Luther; I'll be fine. Besides, I have this gadget." I'd noticed earlier she wore a cord around her neck, and suspected she was wearing a medical alert device. She pulled a plastic medallion from under her blouse. "All I have to do is press this button if I have a problem. Clay had it hooked up for me. I'm perfectly safe staying by myself."

Putting my glass on the tray, I said, "I'll be leaving now. What time should I return tomorrow?"

"Come over in the morning, whenever it's convenient."

"You said you're interviewing a nurse tomorrow morning," Nolah said.

"Oh, that's right. I'll call you when she leaves. What's your room number?"

"In case I'm not there, I'll give you my cell phone number." I dug in my purse for a scrap of paper and a pen. I scribbled the number and put it on the table.

"Good, that's settled." She struggled to stand up. "Hand me my cane, will you please?"

"You don't have to see me out. Please take care of yourself." I patted her shoulder. "It was very nice to meet you, Nolah. I'll see you tomorrow."

"You won't be seeing me," she said. "Luther and I are flying to Chicago to visit with our son and his family. We'll be gone till after Thanksgiving."

After I let myself out, I saw a silver Cadillac parked alongside my car in the driveway. An obese woman with frizzled blonde hair was peering into the window of my rental car. A man with a protruding stomach seemed to be waiting for her at the foot of the steps. She jumped back when he said something to her.

"How do?" he said as he walked up the steps. "Been visitin' Ms. McFadden?"

Not sure what to say to this couple, I nodded without stopping and opened my car door. I wanted to tell them Sudie was too tired to accept guests, but I had no right to intervene.

"You're a stranger, ain't ya?" the woman blurted out. Up close I noticed she would have been pretty if it weren't for her blue eye shadow, heavy mascara, and bright red lipstick.

"That depends on what you mean by a stranger, doesn't it?" Now why did I say that? I got into the car and backed out of the driveway. I had a feeling they were the relatives Sudie had mentioned. Thank God Nolah was there to run interference.

~ * ~

Back in my room, I put on pajamas and studied the room service menu. I was surprised to note the influence New Orleans cuisine had in Arkansas, then remembered Louisiana is a border state. Jambalaya, the house specialty, sounded great, along with a glass of chardonnay.

After finishing the spicy stew, I set the tray outside the door and tried to read. When I found myself reading the same page over for the third time, I turned out the light. Tossing and turning, I pounded the pillow, trying to get comfortable.

Telling Sudie of my experience of being so young when I married and then divorced had been difficult. I then thought of women four hundred years ago. If a woman were Shakespeare, she would certainly have to have had a lot of spunk to oppose the customs of her time. Girls were considered the property of their father; arranged marriages and dowries were the norm, and after the girl was married, she would then become the property of her husband. Could she even be married and still be a writer? I seriously doubted it. But you never knew.

I turned over, thankful I'd been born in the twentieth century.

Six

You have showed a tender fatherly regard
To wish me wed to one half lunatic,
A mad-cap ruffian and a swearing Jack...
—*The Taming of the Shrew*, Act 2, Scene 1

July 1577
Rocester, Staffordshire

"I shall not, I will not!" Ely stomped into the room she shared with her sisters. "The thought of being in the same room with that detestable man, let alone sharing his bed, is beyond belief." Ely flung herself on the bed next to Kate, her face flushed with fury. "Father called me a disobedient shrew."

"Where is he now?" Dorothy looked toward the door as if expecting her father to come storming in.

"I don't know. He ordered me to my room to think upon the proposal." Ely turned herself over and stared at the ceiling.

"Did he beat you?" Kate asked, her eyes wide with concern.

"No, but his tongue is made of nettles. He knows the sole aim of the duke's son is to find a daughter of a rich man. He cares nothing for me—and certainly not I for him. Father surely has me fettered as a squirrel in a snare." She moved across the bed and rose to her feet. Her eyebrows drew together and her shoulders hunched as she began to pace, her brain alive.

"Ely, for shame. You are seventeen years and must marry; else what am I to do? Father will not allow me to marry until you do," Dorothy said, and turning toward her little sister, continued, "or Kate for that matter, unless you marry first. You have turned away many suitors for two years. You must marry..."

"Go ply thy needle and meddle not with me!" Ely faced Dorothy, her hands on her hips. "I shall ponder this." Ely's forehead smoothed and a smile slowly emerged as she sat next to Kate, winding one of her blonde curls around her finger. "How old art thou now, sweet Kate?"

"Nearly fourteen."

"Is there anyone you fancy?"

"Nay." She blushed a rosy red.

"Not so," piped Dorothy. "She visits Sir John Stanhope so oft by now her horse knows the way without prodding."

"I pity him so, sister." Kate turned her back on Dorothy. "His wife dying, leaving baby Phillip with no mother." Kate touched Ely's hand. "He's a fine gentleman. Perchance you shall have him?"

"I have no desire to marry a country squire, even if he is a knight. When I marry, it shall be with a man who desires me, someone who will not forbid me should I want to continue my studies, someone who desires to travel as much as I."

"Be realistic. There is no such man born who would agree to any woman's being his equal. You have no choice. Father will order you to marry Sir Clifford. Have you forgot he will be a duke someday and thou shalt be a duchess, wearing fine gowns, going to soirees? 'Twould be a good match."

"If you believe so, why don't you marry him? Perhaps you would not mind smelling the sow sweat under his armpits. You are of an eligible age. Why not offer this solution to Father?"

"You know he would never agree. You must marry first." Dorothy turned away and began to snivel.

"So that is it. You desire the smelly duke. Begone with you and your sobs. Let me think what I must do."

Dorothy stuck her tongue out at Ely and flounced from the room, slamming the door.

Ely returned to her pacing, pulling at her long red hair. Turning toward Kate, she said, "I will need Mother's scissors. I saw them last in her sewing whisket. Can you fetch them without being seen?"

"What is your plan?"

"You shall see. Hurry now. It is well Francis is in Oxford."

Kate tiptoed down the staircase while Ely moved quietly down the hall and entered her brother's room. She returned carrying a bundle of clothes as Kate was racing back up the stairs.

"Here they are."

"Good," Ely whispered. They entered their bedroom, where Ely picked up a stool and carried it to the window. "It will be dark soon; I must hurry." Ely began to comb her hair, pulling at the snarls. "Hand me the mirror and scissors." Ely balanced the mirror between her legs, pulled a lock of hair forward, and cut it off just below her ear.

"Sister, what are you doing? You've cut your hair..." Kate wrung her hands. "What will Mother say? Ely, you must stop!"

"Stop blubbering and come help me." Ely pulled at her sister's skirt. "There's a method to my madness. Here, cut the rest of my hair at this length."

"But..."

"Do as I say or I will box your ears! Be quick about it. I must leave when it is dark."

Kate took the scissors from Ely's hand and began to cry. "Why so? What do you have planned?"

"Do not cry. You know I am capable of taking care of myself." She lowered her head as Kate snipped off her hair. "I will leave home this night as a boy. I'll wear Francis' old clothing and shoes and use the coins Father paid me for keeping his ledgers—enough to buy food and lodging."

Kate stopped snipping and grabbed Ely by the shoulders, her fingers digging into her soft flesh. "What are you saying? You must not! It is not safe. What if—"

"Hush. Give those to me. I shall finish this myself." She took the scissors from Kate's fingers and completed the haircut, her shorn hair carpeting the floor. "There now, not so dreadful," Ely said as she shook her head, threading her fingers through what was left of her hair.

"Kate. Listen to me." Ely stood to face her sister and looked her in the eyes. "Dorothy will soon be coming to bed. As soon as it is dark and I am sure she is asleep, I will leave the house through the scullery. You must not tell anyone where I have gone. Is that understood?"

"But...where are you going? Toward what destination?" Tears coursed down her face.

"'Tis best you do not know." Removing a cover from a pillow, Ely began to stuff handfuls of hair into the case. "When I am gone, surely Father will allow Dorothy to marry Clifford, and Sir John will make a fine husband for you someday."

She shoved the filled pillowcase under the bed and looked up to see tears running down Kate's face. Ely hugged her tightly.

"Only you shall I miss. Prithee, if only I could take you with me." Ely removed her arms from around Kate. "But you must stay here. Leave me now and join Dorothy. Mother will soon be sending you to bed. I will pretend to be asleep. Remember, not a peep. As good luck will have it, I shall be a far distance by morning light." Kate gave Ely a mournful look but did as she was told.

Even though Ely was beset with strange fears, she remained determined to follow her plan, making sure she kept her wits about her to avoid any mishap. It would soon be dark, and the July sun would rise early; she would leave as soon as all was quiet in the manor. She looked out the window, seeing the trees' long shadows upon the grassy fields. Her father stood at the watering trough washing his hands. Tears sprang to her eyes, wondering if she would ever see him again. She stiffened, remembering his plan to marry her off to the loathsome man. Her father had given her no choice. Her thoughts turned toward her mother, whom she could hear singing softly in the nursery. She would miss her brother Tommy, too. But no second thoughts. She was committed.

She took a ring off her finger and looked at the gold band inset with a small ruby, a present her mother had given her on her birthday last month. She at first thought the ring was too feminine to take with her, but decided she may need to sell it in case her money was insufficient.

Searching the carved chest at the foot of the bed, she found the leather pouch with the small stash of coins she'd been saving, pulled on the strings, and put her ring inside. She shoved the pouch deep into the pocket of Francis' doublet.

She held up Francis' breeches against her waist. The calf-length pants were common apparel for peasant boys, so they would be perfect. She quickly removed her own clothing and put the breeches on over her pantaloons. She gazed down at her slim body, assured the doublet would be tight enough to flatten out her breasts. She quickly slipped Francis' undershirt over her head, pulled on some socks, and then donned her long nightdress. She laid the doublet and boots on top of a gray woolen shawl, then added her own waterproofed cloak and cowl, thinking she could use this as a covering should she be forced to sleep in the fields. At the last minute, she remembered to pack some rags of muslin to use when her moon phase arrived. She removed a stub of candle from its holder and packed it on the shawl as well.

The *Complutensian Polyglot Bible* sat on a table near the window. She wished she could take all six books, but that would be out of the question, as they would surely add too much weight. The Old Testament was in Hebrew, Aramaic, Greek, and Latin, and the

New Testament in Latin and Greek, but those languages posed no problem for Ely. She settled on taking the volume containing Psalms and Proverbs. Those were the verses that had given her the love of poetry.

Thomas Trentham had found the books hidden under the floor where the monk's altar had once stood. The family surmised the monks must have hidden them before their rapid exodus when King Henry VIII abolished the monastery in Rocester.

If only I could have been born during King David's reign and been part of his household as he wrote and sang songs of his love of God! Ely thought of Bathsheba. Had she been forced to marry Uriah the Hittite? *I wonder if he was as repulsive as Clifford.* Perhaps Bathsheba's affair with David could have been justified. Ely chided herself for having sinful thoughts. Her active imagination had taken over and she wanted nothing more than to write down her musings. However, time was growing short.

Ely did not consider taking the volume to be stealing, as her father had promised all the books would be included in her dowry. The volume would not be missed. *I am the only one in the family who studies these books.* She considered taking the penner the queen had given her, but her parcel would be too bulky. She did put in the knife and two quills and inserted several blank sheets of paper into the Bible, as she knew she could ill afford to purchase more of the expensive commodity with her small stash of coins. She could either purchase ink later or use a charcoal mixture.

As she tied the corners of the bundle together, she heard her sisters' voices. She quickly stashed it under the bed, took off Francis' hat, shoved it under her pillow, and pulled on her own nightcap. She jumped into bed and pulled the covers up to her chin.

After the girls had joined her, Kate clung to her beloved sister and wept silently. Ely rubbed Kate's back and kissed her cheek. "Go to sleep now," she whispered.

While Ely listened for their even breathing, she planned her future. She had always wanted to visit the countries of the languages she knew best: France, Spain, then on to Italy, maybe even Greece.

Her plan was to walk the fifty miles west to Chester. She remembered there would be a full moon tonight and she could stay on the road. During the day she would hike through the fields to avoid being found. If she walked a far distance tonight, she calculated it would take two, perhaps three days to reach the sea. She would like to take one of the horses, but knowing her father would organize a search, she would be less noticed if she walked. Since her father would not know which direction to search, she hoped he would follow the old Roman road toward London. She would head west and hopefully connect with the Great North Road that led through Chester and on to Scotland. When she arrived in Chester, she would book passage on a ship headed for France.

Her biggest threat was her Grandfather Sneyd, who lived in Chester, where he not only practiced law but was a former mayor. She'd overheard a conversation between her parents telling of her grandfather's plan to move his whole family seat to Bradwell Hall in the borough of Newcastle-under-Lyme, just twenty-five miles from Rocester. He would join Thomas Trentham in land investment. Perhaps he had already moved. Ely yawned deeply. Even so, she would have to be extra observant while in Chester.

Ely fell into a deep slumber and dreamed she was at sea in a small boat in the middle of a storm. She began to thrash about, waking up with a start. She felt Kate turn over and listened to her sisters' regular breathing, relieved they were still asleep. The moon cast an eerie glow through the window. All seemed quiet in the manor.

She slowly rose from the bed, removed her nightgown, picked up her bundle, crossed the room, and opened the door just wide enough to let herself through. Then she remembered her nightcap. Propping the door open with her bundle, she tiptoed back to the bed and exchanged headgear. Her stockinged feet allowed her to escape through the door and down the staircase without a sound.

At the bottom of the stairs, she paused to listen for anyone who may still be about. Not hearing a sound, she headed toward the rear of the manor, down another staircase, and into the scullery. It was pitch black in the small room and redolent with the smells of smoked meat and aging cheese. Feeling her way to the back door, she opened it wide to let in the silvery moonlight. She sat on the floor and unknotted her bundle. She put on her brother's doublet and boots. They were too large, but it couldn't be helped. Feeling her way around the room, her hand touched the shelf where she knew the cook kept bread and cheese in a tin container. She bumped her foot against a basket of apples that she and her sisters had picked the day before. Placing four apples, a brick of cheese, and a loaf of bread in her shawl, she knotted the corners once more and left the manor, closing the door quietly behind her.

Seven

The music on my cell phone woke me from a sound sleep. Squinting at the clock, I wondered who could be calling at 6:40 a.m.—actually 4:40, my time. I groaned. "Hello."

"Cynthia, it's Sudie. I'm sorry. Drat. I forgot all about the time difference. You go back to sleep and I'll call later."

"Um—that's okay. I'd rather get up." I immediately sat up in bed. "Are you all right?"

"Yes, I'm fine. I had a good night's sleep. Would you care to join me for breakfast? There's so much to be done this week."

"I thought you were interviewing a nurse this morning."

"Well, actually, no. Nolah would not have left on her trip if she thought I'd be on my own. I don't need a nurse."

"But..."

"I don't want you to worry, either. Will you come?" Something in her tone reminded me of my own grandmother's rebellion when my mom had to move her into a nursing home. The last thing I wanted was to get involved in that kind of dispute. And she did wear the medical alert device.

"Sure. Soon as I get dressed."

I pulled the drapes. The sun had just come up and it was a beautiful, sunny day, and to my surprise, frost covered the lawn and bushes. *This is the south—why is it so cold?* I turned up the thermostat. Forty-five minutes later, I was in Sudie's kitchen eating eggs, bacon, and a bran muffin and sipping orange juice.

"More coffee?" she asked.

"Let me get it." I picked up our empty plates and silverware from the yellow placemats and walked to the sink. The sun shining through the kitchen window, along with the smell of coffee and bacon, made me feel as though I'd come home. The wallpaper had a light-blue background scattered with tiny yellow flowers. The dotted Swiss curtains at the windows added to the coziness. The frost outside the window had nearly vanished from the bushes. She held up her hand when I started to refill her cup.

"I'm only allowed one cup a day. I had that before you came."

"You shouldn't have gone to the trouble of fixing breakfast for me."

She waved her hand. "Pooh! There's nothing to scrambling a few eggs and making coffee. Besides, Nolah left my freezer full."

"You're looking much better today." It was true; her face had a healthy, pink glow. She wore gray slacks and a white cotton blouse under a bibbed apron.

"I'm feeling good, too. I tried to do too much yesterday. I went to Mass, had lunch out with friends, and helped Nolah prepare a room for my fictitious companion. I missed taking my nap."

"Then you met me." I reached over to pat her hand. "I'll try not to wear you out today."

"Won't you reconsider staying here? The guest room is ready and..." I must have flinched, because she added, "It's not because I need you to take care of me, either. No matter what others may think, I can take care of myself. It's important we work together on this project. If you stayed here, we'd have more time."

"I gave this a lot of thought last night, and I think we need to continue with the research I started in college. You should know, however, scholars have been trying for years to prove someone other than Shakespeare wrote the plays. The most well-founded opinion is Edward de Vere, the Seventeenth Earl of Oxford. He's been discounted by many because after he died, more plays were written. What makes you think we could come up with a different person, especially a woman?"

"You forget, my dear," she argued, "we have a name and a page, something those so-called experts didn't have." She stood by grasping the edge of the table, and taking off her apron, draped it across her chair. "Hand me my cane." She had propped it near the stove. "Come with me. You need to see this."

Suppressing a smile, I followed her through a swinging door that led into a short hallway. On the left, a doorway led into Sudie's tidy bedroom. At the end of the hall, and on the right, she opened a door into an office. Floor-to-ceiling bookcases covered two walls and a large rolltop desk stood against another. A table with a computer sat between two windows. Another open door led into the parlor.

"This was my husband's office. I had a computer installed." She tapped the top of the monitor with her cane. "I took a lesson on how to use it, but I'm in over my head. I'm able to get on the internet and email, but that's about all."

She took a few steps across the floor to one of the bookcases, and tugged on a shelf. A section of the bookcase swung out like a well-oiled door. Behind it was a safe built into the wall. It was about three feet square with a large combination lock in the center. It looked like it had been installed when the house was built. I had the weird sense I had just entered a 1940s film *noir*. Propping her cane next to the safe, she bent over and turned the dial. After opening the safe door, she pulled out a metal box about the size of a library dictionary.

"Here, take this." She handed me the box.

She closed the safe door, picked up her cane, and walked to her husband's desk. "There now," she said as she seated herself in the wooden swivel chair. "Hand me the box and pull that chair over here by me." She must have noticed my confused look. "Surprised by all this?" She motioned toward the safe and the gaping bookshelf. I set the box on the desk in front of her and rolled the computer chair alongside hers.

"I appreciate your trust, but you don't know me. Don't you think...?"

"Cynthia. When you get to be my age, you learn whom you can trust. We have hit it off so well—I knew yesterday I'd been right to contact you." She pushed the box away. "Before I show you this, you need to know another reason that prompted me to call a stranger."

I was boiling with curiosity and wouldn't have left that room even if a truck had rammed the house.

She removed a snowy white hanky from her sleeve and dabbed her nose. "With my age, arthritic hips, and a bad heart, I knew I had to tell someone who'd appreciate knowing about the page and my special ancestor. I guess I already told you that when I read your essay, I felt in my bones that you were the one."

"And you remembered my essay after so many years," I said.

She looked at me strangely. "That's not quite right. I read your essay right after finding the page."

"Really? But how..."

"After I was able to decipher the writing, I came in here to look up the play." She pointed toward the bookshelf. "When I pulled the book out, the Marylhurst Literary Review fell out and landed on the floor. It was open with your article on 'Shakespeare, Perhaps a Woman' staring me in the face. I knew then and there it was predestined."

Goose bumps covered my entire body—what she said was so eerie, yet I couldn't doubt her veracity. "Now that I've met you," she continued, "I believe something beyond our understanding directed us to meet. That same source led me to the prayer book." She touched the box.

"What do you mean?"

"I wasn't in the attic looking for a picture. I said that because I didn't think you'd believe what actually happened." She stopped talking, looking at me, somewhat embarrassed. "I had a dream. A woman appeared, pointing to a steamer trunk, saying, 'Find a Book of Prayers.'"

Dumbfounded, not sure I should believe the strangeness of it all, I asked, "Is that the reason you asked if I believed in paranormal...?"

She nodded. "I've come to believe all of this has to do with timing."

"What do you mean?"

"The timing is right for the woman to reveal herself. She had to stay hidden until the public was ready to accept a woman behind the pen. Women have been so subjugated by men, especially during her era; I'm sure she must have needed a man to front for her work. Otherwise, the plays never would have been performed—or published, for that matter."

"I reached the same conclusion when I wrote my paper. There was no way anyone would accept the idea a woman would be capable of much—let alone Shakespeare in disguise. Even today, some view feminists as dreary or militant."

"But times are changing. We may even have a woman president soon." Sudie pulled the rolltop down halfway and stretched her arm underneath to reach to the top of the desk. I heard a click, and a small doorway sprang open. She pushed the rolltop back into place, pulled out a tiny drawer, and took out a key. She unlocked the box and opened the lid.

"Here it is."

I scooted my chair closer. "I don't want to remove it from the plastic. You can see how fragile it is."

I pulled the page close to me, wondering with awe if this could be one of the original writings penned by the great man himself—or herself. The page was frayed around the edges, yellowed with age. The ink on the paper had faded and appeared splotchy; the writing extended to the edges. The penmanship was rounded cursive, easily readable except for the Early Modern English. The fact that the page had been pressed between the leather covers of the book probably helped to preserve it.

"The handwriting does look like it was written by a woman."

"Yes, I think so, too," she said. I began to read aloud:

Lys: Made me compare with Hermia's sphery eye?
Hel: But who is here? Lysander! on the ground!
Dead? or asleep? I see no blud, no wound.
Lysander, if you live, good sir, awake.
Lys: Mine eyes. What watery substance this be?
Helena? Are you I see fairly?
What trickery hath brought you to my side?
Oh spirits of love so sweet you appear
As from a dream—my beloved is here.
To mine arms—come near, my dear, so I may
Taste thou sweet lips. Hasten to my arms.
Hel: Are you still at slumber—or are you daft?
Lys: And run through fire I will for thy sweet sake.
Transparent Helena! Nature shows art,
That through thy bosom makes me see thy heart.
       Ely

"Look how it's signed." Sudie pointed her finger. "Ely? I wonder what it means."

"A signature?" I said, continuing to study the document.

"Ely is a Cathedral in England that dates to medieval times."

"Or Ely could be short for Elijah, or Elizabeth. Do you think Queen Elizabeth could have written this? I've heard it speculated she could have been Shakespeare."

"I thought the same thing," Sudie said, "so I compared the handwriting with letters she had written. Here, let me show you." She pulled open a drawer and took out a folder. "Look at these pages I copied from a biography of the queen. They're photographic copies of one of her original speeches and one of her letters." She ran her index finger along one page. "I'm no expert, but see how her handwriting is more sloping?" She pointed back to the page from the play. "This is more symmetrical. Also, see how she signs her name: Elizabeth R., for Regina. She was called Queen Bess, but I've never heard her referred to by the nickname of Ely, have you?" I shook my head. "Also, I think being a ruler of a major country during a very tumultuous era wouldn't have left her much time to be such a prolific writer."

"That makes sense," I replied. "But...if it is a signature, why wasn't Ely spelled E-L-I?" I looked at the page more closely.

"Haven't you noticed? The spelling of that era was not consistent. "Look, the *s*'s look like *f*'s," Sudie said, "and I suspect *i*'s and *y*'s were interchangeable."

"But Ely must mean something. It could be a person or place— hard to speculate with so little to go on." I pointed to the signature. "It's difficult to tell with only three letters, but I think someone else wrote Ely."

"You may be right. There is a difference. The ink appears darker, like it was written with a different kind of ink."

"Or maybe Katherine Stanhope was trying to give someone named Ely credit for the writing." I turned to Sudie. "Handwriting may play a big role in identifying who actually wrote this page."

"You need to compare what's actually written on the page with the published version." Sudie stood and walked to a bookcase. She pulled out a large leather-bound volume of *The Complete Works of William Shakespeare* from a middle shelf. "It's not the same."

I took the heavy book from her grasp. Just then the doorbell rang.

"Oh, drat. Who could that be?" She turned toward the open door that led into the parlor. "You go ahead and study this—I'll be right back." She closed the door behind her.

I put the large book on the corner of the desk, sat in the chair Sudie had vacated, and pulled the plastic-covered page toward me. Looking at the faded script, I could imagine a woman dressed in fine wool, or velvet perhaps, quill pen in hand, head leaning over the paper. If it were a woman, who was she? How old was she when she wrote this? How did she have the courage to defy the culture of her time? She must have been a woman of the upper class to have received an education at all, and her genius must have been recognized and developed by someone—a tutor, perhaps.

Sudie and another woman were talking in the other room, but I was so engrossed in studying the page I didn't pay any attention to what they were saying.

A Midsummer Night's Dream was one of my favorites, but I couldn't remember where this passage appeared in the play. Still studying the page and reaching for the book, I accidentally bumped it with my elbow, sending it crashing onto the hardwood floor. Sudie and the other woman's voices reached me.

"What's that?"

"Stay here. I'll find out," Sudie said.

"Never mind; I will."

The door opened as I picked up the fallen book.

"Who are you?" The same middle-aged woman I'd seen yesterday stood in the doorway. Today she wore plaid polyester pants and an oversized rust-colored shirt. We stared at each other. "I remember you," she said.

Sudie came up behind her. "I'm sorry we disturbed you, Miss Parsons. This is Patricia Springer." I positioned myself between her and the desk. I shouldn't have worried she'd spot the page, because her eyes were focused on the safe.

"So this is where the safe is hidden," she said. "We knew Uncle Paul had one, but I had no idea...how clever." She walked toward it, but before she could reach it, Sudie hurried to the bookcase with surprising swiftness and pushed it back against the wall.

The woman turned to look at me. "What are you doing here?"

"I hired Miss Parsons to help me with, er—my family tree."

"I could have done that for you. I learned how when I was at Ole Miss. No need spending good money on strangers."

"She's an expert, Trisha. You were only there for two terms."

She crossed her arms and sniffed. "I'd have gone longer if I hadn't met Tom."

Sudie took Trisha's arm and steered her toward the door. "Come. Let's leave her alone while she continues her work."

I was impressed with Sudie's quick thinking. I sat back down and scanned through the contents of the large volume of Shakespeare's plays. A bookmark had been placed into *A Midsummer Night's Dream*, act 2, scene 2. Comparing the play with what had been handwritten, I found that ten lines were not in the publication, which struck me as strange. This was probably a draft, unless…Who would have edited out those lines—the writer, or someone else?

I reread the entire scene and referred to the page. I saw nothing wrong with the omitted passage, as it seemed a logical addition to the play. In Shakespeare's day, scribes prepared copies of the script for the actors, and with so many different people playing parts, the publisher may have printed their edition from one of the actor's copies. That would make sense if this were the original. The more I thought about it, there seemed to be any number of reasons why the two passages didn't completely match.

Sudie came into the room. "I thought I would never get her to leave."

"I'm so sorry I dropped the book. I hope her knowing where the safe is won't cause a problem."

"Don't worry about it. She doesn't have the combination. It's okay."

"She and her husband had just driven up when I was leaving yesterday."

"Nolah told me. Trisha is such a busybody—she can't stand it unless she knows everything that goes on in this house. Ever since their boys grew up and left home, she doesn't have enough to do. Tom's not quite so bad, but they both can be a trial. Sudie sat in the chair near the desk. "You saw the difference?"

"Yes, this has more lines than the published version."

"Do you think that matters?"

"It depends. After you have the page tested for age, we may know more."

"I figured it would have to be done, but I hated to have any of it destroyed to do it."

"It's my understanding that only a tiny piece is needed. I know a chemistry professor who could advise us. He's my best friend's partner, but I don't know him that well. I'm not so sure he's the right man." I cringed at the thought Frank already knew about the page. "I worry this could leak out to the press."

"The last thing in the world I want is publicity—that is, until we're ready to prove who wrote it."

"Are you sure no one else has seen this?"

"You're the first. I did tell Clay I found an old book I wanted to show him the next time he comes here. I didn't think I should distract him while he's so busy."

Putting on cotton gloves she had left inside the box, I picked up the book. The leather cover had nearly disintegrated, but the book looked valuable—a museum piece. I picked up one of the blank papers. "Where did you say you found these papers?"

"They fell out with the page. I figured they were used to stiffen the cover—must not have had cardboard back then. I almost threw them out, but decided they probably should be kept, being as how they're so old."

"We could have one of these tested. It may give us the period the book was assembled—or repaired, at least."

"That's a good idea," she said. "I'll get Clay's advice."

We looked at the ancient book together. The printing was dim, but I could make out *The Booke of Common Prayer*. "Do you know the history of this book?"

"It dates back to when my father's family lived in England. They belonged to the Church of England, which is Anglican. That's why we still have this book of prayers. The early 1800s is when he emigrated to the states with his wife and family. Most of his descendants lived in the Northeast and went to the Episcopal Church until my own grandmother converted to Catholicism when she married. My mother and I were both raised Catholic." She wiped her nose with the hanky she tucked into her sleeve. "I've been getting results from a DNA test I took a few months ago. They send me emails whenever they find out more about my relatives. Haven't seen the name Stanhope yet. I'll show you what they sent me."

"Yes, I know. For the past two years, I've been getting the same kind of information from my DNA samples. Wouldn't it be weird if we're related?" I opened the cover and saw the signature of Lady Katherine Stanhope. "My friend Josie researched this name before I came. She found two Lady Katherine Stanhopes, but neither was a contemporary of Shakespeare. Is there anything else from your family history that can shed light on who she was—her maiden name or family history—or what part of England they were from?"

"I remember seeing a journal written by my grandmother, but that was years ago. It was a travel journal she made when she went to England on her honeymoon. While she was there, she tried to research our family tree. I know she visited cousins who still lived in the area—this was in 1906, I think. Her mother, my great-grandmother, was from the Midlands of England. I'm sure Grandma Emma's journal is around here somewhere. It's probably in the attic, too. I know it wasn't in the trunk where I found this. There's another trunk in the attic. Maybe we can search for it together."

"I'd love to." I had a huge grin on my face. This was turning into a regular Nancy Drew mystery.

She gazed into my eyes. "Then you're willing to help me?"

"It will be a privilege." I patted her shoulder and immediately thought of the problem at hand—how would we ever be able to prove Katherine Stanhope wrote the page that was lying openly on the desk?

"Do you suppose she was called Kate? Maybe the same woman in *The Taming of the Shrew*," I said.

"If so, that could give us some insight into her personality, don't you think?" Sudie said.

"Writers often incorporate their own personalities into their work, and people they know...events too. We could be looking for a woman with spunk—someone who had the grit to buck the old misogynistic system—maybe someone like my favorite, Rosalind, in *As You Like It*, who dared to disguise herself as a boy."

Eight

I am glad this parcel of wooers are so reasonable, for there is not
one among them but I dote on his very absence, and I pray God
grant them a fair departure.
—*The Merchant of Venice*, Act 1, Scene 2

After leaving Rocester behind, and with a full moon lighting
her way, Ely quickly followed a path leading west. She found a sturdy
stick and by placing it in the knot of her bundle was able to ease the
load by carrying it over her shoulder. She also felt reassured she had
a good weapon to use against growling dogs or wild animals.

She covered several miles on the packed roadway, thankful it
hadn't rained recently. After many hours, it became more difficult
to see, and she remembered it was always darkest before the dawn.
Spotting a grove of trees, she left the road and waded through grass
wet with dew.

Upon reaching the dark wood, not knowing what sort of night animals might be lurking about, she had second thoughts about the wisdom of hiding in such a dark and fearsome place. She considered lighting her candle, but knowing light would carry a far distance, decided against it. She walked a few steps into the black copse and felt her way from tree to tree. When she believed she was well hidden from the road, she removed her cloak from the bundle and wrapped it around her body. She knelt in a thicket of tall grass and prayed for her safety.

Lying in her makeshift bed, she thought again of her father's resolve to marry her off. *Have I made the right decision? To be or not to be a wife and mother? No! Never the duke's wife.* Hearing a bullfrog croak in the distance, she thought it would better to be a toad with a jewel in his head than to be married to a dim-witted duke with many jewels about her neck. *My wit is far greater than his. He would use his fist to control me or lock me in his castle tower. I would poison him at my first opportunity. No! Would that I were truly a man to be able to go where I pleased. A man...*She rubbed her smooth chin. *I am a boy; my name is Elijah Goodfellow.*

Reassured she had made the right decision to flee from a marriage to a man she would have never been able to tolerate, she closed her eyes. Even if she had only the open road and the sea to call her home, living as a boy meant more to her than marriage. Holding her stick in her fist and using her packet for a pillow, she fell asleep.

With the chirping of birds and the scampering of a red squirrel on a tree limb above her head, Ely awoke with a start. In the dimness of the shadows cast by the tree branches over her head, it was no wonder she had slept beyond sunrise. Fearful the morning was already well advanced, she quickly accomplished her ablutions. She tore off a chunk of bread and a piece of cheese and put an apple in her pocket, then hoisted her bundle across her shoulder, ready to continue her journey.

Leaving the grove of trees and munching her breakfast, she took stock of her surroundings. With relief, she saw the sun was still low in the eastern sky. Her goal was Chester, where she would book passage on a ship headed to France. Her parents would just now be discovering her disappearance. They were sure to start searching for her soon, which meant she should not return to the road. By staying in the woods, she could maintain her bearings by keeping the sun at her back until it was overhead. She would stop for a bite to eat and then walk toward the sun. She returned to the woods, not realizing it was, in fact, a forest.

Trudging along, kicking at dry leaves and twigs underfoot, she tried to focus by reassuring herself she had made the right decision. To keep her mood in concert with the tranquil wood, she sang a merry tune:

Under the greenwood tree
Who loves to lie with me,
And turn his merry note
Unto the sweet bird's throat—
Come hither, come hither, come hither!
Here shall he see
No enemy
But winter and rough weather.
Who doth ambition shun
And loves to live in the sun,
Seeking the food he eats
And pleased with what he gets—
Come hither, come hither, come hither!
Here shall he see
No enemy
But winter and rough weather.

She stopped singing when a hare jumped out of the thicket, gave her a blink, and bounded down a deer path. She licked her lips, chiding herself for not bringing a container of sweet cider. Thinking the trail might lead to a stream, she decided to follow the hare. After several minutes, the path vanished into a thick growth of underbrush. She could not see through the forest canopy to orient herself. Knowing she was lost, her heart dropped like iron on an anvil. She felt the urge to run but stopped, her wits telling her it was a foolish move.

Ely meandered through the woods for what seemed like hours. Even though she had gone horseback riding some distance from Rocester, she could not recall this forest. She could be lost until everyone gave up looking for her. To ease her anxiety, she decided to create a story.

She and Kate would be escaping from a tyrant duke who had overthrown the crown by killing her father, the king. Here she would meet her true love, but since he thought she was a boy, she would tease him merrily before letting him know she was a girl. She entertained herself in this manner during her trek through the dense wood, trying to keep herself from admitting she was lost and thirsty. Eventually, the feeling of panic reasserted itself.

"Have courage and pretend you are a lad on a hunting trip," she said aloud. Looking high into a leafy oak, she thought of Robin Hood, a man she could admire. *I could be Maid Marian and live in these woods forever. He would revere me as his equal, not chattel to be ordered about.*

But she knew better. Finding such a husband would be unlikely, and such a partnership surely would not be found with Sir Clifford. If she were married to him, she would be a prisoner as surely as though she were incarcerated in gaol, shackled by chains, legally bound with no rights, no power of her own to wield in any matter that counted. The duke could beat her, and she would have no defense. She'd belong to him as surely as his house, his dogs, or horses. Above all, she must never, ever lose her virginity, she decided—for it was truly her only possession. She would remain a boy forever if need be and only marry if she were sure the man was her equal and would treat her with respect.

Ely heard running water and walked quickly in its direction, coming across a small rivulet. After drinking her fill, she discovered watercress growing at the water's edge. She pulled up a clump and munched on the peppery herb. Her hunger pangs told her it must be well past noon.

She spread her cloak on a grassy spot near the stream and took stock of her dwindling food supply. She had but a bite of cheese, a crust of bread, and two apples left. She sat cross-legged on the cloak, eating about half of the cheese and nibbling at the bread. It was all she could do to keep from gobbling it all down, but she knew she'd need to save a bit for tomorrow. Who knew how long it would be before she found an exit from these foreboding woods?

A slight movement in the grass a few feet away caught her attention. The grass parted to reveal the head of a gray partridge busily pecking at grass seeds. Thinking what a tasty meal the round bird would make, she slowly raised herself to her knees in preparation to leap and nab it. Just as she propelled herself forward, the bird took flight, leaving but a single feather caught between her fingers. "Oh, fopdoodle!"

Thinking what a wantwit she was for even trying to catch the bird, she shivered. The weather had turned cool, and she slipped into Francis' doublet. The shadows on the ground were long, and dusk was at hand. Knowing she would have to spend another night in the woods, she decided not to wander any further and perhaps become even more lost in the darkening gloom. She wrapped herself in the cloak and was soon asleep. The long walk and stress of being lost had taken its toll, and she slept soundly until daybreak.

After eating the rest of her bread and cheese, she decided to save the two apples until midday. She began to walk in what she hoped was a westerly direction. About an hour later, she climbed to the top of a hill where the trees were sparse. When she reached the top, she looked down, sighting a large meadow many acres across. Laughing out loud, she ran down the hill and a few minutes later, left the wood behind and entered the field.

Spotting a stream, she ran through the tall grass and knelt at the water's edge. Cupping her hands, she drank noisily, chiding herself once again for forgetting to bring a water container. Deciding to rest and eat one of her last two apples, she sat on a flat rock.

I had best be finding a village soon to replace my store, she thought as she hoisted the pack back across her shoulder. Just then she saw a shepherd in ragged clothes prodding a herd of sheep with a staff. He seemed to be heading in her general direction. She thought about hiding in the tall grass to avoid him, but it was too late: he was already hallooing.

"Hey-ho, me lad! What ye be up to?" Ely had lived among peasants all her life and figured she could explain herself by using the colloquial accent. She walked toward the man. "Ye best not be poachin' or the gamekeeper will be havin' yer hide," he said.

"No—'twasn't. Took a cut through the wood an' lost me way. Where be I?"

"Oh, that be Ardeen Forest." He gave a large ewe a whack across the rump with his staff. The ewe looked back at him and ambled away to begin grazing. Ely was unsure of his pronunciation; perhaps he meant Arden. It mattered little except to give her forest a name. She lowered the pack from her shoulder and leaned over to pick up a small twig. She put it between her teeth, hoping the gesture would seem boyish.

"Needin' to find a road—er, west, toward Wales. Perchance ye could point the way?"

"Wales? Don'na know a wale..."

Realizing the man had probably never ventured off this land, she would have to allow for his ignorance of what lay beyond. "Who's ye master? Which way to the manor?"

"Ye be in Shropshire lands." He waved his staff in the air. "Lord George's castle lies yonder." He pointed to the southwest. With a snaggle-toothed grin, he added, "Ye be a bonny lad."

Shropshire? I'm too far south. I should be in Cheshire. "A road nearby?"

"Aye," he said, swinging his staff in what she hoped was a westerly direction. "Don'a wanna natter a spell?"

"Thank ye fer offerin'. Best be goin'." With that, Ely turned her back on the shepherd, heaving a sigh of relief that the man seemed to accept her as a boy. She quickly walked in the direction he had indicated.

She remembered from a traveler stopping by her home in Rocester that there were several castles along the Welsh border. She wondered to which one the old shepherd was referring. Wales must be a day's walk, considering the mountains she could see in the distance. She remembered a George—could it be George Talbot, Earl of Shrewsbury? One of her suitors was an elderly uncle of the earl's who had asked her father for her hand. Even her father would not entertain the notion of having his eldest daughter marry a man far gone into his dotage. As she strode through the tall grass in the meadow, she began to count the number of men who had tried to woo her, arriving at four who were serious and one who desired a mistress. After the many rejections Ely had given her suitors, 'twas no wonder her father would have her marry Sir Clifford.

Seeing a cart path ahead, Ely quickened her step. She jumped across a small stream, and shading her eyes from the sun, continued her journey. Toward evening, the sky clouded over and a cold southerly wind began to blow. Thunder rumbled in the distance, and she knew she would soon be in for a drenching if she didn't find shelter soon. She stopped walking long enough to don her long cloak and pull the cowl over her head, thankful it had been treated with pigs' fat to make it waterproof.

After walking for at least an hour, she seemed to be headed in a more northerly route. The wind had picked up and it began to rain cold sheets. She stopped walking long enough to remove her bundle from the stick and tuck it beneath her cloak. Already her feet were squishing in her wet shoes as the path became a sea of mud. She continued to look for shelter, but only open fields surrounded her.

Toward dusk, the path came to an end when it intersected with a well-used road. Open fields lay beyond either side with no shelter in sight. Hoping she was making the correct decision, she turned right.

Some minutes later, she spotted a stone building with a thatched roof set back from the road in a grove of trees. Seeing candlelight through the window, she quickened her step, relieved she may have found shelter for the night. Drawing near, she saw a barn and could hear the neighing of horses. A sign above the door indicated she had stumbled upon the Lamb's Head Inn. Feeling even more relieved she had found a public house, she pounded on the door.

Nine

I could find in my heart to disgrace my man's apparel and to cry
like a woman, but I must comfort the weaker vessel, as doublet and
hose ought to show itself courageous to petticoat.
Therefore, courage...
—*As You Like It*, Act 2, Scene 4

A portly man with a week's growth of whiskers on his grimy
face opened the door. A welcoming fire blazed behind him. A fat
woman dressed in a gray woolen dress with a frayed hem stirred
the contents of an iron pot. The aroma of mutton stew made Ely's
stomach rumble in anticipation of a hearty supper.

Ely's voice had a naturally low pitch, but she lowered it further.
"Kind sir, can you offer a poor lad a bed and a bit of supper for the
night?"

"Ye have a farthing?"

"Aye."

"Me spare room been took by them gentlemen," the proprietor said, gesturing toward two men who sat at a table near the window drinking from pewter mugs. "Ye can bed down by the fire."

Greatly relieved she wouldn't have to share a room with the men, she readily agreed. The straw on the dirt floor stuck to her muddy shoes as she walked to the fireplace. The woman glanced at her with friendly eyes and a bit of a smile. Ely returned the smile, took off her wet cloak, and hung it on a peg near the fire. She considered taking off Francis' hat but decided to leave it on to maintain her disguise. Setting her bundle on the dirt floor, she looked down, noticing the doublet had become unbuttoned. Turning toward the wall, she quickly rebuttoned it and removed her small purse from a pocket. Sensing she was being watched by the woman, she took a coin and handed it to her. The woman took the coin to her husband, who was refilling a flagon with ale.

After Ely took off her wet shoes and stockings to dry near the fire, she looked around, noticing the two men engaged in deep conversation. She sat on a small stool near them, but she was more concerned with what the woman was whispering in her husband's ear. Fearful she was able to see through her disguise, she tried to appear nonchalant. She sat with her knees pressed together and her hands folded across her lap. Realizing her demeanor was a dead giveaway, she reminded herself she was an actor playing the part of a boy. She quickly extended her bare feet toward the fire and crossed her ankles. She picked up a straw from the floor and began to chew on it.

She glanced toward the two men, noting for the first time one was dressed in black leggings and tunic with a white stiff collar, the somber clothing typical of a Puritan. The other man wore soft buckskin with a forest green ruffle at the neck, the attire of a traveling gentleman. His boots, although muddy, were of excellent quality. Because travelers had often stopped in Rocester on their way to London, she knew a man such as he would not travel without a manservant. As if in answer to her musing, a man of middle years came into the room.

"How now, Toby. Are the horses well-tended?"

"Yes, milord." Toby ambled to the fire to warm his hands.

The nobleman turned toward his companion. "As I was saying, I am curious why you would want to follow the teachings of Calvin and deprive yourself the benefit of becoming a follower of our queen's church. Explain yourself." He took a sip from his cup and stared at the younger man over the rim.

Ely became interested in their conversation and wondered how the man would answer the question. She began to openly eavesdrop.

"Milord, you misunderstand. I am not a dissenter of our Elizabethan Church, but rather I am a dissenter of the Church of Rome. What I would argue for is more departure from Rome, while still complying with the Church's laws and sacraments."

"In what way, pray, would you want to change the queen's church?"

"I would desire a national English church that is not based on Roman rituals—less splendor and pageantry."

The courtier smoothed his pointed beard. "But you must be aware of King Henry's intent to end the pope's rule over our English church. He knew too radical a departure from Roman tradition, as many of those who are called Puritans would suggest, could very well cause dissent."

"Are you suggesting a religious civil war could result?" The Calvinist whispered the final words and look cautiously around.

"I am sure our queen would stifle any sort of rebellion before it started. There could be much unrest if the queen were persuaded to radically change tradition. People will accept change, but it must be done slowly and methodically. She may in time be persuaded to become more moderate, but it is too early in the reformation for her to consider making the drastic changes the Puritans would desire."

The men's conversation was interrupted when the woman put two bowls of stew before them. The innkeeper brought them a plate of yeoman's bread and a wooden tub of butter and refilled their cups with ale. She handed Ely a bowl.

"Boy. Come join us at the table." The religious man was addressing her. Ely judged him to be near her age, as his blond beard was sparse.

In a low voice she responded, "Thank you, kind sir." Ely set her bowl on the table and the Calvinist slid aside to allow room for her to sit.

"What are you called and where are you bound?"

"I'm known as Ely—Elijah Goodfellow. I hope to reach Chester on the morrow." Taking in a spoonful of the stew, she was surprised by how good it tasted. The meat was fresh, not rancid as she had feared.

"May I present Edward Vere, the Earl of Oxenford." Ely's eyes grew round as she quickly rose to her feet, remembering at the last second to bow, rather than curtsy.

"Sit down, boy, and finish your supper," said the earl. "There is no need for formality. Traveling in weather like this makes for strange bedfellows." Elizabeth took her first good look at the earl. He was quite handsome. His hazel eyes seemed to reflect a humorous outlook on life, but she wasn't sure she liked the superior tenor of his voice.

"My name is John Overall," said her bench companion. "I am also bound for Chester to meet with my godfather."

"He has traveled from Cambridge, where he has been studying at St. John's College. He desires to take up the cloth." The earl tore a slice of bread in half and generously buttered it.

"I'm very happy to meet you both," Ely said. She looked at the innkeeper's wife as she brought them wedges of cheese.

"Give this lad ale," ordered the earl. "On such a night, everyone needs a bit of warming."

"His lordship is on his way to Warwick to join the queen's party," John said. Ely was aware of the queen's practice of journeying throughout England during the summer months with her large entourage. Knowing Queen Elizabeth was her godmother gave her a warm feeling. Listening to the men talk, she was thoroughly impressed with their importance and wanted to join their conversation as an equal.

"And what takes you to Chester?" John took a large bite of stew, wiping his chin with his sleeve.

"I am hoping to book passage to Brittany," Ely said.

"Perchance we could travel to Chester together."

"I've been walking, sir. I think it would be—"

"My horse is sturdy, with a broad back. We could manage. I would enjoy the company." The innkeeper interrupted by bringing Ely a mug of ale.

Ely's first reaction was to refuse John's offer, but she reasoned that if she had a traveling companion, she would be less likely be found by those looking for her. "Thank you, sir. I will accept your kind offer."

After they had finished their stew, the woman served dishes of stewed apples and a wooden bowl of walnuts along with a small mallet for cracking. She refilled their mugs.

"I hope you don't take offense..." Ely said. Wanting to emulate the men, she rubbed her mouth with her shirtsleeve. "But I overheard your conversation. It will please me if you continue. I have studied the Bible." She considered showing them the Polyglot Bible she had in her bundle but thought better of it.

"Are you a university student?" John asked.

"Nay. I have been tutored along with my master's children. My father was steward for a squire in...er, Worcestershire."

"Perchance I know him," the earl said. "His name?"

"Squire, ah..." Ely cleared her throat, watching the earl puff out his cheeks in a quiet belch. "Aguecheek. Squire Andrew Aguecheek."

"Never heard of him." He studied Ely with narrowed eyes. "How does it come about you're traveling alone at your age?"

"I am thirteen, Your Grace—not so young. My father died and mother afore him. The squire and me...we had, er, cross purposes. He sent me on my way."

"Cross purposes?" The earl leaned forward, obviously wanting to be entertained. "Explain yourself. What sort of cross purposes?"

"'Twas nothing of import, milord." Ely was becoming a bit miffed at the nosy courtier. "He said I did not know my place—my goals were too lofty. 'Tis best we came to a parting of the ways." Wanting to change the subject, she turned toward John. "I would have wanted to attend university. Studies came easy for me."

"Have you an ear for languages?" John asked.

"Yes. Latin, and the manor's tutor was French. He taught us his native tongue." Ely wanted to boast her proficiency in more languages, but she thought it best not to elaborate for fear they would become suspicious.

"I have spoken Latin so long, it is troublesome for me to speak English in a continued oration." John laughed.

"I would be happy to speak in that language if it pleases my lord," Ely offered.

"I have always excelled in Latin," the earl said. "My uncle, Arthur Golding, was my tutor. I assisted him with the translation of Ovid's *Metamorphoses*. Are you familiar?"

"I am. 'Tis my favorite non-biblical book," John said.

Ely, caught up in the excitement of the conversation, blurted the invocation to the *Metamorphoses:*

Of shapes transformde to bodies straunge,
I purpose to entreate, Ye gods vouchsafe
(for you are they ywrought this wondrous feate)
To further this mine enterprise.
And from the world begunne,
Graunt that my verse may to my time, his course directly
runne.

Both men looked at Ely wide-eyed. She lowered her head and mumbled, "Pray beg your pardon, milord. I forgot my place for a moment."

"By God, boy. You are certainly more learned than I would have imagined. You have quoted my Uncle Golding's translation perfectly."

"You should be proud of your ability to memorize," John said. "That is something I find dreadfully difficult."

"You are a comely lad," the earl said. "Let me look at you." He reached across the table and held Ely's chin, rubbed his knuckles across her cheek, and removed her hat. "Yes indeed, quite comely. Red hair as well; you need to find a better barber." He picked up a lock of her hair and rubbed it between his fingers.

Ely refused to raise her eyes. She was aware of the sexual appetites of some men who preferred a relationship with men and boys to that of women. Obviously, this earl was of that ilk. She wanted nothing more than to stand up and slap his smug face. She clenched her hands under the table, knowing she would need to keep her wits about her to avoid getting herself into more trouble than she was in now. She knew her face was becoming beet red—not from embarrassment but from unadulterated anger.

"You mentioned you are married," John addressed the earl. Ely hoped John was trying to circumvent an uncomfortable situation that seemed to be developing, but whether he was doing it to protect her or himself, she was unsure—nonetheless, grateful.

"What?" The earl pulled his hand away from Ely's hair and leaned back. "Oh yes, Anne. My wife is Lord Burghley's daughter. We are separated..."

He continued to gaze at Ely. She didn't like the smirk that played about his lips. "I sponsor a group of players. With your ability to memorize, you would be suited to the stage. With the right makeup you could pass as a woman without difficulty."

Ely would have been delighted at the suggestion, but a girl pretending to be a boy pretending to be a woman was too farfetched for even her to consider.

"I think not, sir. I have made my plans. Besides, I'd be too fearful to appear on stage." She faked a huge yawn. "I am weary from my long walk. With your permission, I shall retire."

Ely was again relieved the innkeeper had only one room to let and the two men had already been promised the bed. The earl nodded his permission for her to leave. She stood, picked up her hat from the table, and moved toward the fireplace. She only wished John Overall would be safe from Lord Vere's dishonorable advances. She would offer up a prayer for him.

Toby the manservant looked up from a stool where he was sitting and emitted a loud belch. He set his empty bowl on the floor and smiled at Ely. Sir Toby Belch, she thought to herself. This struck her as funny, and she giggled softly. Her musings were interrupted when the innkeeper's wife came in from a back room with two straw pallets. She rolled one on the floor near where Toby was sitting. Ely felt her cloak to see if it was dry enough to use as a cover. It was a bit damp, but even wet wool gave off warmth. The woman rolled the other pallet on the floor a goodly way from where Toby would be bedded down. Drawing close to Ely's side, she whispered.

"Come with me, girl. I will show you to the jakes."

Ely jumped as though she'd been pierced by an arrow. Looking directly into the woman's face, she saw friendliness, not hostility. Ely glanced around to see if anyone had overheard. The innkeeper was looking in their direction, but the two men were still engaged in their conversation. Toby was lazily removing his boots. The woman pulled on Ely's doublet sleeve. "This way," she whispered. She led her through the back door.

Ely found herself in a shed where firewood and other supplies were stored. "Why did you call me girl? I'm not..."

"I know what I knows. Lads don't have bosoms." Ely looked down at herself. "I watched when ye took off your cloak—and you sittin' like a lady."

Ely felt genuinely frightened and, thinking fast, she thought perhaps for a few coins, the woman would keep quiet. "Please, good mother. Do not let it be known."

"What're you running away from? Are ye in trouble?" The woman looked at Ely's midriff. "'Tis plain you're a lady of means. What's yer name?" The woman's expression had lost its friendliness. She had her hands on her hips and a scowl on her face.

"I needed to flee from my father. He intends to have me marry a despicable man. I had to escape." Ely gestured toward the clothes she was wearing. "What are you going to do?"

The woman's look softened. "Ye must understand, this ain't my idea to...I mean, me husband wants paid fer keepin' quiet."

"I only have a few coins. I had hoped to purchase passage..." Her voice trailed off; Ely didn't know what to do. Should she turn over her purse to this woman or take the risk of revealing her disguise to John Overall and Lord Oxford? Perhaps she could leave now, but the rain beating on the side of the shed made her realize the foolishness of that thought. "Right. Yes, well. I will give you my purse, but please let me keep a bit."

The woman looked toward the closed door. "Me husband will have me hide unless I bring back the purse."

"'Tis in my bundle. I'll need to go back in the room."

"Don't lie to me, girl. 'Tis in yer pocket."

Ely reluctantly pulled out the purse. Pulling on the strings, she removed her ring. "Please, let me keep the ring. 'Twas a gift..."

"Let me see." Ely put the ring on her finger and showed it to the woman. "Hmph. I've no use for finery." She reluctantly gave the woman the purse, her lips trembling as she squeezed back tears.

Ten

After Sudie showed me the *Midsummer* page and explained the enormity of the research before us, my move into her house was a foregone conclusion. Even though Sudie had been adamant about not needing anyone to care for her, I easily settled into that role—but she became as much of a companion to me as I was to her. Maybe it was because I missed my mother that Sudie became an important part of my life in such a short time. I still find it hard to understand just how it happened; synchronicity seemed to be at play.

She assigned me to a guest room on the second floor, located directly above her bedroom. I wanted to begin the search of her attic for her grandmother's journal, but it was midafternoon, and she showed signs of needing to rest.

"Tell you what, while you take a nap, I'll visit your city library."

Even though she wanted to go with me, she finally agreed to rest. Armed with her library card and directions, I took off. It was late afternoon when I returned with a book of the Tudor period and two books by authors who had explored their own ideas about Shakespearean authorship. I also purchased spiral notebooks to take notes.

The house was quiet when I let myself in. I assumed Sudie was still asleep as I tiptoed into the kitchen, set my books on the table, and made a small pot of coffee. I began to read a book by an author who was convinced Edward de Vere, the Seventeenth Earl of Oxford, was the true playwright.

A half hour into the book, I thought over what I'd just read. The author speculated Shakespeare, who was from meager beginnings, must have known someone connected to the royal courts to have been able to write of England's kings and have intimate knowledge of their politics. For a woman playwright to have access to royalty, she could have been a lady in waiting. I made a note to myself to see if I could find a list of the queen's ladies. I also noted: If Shakespeare retired in 1612, but lived until 1616, why didn't he continue to write? It made sense that whoever it was who had allowed him to take credit, that person died in 1612. I drew circles around that year.

My musings were interrupted by the sound of Sudie's cane tapping against the swinging door into the kitchen.

"I smelled coffee and knew where to find you." Her hair was flattened on one side from her nap. "I'm glad you're making yourself at home." I pulled out a chair for her.

"Would you dare have a cup?"

"I better not." She smiled mischievously. "But I am looking forward to having a glass of wine before dinner. It's supposed to improve my appetite." She picked up one of the books. "I see you've been busy."

"We need to come up with Katherine Stanhope's maiden name. Would it be okay if I reviewed your DNA ancestry?"

"Of course you may. My password is on a note pad next to the computer. But I think Grandma Emma's journal may be a better source."

"Providing it dates back four hundred years. We'll need to search your attic."

"It's a jumble." Her hands fluttered. She mumbled something that sounded like, "She mentioned…" but then caught herself, her eyes wide with mystery.

"Is something wrong?"

"No, no. It was another dream—nothing of any consequence." She shook her head as if to clear it. "Even though I can't remember the family name, I do remember my grandmother telling me that at one time her ancestors were wealthy landowners in the Midlands of England, and we are direct descendants of someone important."

I could tell she was deep in thought and I sat quietly, hoping she'd remembered something I could research.

"Yes. There was a knight in the family. I remember my grandma telling my mother that this ancestor was one of the shire knights responsible for the custody of Mary, Queen of Scots, during the years Queen Elizabeth held her captive." Sudie paused, her forehead wrinkled in thought. She then looked at me, her eyes shining with excitement. "We've the right era, don't we?" I didn't respond, busily writing down what she had just told me. At least that information could be researched for names and the different locations Queen Mary had been held prisoner.

Sudie went to the cupboard and removed a bottle of red wine along with two wine glasses.

"The puzzle pieces may be falling into place," she said.

"Have you given any thought it could have been someone other than Katherine? What I mean is—if Katherine were the writer, why not leave something behind more substantial than just one page? What if she did it for someone else—someone she cared for deeply—someone who was truly Shakespeare?"

"Maybe there's more evidence hidden in a different place," Sudie said. She handed me my glass and joined me at the table. "We do need to look through more stuff in the attic."

"Let's see what we can find tomorrow." I looked at my notes and shared more information with her. "To prove someone other than Shakespeare was the true playwright, we first need to include why he lacked the right qualifications."

"You've already done that in your essay—" she said.

"And it is also included in this book." I showed her the book by the author who supported de Vere. "One thing I forgot to include in my essay is the only writing ever found attributed to Shakespeare is five signatures." I located the page in the book and showed her.

Sudie studied them. "Look. These signatures aren't even spelled the same—and the handwriting is terrible." She looked up at me. "As a former school teacher, it looks like he could barely write his name, let alone be the author of such wonderful works."

~ * ~

Before I went to bed that evening, I peeked into Sudie's room. She was sound asleep, with a rerun of *The Golden Girls* on the television. She sat in a recliner wearing a flannel nightgown with a knitted afghan covering her legs. I gently shook her shoulder and whispered that perhaps she should get into bed. She awoke with a start. She smiled as I helped her out of the chair. Her medical alarm lay on the nightstand.

After I tucked her in, I spent an hour on the phone talking to Josie. Coincidently, we both had figured out the lady-in-waiting angle. "Do you know the difference between lady-in-waiting and maid of honor?" Josie asked.

"No, unless maid means someone not yet married," I opined.

"Yes, that's correct. It was created during Elizabeth's reign for unmarried girls. It gave those young women recognition, power, or a good marriage. They also received a liberal education—including languages. They were trained in the arts of music, dance, and poetry, so they could entertain the royal court."

"So, it's possible a woman of her court would have been allowed to write the plays as well as poetry?" I shifted the phone to my other ear.

"Perhaps. I read where they would have attended masked balls, seen plays performed for the queen's court, and accompanied her when she traveled, plus had any number of other opportunities. She could have caught the acting bug as easily as any person of our age. Of course, she wouldn't have been able to act, since only men could perform on the stage, but writing plays could have been an outlet."

"She would have had ample opportunity to become politically savvy—through eavesdropping, if nothing else," I said. "Who knows how many titled men she'd have met."

"That brings up something else I learned. These maids had to get the queen's permission to marry. There were at least two who were banished from the court, even though they had married earls."

"Yes, I've heard the stories."

After another few minutes of conversation, I asked how she was doing. "I have a feeling not all is well between you and Frank."

"You're very perceptive," she said. "It's his gambling—he's in so deep, he wants me to sell my house."

"You're not going to, are you? He's the one with the problem, not you."

"I know, Cynthia. But I do love him and would like to help—but I have dreams of raising my family here. I grew up in this house." I doubted Frank would want a family at his age. I didn't share my cynical thoughts. She paused like she wanted to say more, then said, "It's my problem. I'll figure something out."

~ * ~

It was after midnight before I went upstairs. The brass bed was covered with a yellow quilted comforter. I could hear Sudie snoring. I was standing near a heating vent and remembering her bedroom was directly under this one. I crawled into bed and read more of the de Vere book. I was especially interested in learning about his second wife, Elizabeth Trentham. I laid the book aside, wondering if there was a connection between her and Katherine Stanhope—good friends or a relationship? I turned off the bedside lamp and lay in the dark with my eyes wide open.

I couldn't seem to get my mind off Katherine Stanhope's maiden name. Could it possibly be Trentham? I laughed silently. That would certainly be a weird coincidence. Where the heck was Sudie's grandmother's journal, anyway? Finally, giving in to temptation, I got out of bed and pulled on a robe. Barefoot, I tiptoed to the attic stairs.

When I pulled a chain connected to a bare light bulb hanging from the ceiling, I could see what Sudie meant by a jumble. I picked up a flashlight that had been left behind on a box near the door. The room was like any other unfinished, windowless, airless attic, except it was long and narrow, taking up the entire area under the sloping roof of the house. It was filled with cardboard boxes and old furniture in various stages of disrepair, including a full-length cracked mirror in a scrolled wooden frame. There were several boxes labeled "Xmas," and a huge wicker basket overflowing with blankets and coats smelling strongly of mothballs. A steamer trunk sat off by itself in front of a small rocking chair. I switched on the flashlight and looked inside, assuming this is where Sudie had found the prayer book. The trunk seemed to be filled with family photographs and an assortment of linen and lace.

I didn't know what I was looking for, but I assumed it would be a notebook or a ringed binder. I flashed the light around the room, casting shadows in the dimness, and spied a trunk against the wall with two large cardboard boxes stacked on top. I wended my way across the room and nearly bumped my head on the sloped ceiling. I had started to lift the first box down when I paused. Now, I've never been a particularly superstitious or afraid-of-the-dark type, even when I was a kid, but standing in that musty-smelling attic, an eerie feeling came over me—as if I were not alone.

My heart sped up as I lowered the box to the floor. Almost afraid to breathe, I turned around and slowly scanned the shadowy interior of the room with the flashlight. Seeing nothing but more storage containers and cobwebs between the rafters, I decided I was letting my imagination run wild. Chalking it up to too much thinking about dead people, I turned around and shifted the second box on top of the first one. This trunk, like the other, was made of wood with wide metal strips. I tried to open the lid, but it was stuck. I flashed the light on the hasp lock, wondering if it was just rusty. Getting down on my hands and knees, I tried to pry it loose with my fingers when I heard something.

My fingers froze. It was barely a whisper, or maybe just the creak of an old house, but it was enough to frighten the bejesus out of me. I jerked around and caught a glimpse of a slight shimmer on the far side of the room. It couldn't be a shadow because the flashlight was on the floor. The shimmering seemed to float toward me, like the faintest puff of glimmering fog. I stood and backed away, stumbling over my own feet. My heart pounded and my mouth was so dry I couldn't swallow. Without any logical reason, "Ely" popped into my mind and suddenly I knew Ely was the name of a person. *Is it Elizabeth Trentham?* I didn't know for certain if I'd asked that question out loud or just thought it, but I had my answer when I heard a woman's voice say faintly, "Yea, my hour is almost come."

I swallowed. Had I just heard a line from Hamlet's dead father...spoken by an actual ghost?

I slammed the attic door behind me, ran down the stairs, and hotfooted it back into bed. I felt like a ten-year-old shaking under the covers. After I calmed down, I wondered if I had actually witnessed a ghost or just imagined it. It was past midnight—when things go bump in the night—and I'd been sneaking around a strange house as if it were my own. After replaying the moment in a room crowded with relics from the past, I decided it must have been my imagination. But why did the name Ely pop into my mind for no reason? I hadn't thought of the name since I had read it on the *Midsummer* page.

The next morning, I couldn't decide if I should tell Sudie about my ghost, but eventually I thought it best to keep it to myself. I didn't want her to think she had asked an overly imaginative weirdo to help her. I did confess I'd been poking around in her attic in the middle of the night, and explained we needed a screwdriver to pry open the lock on the trunk. Sudie didn't seem surprised at my confession. Armed with the tool, we headed back into the attic. I let Sudie lead the way.

"The light is on," she said.

"I must have forgotten to turn it off." Sudie shot me a quizzical look, but I still couldn't bring myself to tell her about my ethereal experience. "Sorry."

"It's okay, my dear."

I scanned the attic from end to end, wondering if the ghost were still hanging around. Luckily, all seemed normal, or at least nothing was moving in the crowded room. "Over there," I pointed. "I took the boxes off the trunk. Let's see if I can get the lid up."

After prying, the latch popped loose and I opened the lid. But unlike pirate tales where a sailor opens a trunk to a treasure trove, all this one held was an odd assortment of toys and board games.

"Oh, I remember now." She picked up a stuffed Smokey Bear. "We kept toys for Clay when he came to visit. Nolah's children used to play with them, and Tom and Trisha's boys. Maybe I should give these to Trisha. She's going to be a grandmother soon." Her mind seemed to wander into the past as she sorted through the trunk. Looking over her shoulder at the collectibles, all I could think of was what they'd sell for on eBay. She turned a crank on a box. Tinny music began to play: *All around the mulberry bush, the monkey chased the weasel, the monkey stopped to pull up his sock—pop goes the weasel.* A clown jumped out of the box. "This used to be Clay's favorite toy," she said.

An hour later, after we'd searched through most of the boxes, Sudie said, "Let's give this up. Next time Clay comes, I'll have him look for it. We should be getting rid of most of this stuff anyway."

After we returned to the kitchen, Sudie was drinking herbal tea and I sipped a cup of reheated coffee. I picked up one of the library books. "Remember yesterday I showed you this book, where the author gives a history of Edward de Vere, the Seventeenth Earl of Oxford?"

"Yes, I do."

"Well, Edward's second wife was Elizabeth Trentham." I flicked to the pages where Elizabeth Trentham was mentioned. "Here, read this." I pushed the book across the table.

After Sudie finished reading, she surprised me by saying, "Trentham. Now I remember! That name is in my family tree. I bet there's a town with the name *Trentham*. I have an atlas in the office."

Sitting in her office a few minutes later, we confirmed there was a Trentham Township in the North Midlands of England.

"Do you suppose Elizabeth Trentham was related to Katherine Stanhope?" I asked.

"Depends on the years they lived. I suspect the names Elizabeth and Katherine were even more common then."

"You're right, but the page is signed Ely, which could be a shortened name for Elizabeth. Here's what I think could be plausible..."

"Go on—I'm listening," Sudie said.

"Prior to Elizabeth marrying de Vere, she was a maid of honor for ten years. Ten years is a long time to remain unmarried, especially since it's reported she was very comely. In such a position, she would have had the queen's ear, been involved in the court—especially since she later married an earl. He traveled to the continent often. Many of the plays take place in locations visited by de Vere. Even if Elizabeth never traveled, he could have shared some of his traveling experiences. Maybe they even collaborated. Also, her marriage to Lord Oxford gave her access to the stage. Did you know he owned a group of players?"

Sudie picked up the book. "I need to read this."

"Yes, please do. There is one other fact that makes this even more plausible. She died in 1612, the very same year Shakespeare retired, never to write again, even though he lived until 1616."

I was feeling jazzed and wanted to dance around the room with her, but settled for squeezing her fingers. "I think we've had our first breakthrough!" Then something caught my eye and I let go of her hands. That same shimmering fog I'd seen in the attic appeared against the office window, which I happened to be facing. In fact, it obscured the view of the back yard. The shimmering seemed to be vibrating as if it were caught up in our excitement.

"What are you looking at?" Sudie turned toward the window, but by then the mirage, or whatever it was, had vanished. I shook off the feeling of foreboding and brushed my hand through my hair. "Your eyes were as big as saucers. What was it?"

"Oh, nothing. I thought I saw something in the window—it must have been a shadow." By then I had come to believe I was truly being haunted.

Eleven

Here's ado, to lock up honesty
and honor from th' access of gentle visitors!
—*The Winter's Tale,* Act 2, Scene 2

It was hours later when Ely felt the toe of a boot. "Boy, get up if you expect to travel with me." Her sleeping mat crackled as Ely sat up with a start. She momentarily forgot where she was, but it came back to her when she looked up into the smiling face of John Overall.

"How late is it?" Ely rubbed her eyes. She had lain awake most of the night and only dropped off at the first glimmering of daylight. "Where is everyone?" she asked, looking around the room. Her hand brushed against her breast. She turned away from John and quickly rebuttoned the doublet.

"An hour past sunrise. Lord Oxenford left at daylight, and the innkeeper is seeing to my horse."

Ely nervously scrambled to her feet and then sat back down to put on her shoes. "I will only be a minute." She folded her cloak to add to her bundle.

"You have a Bible." Ely began to panic—what excuse could she justify for having it? John picked up the book and turned it over in his hands. "It's one of the Polyglots." He looked into Ely's eyes. "Did you know there are six volumes? Where are the other five?"

"I don't know, sir." Ely looked at her feet, afraid to face him for fear he would see through her lie. "I found—I mean...'twas part of my inheritance from me pa."

"'Tis unfortunate you do not have them all. I have always wanted to own them myself."

He handed it back to her. "The woman left bread and milk for you on the table. I'll be outside." She let out a sigh of relief that John had not questioned her further.

Her thoughts returned to the innkeeper's wife with mixed emotions. On one hand, she resented the woman for revealing her gender to her husband, but on the other, she knew the woman was probably a victim of her husband's tyranny. At least she was kind enough to leave a bit of breakfast for her. She donned her hat and picked up her bundle. She drank the milk still warm from the cow. Putting the bread and one remaining apple in her pocket, she went outside into the gray morning. The rain had stopped, but the ground was soggy with clumps of mud the horse hooves had kicked up.

After she had visited the jakes and cleaned her hands on the wet grass, she saw John standing near the innkeeper. She held back for a minute, fearful the hateful man was telling John she was a woman grown. As she drew near, her fears were allayed when she saw John get on his horse and motion toward her.

"Hand me your bundle," he said. She did as she was told with some trepidation. "There is no room in my saddlebags. It will be safe here." He tucked it in front of the saddle. He bent down and held out his arm. They linked elbows and he hoisted her up. She found herself straddling the wide horse and had to grab John's coat to keep from slipping off the other side. It wasn't as if she had never sat astride, but for the past five years she had only been allowed to ride side-saddle. She reminded herself that she was a boy now and she'd better start playing her part or her identity would surely be revealed for everyone. She looked down at the innkeeper's smug face and wanted to kick him in his unshaven jowls.

"How far to Chester?" she asked, after they were on the road.

"We should be there by evening." John started to quietly sing a joyful tune she had never heard. He had a soothing singing voice, and her lack of sleep during the night finally took its toll. She fell asleep, her head resting on his back.

She awoke with a start when John leaned back to rein in the horse. The sun, peeking out between fluffy white clouds, and her growling stomach told her it was high noon. They had arrived at a village not too dissimilar from Rocester with a community well in the center of the square and a few thatch-roofed houses. A gaggle of geese scratched for seeds under a tree.

"This is Bidston. We'll stop here to give my horse a rest." With that, John linked his arm with hers so she could dismount. Her legs were numb from the ride and she grabbed onto one of John's legs to keep from falling. After she had righted herself, he dismounted and led his horse to the well. He brought up an oaken bucket and put it on the ground for the horse to drink.

"You were supposed to keep me company on this trip," he teased. "Instead, you fall asleep on my back."

"I'm sorry, sir. I didn't sleep well last night, and..."

"'Tis all right," he said as he patted the horse, "providing you stay awake for the rest of our trip."

"I promise I will, sir."

"Would you care for something to eat? There's an inn over there," he said, pointing to a two-story stone house with a goose painted over the door.

"I think not. I have food from yesterday. I'll wait here."

"As you wish. I'll bring you something to drink." He removed a tin cup from his saddlebag. She watched him walk away and enter the inn. A few people walked by, but they paid little attention to her.

Ely removed the bread and apple from her pocket. She drew up a fresh bucket of water from the well and washed her hands. The water looked clear and appetizing, but she remembered her mother's warning about drinking water from an unknown source. She ate her bread while gazing at the countryside.

She felt she had been there before and tried to recall if her family had traveled this road on their way to visit her Grandfather Sneyd when her grandmother died ten years earlier. She would have been seven at the time. Feeling the call of nature, she spotted a jakes nearby. She threw the apple core to the geese and watched them fight over the tasty tidbit. Upon her return to the well, John was waiting for her. He handed her a cup of weak ale. She thanked him and drank thirstily.

"Come lad, we still have a bit of a ride afore us."

A few minutes later, she asked him if he was familiar with the manor on the hill.

"Bedston Hall. The River Dee is close by. Soon we'll cross a bridge that leads into the walled city." He turned in the saddle to look at her. "Did you know Chester was originally a Roman fort?" Ely was aware of the history of her grandfather's home, but encouraged John to continue.

"The city has always been important because of its geographical position near the Irish Sea. It was first settled by the Romans, when they built a walled fortress and an amphitheater. Their purpose for settling this area was to establish a port for the Roman assault on Ireland."

Ely listened quietly, and even though John repeated many facts she already knew, she didn't interrupt because she liked his melodious voice as he described the history of the area. He would make a wonderful teacher and parish priest, she decided.

"You'll be interested to visit the great cathedral of St. Werburgh, Chester's patron saint." He prodded the horse with his heel when the mare decided to munch on the tall grass growing along the road. "Since Chester is some distance from the sea, it offers ships shelter from the storms. The river often fills with silt, and many ships have been stranded waiting for a high tide."

She hoped there was a ship in port when they arrived; otherwise, where would she find food and shelter—and would there be anyone wanting to buy her ring? She knew she could be arrested for vagrancy if luck wasn't with her. The plight of a dismal future was near at hand, and she trembled, trying not to sniffle. Wiping tears away with her arm, she forced herself to pay attention to what John was saying.

"Chester is not as cosmopolitan as London, but it is still a prosperous seaport with trading routes to Ireland, Scotland, and the Continent." Ely needed to get her mind off her future, and encouraging John to continue to talk would help. She cleared her voice.

"I would be interested to know about your parents, sir—and where you were born."

"In Hadleigh in Essex. I never knew my father; he died when I was a baby. I became a ward of Sir Thomas Heneage—he took my mother and me into his home. It was he who opened the door of St. John's College in Cambridge for me. I am to meet him in Chester where he is visiting a friend." He turned around in the saddle to look at Ely. "Am I boring you with all these names? You are probably not interested in my life."

"Not so, sir, and I would inquire more of your experiences in Cambridge. I would greatly desire to attend university...if I had more learning." Ely longed to tell him of her brother Francis, who studied at Oxford.

John heeled his horse and was quiet for some minutes.

"You may lack an education, but it is obvious you have God-given intelligence. What you need is a sponsor. Someone like Sir Thomas. Yes, I will speak to him of you, perchance..."

Ely squirmed. "No, please, sir. Thank you for the offer, but 'tis not necessary. I've made plans to travel." *Oh, if I only were a boy! To be able to continue my studies under the great learned men of Oxford or Cambridge...why do boys have all the advantages?* But there was no use pondering the impossible. She would have to accept what fate had in store for her. "When we arrive in Chester, I shall take my leave and make my way to the docks. Hopefully, there'll be a boat needin' a cabin boy."

"Cabin boy? Did you not mention you intended to book passage?"

"I'm sorry to say my purse is missing. It was in my pocket last eve, but when I awoke this morn, 'twas gone."

John turned in the saddle. "Stolen? Why did you not tell me sooner? It wouldn't be the first time an innkeeper has taken advantage of—"

"I did not want to cause trouble. I did not know what to do."

John leaned back in the saddle. "'Tis too far to return to the inn. How much did you have in your purse?"

"All my father left me afore he died—two half crowns, five shillings, a tuppence, and a ha'penny."

"That much! That settles it. I'll take you with me until we can figure out what to do. We'll be staying in a great house owned by Sir Thomas' friend. I will speak to him. He may know of work. There are schools in Chester you could attend until you are ready for university."

Ely pondered his suggestion, thinking perhaps it had merit— not to continue her education, but to stay in Chester just long enough to sell her ring.

"Thank you, sir. You are kind to take pity on me." With every passing mile, Ely became more and more apprehensive of what may be in store for her. Could she possibly deceive John's foster father and his friend?

By then they had reached the bridge crossing the Dee River into the walled city. As they traversed the narrow cobblestone streets, she vaguely remembered the month her family had stayed there when her grandmother died.

Today was market day, and being on toward late afternoon, the vendors were loading what was left of their goods into pull carts. She saw a man imprisoned in a pillory and wondered what sort of crime he had committed. She knew prisons were not used for punishment but rather as holding places until an inmate's trial and some form of physical punishment could be decided. Two boys were throwing bits of vegetables that had fallen to the ground at the poor prisoner.

"You lads—stop this instant," John yelled as he pulled the horse to a stop and started to dismount, but the boys had already bolted out of there. "Young rogues," he said. "Let that be a lesson to you, Ely. The man is suffering enough without heckling him further."

"I would never hurt someone intentionally."

"I would hope not." John's act of chasing off the boys endeared him to her. Her heart pounded, thinking this was the sort of man she would like for a husband. Someone kind and caring—and a learned scholar.

She looked around, trying to locate the way to her grandfather's home. If memory served her right, his estate was located along a meandering road of well-kept homes beyond the Roman wall, on a hillside overlooking the river. They left the narrow streets of the city behind. John turned his horse up a hill. Did this road also lead to her grandfather's estate? After several minutes, she felt relieved she could not identify any of the stone manors.

They reached a high hedge on either side of an iron gateway. John reined in the horse. "Open the gate for me, will you, Ely?"

She slid off the horse and as she pulled the gate wide, she realized with horror that they were at the entrance of her grandfather's estate. Was John's foster father her Grandfather Sneyd's friend? Her hands shook. She didn't know what to do. Should she take flight and risk being on her own without a farthing to her name, or should she go into the house where she might be recognized? She quickly considered the options. She hadn't seen her grandfather for two years. Not since he'd come to Rocester to meet with her father. If she played her part, perhaps he would not recognize her. Before she could make up her mind, John rode the horse through the gate and dismounted.

He stared at her as she continued to cling to the gate latch. "What is the matter, lad? There is no need to be afraid. I am sure Sir William Sneyd will be a kind man. Come now, close the gate."

Ely gazed at John. If her disguise was enough to deceive him, perhaps she could fool her grandfather as well. There was another member of her family who lived here: her grandfather's spinster sister, her own favorite great-aunt Dorothy. What was she to do?

Her decision was made for her as John spoke in a loud voice. "What is wrong with you, Elijah? Shut the gate. Here comes Sir William's man." Ely quickly closed the gate and watched John talk to the servant before handing over the reins of his horse.

"I should enter by the back entrance," Ely said.

"Don't be foolish. How are they to meet you unless you come with me?"

He linked his arm through Ely's as they walked to the front entrance. Ely first saw her grandfather with his thick eyebrows over dark piercing eyes, his beard now completely white. Her eyes swung toward the other man standing at the wide door. Slipping free of John's arm, she pulled her hat low over her eyes and moved behind him as he shook hands with both men.

"We expected you earlier, John. What detained you?"

"'Twas caught in a rainstorm and was forced to stay in an inn last eve. This lad was also on his way to Chester. We rode together." John turned, but Ely scooted further behind his back. "He is a bit shy." He moved aside, grasped Ely's arm, and pulled her forward until she was standing directly in front of her grandfather. "He planned to book passage on a boat to Brittany, but was robbed. I hope you don't mind me bringing him here." John put his arm about Ely's shoulders. "This is Elijah Goodfellow from Worcestershire. Ely, this is my godfather, Sir Thomas Heneage, and the home of Sir William Sneyd." Ely hung her head so low the only thing the men could see was the top of her cap.

"You always did bring home stray dogs and cats," laughed Sir Thomas. "I see you've graduated to lads now." Ely glanced at Sir Thomas through her eyelashes, afraid to lift her head.

"Come in, boy," Sir William said. Turning toward a servant behind them, he said, "Take this lad to the kitchen and tell the cook to give him food."

The haughty servant looked Ely up and down as if he were afraid a flea would jump off her and onto him. They moved into the great room, dominated by a huge fireplace with a chimney that extended to the ceiling. Pieces of heavy oak furniture were situated around the room, and heavy rugs hung upon the stone walls.

The servant led her across the room and down a flight of steps. When they were out of earshot of the men, he said, "Remove your hat. Where are your manners?" Ely quickly doffed the cap. "After this, you must enter through the back door." Ely stiffened her back; she would have liked nothing better than to give this overbearing servant her identity and properly put him in his place, but she dared not spoil her cover.

She followed him down another flight of stairs and into a scullery not too dissimilar from what she was familiar with at home in the Rocester manor. Her great-aunt Dorothy was talking to the cook. Ely recalled her grandfather's sister was now his housekeeper.

"Sir William said to feed this lad," the servant said as he gave Ely a shove. He turned and left while both women stopped talking to look at Ely. The strain of the past two days became unbearable when Ely saw her favorite aunt. Unable to control her emotions any longer, tears coursed down her cheeks.

"Whatever is the matter? Did Hayden say something to upset you?" The cook took Ely's arm and steered her toward a bench near the large fireplace. "What's your name, lad?"

Ely allowed herself to be led by the cook, but she couldn't take her eyes away from her aunt.

"Elizabeth, is that you?" Dorothy took a step toward her and held out her hand. "Yes, I believe it is." Ely took her aunt's hand in both of hers and placed it on her breast, then sobbed in earnest.

"Oh, my sweet lass, whatever have you done to yourself?" Her aunt put her arms around the tearful girl. "Your beautiful hair and those clothes. Whatever possessed you?"

"Please, Aunt. Don't tell Grandfather." She pushed herself away and gazed into the older woman's eyes. "He'll force me to marry the smelly duke. I cannot—I will not." Ely picked up a rag lying on the table and wiped her eyes. "How did you know 'twas me?"

"Your father's stable master arrived yesterday to tell us you had run away. He also alerted the sheriff to be on the lookout for you."

"How did Father know to search here?"

"He did not. He and other men are searching all the roads leading from Rocester." Dorothy turned toward the cook. "Do not tell anyone the lad is Elizabeth—at least not until I find out what this is all about." The cook nodded her consent.

Dorothy put her arm around Ely's waist. "Come to my room where we can talk in private." Turning toward the cook, she said, "Mary, bring a supper tray to my room. Let us see what we can do to help Elizabeth out of this dilemma."

Twelve

Give salutation to my sportive blood?
Or on my frailties why are frailer spies,
Which in their wills count bad what I think good?
No, I am that I am, and they that level
At my abuses reckon up their own...

—Sonnet 121

Dorothy Sneyd sat quietly before an open window that overlooked the river and pondered Ely's story. A large sailing vessel was anchored in the bay. The gentle northwesterly breeze brought in the smell of the sea. Dorothy breathed in the freshness while she mulled over various options for Elizabeth.

She turned to gaze at the young woman sitting naked in a hip bath. Mary poured warm water over Elizabeth's soapy hair. In her own youth she had possessed the same lithe body—small breasts and narrow hips. It was the body the king had taken a fancy to when she was a lady-in-waiting to Catherine Parr, his final wife.

Shaking off the sudden melancholy, Dorothy vowed to do something to help Elizabeth, even if it meant going against her brother's will—even if it meant banishment from his house. She did have one weapon at her disposal: the secret her brother had promised never to reveal. She would use that secret as blackmail if need be.

"Master John Overall came into the kitchen looking for her, er, him, a while ago," Mary said, turning toward Dorothy.

Ely grabbed Mary's arm. "What did you tell him?"

"Ye were sleepin' on a pad in the pantry." Mary finished drying Elizabeth's back with a towel. "He said he'd see you in the morn." Mary pushed the bath tub out into the hall and came back into the room.

Looking at the short, wet curls on Elizabeth's head, Dorothy concluded they'd have no choice but to let her continue to play the part of a boy. But tonight, Elizabeth would once again be the lovely girl she had remembered from two years ago, when she had seen her last. She walked to a chest at the foot of her bed and removed a fine woolen nightdress. She draped the gown over Elizabeth's head, letting it fall loosely around her bare feet.

"What shall I do with these?" Mary asked as she gingerly picked up the soiled doublet, trousers, and undergarments.

"Launder them and bring them back to me." The cook looked at Ely with surprise.

"Are you expecting the girl to continue with the deception?"

"That is precisely what we will have to do for the time being," Dorothy replied. "But tonight, Elizabeth will share my bed while we plan our strategy." Mary turned to leave the room. "You come back early before the others have risen, and don't forget to bring the clothes with you."

After Mary left, Ely continued to comb her hair while gazing at her aunt. "What is it you would have me do?" She shivered from the cool evening air blowing through the open window.

"Close the shutters if you are cold." Dorothy proceeded to snuff out candles in the wall sconces positioned around the room. She picked up two metal candleholders and handed one to Elizabeth. "I have a plan, but it will mean we will have to confide in my brother."

"I feel certain he will have me return to Rocester to wed...I'm surely in a pickle."

"Get into bed and let me explain what I have in mind." Elizabeth clambered into the soft bed and put a pillow against the headboard so she could sit rather than lie down. Dorothy did the same, pulling the quilt over their laps. "It is quite clear you have no intention of marrying since you have resisted many suitors for the past two years, is that correct?"

"'Tis true. I cannot tolerate being obedient to any man, much less a man who is an ass and a bore. I would probably be beaten into submission and end up running away. It is best I become a spinster, like..." Ely turned toward her aunt and blushed.

"Like me? Is that what you were going to say?"

"I am sorry, Aunt, I meant not to dishonor. I admire you greatly. But I want to have experiences that would be denied to me as a wife and mother." Ely yawned and stretched out her legs. "I have learned much from my mother. I can sew, identify healing herbs, play the lute, and I know all the country dances. I want to continue to write poetry and stories—create entertainment. I have read every book in my father's library and our priest's home. Yet these books only whet my appetite for further knowledge. I have learned languages, but have yet to practice them in ordinary usage. My desire to travel is keen. I could still follow my plan to hire on as a cabin boy."

"Don't be ridiculous," Dorothy said. "Sailors are a brutal lot. The very idea is alarming. Do you realize what could have happened to you?" She sniffed. "You may have advanced intellect, but you are a foolish, naive girl. Now listen to me. William is making plans to move us to Bradwell Hall—did you know that is our ancestral home?"

"Yes, I knew that was his plan."

"My nephew Ralph and his wife left a fortnight ago. This household won't be able to take up permanent residence until

William has finished putting his legal affairs in order. That may take another year. He has been searching for a capable man to assist him. Since John Overall concluded his studies at Cambridge, William hopes he will agree to become an apprentice in his law practice. That is the reason Sir Thomas arranged the meeting between John Overall and William."

"But John has made his plans to become a parish priest. He said he was able to secure a position near Cambridge." Elizabeth scooted down into the soft bed and pulled the covers over her shoulders and yawned. "'Tis doubtful he will want to change his plans—that is, unless Sir Thomas insists."

"Excellent." Dorothy grinned. "That may solve the only obstacle I could not give answer to."

"What obstacle? What do you mean?"

"I believe I can convince William to have you become his clerk. It would mean you will have to continue your disguise, but you would have an opportunity to learn the common law of England and the laws of Europe as well. William's affairs reach far and wide. A trip abroad could well be in the offing."

Ely scooted back into a sitting position. "Aunt! How wonderful that would be. If only it could be so. I will need more manly garments, and my hair needs a proper cut, and..." Her mind jumped from living the life of a boy to wondering what sort of employer her grandfather would make. "Everyone would have to get used to calling me Ely—the name my sisters already use." Turning toward Dorothy, she impulsively hugged her. "Do you truly think you can convince grandfather?"

"Yes, I believe so." She kissed Ely on the cheek. "Now, blow out your candle and get some sleep. I must think on how best to approach my obstinate brother." Dorothy gazed at the happy girl squirming beside her. She wanted nothing more than to entrust this beloved girl with her secret, the one she had held in her heart for so many years. But she dared not. She was bound never to reveal her true past to anyone.

Thirteen

Dressed in a little brief authority,
Most ignorant of what he's most assured,
His glassy essence, like an angry ape,
Plays such fantastic tricks before high heaven...
—*Measure for Measure*, Act 2, Scene 2

Ely sat alone at a small table in the kitchen eating her breakfast. She had Francis' clothes back on, now smelling fresh from the wash. The cook was busy plucking a chicken just outside the door that stood open to let in the sun.

Ely felt restless, wishing she were a mouse in the corner of the room where her great-aunt Dorothy was meeting with Sir William. She was trying to fathom what sort of power her aunt had over her grandfather, when John Overall arrived.

"Here you are," he said. "How are you faring?"

"I am doing well, thank you." Ely quickly stood and nearly curtsied, remembering to bow. She smiled, showing her even teeth. "The cook has given me boiled eggs to eat this morn. Sir William's sister is very kind."

"It appears you are well treated." He looked inside her bowl, which still had a few scraps of egg in the bottom. "With your face all shiny and roses in your cheeks, you look like a pretty girl." Ely could feel her face heat up. "And you blush like a girl, too."

Her heart leapt, thinking John had seen through her disguise, but his smile made it clear he had been jesting. She lowered her head, unsure how to answer him. With alarm, she realized she only had Francis' undershirt on this morning as the doublet was still damp. She saw the padded garment hanging on a hook near the fireplace and thought frantically of retrieving it to hide the thrust of her nipples against the shirt, but it was too late.

"What is this?" John said, grabbing her by the arm. He started to put his hand on her breast, but quickly withdrew it. "What is this!"

With his question repeated, he appeared more flustered than she. "What do you think it is, kind sir?"

"You are not a lad." He looked her in the eyes. "You...you are not a lad at all!"

Ely walked to the fireplace and pulled down the doublet. "Why do you keep repeating yourself?" She put on the padded vest. She watched as John noisily swallowed. He straightened his shoulders, taking on the stance of a soldier. "Explain yourself, Mistress..."

"Elizabeth," she finished for him. "Elizabeth Trentham of Staffordshire. Please continue to call me Elijah, or Ely." She looked toward the steps that led to the main part of the house. "We should go into the garden where no one can overhear. I will explain."

When they walked past the cook, it was obvious the woman had overheard their exchange. "Please tell Aunt Dorothy I will be in the garden with Master John." The cook nodded and entered the house.

"You are becoming more and more mysterious by the minute. Who are you to be ordering a servant in the house of a gentleman?" John demanded as they walked down a path.

"Pray lower your voice." Ely walked on ahead, down a gentle slope into a kitchen garden consisting of clipped hedges and gravel paths. She led him to a stone bench at the entrance to a formal garden beautifully landscaped with rock work, a fountain, and a statue of a stag.

"Pray, sit here." Now that her masquerade had been uncovered, she could relax and be herself. However, she still felt uneasy being alone with an eligible man who was fair to look upon.

"I do not feel like sitting," he said.

"As you please," she said, sitting down. He put his foot on the bench and bent toward her.

"Well?" When she didn't respond, he straightened himself and stomped off for a few feet before returning, only to walk away again.

"Please sit. You are making me ill at ease with your pacing." He whirled around.

"I do not appreciate being made the fool, Mistress Elizabeth," he snarled. "Here I thought I was assisting an orphaned boy, only to find he is not a boy at all, but a—"

"What I am going to tell you, sir..." Ely rubbed the palms of her hands against her breeches. "I want to confide in you—not as a friend. I mean...I should like to be your friend, but what I have to say must be kept in confidence. Will you hear my confession as a man of the cloth?"

He seemed to think about what she had said, took a deep breath, and sat on the bench beside her. She breathed a sigh of relief. "Go on," he said.

Ely then told him everything, starting with her plan to escape from being forced to marry a man she detested. Moments later, when she related her anxiety of finding herself at the entrance to her grandfather's estate, he interrupted.

"You mean to say I unwittingly brought you to...to your own grandfather's..."

"Yes. Can you imagine my state of mind? Either run away to the docks or enter the house with the hope Grandfather would not recognize me. I was all in a muddle, and when I saw my Aunt Dorothy in the kitchen—she is my grandfather's sister and housekeeper—I felt overwhelmed with the thought of continuing my deception, especially to someone who knows me well. She recognized me at once."

"I met Misstress Dorothy this morning. I had an appointment with Sir William, but our meeting has been delayed."

"Aunt Dorothy is talking to him about my continuing with my disguise."

"Continuing with your...? You cannot. It is unseemly for you to..." He looked her over, from doublet to baggy breeches. He looked quite dapper in his flared velvet breeches, drawn tight under his knee, and hose held up by garters. A ruffled collar peeked from beneath his embroidered green doublet.

"You do not understand. I could never be a girl again—at least not until my hair grows." Ely threaded her fingers through her ragged red hair. "My grandfather needs help in his law practice, and a woman would never be accepted working for him."

"That is the purpose of my coming here—to be interviewed for that position."

"You said you hope to have a parish in Cambridge—surely you do not want to work as a law clerk, do you?"

John stood and began his pacing again. "No, I do not, but Sir Thomas expects me to do so. I owe him much for his trust in me. Howsoever..." a smile slowly appeared around his mouth. "Perhaps what you have in mind may solve my problem, too."

Their conversation was interrupted by the crunch of footfalls on the gravel path. Sir William and Dorothy Sneyd were headed their way. Ely could not help but notice the smug expression on her aunt's face.

"Good morning, Sir William—ma'am," John said, bowing at the waist. Ely stood and bowed as well.

"John, would you excuse us. I must talk to my grand...this person."

"Certainly, sir." John turned toward Ely and winked, then quickly left the three of them alone.

"Ely, is it?" He said looking her up and down. "I would never have agreed to this shameful exhibition if I did not know of your, er...ability. I always felt intelligence was wasted on you." Ely sat back down with Dorothy next to her.

Sir William crossed his arms and glared. "Understand this, my girl. I will brook no slack because you are..." He harrumphed. "My grandchild. You will be treated the same as any man in my employ." With that, he abruptly left and stormed back to the manor in such a huff that Ely did not have an opportunity to thank him.

She turned to her aunt. "How ever did you convince him?"

"'Tis best you do not know." With that, she chuckled under her breath. "Someday, we will discuss it, but not now. Shall we return to the house?"

~ * ~

Sir William ordered Ely to confine herself to a room in the servants' quarters until Sir Thomas departed. Much to her chagrin, she learned John Overall also planned to leave at daybreak. He had told Dorothy he was anxious to begin his career as apprentice parish priest in Cambridge. Hearing this, Ely sent word to have him meet her in the garden before he partook of his evening meal.

When he approached her, she grabbed his hand, and pulled him down the path to the bench they had occupied that morning. He pulled his hand from her grasp.

"Please, Mistress Elizabeth, holding hands is not proper." She was surprised to see him blush a rosy red. "I must not be tempted."

"Oh John, do not be a prude. Please treat me as the boy you first met."

"'Tis not the same. I know you are..." He lowered his voice to a whisper. "...a lass."

"For pity's sake. I am not trying to seduce you. I only wanted you to know how sorry I am that you are leaving. I had so hoped to spend more time with you." When he backed away from her, she quickly elaborated. "I long to have many more intellectual conversations. I so rarely meet anyone so well educated...someone I can converse with on an equal level."

"'Tis not seemly for you to be equal to—I mean...perhaps you have been acting as a boy too long. You must have quite forgotten your place in society."

"John Overall, you are quite perplexing. Is it not possible for you to view me as your friend and forget I am a girl?"

He stared at her for a few seconds before responding. "I shall try. 'Tis easier for me to do so since you are still dressed as a lad."

"Good. Let us sit. I have something for you." She picked up a book she had left on the bench. "Here, I want you to have this."

John took the book from her. "'Tis your Polyglot Bible!"

"I have the other five books as well. They are all promised to me when I marry...or become of age."

He tried to return the book to her. "Then you should keep this one. 'Tis a shame to have them separated."

"You don't understand...I intend to give them all to you eventually. Who better to have them than a future priest in our queen's church? 'Tis the least I can do to thank you for taking care of me on the road. If it had not been for you, I am at quite a loss of what would have become of me. I can now live as a boy for a while longer and learn law from my grandfather. I truly believe God led you to me."

"Even so, I am not sure 'tis proper for me to accept such a valuable gift as this." John held the book tightly in his arms, and she could tell he had no intention of returning it to her. She smiled, assured he would always remember her whenever he read the book.

"Would it be proper for us to exchange letters?" Ely asked. "I would not like it if we could not keep in touch with one another. I would so like to know what becomes of you."

"And me of you." He smiled into her eyes. "Methinks you are to lead a more exciting life."

"Perhaps so." She laughed merrily. "Will you write first? I will be living here in Chester."

"Yes, as soon as I return to Cambridge." He took her hand as they began the walk toward the house. "And when and if we meet again, I promise I will not be such a...prude. Is that not what you called me?" They were both laughing. "Wherever did you come up with that word?"

"I made it up when...'tis similar to a French word." They were still laughing when they entered the manor.

Fourteen

Though justice be thy plea, consider this—
That in the course of justice none of us
Should see salvation. We do pray for mercy,
And that same prayer doth teach us all to render
The deeds of mercy.
      —*The Merchant of Venice*, Act 4, Scene 1

The first assignment William Sneyd gave Ely was to become familiar with the *Nova Statuta* that had been printed in Latin and French in 1507. During her free time, she read every book in her grandfather's law library. She would jot down points of law she didn't understand and ask him to explain. She quite enjoyed working with him and listening as he gave her examples of cases he had handled in the past. He must have been pleased with her work, because he turned over the writing of wills entirely to her.

Ely had been working under her grandfather's tutelage for nearly five months. There were times he must have quite forgotten she was a girl, and true to his promise, he gave her no favoritism. She even detected a pleasing demeanor to his countenance whenever she took the initiative to offer her opinion on certain points of law.

Sir William became mayor of Chester in 1567 and had become a backer for a law that would provide relief for mariners who had become sick, hurt, or maimed. It was common practice for ship owners or the captain of a ship to discharge a seaman who was no longer fit. These men were often homeless and forced to beg. Sir William had stated many times, "'Tis not a fit ending for the men who have served her majesty so faithfully." Ely quite approved of her grandfather's position on the matter.

So was the case of an Irish seaman by the name of Dennis O'Leary, when he was put to shore after losing an eye and his left leg during a battle with Spanish pirates in the Irish Sea. In addition to his injuries, Dennis developed a sweating sickness. When the ship limped into port in Chester, Dennis was at death's door. The captain gave the owner of a popular ale house near the docks a few coins to provide Dennis a bed in his storage room until he died or was well enough to make it on his own. The inn owner well remembered his own past shipboard experiences and felt a kinship with the suffering sailor. The owner's wife was skilled in the use of tonics and simples, and with nourishing soup, soon had Dennis on the road to recovery.

After Dennis was up and about, and being skilled in wood carving, he made himself a peg leg with leather straps that fastened tightly around his thigh. He became more and more proficient in its use, lessening the need for crutches.

Since Ely's grandfather's office was in the walled city close to the seafront, Ely had many occasions to walk along the waterfront. Ships with furled sails anchored in the bay while others, with their sails fully extended, departed for open water. She loved to imagine what it would be like to sail on one of those ships.

Her grandfather had not mentioned traveling to other countries, but she felt sure he would soon. His venture into importing and exporting needed to be curtailed, if not outright liquidated, if he intended to move to Bradwell Hall in Newcastle-under-Lyme. She had overheard him discuss plans with his son, Ralph. He said that between pirating on the seas and storms destroying ships, his shipping business had become too risky. Since Thomas Trentham had already amassed a fortune in land management, both the Trenthams and the Sneyds were assured they would see even higher profits by forming a partnership.

Ely first met Dennis O'Leary sitting outside the Sailor's Port Inn, a wooden bowl before him, ready to accept a coin that may be flipped his way. Never idle, he occupied himself with his carving. Ely paused, put a farthing into his bowl, and became fascinated with how a little wooden bird was seemingly coming to life under his skillful fingers. Ely was so entranced watching the disabled sailor that she became oblivious to the ugly scar that ran from his empty eye socket to his chin. Finishing his carving, Dennis stood with the help of one crutch and handed the bird to Ely. It was on this chance meeting Ely came to know the former seaman, and often stopped to pass the time of day.

Ely and Dennis became friends as he entranced her with stories of his adventures on the high seas. She in turn told him of her original plan to be hired on as a cabin boy.

"You have received good fortune to be allowed to train with Sir William. Cabin boys are often badly abused by sea captains and their officers." She wanted to ask him in what manner of abuse, but sensed she should not inquire further. Ely had become quite skillful playing the part of a boy and Dennis was bluntly forthcoming. Through him, she learned the colorful vocabulary of the sea. She also learned by being observant of other sailors as they arrived or departed the harbor.

One day, as Ely was using Sir William's notes to write a letter to a client, she was interrupted by a commotion in the street. She thought she heard Dennis' name being shouted, and she moved to the open door to observe a crowd form near the quay. Curious as to what was taking place, she ran down the cobblestone street to where the crowd was standing. She was horrified to see Dennis being pulled away in the same manner as a dog, a rope about his neck.

"What is this—I know this man! What crime has he committed?"

A toothless sailor answered, "He be arrested for vagrancy."

"Vagrancy! Surely a mistake has been made."

"He be deemed able to work by the justice of the peace."

Ely ran down the street trying to catch Dennis. Gasping for breath, she was finally able to grab his arm. "Dennis. Don't be afraid. I will help you."

"There's nothing ye can do, lad. This be my second offence."

The man dragging Dennis by the neck turned around. "Get away from this man afore I haul you in, too!" The man had a whip in his other hand and made a threatening move toward Ely. He gave such a violent tug on the rope that Dennis' peg leg gave way. Ely ran to his side to help him regain his footing, only to receive a whiplash across her back for her trouble. Ignoring the pain, she refused to move until Dennis was back on his one good foot and the peg was firmly planted on the ground.

"Leave me, Ely. I don'na want ye harmed."

"I will provide a defense for you. 'Tis not right for you to be arrested."

Even though Ely had good intentions, she did not know how she would be able to fulfill her promise, since her grandfather was in Scotland and wasn't expected to return for a fortnight, but she would think of something.

It didn't take long for her to decide what to do. She knew the statute for vagrancy. The first offence was punishable by being whipped and burned in the right ear with a red-hot iron—unless someone came forth with meaningful employment. She remembered seeing a bandage on Dennis' ear and wondered at the time what had happened. On Dennis' second offence, he would be hanged—again, unless someone was willing to hire him. For the third offence, however, he would be hanged regardless. She was familiar with the new Poor Law act the queen had passed in 1576, just three years ago. Perhaps she could use this law to defend Dennis.

Sir William left several blank pages with his signature at the bottom for her to use when writing to his clients. She would use one of those pages to send a letter to the magistrate. The letter informed him that he (Sir William) would have taken up Dennis' case; however, he was being called to Scotland on the queen's business. In his stead, an associate of his, a Mister Messenger, would be coming to Chester on the morrow to stand for Dennis' defense. Ely melted the sealing wax and stamped it with Sir William's own seal, and then she closed the office. After she retrieved her horse from the stable, she delivered the letter and rode home.

Her great-aunt Dorothy's carriage arrived at the same time Ely was walking in from the stable. She greeted her with a warm smile.

"Home early, are you not? Is something amiss?"

"Yes, Aunt, there is—" A servant hurried down the stairs to take a large package from the carriage driver. "I see you've been shopping. Buy anything interesting?" Ely asked, looking at the large parcel tied with string.

"I've picked up a new frock from the dressmaker. Wish that I could have purchased one for you as well," she whispered behind her hand.

"Perhaps soon, Aunt, when my hair grows longer," she whispered in return. "May I beg your leave to engage you in a plan to save someone's life?"

"That sounds exciting. Come to my room so I may remove my shoes. They are a torture." Dorothy interrupted a maid's dusting with orders to bring two flagons of sweet cider and sweetmeats to her room.

Ely sat on the floor and carefully eased Dorothy's shoes from her feet. "Ooh, so much better. The older you grow, the more misshapen your feet become," Dorothy said as Ely massaged oil onto her aunt's feet. "At your age, 'tis best to go without shoes whenever you have the opportunity." Dorothy pulled her feet away from Ely's massage and stood to let in a maid carrying a tray.

After the maid left, Ely and Dorothy sat across from each other at a small table near the window. "Tell me, my dear, what is happening? Who is it you need to save?"

"His name is Dennis O'Leary, a seaman I happened to meet. He has been arrested for vagrancy, but he is not a vagrant; he is but a poor beggar. Just because he has been able to walk with the use of a peg leg, they expect him to work."

"Who...what is his name?"

"Dennis O'Leary. An Irish sailor put ashore by his captain when he lost his leg and eye in a battle. He is an excellent carver— and very intelligent. He knows how to write and cipher, and he tells wonderful stories of his adventures at sea and..."

"I thought him dead," Dorothy said.

"You thought him...? Do you know him, Aunt?"

Dorothy's face became pale and the hand holding her flagon began to shake, forcing her to set it on the table. She stared into Ely's face, seeing before her a pretty girl dressed as a boy in tights, doublet, and ruff. Her hair now fell to her shoulders but was kept hidden beneath a cap in public.

"Aunt, you look as if you'd seen a ghost. What is amiss? Do you know Dennis?"

Dorothy's linked fingers showed knuckles white with tension. "Yes, I did know him—there was a time he was my kin."

"Your what...? Aunt, you cannot be serious. This man is a beggar, a poor—"

"That was not always the case." Dorothy leaned back into her chair. "Let me tell you his story." She took a long drink of cider. "You did not know I had a daughter?"

"No...Aunt, I thought you never married."

"Yes, that is quite true, but nonetheless, I did have a daughter. Her name was Ann. She died in chi—that is, when she was eighteen. Ann was but an infant when I brought her to Chester. William agreed to be her guardian. She was raised in this household with the same privileges as Ralph and Jane, your mother. Jane and Ann were cousins of the same age and best friends."

"I never knew Mother had a cousin named Ann. Why has she never told me?" She couldn't understand. Ely wanted to ask who Ann's father was, but she knew if her aunt wanted her to know, she would tell her.

"Because I never married," continued Dorothy, "Ann was a bastard and an outcast. Her prospects for a good marriage were nil, and I thought she would have to remain a spinster—like me. You are like Ann in many ways, and like you she loved to go for long walks and often found her way to the docks. She had an active imagination and could see herself traveling to another country to live. Had I been willing to finance her passage, I am sure she would have left Chester forever. However, fate took a hand when she met Dennis and fell in love."

It was difficult for Ely to imagine anyone falling in love with Dennis, but she realized that at one time he could have looked quite different, perhaps even handsome.

"Dennis was first mate aboard a ship that sailed routinely from England to Ireland. I am sure Dennis must have sought out Ann's acquaintance. She was very young and became enamored with the sailor. She discovered he was from a good but poor family in Ireland. He was educated by a learned monk, and had he the resources, he could have attended a university. But he was overly fond of the sea. It wasn't long before Dennis was asking my brother for permission to marry Ann. William was quite against it at first, but when he realized Ann could probably do no better, he relented. With William's influence and money, Dennis could have become master of his own ship in time. Ann and Dennis were married for only three months when he went to sea. While he was away, Ann became ill and died."

"What happened to Dennis?"

"When his ship returned and he discovered Ann had died, he was quite beside himself. His ship needed repair and wasn't due to depart for several weeks, but Dennis could not bring himself to stay in a city where he and Ann had been happy. He secured a lesser position aboard a different ship and departed within a week. We never heard a word about him until two years later, when the captain of his ship came to tell us Dennis had been killed and buried at sea."

"He must not have wanted Ann's family to know of his injuries. I am sure you would never recognize him now."

"Perhaps not. Dennis was a proud man—he would not want to take charity from us. But to become a beggar...'tis more than I can fathom. We must do something to help him.

"It is what I intend to do. To think he and I were once related..." Ely noticed tears forming in Dorothy's eyes and reasoned it was because of the memory of her daughter. Wanting to change the subject, she told her aunt of her plan to pose as a lawyer from another town. To do so she would need to dress the part of a man from a higher position in society.

"I intend to be Mister Messenger. Will you help me secure the necessary look? I was thinking of a mustache and chin whiskers to make me look older—but am quite at a loss as to how to paste them to my skin. I will also need help with my attire."

Fifteen

After four days of steady work, I had filled a notebook with research material. My goal was to accumulate enough information to write a book. Eventually, I would put everything into some sort of an organized format. Even though Josie and I might find evidence Elizabeth Trentham possessed the requirements needed to be Shakespeare, I was enough of a realist to know that to prove she actually wrote the plays would be nearly impossible. I had no intention of sharing my skepticism with Sudie. She had such high hopes.

Josie and I kept in close communication, and I looked forward to comparing our notes when I returned home. Which brought me back to where in the world would I live when I got back to Oregon? I no longer had my mother's house to go to and I'd declined Josie's invitation to move back in with her. With Frank there, that wasn't an option, as far as I was concerned. I was relieved when my realtor called recommending a bed and breakfast in the Oregon wine country, just a few miles outside of the city. I made reservations, happy to note it was off-season with lower prices. At least now I knew where I was going when I went home.

~ * ~

It was Saturday, the last day of my visit, when Sudie said she wanted to show me something. I followed her into her husband's office. She picked up a worn and faded notebook from her desk.

"Look what I found! Grandmother Emma's journal. It was in this room all along."

I hugged her tightly. "This is great. Tell me, what did you find out?"

"I haven't taken the time to read it thoroughly, other than to prove Katherine and Elizabeth were sisters. They grew up in Rocester, a small township in Staffordshire. There were five children, with Elizabeth the eldest, followed by a boy, Francis. Besides Katherine, there were Dorothy and Thomas the fourth, the baby of the family. There was another daughter, Lettice, who died shortly after birth. Please take this home with you." She handed me the bound book.

"I'll copy it and send this right back to you." I took a good look at her, just now noticing how tired and frail she seemed to be. "Would you care for your glass of wine? I put one of Nolah's casseroles in the oven. It should be ready shortly."

"I think I'll skip dinner tonight. I'm very tired. Could you help me to my room?" I put my arm around her back as we walked the short distance to her bedroom.

"Will you be okay?" I asked. "Should we call your doctor?"

"No, no." She sat on the edge of her bed. "Maybe I'll get up later, after I've rested a bit." She picked up her nightgown that had been placed at the foot of her bed. "Could you help me undress?"

"Of course." After she was in her gown, I said, "My flight leaves at seven in the morning. I'll have to leave for Little Rock around four to make it. In case you're still asleep when I go to bed, I'll say my goodbyes now."

"I hate to see you leave." She swallowed her nightly pills with a glass of water she had sitting on her nightstand.

"I'll call often to let you know how the research is progressing."

"Just one more thing. Have you been visited by...the woman?"

"What do you mean?" Confused, I sat on her bed and took her hand.

"Three times now...in dreams...I thought it was Katherine, but now I think it may be Elizabeth—maybe both, I don't know." She squeezed my hand. "Have they come to you, too?"

"No, no dreams." She seemed disappointed, so I quickly added, "I've sensed a presence though..." I hesitated to tell her about seeing the aberrations. Even to me they seemed too ludicrous. "Perhaps I still will...in my dreams."

"Yes, I'm sure you will. Please don't give up on our project, no matter what happens to me." She squeezed my hand tightly. "Promise me you won't."

"Of course. I promise." I brushed her hair back with my hand. She smiled weakly.

"It's been such a pleasure to get to know you. You're like the daughter I never had." My eyes misted over when I bent down to kiss her creased forehead. I felt helpless, knowing it was only a matter of time before she'd be gone. I placed her medical alert pendant on the nightstand.

~ * ~

It was early when I climbed into bed. I propped myself up with pillows and opened Emma's journal. The first part covered several pages of train travel to New York, then a steamship across the Atlantic. They landed in Plymouth and traveled to London by rail. She wrote of several places they visited before taking the train north to Staffordshire. She gave a history of Rocester having first been a Roman fort and later a monastery for several hundred years. The monastery was vacated on the orders of King Henry VIII and Thomas Trentham had it remodeled for his home after marrying Jane Sneyd. Her family was from Chester where her father, William Sneyd, was an attorney and former mayor of the coastal city. Emma wrote of how the wealth of both families had grown when they formed a partnership in land management techniques.

"Cynthia..."

It was Sudie's voice coming through the heating vent. I threw Emma's journal aside, jumped from the bed, and raced down the stairs.

Sudie tried to sit up from the floor where she had fallen. I rushed to her side and put my arm around her shoulders.

"Sudie! What happened?"

"Pain—in my chest. Need to find my nitro and..." With strength I never knew I had, I picked her up from the floor and laid her on the bed. My elbow brushed against her medical alert device. I pushed the button.

"Send an ambulance. Sudie McFadden...it's her heart." I found a brown pill bottle of nitroglycerin behind the lamp. I carefully shook out the tiny pill into my palm and placed it under her tongue. I ran to unlock the front door and turn on the porch light.

I let the EMTs into the house only minutes later, though it seemed like an eternity. I gave the pill bottle to one of the men and told him what I had done.

"I've got a pulse," an EMT said.

I watched as they put her on a gurney.

"Where are you taking her?" I followed them from the house.

"Saint Joseph's." I watched as they loaded Sudie into an ambulance and sped away.

I got dressed and had just put on my coat when I remembered to call her nephew. Clay...something. Phone number? Where? In the office. Hurrying to the room, I turned on the light and searched through the desk. Finding her address book, I saw the name Clayton Darnell. While his phone was ringing, I glanced at the clock: 10:13. Just after eight in Portland.

"Hello." A female voice answered.

I thought Sudie had said Clay was a widower.

"Clayton Darnell, please. It's an emergency."

"It's for you. Some sort of emergency."

"Yes. Who is it?"

"Mr. Darnell? I've been staying with your aunt Sudie. I think she's had a heart attack. The ambulance just left. They're taking her to St. Joseph Hospital."

"How is she?"

"They had her on oxygen. I'm leaving for the hospital now."

"Wait a minute. Who are you?"

"Cynthia Parsons. Your aunt invited me to stay with her."

"Oh yes, she told me about you."

"Will you be able to come?"

"I'll get the first flight available, probably in the morning." I put her address book in my purse so I could call the Springers when I got to the hospital.

~ * ~

When a nurse confirmed Sudie had suffered a heart attack, I called Tom Springer. I expected them to come to the hospital, but they didn't show.

After I rescheduled my flight for the following day, I tried to sleep in a waiting room chair, but finally gave up. The time crawled by. It was nearly six when a doctor came to tell me Sudie's condition had stabilized, but she was still critical. He allowed me to see her, but for only a minute.

Multiple machines monitored her condition. Someone congratulated me on the quick response; otherwise, she may not have made it. I pulled a chair near the bed and took Sudie's hand in mine. The scene reminded me of just over two months ago when my mother died. Hot tears stung my eyes.

A half hour later, I was back at Sudie's house, took a quick shower, and fell into bed. I woke up mid-afternoon. An hour later, I was waiting for Clay in the hospital lobby. I had been told Sudie's condition had improved enough to move her to a room. I saw a middle-aged man standing at the information desk, and wondered if this was Clay. He was tall, at least six-two, had dark-hair with a smattering of silvery gray. His appearance put me in mind of Gregory Peck in *To Kill a Mockingbird*, but perhaps that was only because he too was an attorney, perhaps not so handsome, but still compelling.

"Excuse me, are you Clay Darnell?" Deep blue eyes stared back at me.

"Yes, and you are?"

"Cynthia Parsons."

"Thanks for calling me. How is Sudie?"

"She's in a private room now. I'll show you the way."

A nurse met us in the hall. "Miss Parsons, Mrs. McFadden has been asking for you."

"This is her nephew. He just arrived."

"I'll take you both in, but please stay for only a few minutes."

Clay allowed me to enter first as we approached Sudie's bedside. The nurse left the room. Sudie held out both hands and we each took one. I was happy to see she no longer needed oxygen.

"I'm so happy to see you two together." Speaking in a soft voice, she continued, "Clay. There's so much you need to know. Cynthia has been staying with me while we..."

"Don't try to talk now. You'll need to get your strength back before—"

"But I need to tell you." Sudie looked at me. "What Cynthia is doing is vital..."

"Cynthia can tell me about it. You need to rest. Why don't you wait until tomorrow when you feel stronger?"

She turned her head toward me. "Show him the book—tell him what we've been doing. And don't let him talk you out of continuing with our project."

"Okay. I promise."

The nurse reentered the room and motioned for us to leave. I kissed Sudie's cheek. Clay followed a couple of minutes later. I saw him knuckle a tear from the corner of his eye as he walked toward the nurses' station. He asked to have Sudie's doctor call him and handed the nurse a business card.

He took my arm as we walked down the hall. "Other than my step-daughter, Sudie's the only family I have left."

"She's a wonderful lady. I only wish I had met her years ago."

"What's this business about a book, and what project?"

"It's an ancient book of prayers. Shall we go somewhere for a cup of coffee and I'll tell you about it and my involvement."

He scrubbed the stubble on his jaw. "I need to clean up. Let's go to Sudie's. I feel like I've been put through a wringer."

"Sure. Meet you there?" He agreed. I wondered about this man. It was obvious he had a great affection for his elderly aunt.

We arrived back at the house about the same time.

"Which room are you in?"

"The one directly above Sudie's. I'll drive to Little Rock tonight—I have a morning flight."

"Stay here. There's plenty of room." He picked up a suitcase and a garment bag from the floor. "If you make a pot of coffee, I'll join you in a few minutes." I watched him walk up the curved staircase and wondered if I should have allowed him to tell me to stay here for the night, but there was no sense arguing over a minor detail. When he arrived at the top, he looked down at me. Feeling embarrassed he'd caught me staring at him, I hurried to the kitchen.

He joined me a half hour later, his hair damp from the shower. He had shaved and changed into a russet-colored golf shirt tucked into dark blue Dockers. I figured with his athletic build and flat abs, he probably belonged to some exclusive recreation club.

"That smells good. I could sure use a cup." I handed him a mug filled with strong black coffee.

"There's milk in the fridge."

He sipped the coffee. "This is perfect, thanks. Shall we sit down?" He pulled out a chair from the kitchen table and I joined him.

"Okay. Let's hear the story."

I took a drink of coffee first. His abrupt tone of voice bothered me, but I didn't want to be defensive, for Sudie's sake. "I imagine you're aware that Sudie had your secretary find me?"

"Yes, something to do with an article you wrote."

"The topic of the piece was of great interest to her. It had to do with my theory Shakespeare was a front for a woman writer. She wanted me to help her prove..."

"Help her? Help her with what?" His voice was low—probably an excellent public speaker.

I squirmed a bit, wondering if he were another chauvinistic male who would never believe a woman could be Shakespeare. He looked straight into my eyes—his were mesmerizing. I wished I didn't feel like I was on a witness stand. "Are you by any chance a criminal lawyer?"

"Trial attorney. How could you tell?"

"It isn't hard."

He smiled. "I'm sorry if I seem too abrupt. So you agreed to come here based solely on some sort of theory?"

"You may know of the Shakespeare authorship dispute—that William Shakespeare may not have actually written—"

"Yes, I know. I did take a Shakespeare course in college." He took another drink of coffee. "There's a popular opinion that some earl may have been behind his works."

"Yes, that's right. My essay offered a different opinion—that it wasn't necessarily a man who wrote the plays, but a woman." I immediately saw skepticism in his expression. "It may not be as farfetched as you think. In fact, Sudie found proof I could be right."

"Proof? What proof?" I had his full attention.

"It has to do with a prayer book originally owned by one of her...one of your ancestors. Her name was Katherine Stanhope. We're certain she would have been a sister-in-law to Edward de Vere, the seventeenth Earl of Oxford."

"Yes, that's the name of the man who...wait, that's unreal! Do you mean the Earl of Oxford could be related to Sudie—and me? I'll be damned." He leaned across the table. "Okay. What about the book?"

I went on to tell him of the events that led Sudie to call me, including the dream telling her to look in the trunk, finding the prayer book and the *Midsummer* page, and why she thought I could help her.

"Do you mean Sudie may have found an original page written by Shakespeare? I can't believe it!" He ran his hand across his hair. "Holy sh—! Where is it now?"

"In her safe."

He stood. "Good. Let's go get it."

"Wait a minute. Don't you want to know why she called me instead of you?"

"Right. Why did she?" His eyes narrowed as he looked down on me.

"She had every intention of telling you, but you're busy with a trial and she didn't want to sidetrack you." I stood up, trying not to look intimidated.

"She's right about that." He walked toward the office with me trailing behind. He went directly to the bookcase and pulled it forward.

"Locked. Do you know the combination?"

"Haven't the foggiest."

He looked around the office. "She would have it written down—it must be around here somewhere." He walked to the desk and began looking through the drawers. "I probably have it at home, but it has to be here somewhere." He paused for a second. "I remember now. Uncle Paul showed me a secret..." I watched as he reached under the roll top on the desk. The tiny door opened, revealing the drawer. "There's only a key in here."

"That's the key to the strong box where she put the book."

"So, we're back to square one." He sat down in the chair behind the desk. "I'll get the combination from Sudie tomorrow." He looked at his watch and then grinned, showing straight white teeth, deep dimples creasing both cheeks and laugh lines crinkling at the corners of his eyes. I felt my heart beat faster.

"I'm starved. What say we go out to eat and get better acquainted?"

We drove along a lake to a beautiful home that had been converted into a restaurant. The steaks we ordered were exceptional. Now that the original clumsiness of our first meeting had passed, I began to feel more comfortable with him, especially after two glasses of an excellent cabernet sauvignon. When I asked about his practice, he told me he was with the Morgan-Tessler law firm in Portland. I was aware of the large law firm with its reputation of defending difficult cases.

"Sudie's heart attack couldn't have come at a worse time for me. I can't afford to stay here for very long." He removed his glasses and cleaned them on a napkin. The dark circles under his eyes made it obvious he needed sleep. "I don't feel right in asking you, but is there any chance you could extend your stay?"

"I'd like to, but I can't. I have an early morning flight tomorrow." He frowned and I quickly said, "My mother died not long ago and I'm involved in settling her estate. It was difficult for me to come here even now..."

"I shouldn't have asked. Sudie's my responsibility." He picked up his coffee cup and took a sip. "So, what have you and Sudie been doing this week?"

"Mainly research...a lot of reading and planning how we want to proceed. Sudie's grandmother kept a journal when she traveled to England about a hundred years ago to trace her family tree. I was reading it when Sudie had her heart attack. I'm going to return it as soon as I have a chance to make a copy."

"I'd like to read it, too, but what I really want to see is the page she thinks is an original..." He seemed to ponder what he had just said. "Perhaps Sudie should just make it public."

"No, not yet. We're still working on trying to prove a woman is the real Shakespeare."

"But why a woman? The page could have been written by William Shakespeare himself."

"Well, yes, that could be true, but there is definite reason to believe it was not only unlikely, but in some respects even impossible for Shakespeare to have..." I noticed his eyes had a teasing aspect to them, and I realized trying to convince him otherwise would take more time to explain than I cared to get into. "Do you realize the importance of finding an original page of a Shakespeare manuscript?"

"Right now, I'm too tired to realize much of anything. How long do you think it will take you to do the research?" He looked at the bill the waiter brought and placed his credit card on the tray.

"It's difficult to tell," I said. "Several months, and I still may never find absolute proof. It's a very interesting research project and I promised Sudie I'd continue, even if..."

"I'll talk to Sudie tomorrow." He signed his name to a charge slip. "Let's go—I'm beat."

Sixteen

It was nearly six p.m. when I arrived at the White Dove Inn, rumpled, tired and hungry. The home was a large, renovated farm house. After signing in, I was led into a large room with a beautiful river rock fireplace with heat from real logs blazing cheerily. Comfortable sofas and overstuffed chairs were situated randomly around the room, with books in an ornate bookcase. A modern desk sat off to the side with a computer and printer. Stemmed glasses and a carafe of red wine along with white wine in an ice bucket sat on a small table near a window, and an assortment of cookies.

I left a briefcase, bookbag and large suitcase in the car, and only brought in an overnight bag. We walked up a staircase into a long hallway. It appeared there were three rooms on this level. My room was perfect. A double bed was covered in a beautiful comforter and matching sham. Besides a chest of drawers, a desk sat in an alcove. Perfect for my needs. The owner's name was Lisa

Nyberg, a woman a bit older than me, maybe in her fifties. I asked if she could recommend a nearby restaurant.

"Nothing very close. Have you been traveling a long way?" she asked.

"Yes, I flew in from Arkansas with two layovers, then had to pick up my car in the long-term lot. I'm exhausted."

"I thought so," she said. "This time of year, we are not at all busy. My daughter and I were just about ready to sit down to dinner. Would you care to join us? I made chicken parmesan."

"That sounds wonderful. I'll freshen up a bit and then join you, if that's okay."

"Come through a door off the dining room."

Just then my cell phone rang. She left me alone.

"Hello."

"What kind of game are you playing?"

It wasn't what Clay said, but the contempt in his voice that shook me. My hackles immediately rose. What right did he have to put me on the defensive when I didn't even know what he was talking about? I shouldn't have answered the phone in the first place.

"Who is this?" I snapped back.

"You know perfectly well who this is. Where are the contents of Sudie's safe?"

"Safe? What do you mean?"

"The goddamn safe's empty, that's what I mean!"

"Well, I didn't do it." I heard him grouse back at me. "Wait a minute. Let me think." I tried to remember the last time Sudie used the safe. Who could have...? Then I remembered.

"The Springers!"

"What! Are you trying to blame this on Tom and Tricia?" Clay's voice reeked with disdain. I couldn't believe I'd been attracted to this jerk.

"Now you listen to me, I want to find the contents as much as you." My heart pounded like a trip hammer. I took a deep breath. Thinking out loud, I said, "Maybe Sudie forgot to lock it." When he didn't respond, I continued.

"I called the Springers to let them know about Sudie. I expected them to come to the hospital, but they never showed up. They had plenty of time to go to Sudie's..." I went on to tell him about Tricia seeing the safe when I first arrived. "She saw it behind the bookshelf."

"Hmm. Okay then, I'll give you the benefit of the doubt. If the Springers believed Sudie was going to die, they'd want to know what was in her will." I had been gripping the phone so tightly my fingers felt numb. "I'll call you back." With that, he hung up.

"Damn him. He didn't give me a chance to ask how Sudie was doing," I mumbled to myself.

I was still fuming when I went down to Lisa's living quarters off the dining room. But the wonderful smell of chicken in garlicky marinara sauce improved my mood significantly. Lisa introduced me to her daughter, Karen, a teenager with Down syndrome, somewhat overweight and very shy. Such a sweet girl and after we talked a bit, she opened up, keeping me entertained as she explained how she and her mother ran the inn. I told them I was planning to work with a realtor to try and find a place to live.

"November through April is our off-season and we can give you a special rate," Lisa said. I decided that would be ideal, since I didn't know if I'd find a place, or even be able to move in right away. We discussed a monthly rate and the figure quoted would fit into my budget for at least two months. "Have you made plans for Thanksgiving?"

"You know, I've been so preoccupied I completely forgot."

"Please have dinner with us," Karen pleaded. She had such a soulful look, I glanced at her mom.

"Yes, please. We'd love to have you. Two good friends will be joining us. They live in a small house here on the property. We work together managing the inn. You're more than welcome."

"Thanks. I'd love it."

The next day was Wednesday and I drove into Portland, met with the realtor at the escrow office and signed papers. One half of the proceeds of Mom's house would be sent to my brother in

Montreal and the other half deposited in my bank account. Since it was a long holiday weekend, we agreed to wait until Monday before I looked for a permanent residence. Then I called Josie and made plans to meet her at the Multnomah County library after school.

Working quietly at a table in the library surrounded by books and my notepad, I didn't notice Josie until she tapped my shoulder. I quickly stood and we hugged. The library was crowded, and she whispered, "Let's go to my house where we can talk. Frank's out of town until next week."

A few minutes later, we were sitting at her kitchen table. She had poured each of us a glass of white wine, and I was filling her in about my visit to Arkansas when my cell phone rang. It was Clay.

"Hello, Cynthia." He sounded subdued. I put my phone on speaker so Josie could hear.

"It's Sudie, isn't it?"

"She had another heart attack about two hours ago. Had orders—about life support..."

"Oh, no. Not again." Josie put her arm around my waist. "I only knew her for such a short time. A dear, dear person." I couldn't stem the tears. "I felt terrible when I had to leave, not knowing if she would recover. I should have stayed."

"No, there was nothing you could do. I've been expecting..." We both paused and then started to talk at the same time.

"You go ahead," I said.

"I was just going to say, I got the contents of the safe back."

"Thank God. Then the Springers...?"

"Yes. They admitted they'd found the safe door unlocked. At first, they only intended to read Sudie's will, but they ended up taking everything. Fortunately, except for the box, there was nothing of value, just personal records mostly. I have her will. They're lucky I'm not going to bring charges—not that I didn't threaten them."

"Did they try to open the box?"

"They sure did." He chuckled. "When they realized they'd have to destroy it to see what was inside, they changed their minds.

They tried to return everything to the safe, but when they found they'd accidentally locked it, they tried to blame you."

"Why didn't you believe them? The way you acted when you found the safe empty, you seemed only too ready—"

"After I had a chance to think it over and talked to Sudie, I realize I'd jumped to the wrong conclusion."

"As an attorney, you should know better," I retorted.

"Yes, you're right. I am sorry."

"You saw the page and the book, then?"

"Yes. It's a good thing Sudie had them in that box. There's no saying what the Springers would have done if they had realized what they'd taken."

"That's a relief."

"I am truly sorry for thinking you took it."

"I understand. You don't know me." I never was one to hold a grudge. Besides, I'd be stupid to alienate him.

"When's the funeral?" I asked.

"A Mass will be held on Saturday. Luther and Nolah will be back by then."

"I'd like to be there."

"Please don't feel you have to. You said your goodbyes at the hospital. Sudie and I managed a long talk the day before she died. She knew she wouldn't see you again."

I choked up and tears began to flow. I wanted to explain why Sudie meant so much to me, but he seemed to sense I couldn't talk about her right now. "I'll be reading the will after the funeral and expect to be back in my office on Monday. I've hired a local attorney to take care of her estate. Sudie gave me instructions about your project and we need to talk. Would you mind calling my secretary for an appointment? I'm going to be busy with the trial, but I'll find time on my calendar for you next week."

After we hung up, I was crying in earnest. "I'm so sorry, Cynthia. You must have developed a real fondness for the woman."

"Oh, I did. Josie, she was the dearest person, it felt like I had my own mother back again, and now she's gone, too." Josie patted my shoulder. "I'm okay. Do you mind if I leave now?"

"No, not at all. But wouldn't you like to stay here? Your old room is available."

"Thanks, but I don't think so." Then I remembered a conversation we'd had when I was still in Hot Springs. "Didn't you say Frank went to Chicago to be with his parents for Thanksgiving, and you were going to Salem?"

"Oh, that's right. Tomorrow is Thanksgiving. My aunt and uncle are expecting me. But let me make you a sandwich before you leave."

When I was back in my room at the inn, I changed into flannel pajamas and sat at the desk to review my research notes and re-read the section in Emma's journal about the Trentham family. The enormous task before me suddenly sunk in like a bullet to my chest. The thought of continuing with the project without Sudie seemed overwhelming. Should I abandon the whole effort? A big part of me certainly wanted to, but I'd made a promise to Sudie. Besides, with Clay in possession of the Shakespeare page, he'd probably want to make it public and let professionals figure out the authenticity. My head began to pound. I pushed aside the sandwich Josie had prepared for me. Tears stung my eyes and I wanted nothing more than to go to bed, pull the covers over my head, and give in to a good old-fashioned bout of depression—so that's what I did.

It seemed as if I'd been in bed for only a few minutes when the gloominess left me like a cloud shifting from the sun. Feeling warm and cozy and not wishing to break the mood, I took a deep breath and gave into it. I seemed to sink deeper into my body until I felt transported—a peaceful feeling of release, of solace in a turbulent world. I sighed and turned on my back.

"Cynthia." For some unknown reason, I wasn't frightened when I heard the woman's voice. "Look to the Psalms over all." I opened my eyes and watched as the shimmering dissipated.

I threw back the covers and sat up. I jumped from the bed and grabbed my notepad and wrote: Look to the Psalms over all.

What did she mean by that? There must be a clue in the Psalms, but the Psalms had many chapters. Which one did she mean? I guess it wouldn't do me any harm to read them all. At least our pastor would have approved.

I chewed on the end of my pen. Only minutes ago, I was willing to abandon the project. Was that the reason the ghost appeared? If so, it worked; my eagerness to continue was reborn, although the trepidation I felt when I considered the magnitude of my task also returned. Knowing I was being observed from beyond gave me hope—or was my flight of fancy working overtime? If my friends knew I believed in ghosts, they'd surely think I was unhinged.

~ * ~

I had a lovely Thanksgiving with Lisa and Karen. Meeting their friends and employees, Randy and Annette Phillips, made for an interesting day. On Friday, I visited an Apple store in the mall and bought a laptop—a big investment for me, but necessary. My old desktop computer was in storage and I was due for a new one anyway.

On Sunday, Josie came over and we visited a few wineries in the area and went back to the inn to relax in the comfortable common room. I helped myself to a glass of wine, but Josie declined.

"I was doing more research from a book on Edward de Vere, and ran across a satirical 1594 poem called 'Willobie His Avisa' that is supposed to parallel Elizabeth Trentham's life," Josie said, and reached into her purse. "I made a copy for you."

After I read the poem, I looked at Josie. "This poem must be about Elizabeth Trentham."

"How do you know?"

"See, it says, 'Between rivers, Churnet and Dove, Where Augustine pitched his monkish tent.' In Sudie's grandmother's journal, there is mention the Trentham family lived in a village named Rocester, in Staffordshire. It lies between two rivers, the Churnet and Dove. The land was originally an abbey until King Henry the Eighth abolished all the Catholic churches. This poem must be autobiographical, which is proof she wrote poetry." I reread it. "In your opinion, do you think this rises to the level of the sonnets?"

"I don't know," Josie said, taking it from my hand. "Perhaps." She read it through again. "But it's about where Avisa lives."

"I doubt she would want to use her own name...would she?"

Seventeen

The realtor picked me up on Monday and we looked at five different condos, but to no avail. All of them had aspects that didn't appeal to me, but the issue was mostly the cost. I couldn't believe they could be more expensive than houses. The realtor told me the best choices were in retirement communities, but I didn't yet meet the over fifty-five age requirement. We decided to look again later in the week. When I got back to my room, I called Clay's secretary for an appointment. I was disappointed he couldn't see me until Thursday.

It was Tuesday morning and I had decided to work in my room, trying to get used to my new laptop when my phone rang.

"Cynthia, this is Clay Darnell. Would it be possible for you to meet with me today at my office? I have free time around four thirty." I agreed. "Good. My office is in the US Bancorp Tower, thirty-seventh floor. It's the big pink building."

"Yes, I know it. I'll see you later."

I was a bit early for the appointment, but didn't mind waiting. It gave me a chance to settle my nerves and observe other people coming and going. It was obvious Clay's firm had a busy practice. The opulence of the office was impressive: floor-to-ceiling windows overlooking downtown Portland and the Willamette River. Mount Hood and the other snowcapped mountains of the Cascade Range seemed pristine silhouetted against the clear blue sky. I was enjoying the view when Clay came to stand beside me.

"Beautiful day, isn't it? The snow on the mountains is a constant reminder that I'd rather be skiing."

"Yes, I agree. However, I haven't skied in years—not since my husband..." I considered telling him about Alan, but it was still a sensitive subject. And I didn't know him well enough to share my past. "You've quite a view." I turned around to shake his hand. He seemed different than he had in Hot Springs—more professional in his suit and tie, but there was something else. Bookish? But when his eyes crinkled behind his black-framed glasses, I changed my mind. He was handsome in his own way, and at least six inches taller than me, which is always a plus.

"Come to my office. This way."

We walked down a wide hallway and when we reached his office door, he stood aside to let me enter.

"Have a seat," he said, pointing to one of the two maroon leather chairs opposite his desk.

The view from his office windows was also spectacular, but it looked out from the north side of the building with the river and Mount St. Helens clearly visible. His desk was large, with file folders neatly stacked on one side. A computer was within easy reach. He opened a folder and removed several legal papers. It was obvious he wasn't taking time for pleasantries.

"This is Sudie's will. She added an addendum the day before she died that directly concerns you. But I have a couple of questions." I nodded for him to continue. "It was obvious Sudie intended for you to go on with the research you had started, but there's something I've been thinking about."

"Oh, really?"

"Do you feel qualified to do the research?" He must have noticed my shocked expression and quickly added, "I mean, you're a high school teacher, and I don't know how..."

"I suppose you're right about my lowly position as a teacher... but Sudie didn't have any qualms about my—"

"Now, don't get defensive," he said. "What I'm trying to ascertain is how serious you are about continuing. I mean, if you think a professional researcher could do a better job, are you willing to turn the project over to someone else?"

"Why don't you tell me what you want? Now that you own the page, it's your decision." I was about ready to leave, when he leaned forward. "Cynthia, please. I have no intention of taking you off the project. I'm just trying to make the right decision here."

I didn't want to answer him until I could figure out which side of the question he preferred, but he had such a poker face, I couldn't read him.

"What did Sudie think?"

He tapped his pen against the desk and stared at me. "I think you know the answer to that. She had some sort of opinion your doing the work was predestined—which surprised me. I would never have suspected Sudie of being irrational."

"I don't believe she was. She had a real ethereal experience, one that was beyond belief...even paranormal."

"Yeah, I know. But can you honestly believe it?"

I took that as a rhetorical question and didn't reply, since I didn't want him to know about my own ghostly experiences.

"Anyway," he continued. "My question still stands: do you want to continue with the project?"

"Yes, I do, but there are hurdles in my way of finding historical answers. I don't know if it's possible to...that is, other than trying to work through the internet and our own local libraries, I don't know how..."

"That's where Sudie's will comes in. She knew how limited you are personally to complete the work—your...er, you have financial limitations." He shuffled the papers in the folder and did a bit of reading as if to refresh his memory. "The addendum to her will proposes you continue with the research and when you have either found enough to offer credible evidence Elizabeth Trentham was the true Shakespeare, or have exhausted your ability to conduct further research..." He lifted his head. "Which in my opinion is probably more likely, but that's neither here nor there." He glanced at me. I didn't react. "At any rate, Sudie made it clear that you are to make the determination as to how and when the evidence is to be presented to the general public. She also instructed we work together. Now, as far as the Shakespeare document and the prayer book are concerned, they will remain in my custody until your paper is ready for publication." He looked up. "Does that meet with your approval?"

"Absolutely. Did she mention having the paper tested for authenticity—and perhaps the ink as well? Those findings will prove the document fits into the correct time frame."

"She mentioned you knew a chemist, or someone who could conduct the proper testing."

"Yes. His name's Frank Hacker. He's a chemistry professor at Portland State—a significant other to one of my best friends. I'm a bit leery of having him, or anyone else for that matter, actually see the page until we're ready to publish on the off chance it could be released to the media prematurely." I omitted my biggest fear: that it would be stolen.

"That seems wise. I'm keeping everything in my safe at home. Now we need to discuss how Sudie's instructions are to help with your financial needs. She has left you enough money to offset your expenses, including a trip to England."

"Oh, my!" I couldn't believe it. The thought of Sudie leaving me money brought tears to my eyes. I scrounged around in my purse looking for a tissue. "I'm sorry, I had no idea she'd do something like that." I blotted my eyes and blew my nose. Looking at Clay, I wondered how he felt about the bequest. "I appreciate what she's done, but is it fair? I mean, you're her only living relative. That money should rightfully belong to you."

He smiled and settled back in his chair. "As an attorney and her heir, I could very well contest it, but I loved my aunt. She knew exactly what she was doing, and you shouldn't feel sad about it. I was by her bedside when she made the decision and I helped her arrive at the proper amount."

"You should know, I'm far from being destitute. With the sale of my mother's house in St. Helens, even after my brother received his half, I have enough for a large down-payment on a condo here in Portland. I will need to find a full-time teaching job, but I want to find a place to live first. I'm giving myself two months before I need..."

"Perhaps you will want to make other plans after you hear the amount Sudie left you." He smiled. "I won't keep you in suspense. I'm authorized to give you fifteen thousand today and an additional fifteen thousand in January. This is so you don't have to declare the income on your taxes." He reached into the file and pulled out a check. "I need you to sign this release, verifying you have the first check."

"Thirty thousand. My God! Was she that wealthy?" I blurted out before I had a chance to think about it.

He stood and came around to my side of the desk. "Not so you'd notice. Let's just say her total assets fell below the probate law." I must have looked confused because he explained. "Her largest asset was the house, and she had the title transferred two years ago to Nolah and her husband. The balance of her estate was not large enough that it required probate." He handed me a release form and a certified check for fifteen thousand dollars. "Sign here."

"Since her estate isn't large, that's even more reason for you to contest her will." I signed the release and handed it back to him.

"No, you're not looking at the total picture."

"What do you mean?"

"Have you forgotten about the Shakespeare page? If it's authentic, it could be worth millions." He returned to his side of the desk.

"Of course. Now that you own the page, you could easily make it public whenever you want to."

He sat back down. "There's another stipulation to guard against my doing so. The page is now owned by us jointly, as well as any proceeds that might be forthcoming from its release."

"My God, why didn't you talk her out of that?"

He leaned forward and gave me that trial attorney stare again. "It was her wish. Sudie had only known you for a week. To say I didn't worry you had taken advantage of her would be a gross understatement."

"That's understandable, but honestly I didn't try to."

"We'll see. I intend to monitor your progress and activities closely until I'm sure you're on the up and up."

His tone of voice lacked any warmth, and maybe I should have felt insulted by that remark, but I understood why he would have reservations about me. I would too, if the positions were reversed. "Fair enough," I replied. "Anything else?"

"That about does it." He looked at his watch. "It's quitting time around here. Can I buy you a drink? No time like the present for us to get better acquainted."

I didn't know if this was an olive branch to make up for telling me he didn't trust me, or something else. I didn't really care, because two could play that game. "I'd like that."

After we were seated in the bar on the top floor of the building, Clay ordered a sushi appetizer, scotch and water for him and white wine for me. I asked how the trial was going.

"Not so great for my client. We were forced to plea bargain," he said. "While I was in Hot Springs, my paralegal found the witness we were looking for—which unfortunately did not go well for our side. That's why I had free time to see you this evening." The waiter brought the drinks and sushi as he answered my questions about plea bargaining.

The conversation shifted to me and he asked if I'd given any thought to the course of action I needed to take. I explained I hadn't thought beyond confining my research to the internet and libraries. I also repeated my intention to live in Portland and look for a full-time teaching position.

"Can you do that and still do justice to your task?"

"Possibly not. I'll have to think about it. I'd like to take a trip to Washington, DC, and spend time at the Folger Shakespeare Library. I especially want to see the Geneva Bible that was owned by Edward de Vere."

"Why is that?" He took a sip of his drink.

"I've read there are writings in the margins. That would be a source for comparing the handwriting with that on the *Midsummer* page."

"Good idea. By the way, who else knows about Sudie's finding the page?" He picked up a crab roll and took a bite. He pushed the plate toward me. "Here, help yourself."

"The only others who know are Josie Jenson, a librarian and my best friend, and Josie's friend Frank, the chemistry professor." He had that deadpan expression on his face again. "I've sworn them to secrecy."

"I'd like to be involved, too—as much as my schedule will allow. I was both prelaw and a history major in college." I smiled, thinking it would be fun to have both him and Josie on our research team. "You're in charge, though. Just give me an assignment, and I'll see if I can help—we're in this together, you know."

Clay looked at his watch. "Oh God. I didn't realize how late it was getting." He picked up the bar tab and pulled out a credit card from his wallet. "I need to get back to my office and prepare for tomorrow."

"What time is it?" I asked as I reached for my coat and purse.

"It's six-thirty. Sorry we can't have dinner, but I do need to get back to work."

"No problem."

"I'll ride down with you," he said.

On our way to the elevator, a thought came to mind. "As a lawyer, perhaps there is something you could do to help me with the research."

"What is that?" he asked as he pushed the down button.

"One attribute Shakespeare needed was knowledge of the law. It would seem unlikely women four hundred years ago would know anything about the law, since they weren't even allowed to attend school. I just wonder how she could have learned..." Just then the elevator doors opened.

"My guess would be that she knew someone—perhaps she had a relative who was a lawyer," he mused. "One of our senior partners married his paralegal, and I'll wager she knew as much about the law as he did."

I turned to him. "Of course. That makes perfect sense. During my research of Elizabeth Trentham, there was mention her grandfather was a lawyer—in Chester, I believe."

"There you go," he said as the elevator proceeded to descend. "Now if you only knew how much contact she had with him." The elevator doors opened again. "I'll call you. Can we plan to have a regular time to get together to share notes?"

"I'd like that." We shook hands.

Eighteen

Age cannot wither her, nor custom stale
Her infinite variety. Other women cloy
The appetites they feed, but she makes hungry
Where most she satisfies, for vilest things
Become themselves in her, that the holy priests
Bless her when she is riggish.
—*Antony and Cleopatra*, Act 2, Scene 2

August 1580
Bradwell Hall,
Newcastle-under-Lyme, Staffordshire

"Sister, sister, come quick. She's coming, she's coming!" Tommy Trentham called out as he raced into the library.

"Who is coming?" Ely asked as he tugged on her hand.

"The queen. Mother said for me to fetch you." Ely allowed herself to be pulled from her writing, through the doorway, and into the wide hallway. Tommy let go of her hand and ran to the front entrance.

Ely's parents, her brother Francis, and her sisters Dorothy and Katherine and their husbands, along with her great-aunt Dorothy Sneyd and Uncle Ralph Sneyd, stood along the circular driveway leading into Bradwell Hall. Cousin Ralph's servants, decked out in their new black-and-gold finery, stood at attention waiting to assist with the horses.

When the royal harbinger had arrived a month ago to check out the suitability of Bradwell Hall for the queen's visit, it had not only put the Sneyd household, but also all of their servants and the whole community within a twenty-five-mile radius, into a frenzy to prepare for the queen's arrival.

The Trentham family and their servants had arrived the week before from Rocester, on the same day one hundred of the queen's servants showed up. After much haggling and practically coming to blows over who would take charge of the preparations, Dorothy Sneyd stepped in and resolved the dispute, giving each servant specific duties. After a few days, Dorothy finally felt reassured that the queen would be well taken care of, as well as her courtiers, ladies-in-waiting, and members of Parliament. They would be fed the finest of food with evening social activities, including a play, musicians, and dances. During the day Ralph Sneyd had planned various sporting activities, including stag hunting and falconry.

The arrangement Ely found most worrisome was her interview with the queen. She was now twenty and worried she would be considered too old to join the other unwed ladies as one of the queen's maids. Dorothy reassured her, saying she was positive the queen would have no difficulty accepting her in her court. Ely should expect to join the queen's entourage immediately after being approved. In anticipation for such an eventuality, several seamstresses and shoemakers were put to work on Ely's wardrobe.

However important her impending interview with the queen was, it was incidental to the primary reason for the queen's visit. Queen Elizabeth had heard of the great wealth the Trentham and Sneyd families had acquired through their land investments and other commercial activities, and she desired to learn their strategy.

When the queen's horse emerged from the trees surrounding the estate, Ely took Tommy's hand and joined Kate and Dorothy. Kate's husband, Sir John Stanhope, and Dorothy's husband, William Cooper of Thurgarton, stood with the other members of the Trentham and Sneyd families. A city of tents had been set up in the acres of fields surrounding the hall. It appeared to Ely this must be how soldiers set up an army field base. The queen's extensive entourage of over a thousand followed in her wake, along with herds of various animals and a long line of carts of provisions and finery. The queen's walnut state bed and personal hip bath had arrived earlier that morning and had already been installed in the upper floor of the hall. The sound of trumpets, the creaking of leather, and the animal odors associated with the long parade took over the peacefulness of the surrounding area.

Ely was amazed to see the queen's horse's tail and mane had been dyed the same red-gold color as her hair. Now forty-seven, the queen was still a beautiful woman, notwithstanding her heavily made-up face. Ely would later learn the queen had her face painted with a mixture of white lead and vinegar with red rouge on her lips and cheeks to hide smallpox scars. She sat side-saddle on her horse with a purple velvet cloak completely covering the horse's rump. She wore boots and gloves of the finest buckskin and a tricornered lavender hat decorated with green ribbons and a peacock feather.

The queen dismounted with the assistance of a courtier dressed nearly as fine as she. The man was well over six feet tall, and his hair as black as a raven's wing. His perfectly shaped legs were encased in close-fitting hose, and a yellow-and-black leather doublet flared over his bombasted breeches. "Methinks he is Robert Dudley, the Earl of Leicester, the queen's favorite," Kate whispered in Ely's ear.

But Ely's attention had been drawn to another handsome man with a pointed, sand-colored beard. It was Edward Vere, Lord Oxenford, whom she had met three years earlier on the road to Chester. She didn't fear he would recognize her because he had thought her a boy at the time. She did remember his pompous manner and her embarrassment when he fondled her hair. She detested him and vowed to stay away. When the queen approached, the Sneyd and Trentham ladies curtsied deeply and the men bowed.

"Mistress Dorothy, it is good to see you again." Queen Elizabeth took Great-aunt Dorothy's hand. "You may rise."

"May I present my family, Your Grace?" Dorothy said. She first introduced the men and then the women. When she came to Ely, the queen lightly touched Ely's hair and then turned to face Ralph Sneyd. "You may show me to my quarters."

"We have given you the upper level with a view of the countryside," Ralph said. "May I lead the way?" The queen gave her permission by waving with the back of her hand.

The next morning, Ely was summoned to meet Lady Mary Dudley Sidney in the library. The elderly woman was the queen's closest friend and one of the few ladies-in-waiting who had access to her private quarters. Lady Mary wore a gray dress trimmed in rose-colored braid and buttons to match; a heart-shaped, close-fitting linen coif with a sheer veil covering her face. Lady Mary had nursed the queen during a bout of smallpox only to succumb to the dread disease herself. But when Mary lifted her veil, her blue eyes held such warmth and sparkle that her pockmarked face seemed trivial. "The queen will meet with you anon, but I thought it best to prepare you for your interview."

"Thank you, Lady Mary. I am anxious to meet the queen and will do my best to impress her."

"I am sure you will. Of course, you have an advantage, being as how you are her kin."

Ely thought the elderly woman must be confused. She was not related to the queen, but thought it best not to correct her. Lady

Mary looked around the room and motioned toward two chairs near a window. "Let us be seated and get acquainted."

After they sat, Lady Mary said, "Yes, the queen was correct. You do have her coloring...the same red hair and fair complexion."

"My coloring is not unusual in the North," Ely responded.

Lady Mary cocked her head and spoke as if to herself. "Perhaps you do not know."

"Know what?" Ely asked.

"Ahem." Lady Mary straightened her back. "It matters little. Tell me something about yourself—something the queen might find of interest."

Ely crossed her ankles, the toes of her green slippers peeking from beneath her best dress of light green made of fine Egyptian cotton. "I believe we share our love of writing verse. I find music enjoyable and play the lute and pianoforte. I have tried my best to learn to sing, but I am fearful my voice sounds much like the croaking of a frog." Lady Mary smiled and nodded for her to continue. Ely put a finger to her chin, thinking what the queen would find impressive. "I ride well and learned falconry from my father."

"What of marriage? I daresay, every one of the queen's maids have dreams of marrying well, which is their primary purpose of wanting to join her court."

"That may be well and good for other maids, but it interests me little," responded Ely. "My desires are many, but to find a husband is not one of them." She went on to tell Lady Mary of her education and her desire to have access to the queen's libraries. This led the conversation to reading and writing, a common interest of both women.

After several minutes, the conversation shifted to Lady Mary telling her what to expect at court, using her own experience as an example. She ended the conversation by saying, "Even though I am married with seven children, I still serve at the pleasure of the queen. My husband, Henry Sidney, is the lord president of the border countries, and I was at his side in Wales when the queen summoned me. Perhaps you saw my brother, Robert Dudley, ride in with the queen? My son, Sir Philip Sidney, is here as well. The queen values him at court, as he is well versed and writes beautiful poetry. I will have you meet him later."

"Thank you, I know of him. I would enjoy a conversation with a learned man."

Lady Mary shifted in her chair. "Perhaps we should depart and see if the queen is ready to have us join her." She stood and took Ely's hand. "As far as I am concerned, Mistress Elizabeth, you will be an asset to the queen's court."

~ * ~

The queen settled herself in an ornately carved oak chair. A maid clothed in silver and wearing a dour expression, whom Ely later learned was Anne Vavasour, stooped to straighten the skirts over her majesty's black slippers.

"Stop fussing," she ordered as she slapped Anne's ear. "Fetch me something to drink and sweetmeats." Elizabeth watched in fascination the hoops the queen's maids had to jump through to satisfy their queen. She wondered who had tacked the title of "Good Queen Bess" onto this shrew. She thought briefly of changing her mind about becoming one of Elizabeth's maids, but before she could give it serious consideration, she realized the queen had said something to her.

"I'll call you Ann. One Elizabeth in my court is quite enough, don't you agree?" Ely was surprised to see a smile flitter across the queen's face. Her finger poked from beneath a lace and black velvet sleeve, pointing toward the fireplace. "Bring that footstool closer." Ely quickly did as she was commanded and nervously moved toward the queen. "Sit." Ely perched herself on the short-legged stool.

The queen put her hand under Ely's chin and forced her eyes to meet hers. "You're comely. Your hair will fade as you grow older." She loosened her grip on her chin, but Ely did not lower her face. "Good. I like a girl who is not afraid to look me straight in the eye, unlike these simpering maids." She shot a disdainful look at the two servants who stood at either side of her. "How old are you, Ann?"

"Twenty last May, Your Majesty."

"And still not married. What is wrong with your father? Can he not find a suitable man for you?" Jane raised her arm as if to defend her husband, but lowered it without saying a word.

"No, that is not the case. Several men have offered me their hand, but I declined."

"You refused? Do you hear that, Mary?" The queen turned toward Mary Sidney. "How old was your Mary when she married?"

"Fifteen, Your Majesty, but—"

The queen looked at Ely and said, "Her daughter is now the Countess of Pembroke. Is that what you want—for me to find you a titled man?"

"No, Your Majesty."

"Oh! And why not, pray?"

"Why should I be the smoke for some man's chimney or have him put his foot upon my neck?"

"Ho, ho, ho!" The queen's laugh was infectious, and all the women in the room joined her in laughter. Elizabeth squirmed on her small stool, not appreciating their reason for humor.

The queen's laughter suddenly stopped, and she pinched Ely's chin. "Are you chaste?"

"I've known no man, Your Majesty." Ely folded her hands into her lap but continued to look into the queen's eyes, resenting the question. She noticed that not only was her hair the same color as the queen's but her eyes were also the same shade of green with amber specks.

Anne Vavasour and a servant re-entered the room with trays of confections. Anne must have heard Ely's comment, because she had a strange smirk to her lips. A servant followed close behind carrying glass cups.

"I cannot abide holding a cup in mid-air with no table to sit it upon. Put it on the table," the queen ordered.

It took four of the queen's ladies to move the solid oak table and four chairs to where the queen was seated. After Lady Mary, Jane Trentham, Dorothy Sneyd, and Ely joined the queen at the table, she ordered Jane to pour. The steaming liquid released the pungent aroma of crushed wild mint as Jane poured each of them a cup.

"Dorothy tells me you have an excellent education with a flair for languages. What have you studied?" the queen asked as she spooned a generous amount of honey into her tea.

Ely pulled her shoulders straight and responded. "I have studied French, Italian, Spanish, Greek, Hebrew, and Latin. I have often wished for a teacher so that I may learn the Germanic tongues."

"Impressive. What other subjects?" The queen's long fingernails clicked together as she brushed crumbs from her fingers.

"Rhetoric, geography, history, and astrology from our tutor. My father's steward taught me to cipher, and I have assisted him in keeping my father's ledgers." Ely debated whether to tell her she had studied law from her grandfather, but decided it was more judicious to be secretive than boastful. "I write poetry and plays."

"So I hear. You perform, do you not?"

"Only for my family, Your Grace."

"Recite a sample of your writing."

"Shall I play the lute, as well?" The queen nodded her approval. "I have written a verse of my home in Rocester." Ely stood and bobbed a curtsy before moving across the room to pick up her lute. Strumming quietly, she talked through the verse rather than sang:

Between rivers, Churnet and Dove,
Where Augustine pitched his monkish tent,
Where shepherds sing, where muses smile,
They all admired so sweet a sight.
The nymphs frequent this happy dale
Where Helicon spreads his wings again.
Here muses sing, here Satyrs play,
Here mirth resounds both night and day.
At east of this, a castle stands
By ancient shepherds built of old,
And lately was in shepherd's hands,

Though now by brothers bought and sold,
At Westside springs a Chrisfall well.
There doth this maid Avisa dwell.

Ely finished her prose and strummed a few more chords before setting the lute aside.

"Is that all to the story?" the queen asked.

"That is what I have completed thus far. Perhaps I will decide to add verses later."

"Until you have more experiences, I suspect." The queen chuckled. "Why Avisa?"

"It is a pretty name and goes well with the verse. I think it best not to identify oneself."

"Very wise. Tell me, what poets do you admire?"

"Oh many, Your Grace. Homer and Cicero, of course. I am a true Protestant, but confess I have a love of Greek and Roman mythology. I recently reread Chaucer's 'Legend of Good Women.' Perhaps I could recite for you."

"Do you know the story of Dido and Aeneas?"

Without hesitation, Ely moved toward the center of the room and began to recite Chaucer's poem "The Legend of Dido." Toward the end of the poem, where Aeneas has deserted Dido, leaving her pregnant and ashamed, Ely recited the final lines:

I may well lose on you a word or letter,
All be it that I shall be never the better,
For the wind that blew your ship away—
The same wind hath blown away your fey.
But who would all this letter have in mind,
Read Ovid, and in him he shall it find.

With the reciting of the final line, Ely stabbed her chest with an imaginary knife and slumped to the floor.

The queen clapped enthusiastically. "Excellent, excellent. I've never heard Chaucer quoted so well." A high compliment from this queen. After Ely stood, she knew she should have curtsied, but making a small gesture of defiance, she bowed. If the queen noticed, she made no comment.

"Your Majesty, you must forgive my daughter," Jane said. "She has been taught never to bring attention to herself. I do apologize."

"Nonsense! She is among women. I will expect her to entertain in my chambers regularly when she comes to court."

"Then you approve my application?" Ely said.

"Of course. I hear you assisted Sir Ralph's father in his legal matters."

"Yes, Your Majesty, in Chester, before and after his death." Ely blushed, wondering if the queen also knew she had disguised herself as a boy to work as a clerk in her grandfather's law office.

The queen asked Lady Mary something, but Ely paid little attention as her thoughts turned to the sorrow she had suffered when she received word of Sir William's death. It had happened on his return trip from Scotland during the time Ely was in court successfully defending Dennis O'Leary's arrest on charges of vagrancy.

When Ralph Sneyd returned to Chester to manage his father's estate, he learned for the first time that the boy who had been clerking for his father was Ely in disguise, and that she had been doing so for over a year. Notwithstanding his Aunt Dorothy's argument, he would not hear of Ely continuing the deception. He sold Sir William's office in the walled city near the docks, but Ralph was ill-equipped to close out his father's law practice. Much to Ely's delight, he had no alternative but to ask her to continue to work as Sir William's agent—on the condition that she remain out of the public eye, confined to Sir William's home in Chester.

It took another six months for Ely to finish the work, but she had learned much of the legal profession. She often railed to her family about the unfair plight of women, in their not being treated equally with men. Her vocal arguments brought a rebuke from Dorothy. She had been reminded repeatedly not to overextend the reality of where women fit into society. Ely yearned for the leniency to pursue her own interests when she joined the queen's court.

As if the queen could read her mind, she said, "Perhaps I will use you as a scribe from time to time." She turned toward Lady Mary. "Is Chester wherein we return to London Town?"

"Yes, Your Majesty. You are to sail with Sir Francis Drake. I believe his ship is in harbor now and awaits thee."

The queen smiled secretively, and with a gleam in her eyes she said, "He can bide his time a fortnight longer." The queen paused. "No, I have changed my mind." She motioned toward one of her ladies-in-waiting. "Send a rider to fetch him. I desire his company here on out."

Ely felt like jumping for joy and her eyes sparkled as she grinned widely. The queen looked at her strangely and said, "It appears you are looking forward to meeting Sir Francis."

"Oh no, Your Majesty. I do not know the man—I don't care about him." Ely felt all the women in the room stare at her in disbelief. She blushed. "I am sorry, of course I would like to meet him, but what I am excited about is a journey by sea. I have longed to have the experience and—"

"You don't understand." Lady Mary spoke. "You will travel to London by land with the queen's other attendants."

"Nonsense. If Ann desires a sea voyage, that is what she shall have." She turned toward Ely. "You may serve me while aboard ship." She took another sip of her tea. "You are truly remarkable. A gel of many talents, it would appear. And still chaste...how extraordinary. It must come from reading Chaucer, hey kinswoman?"

The queen stood from her chair and kicked her long skirt away from her feet. The other women quickly stood and curtsied. The queen was still chuckling when she left the room, her ladies following in her wake.

Nineteen

I must be cruel only to be kind.

—*Hamlet*, Act 3, Scene 4

After the queen and her ladies had left the room, Ely, Jane, Dorothy, and Lady Mary re-seated themselves at the table. Lady Mary turned toward Ely. "The queen desires to rename you Ann; does this meet with your approval?"

"Nay. My sisters call me Ely. I would prefer—"

"Elizabeth! You cannot dictate to her majesty. You will do as she wishes," Jane interjected. "It will take an adjustment for us all, but Ann is a pleasant name."

"Do not be concerned," Lady Mary said to Jane. Turning toward Ely, she continued, "You won't be sent to the Tower for suggesting Ely for your court name." Lady Mary refilled her cup with the aromatic tea. "However, I am surprised you do not desire to have your mother's name."

"My mother's name? No, you are mistaken. My mother's is Jane." Ely looked toward her mother, surprised to see Jane's face turn pale.

"Have you not told Elizabeth the truth of her birth?" Jane turned her head from Lady Mary's questioning gaze.

"The truth? What do you mean, the truth? Mother—what is she saying?"

Jane turned toward Ely. "Elizabeth, my sweet. You are my daughter in every sense of the word—except by birth." Tears began to flow from her eyes.

Ely felt her heart sink. Mary's comment about her being the queen's kin came back to her. "Say 'tis not so." Ely stood from her chair and knelt at Jane's side and gripped her shoulders, forcing Jane to look into her eyes. "Mother, am I a bastard?" Ely remembered a young girl in the village—a girl born to a woman with no husband. The townsfolk had spit on her and called her baby a bastard. Jane placed her hand on Ely's tawny curls. Both women were crying in earnest.

"Nonsense! Elizabeth, halt this display," Lady Mary said. "No one will know the truth of your birth unless you tell them. You are not illegitimate. Your mother was born on the wrong side of the blanket, but thou are not." Lady Mary handed Ely her lace handkerchief. "When the queen called you her kin, she was not being flippant. You are of her blood. You should be proud to be born a Tudor. Stand and comport yourself appropriately."

Ely stifled a sob and stared at Jane.

"'Tis true. You are the daughter of my cousin Ann."

"Ann?" Ely slowly turned toward Dorothy, who had been silent during the exchange between the other women. "Do you mean Aunt Dorothy's daughter?"

"Yes," Jane said. "Before Ann died, she asked me to become your mother. My husband was willing to be your father." Jane held Ely's face between her hands. "I pretended to be with child by wearing loose frocks. Your granddame is Dorothy."

"Dorothy?" Ely turned to the older woman. "You are...you are my grandmother?"

Dorothy smiled warmly. "I wanted to keep you in Chester, but it was not Ann's wish. She did ask Jane to take you as her own daughter."

Part of her did not want to hear the truth, but on the other hand, Ely was intrigued with the knowledge she had been born to royalty. She let loose Jane's shoulders and resumed her place at the table, pondering what she had learned with mixed emotions. "How am I related to the queen?"

"Did I not tell you of Ann?" Dorothy said.

"Yes, I do remember," Ely said. "You served as a lady-in-waiting to Catherine Parr when she was married to King Henry."

"Yes. The king desired me, and I became with child," Dorothy replied.

Lady Mary interjected. "The king sent Dorothy to Richmond Palace, where she secretly gave birth to Ann, your mother. Our queen was still a young princess also in residence there, and she developed an immediate fondness for her new half-sister. She was very sad when Dorothy and baby Ann left for Chester to live under the guardianship of Sir William Sneyd, Dorothy's brother."

"Let me sort this out in my mind." Ely played with the small ruffle that surrounded her neck. "Sir William was not my grandfather."

"'Tis quite true. However, my father was very proud of you," Jane replied. "I think we have all quite forgotten you were not born to me."

"Then our queen and my mother..." Ely stood and began to pace the room. Turning toward Lady Mary, she said, "My birth mother and Queen Elizabeth were half-sisters, and King Henry the Eighth—my grandfather?"

"Yes, 'tis true," said Lady Mary. "That is the reason the resemblance between you and the queen is remarkable. She is your aunt by birth."

Jane interrupted. "Dorothy told me the king held his baby daughter..." She glanced at Dorothy. "That is, he held baby Ann in his arms and kissed her before Dorothy took her aboard a ship that would soon set sail for Chester."

"You may be the dead king's only surviving grandchild," Lady Mary added.

"Ann and I were of the same age and I always considered her my sister—we were raised together. When she married and was with child, she was the happiest woman in Chester. Just before you were born, she received word her husband had been killed at sea during a battle with Spanish pirates."

"Oh, this is more than I can comprehend." Ely turned toward Dorothy. "Dennis O'Leary was my father, that poor sailor, the man I helped?"

Dorothy seemed frozen, staring at Ely. Her face paled as tears formed in her eyes. "Dennis O'Leary married Ann, 'tis true."

"Dennis was not killed at sea?" It was now Jane's turn to look bewildered.

"That is what Dennis wanted Ann's family to believe. He was badly disfigured from his injuries. When we discovered Dennis was alive and living as a beggar on the streets of Chester, we brought him home. Sir Ralph and I gave him employment as a carpenter. He died of a stomach malady shortly after Ely moved back to her home in Rocester."

"But why wasn't I told Dennis was my true father before he died?" Tears coursed down Ely's cheeks.

"Dennis never knew you were his daughter, until I told him on his deathbed. I wasn't at liberty to tell you the truth. I had promised Jane and Thomas you would learn the truth from them," Dorothy responded.

Ely turned to Jane. "Why did you not tell me? Surely Dennis would have wanted to know sooner, and I too..." Ely choked back a sob.

"I had hoped you would never find out," Jane admitted.

Lady Mary cleared her throat and spoke, wanting to end the emotional scene that was being played out before her. "Dorothy, tell me more of Ann."

Dorothy cleared her throat. "Ann had a difficult delivery, and she suffered from melancholy. So deep was her despair upon hearing of Dennis' death, she could not seem to recover her health. She died a few days after Elizabeth was born." Dorothy's voice became hoarse with unshed tears.

Regaining her composure, Dorothy continued, "Princess Elizabeth and I corresponded regularly. Early on she wanted to be kept informed of Ann's progress, and later, Ann's baby—you, Elizabeth." Dorothy patted Ely's hand. "Even before your interview today, Queen Elizabeth knew of your scholastic aptitude. I suspect she is secretly very proud of you; you two are very much alike." She chuckled under her breath. "I am pleased your performance today was proof my letters to her were true." Dorothy paused to take a sip of her tea. "The queen wanted to be your godmother after she learned Ann had named you after her. These are the reasons the queen desires to have you with her in court. As far as we know, you are her only living kin."

Ely felt hollow, believing her whole childhood had been a sham. Her father was not even a blood relative, and her sisters and brothers were cousins—nearly too much to comprehend. She turned toward Jane. "Who knows? Francis, my sisters...?"

"They know nothing of this. 'Tis best no one ever knows."

"That is very important," Lady Mary said. "No one must know your true heritage. In fact, it would be best if you learned to forget it as well. Obviously, you should feel proud to be a Tudor and the queen's niece, but this knowledge must be kept to yourself."

"But what of my father?" Ely turned toward Jane.

"How Ann met Dennis, I do not know, but they became friends—he was indeed a fair young man. My father objected to her becoming wed to a lowly Irish seaman, but he finally relented when Ann reminded him no better suitor would consider marrying a bastard, notwithstanding her royal parentage. Methinks your independent streak must come from her."

"I am sure I would have loved her." Ely gazed into Jane's somber face, and then she knelt at her side and embraced her. "But I am fortunate to have a mother who loved me as her own."

Ely now knew why Dorothy had given her more attention than Jane's natural children. She was anxious to question Dorothy more fully—Dorothy, her newly discovered grandmother, and one of King Henry's paramours.

~ * ~

The same evening, following the ball given in honor of the queen, Ely departed Bradwell Hall through the scullery and into the gardens at the rear of the estate. She could see cooking fires at the campsites in the acreage below the mansion. Music and laughter floated on the evening air from the queen's many servants. As Ely strolled along a row of rose bushes, her thoughts were filled with the events of the day, trying to make sense of it all.

It was difficult for her to imagine Dennis O'Leary being her own true father, but what was even more unbelievable was her relationship to old King Henry VIII and Queen Elizabeth. Had everyone been truthful with her, or was there more of the story yet to be told? She stopped in mid-stride, suddenly wondering if she could be in contention for the crown upon the queen's death. Spotting a bench that had been placed against a tall laurel hedge, she sat down.

"The queen is beyond childbearing years," she whispered to herself. "Am I closest to the throne upon her death?" Her thoughts immediately went to Lady Jane Grey. The story was well known of the attempt by many Protestants to put Lady Jane on the throne following King Edward's death instead of the Catholic Mary Tudor, King Henry VIII's eldest daughter. Jane Grey was proclaimed queen, but Mary staged a coup with her supporters and Jane was deposed to the Tower of London. Lady Jane had reigned for only nine days before she was beheaded in 1554 at the age of sixteen.

The magnitude of Lady Jane's fate suddenly hit Ely like a cannonball to her midsection. A rose brushed her arm and she unconsciously grasped a blossom, pulled the petals loose, and crushed them in her fingers. She knew the illegitimacy of her mother's birth, not to mention her father's being a mere seaman from Ireland, may prevent her from any claim to the throne. However, there could be those who would try to assert her birthright for political reasons. Even if those facts could be ignored, what about her own desire?

No, I do not want it, she thought vehemently. Never, never, never! It must remain a secret.

Realizing she had spoken aloud, she quickly looked around. She saw no one, but could hear the voices of a man and woman coming her way on the other side of the hedge. She recognized the man's voice—it was Edward Vere, Lord Oxenford. The laurel was too high for her to be seen, so she remained seated and purposely eavesdropped.

"My thoughts have been so consumed with you and our problem, I wrote a poem," Edward said. "Let us sit here."

Ely jumped, thinking they were referring to the bench she was sitting upon, but then she realized there must be a bench on the other side of the hedge too. She heard the rustling of clothes as they sat down.

"My lord. A poem, for me?"

"Yes. I shall read it to you."

"Oh yes, please," the woman said.

"There is only enough light left for me to barely see it." Ely heard him clear his throat.

> In the old age black was not counted fair
> Or if it were, it bore not beauty's name.
> But now is black beauty's successive heir,
> And beauty slandered with a bastard shame.
> For since each hand hath put on nature's power,
> Fairing the foul with art's false borrowed face,

Sweet beauty hath no name, no holy bower,
But is profaned, if not lives in disgrace.
Therefore my mistress' eyes are raven black,
Her eyes so suited, and they mourners seem
At such who, not born fair, no beauty lack,
Slandering creation with a false esteem.
Yet so they mourn, becoming of their woe,
That every tongue says beauty should look so.

"How you must pity me. The mere mention of a bastard tears me apart. How can you allow me to suffer so? The babe will be born in three months and I had to have my dresses altered. Is there no way for you to divorce your wife so we may wed?"

"My sweet girl, if only it could be so. There is no way—perhaps if my wife were not the daughter of William Cecil, but he is too powerful. He and the queen are pressuring me to re-establish my residency at the Burghley household and fulfill my vows of a loyal husband and father."

"But what of me? I carry your child—what if it is a boy, an heir Anne Cecil may never give you?" The woman began to weep loudly. "You talk of the queen—what of me? I serve her daily and her eyes are like her falcons; she misses little of what goes on about her."

"Be still, my love. Someone may hear."

Ely was consumed with curiosity. Who is this woman?

"Here, wipe your eyes. I will think on this. We will find a way out of this dilemma. Even if we never marry, you must know you will always be my lady, my love." The sound of kissing could be heard with whispered endearments coming from Vere for several minutes. "Come, Anne, we must return before someone sees us together. If you have an opportunity, come to my room. I will leave a candle lit for you."

When Ely heard their footfalls on the loose gravel, she gave a huge sigh, not aware she had been holding her breath with the realization that Anne Vavasour's black hair, olive skin, and dark eyes fit the description of the lady in the poem.

Anne, a maid of honor to the queen, the same woman who had brought tea to the queen earlier this day. And he wants Anne to meet him in his bedchamber again...'tis shameful, Ely thought. Edward Vere—the cad—the shameful rogue—he has no honor! What has he done to the poor girl?

Edward had made a bad impression with Ely during their first meeting when he thought her a boy, but now she despised the man. If only she could rebuke him as he deserved. Perhaps there would be a chance when she was in residence with the queen. I will treat him as the blackguard he surely is, she vowed. Thoughts of her own circumstance seemed miniscule compared to the trouble Anne Vavasour faced. Ely became determined to befriend the woman, should the opportunity arise upon her arrival at the palace in London.

Twenty

Sigh no more, ladies, sigh no more,
Men were deceivers ever,
One foot in sea and one on shore,
To one thing constant never.
Then sigh not so, but let them go,
And be you blithe and bonny,
Converting all your sounds of woe
Into hey, nonny, nonny.
—*Much Ado About Nothing*, Act 2, Scene 3

On their journey to Chester, Lady Mary Sidney briefed Ely on her duties to the queen. "Generally speaking, a lady-in-waiting will not assist the queen in her daily toilet, which would be left to servants. Kat Ashley, whom you have already met, is the chief lady of the queen's bedchamber. She has been with the queen for many years and oversees her majesty's female servants. Never forget you are not a servant; do not allow anyone to treat you so unless you receive a direct order from the queen. A lady of the royal court is, without exception, of high noble status. Because of her royal birth and training, a lady-in-waiting is in a better position to advise her majesty. They are also expected to participate in court entertainments, such as masques, dances, and musicals."

"But I am not highborn—that is, no one knows of my true birth. The other ladies may suspect something amiss, considering they know my father is not of noble blood...unless the queen announces my kinship to her."

"No, be assured, she will not. Your true relationship to the queen will remain confidential. Other than your grandmother Dorothy, I am the only one of the queen's ladies to know the truth, and I have no intention of telling anyone. But remember, you are not yet a queen's lady-in-waiting. Being unmarried and inexperienced in court matters, you are considered one of her maids of honor, notwithstanding your advanced years."

"What will be expected of me?"

"As I said, you will participate in court activities and be expected to provide entertainment and attend royal functions. You will receive training in court decorum. The younger maids have lessons in languages, elegant sewing, and music. I cannot imagine you will be expected to attend those classes." Lady Mary drummed her fingers on the arm of the chair. "Perhaps the queen may want to use you as a tutor for the young maids. I will ask the queen."

"I will do whatever the queen wishes." Ely only hoped she would have the time to explore the many palace libraries and be allowed to pursue her own course of study and writing.

"As a maid of honor, you are to remain unmarried until the queen gives her permission. You must not take this lightly. Failure to receive her approval before marriage could most likely lead to expulsion from the court, or imprisonment in the Tower."

"The queen will have no reason to doubt my loyalty to her." Ely's thoughts turned to the plight of Anne Vavasour. She wondered what the queen would do to her and Lord Oxford when she learned of Anne's pregnancy.

Upon their arrival in Chester, the queen's party boarded the *Golden Hind*, Sir Francis Drake's ship. The others of her entourage traveled from Newcastle south to London. Besides Ely and the queen, there were five of her courtiers, including Edward Vere and Robert Dudley, four ladies, and two of the queen's personal servants. The plan was to have the queen and her party leave the ship in Bristol, at which point they would travel by foot and horseback to Lechlade, where the queen's barges would wait until she arrived. It would be a slow sail on the Thames as they waited for outgoing tides. There would be stops at various locations so the queen would have an opportunity to greet more of her people. The palaces and grand homes where they would spend their nights in comfort had already been selected. With good winds and tides, they expected to arrive at Windsor Castle by mid-September.

When Ely met Sir Francis Drake, she was impressed with his manliness. He was taller than any man she knew, and his angular face was like leather, having been exposed to the elements of the sea and wind for many years. She could well understand how this man was able to lead the rough lot of sailors.

Francis had received his knighthood from the queen in April after completing his historic voyage around the world in less than three years. Now the queen had a new champion and she was pleased with his accomplishments, not just because of their historic value, but because he brought back riches from his plunder of Spanish ships. Sir Francis' first conquest was in Valparaíso, where he captured a Spanish ship carrying gold and wines. Later, he overtook the Spanish ship, *Nuestra Señora de la Concepción*—nicknamed *Cacafuego*—gaining an additional eighty pounds of gold, thirteen chests of pieces of eight, and twenty-six tons of silver, jewels, and pearls.

There were three other sponsors of Drake's voyage on board. One of those was Sir Christopher Hatton, who was the principal backer. Hatton had promoted the idea of the expedition and recommended Drake to be the leader. The other two were Robert Dudley, the Earl of Leicester, and John Hawkins, Drake's cousin. It was rumored that all seven backers became even wealthier at the conclusion of Drake's voyage, having received a 4,700 percent return on their investment.

When Ely came aboard, she was told she would share a cabin and berth with Blanche Parry. Ely acquired an immediate fondness for the elderly woman when she learned that Blanche had been with Elizabeth since the queen's early childhood. Blanche's eyesight was failing, but the queen had such a love for the woman, she made sure she was well tended and rarely out of her reach.

One trait Ely learned almost immediately was Blanche's proclivity for gossip. This suited Ely nicely, since she was full of questions about everyone who was close to the queen. On their first night at sea, they conversed late. Ely was interested to learn Edward had suffered great disappointment because he did not have the necessary funds to invest in Drake's exploration.

"Why is that the case?" Ely asked. "I would think Lord Oxford would have a great fortune, since he is the queen's lord great chamberlain."

"You would have thought so, but I know Edward had to sell twelve of his estates last year to pay off his debts. Perhaps he is well-heeled now, but he was nearly destitute before. That is why he was unable to invest in Sir Francis' voyage three years ago."

"It is surprising he would find it necessary to sell his inheritance."

"Yes, 'tis true. Edward managed to spend his fortune like it was shot from a cannon," Blanche whispered. "He has always had an extravagant lifestyle. He seems to think he needs the best of everything." The woman turned over in the berth and groaned. "Oh, my back does ache. Would you rub it for me, my dear?" Ely began to massage Blanche's bony back.

"After his marriage, Edward left England without the queen's permission. She forced him to return. He must have been able to persuade her later, because he did tour the continent the following year. He brought back a new fashion in men's attire. He gave the queen a pair of scented gloves."

"I have so wanted to travel. There have been many occasions I have wished to be born a man."

"We women do have a poor lot in life, but you should be happy to be accepted at court. If you choose carefully, perchance the queen will allow you to marry someone like Lord Oxford." Blanche sighed, telling Ely she could stop rubbing her back.

"Hmph. I would hope to never marry someone like the earl. You could never trust him to be true to his wedding vows. I have no respect for someone who..." Ely caught short her comment as she nearly told Blanche about Anne Vavasour's pregnancy.

"You have heard of Edward's indiscretions, have you?" Blanche said. "Being raised in the country, perhaps you did not know that keeping a mistress is an acceptable practice among the queen's courtiers. However, if the queen discovered such an alliance between one of her maids of honor and a courtier—woe betide that poor girl." Blanche yawned. "Did you know when Edward returned from the continent, he refused to reunite with his wife, thinking the daughter she had borne while he was gone was not his? Yet he has a notorious reputation with other women."

"Yes, I can believe it," Ely said. "Was his suspicion—I mean, do you think the child is his?"

"Of course Elizabeth is his daughter. She resembles him, yet he chose to believe gossip." Blanche yawned loudly. "Anne Cecil was a maid of honor for the queen before she married Edward and is still a lady-in-waiting. She continues to live in William Cecil's house, but I am sure you shall meet her. A sweet little thing, but unfortunately, she inherited none of her father's strength. Did you know he is the queen's lord treasurer—the most powerful man in England?"

"I was told. If you are not too tired, I would like to hear how the earl and Anne Cecil came to be married."

Blanche said, yawning again, "Edward became a ward of William Cecil following his father's death—he was about twelve at the time. I believe Edward and Anne's marriage was arranged at the time of her birth. She was fourteen when they married and he was twenty-one, as I recall. Edward resisted the marriage, but the queen interceded." Blanche's voice faded and, in a few seconds, Ely could hear her soft snore.

Ely stayed awake for several minutes thinking about Edward Vere and the way he had put Anne Vavasour in an untenable situation, and his young wife as well. To think Anne Cecil was not only pregnant while her husband was cavorting about the continent, but then he refused to acknowledge his child as his own. If it were possible for Ely to have a worse opinion of Lord Oxford, she did now.

~ * ~

On the first full day aboard ship, Ely was summoned to the queen's quarters with the other ladies. Their conversation with the queen was interrupted when Robert Dudley came into the cabin unannounced. Ely had already been informed that Robin, as the queen called him, was given special privileges, including access to her inner rooms. The queen's eyes beamed; her entire attention was now placed on the handsome young man. The queen waved the women out of her cabin.

Ely was not disappointed to leave, as she looked forward to being on the top deck. Her time aboard the *Golden Hind* and her dream of sailing on the open sea was being fulfilled. She gathered a shawl closely around her. She again longed to have been born a boy and be allowed to climb to the crow's aery if for no other reason than to experience the view and the thrill of danger. But she was forced to be content to watch the sailors run barefoot up the ropes to raise and lower the sails. She walked slowly to the bow and let the wind whip through her hair and long skirts.

She spied the first mate talking to Bess Hardwick, the Countess of Shrewsbury, and Kat Ashley. She overheard him tell them the ship was originally called *The Pelican* and Captain Drake changed the name to the *Golden Hind* during their expedition. When he saw Ely, he invited her to join them on their tour of the deck. He continued his lecture. "This type of ship is called a galleon due to our three masts and five decks."

"How is the captain able to keep the ship on course?" Ely asked.

"We have many navigational aids," he said. "Come with me and I will show you." He led them to the uppermost deck near where a sailor manned the wheel. "Charts are kept in the captain's quarters, but here we have a compass." He further explained how a compass functioned, something Ely already knew, but she listened attentively anyway. "At night we navigate by the stars, using a mariner's astrolabe." The other ladies seemed to lose interest hearing about the technical apparatuses and soon wandered off to explore on their own, but Ely was very interested in what he was explaining. She thought of her natural father, Dennis O'Leary, as she listened to the first mate.

His name was Tom Moore. He had been captain of one of the exploration ships. "My ship, the *Christopher*, broke up in a storm off the east coast of South America. Captain Drake brought me aboard the *Golden Hind* as his first mate."

"How many ships were in the expedition?" Ely asked.

"We started out with five. Besides the captain's and my ship, there were the *Elizabeth*, the *Marigold*, and the *Swan*. The *Swan* broke up in the same storm as my ship. The *Elizabeth* was borne off course during a violent storm off Cape Horn, and she left the expedition to return home. We never learned what happened to the *Marigold*. She was lost, and we assumed she never made it through the storm." Their conversation came to an end when the mate was called to fulfill a duty and Ely returned to her cabin.

~ * ~

On their second day at sea, Ely stood at the rail watching several dolphins following along the side of the ship, when she felt the nearness of someone standing at her back. She was the youngest unwed maid aboard the ship, which made her a target for flirtation. She feared this must be another occasion where she would be required to spurn unwanted attention.

"You are enjoying the voyage, are you not, Mistress Elizabeth?" Ely quickly turned around to come face to face with her nemesis, Edward Vere. She felt trapped with her back pushed against the railing.

"Pardon me, sir. I do not wish to converse with you." She felt the urge to push him away, but she instead made a quick sidestep to avoid contact. He grabbed her upper arm.

"What is this, pray tell? My courtesy met with disdain? Your rudeness is beyond understanding." She pulled her arm free from his grasp, but he continued to gaze upon her face. "Have we met before?"

Ely felt the urge to give him the tongue lashing he deserved, but realized she was acting without thought. As far as Lord Oxford knew, this was the only time they had ever met except when they were introduced when he first arrived at Bradwell Hall, and he had taken little notice of her then. She took a deep breath, knowing she should apologize, but not wishing to do so. He touched her hair and moved down to touch her temple where veins showed through her fair complexion. "Yes, I believe we may have met in the past. Your face seems familiar."

"No, we have never—" Ely's intended sharp retort was interrupted by his laughter.

"Yes, how could I ever forget! The girl dressed as a boy. Elijah Goodfellow?" He continued to laugh.

"You insult me, sir." She stiffened her shoulders in defense, but she could feel her face turn a beet red. "Whatever are you...?"

"Good lady, you insult me by feigning ignorance. Come now, admit it. You are Elijah Goodfellow, are you not? I've seen many performances on stage and the part you played was exceedingly wonderful; I long to hear your story."

"You are mad, sir. We have never met." She turned in a flounce, anxious to escape this insufferable man and go below decks.

"Come now, Ely. Won't you admit it?"

Ely turned to face him again. "Ely? How do you know I am called Ely?"

"I overheard your sister call you so."

"Hmph!" She had reached the steps and proceeded to go below.

"You may depart, my good fellow, but never fear. I will hear your story." She could still hear Edward laughing when she reached the door to the cabin she shared with Blanche.

Twenty-one

Come, bitter conduct, come, unsavoury guide.
Thou desperate pilot, now at once run on
The dashing rocks thy seasick, weary bark.
                    —*Romeo and Juliet*, Act 5, Scene 3

Ten people sat around the captain's table, the queen at one end and Captain Drake at the other. Robert Dudley, Edward Vere, Christopher Hatton, and John Hawkins were on one side; Ely, Blanche, Bess, and Kat Ashley on the other. She felt her face flush as Edward Vere glanced her way with a silly smirk upon his lips. She tried to avoid his attention by focusing on the meal before her. She prayed she would not be made a target for ridicule should he announce how they had first met.

Fortunately, the discussion centered on Captain Drake and his sea adventure. The informality of shipboard with the steady pour of wine kept the talk lively. Eventually, the conversation led to England's conflict with Spain.

"Our ability to outwit the Spaniards and relieve them of the riches they bring from the New World may bring wider conflict," Robert Dudley remarked.

"Not to mention the conflict of religion," Vere said. "I would suspect they would view a war with England as a Catholic crusade."

"Enough discussion of politics," the queen said. "I had hoped this voyage would release me from my duties as queen, if only temporarily. Robin, you may escort me to my cabin."

Ely felt relieved Edward had not embarrassed her in front of the queen; however, she feared he would do so at some point. She decided to take the first opportunity to explain the reason she had felt the need to travel as a boy three years earlier and beg him to keep her confidence. Not that she cared a fig what others may think, but the thought the queen would find out would be embarrassing. She looked forward to what the future held for her and did not want to disappoint.

A summer squall blew in that night, setting the ship to rocking. Nearly every one of the queen's party became seasick. By midmorning, Ely felt recovered enough to take care of Blanche, who suffered miserably. Ely herself felt exhausted from fighting her own nausea plus caring for her cabin mate. She had rubbed her back as the woman held her head above a slop bucket until her vomiting produced nothing but dry heaves. Even though Ely had learned much from her mother in the preparation of simples and herbs to alleviate many ailments, seasickness was one illness with which she had no experience.

It was evening before the worst of the storm had passed, and with the easing of the ship's rocking, Blanche was finally able to drop into a fitful sleep. Because of her advanced age, Ely became concerned she would not survive should she start to vomit again. Ely quietly left their cabin to seek out the ship's doctor and see if he could prescribe a tonic that may alleviate the old woman's suffering.

Ely walked to the end of a passageway and climbed a ladder to the next deck above, where she saw one of the ship's crewmen. After inquiry, he gave her directions to the doctor's cabin, but she found it unoccupied. Another one of the sailors told her the doctor had been tending the queen, as she was also stricken with *mal de mer*. He suggested she seek counsel from the cook. Following his directions to the galley, Ely found the cook, who along with his small crew was preparing the evening meal.

"Ginger is what ye need," the cook said after Ely had made her inquiries.

"Ginger? I am not familiar," she said.

"'Tis a root. Let me show you." He reached into a tin and removed a piece. With a sharp knife he peeled a small slice and handed it to her. Ely smelled it and took a tiny bite. When she chewed it, she found it hot to the tongue but pleasant.

"Where do you find this ginger?" she asked.

"It comes from the east, where the Hindis use it in their cooking. 'Tis tasty crushed into ale or sherry. Your ladyship would find it helpful to ease the heaves." He opened a spigot from an oaken barrel to release a portion of ale into a tin container. "Crush some into this ale and have her sip on it slowly."

While Ely prepared the mixture for Blanche, the cook ladled out a bowl of chicken broth with carrots, potatoes, and onions, and placed it on a tray with a slice of bread. She thanked the cook for his help, and he rewarded her with a toothy grin—minus several teeth—and ordered one of his helpers to carry the tray back to the cabin she shared with Blanche.

Blanche had much improved following Ely's ministrations, and she slept peacefully. It was nearly noon when Ely was awakened by a knock on the door. "Yes, who is it?"

"Kat Ashley," was the reply. "The queen is asking for you."

"Anon." Ely got up, and careful not to wake Blanche, she quickly put on a fresh dress after splashing her face with water and brushing her hair.

A few minutes later she was admitted to the queen's cabin. Ely was surprised to see her still in bed. She was free of the white makeup she wore in public, and her head was covered with a lace cap. Blanche had already told her the queen had many wigs, as she had lost most of her hair following a fever sickness many years prior.

Ely dropped into a deep curtsy. "I am sorry to see you unwell, Your Majesty."

"'Tis my own fault for desiring a sea voyage. I had hoped for a smooth sailing." The queen motioned with her fingers for the doctor to leave. He quickly bowed out of the cabin. "I am concerned for Blanche. I was told you have been caring for her. Is she worse?"

"No, Your Majesty. She is much better and sleeping peacefully. The ship's cook showed me how to prepare a potion that has helped."

"I am relieved. She has always been a dear person to me, perhaps closer to me than the mother I never knew." The queen shifted in bed and tried to straighten her pillow. "Help me with this." Ely quickly approached the queen's bed and fluffed the pillows more comfortably behind her back.

"That is something we both have in common, Ann." Ely remembered the queen's plan to call her by that name and she considered asking her then to call her Ely, but decided perhaps today wasn't the best time.

"We have in common? I am sorry, I am not sure what you mean," Ely said.

"Not knowing our mothers is what we have in common. You may sit down."

"'Tis true, but I never knew Jane was not my mother until a few days ago." Ely sat in the chair vacated by the doctor. "I wish I could have known my birth mother." Ely then realized the reason the queen wanted to call her Ann.

It was as if the queen could read her mind when she said, "Yes, that is something else we have in common. Both our mothers were named Ann."

"Did you know my mother?" Ely asked.

"Know your mother?" The queen stared at the ceiling with a faraway look in her eyes. "I knew her briefly when she was a babe, but I remember...and loved her well."

"My Aunt Dorothy told me of her birth—and mine. How I was adopted by—"

"Dorothy has told you of your mother's birth?" The queen leaned forward. "What did she tell you?" Ely was surprised at the vehemence of her question. *Does she not want me to know of our kinship?*

"Only that Dorothy had...an alliance with King Henry and conceived a child...Ann, my mother. She and the baby were sent to live with her brother in Chester. When Ann became of age, she married my father. He was an Irish sailor, who she thought had drowned at sea before I was born. Before my mother died, she asked my adoptive parents, Jane and Thomas Trentham, to raise me. I knew nothing of this until—"

"You believe King Henry is your rightful grandfather—is that what you were told?"

"Yes, Your Majesty."

"'Tis true. He was your grandfather." The queen looked directly into Ely's eyes as if she wanted to say more, but before she had an opportunity to open her mouth, there was a tap at the door.

"Enter," the queen said. "We will discuss this in more detail some other time." Ely was summarily dismissed as the queen welcomed Sir Francis Drake.

The following day found them off the southern coast of Wales, when the weather turned foul again. After one full day and night sitting at anchor in a cove near the entrance to the bay, the weather further delayed their trip. When they finally sailed into Bristol Bay, all the passengers were relieved to be at the end of their sea voyage. Ely filled her diary with her experiences at sea, especially noting the terminology used by the sailors. She looked forward to their trip overland to Lechlade, where barges would be waiting for the queen and her party to travel down the Thames to London.

Sailing into port, Ely stood at the rail with Blanche to watch another ship headed toward them on its way to open sea. As the ships sailed abreast, the wind brought in a horrible stench from the other ship. Ely asked a sailor working nearby if he knew anything about the ship.

"They be slavers, milady," he responded. "The Portuguese capture natives in Africa and take them to Madeira and Azores Islands to work the plantations. Ye won't be seeing me volunteering to serve on one of them ships, no matter how much they'd be payin' me," he said. "They pack them poor devils in the hold like any other cargo. I am surprised to see one of their ships in Bristol Bay. Perchance for repairs."

Blanche held a handkerchief to her nose until the ship was well passed.

"I did not know such a business was being practiced," Ely said. "Surely they are as human as anyone else."

"Nor did I," Blanche said.

Both women grabbed hold of the railing when the wake of the ship passed under them.

Ely could not get her mind off the suffering of the black people aboard that ship. Perhaps she could write a story to show a black person had as much humanity as any white. He could have a high position in court—maybe even married to a white wife.

She thought Edward's belief of his wife's indiscretion could also be included in the story. She would focus on jealousy.

She thought again of Edward's refusal to acknowledge a child as his own. Whoever told him of the gossip must not have wanted him to be tied down to a wife and child, and made up the story of her unfaithfulness, so the earl would continue to spend money on frivolity. A fair-weather friend indeed.

Twenty-two

Foul whisp'rings are abroad. Unnatural deeds
Do breed unnatural troubles. Infected minds
To their deaf pillows will discharge their secrets.
More needs she the divine than the physician.
God, God, forgive us all!
— *Macbeth*, Act 5, Scene 1

During the two weeks the queen's barge floated down the Thames, Ely felt more and more excited about the new life on which she would soon embark. The balmy weather made the trip even more enjoyable. As they floated by, people would crowd the shoreline to get a glimpse of their queen. Ely was impressed with how adept the queen was at influencing public opinion in her favor. A harbinger on horseback was always a few days ahead of her entourage to plan for her stay.

The queen's comfort was always foremost, which meant her nightly sleep came before good tidal conditions. As a result, the trip took twice as long as it should have. Her party had narrowed down to mostly women as the courtiers preferred to ride horseback to London.

The queen had planned on stopping at Windsor Castle for the month of October before traveling on to London, but the night before they were to arrive, a messenger had been received by the queen. None of the ladies knew what was afoot, only that an emergency had arisen, and the queen decided to bypass Windsor and travel directly to Whitehall Palace.

Even though London Town lay beyond a high wall, it appeared Westminster was a separate city. Ely knew it was there the seat of government was located, and she was most anxious to see Westminster Abbey and Whitehall.

The queen's barge was brought to shore below the palace where a coach was waiting. Blanche was the only one of her ladies allowed to accompany her. The other barges floated further downstream to a dock large enough to unload more passengers, their baggage, and supplies.

When Ely first saw the great London Bridge spanning the river, she was amazed at the size of the stone structure. It looked much like the other thoroughfares in the city, with stores and living quarters encompassing the entire span. She knew beheading was the chief means of execution, with heads mounted upon spikes along the bridge railings. Ely nearly vomited seeing the gruesome sight. She personally felt the beheading alone would be ample deterrent without the display of heads.

Ely, Bess Hardwick, and Kat Ashley, along with the queen's servants, were the first to disembark. They were met by four soldier guards who would accompany them on their stroll to the palace. Ely felt overwhelmed with the number of people crowding the cobblestone streets. Except for the main boulevards, the streets were so narrow the houses with their projecting upper floors nearly touched the houses on the other side of the street. Garbage and refuse produced rats the size of cats. The ladies held perfumed handkerchiefs to their noses when they passed by the squalor.

Ely was beginning to regret her decision to serve the queen, remembering the clean air and lush, grassy fields of Staffordshire. She could well understand why disease was so prevalent in the city. She changed her mind, however, when they entered through the high gates of Whitehall Palace.

Ely had seen many castles on their trip along the Thames, but nothing as grand as the buildings and grounds that stood before her. Westminster Abbey caught her eye first, and she paused to stare at the magnificent church. The other ladies continued to walk toward the palace, and she had to hurry to catch up. The palace was not just one single building but many interlocking structures. The main palace had three stories aboveground with eight identical windows on two levels and a long balcony below a slate roof. She had already been told that the palace grounds consisted of royal apartments, offices, stables, gardens, storehouses, tiltyards, tennis courts, and fields. Close by were great parks with numerous opportunities to ride horses. Acres of hunting grounds and forests could be seen beyond the city walls with numerous groundskeepers to keep out poachers. Hunting was allowed only by elite society.

Turning toward Kat, Ely said, "I did not expect the palace to be this..." She spread her arms wide. "...So massive. 'Tis like entering another city. How many people live here?"

"I should imagine many thousands year-round," she said. "I have never counted the rooms, but I would suppose the entire palace must have many hundred. The queen uses this as her winter residence, but something must have happened to cause her to come here a month early."

"I wonder what it could be."

"We are not to be concerned with the politics of the court," Bess said. "I would curb your curiosity, if you do not want to be reprimanded for being too meddlesome." The older woman strolled on ahead; Ely waited until Kat came alongside of her.

"Why in the world would I be chided for being interested in government affairs?" Ely whispered to Kat.

"Hmph, watch out for Bess. She can be a shrew when it comes to the code of behavior for the queen's ladies. As chief lady of the queen's bedchamber, she is quick to discipline the newer maids. My advice is to stay clear of her. She is already envious of you for being selected to accompany her majesty aboard the *Golden Hind*, being as how you are her newest maid. I have also wondered why you were favored over so many others."

Ely shrugged. "I do not know." Ely thought of telling Kat of her relationship to the queen, but she bit her tongue, remembering being cautioned about keeping the knowledge to herself. Besides, she suspected, gossip among the ladies was perhaps a dangerous practice.

When they reached the entrance to the great palace of Whitehall, the servants left them to walk down a long, covered footpath to the entrance for servants and tradesmen at the back. Their soldier guards took different directions. Two splendidly dressed guards stood on either side of the massive gates. One of the men left his post to open one of the heavy doors. Blanche was sitting on a bench that had been positioned against a wall, and when the women came through the door, she came forward to take Ely's arm.

"The queen has given permission for you to share my room. I will show you the way." Bess sniffed loudly, and holding her back ramrod-straight, she marched down a marbled hall with Kat following in her wake.

Ely caught only a glimpse of the beautiful tapestries and grand furnishings before a liveried servant conducted them down a long hallway. "Our servants have quarters up there," Blanche said, pointing to a stairway that led to an upper level. The servant bowed and left them at the entry to an inner chamber of a complex of rooms. Ely surmised she was in one of the attached buildings to the main palace.

"This is the common room where we take our meals and receive guests." The furnishings were pleasant, but not nearly as grand as those she had passed by in the main palace. Two divans with colorful cushions were positioned in front of a large fireplace, upon which two women were seated doing embroidery. A dining room table with twelve chairs took up most of the center of the room. Three smaller tables and chairs were positioned near the windows. French doors opened into a garden with a central fountain.

Blanche pointed to one of the two large tapestries hung on the stone walls. It was a brightly-colored scene of a forest with hunters on horseback chasing a large stag. "These tapestries were stitched by court ladies. It took many women years to complete. I stitched this area," she said, rubbing her fingers over a section of the forest.

Ely touched the smooth green silk. "You have a fine hand with the needle." The compliment seemed to please the old lady.

Blanche led her down one of the halls that branched off from the common room. They passed by four doors, two on either side of the hallway, and another stairway. Blanche's rooms were located at the end of the hallway. She inserted a large key into the door and swung it open. "I do believe I have the loveliest of all the rooms assigned to the queen's ladies."

Ely was pleased to see how light it was, due to large windows on two sides of the room. Heavy drapes would be pulled at night to hold out the draft. Furnishings were sparse, but beautiful. A small, canopied bed was covered with a yellow woolen blanket and one large pillow. Two wooden chairs with cushions, one with a footstool, were positioned in front of a small fireplace. Blanche pointed toward an archway that led into a small, windowed sitting room. "This will be your room; you must share my bed until one can be brought in for you." Ely nodded her approval. "Since we have already shared a bed aboard ship, we should be used to sleeping together by now. During the winter months, we will appreciate the warmth."

"You are very kind to share your quarters with me." Ely put her arm around the shoulders of the smaller woman. "I will be most happy to assist you in your dress."

"'Tis not necessary. Harriet has a cot in the servant quarters upstairs. She will be able to take care of us both. She is also adept at hair curling and is in demand."

"I shall be most anxious to meet her."

"I will value your company, especially when you read to me. I so enjoyed your poetry and stories aboard ship. I believe I shall be the fortunate one. I will tell you the truth...the queen suggested we room together. I believe it is because you took care of my discomfort aboard that dreadful ship. And I shall be able to orient you to your new duties."

Twenty-three

Friendship is constant in all other things
Save in the office and affairs of love.
　　　　　—*Much Ado About Nothing*, Act 2, Scene 1

Blanche sat before her embroidery frame, her slight figure encased in a heavy, brown silk dress, talking nonstop. Ely paid little attention to her rambling and tried to concentrate on writing a letter to Jane, but when Blanche mentioned what had brought the queen to Whitehall a month early, she had Ely's attention.

Sir Francis Walsingham had arrived from France. He was the queen's principal secretary overseeing both foreign and domestic policy, having served as England's ambassador to France during the 1570s. He was also known as the queen's spymaster, and lately he had been overseeing operations that penetrated the heart of

Spanish military preparations, gathering intelligence concerning Spain's increasing hostility toward England.

"Ever since the loss of Calais during the reign of Queen Elizabeth's sister, Mary Tudor, and with France now controlling the northern coastland, our queen's problems with France have increased. And then when Elizabeth had Mary, Queen of Scots, imprisoned, the situation became even more dire."

"Yes, I know. It all seems to hinge upon religion, doesn't it?"

"I would not say this to anyone else," Blanche whispered, "but ever since King Henry broke with the pope, it has caused nothing but trouble. But that was not the major problem between England and France. Did you know Mary was married to King Francis the Second and when he died, she returned to Scotland? She has French supporters who believe she should be the rightful Queen of England. That is why Mary is in prison now."

"But was not the conflict with France lessened when Elizabeth nearly married the Duke of Anjou?"

"That caused much excitement in court," Blanche giggled. "He was a fair young man and the queen seemed fond of him, but she was nearly twice his age—plus he's a papist. There was much opposition to the union, so it never came about."

"I would assume that France and England have resolved much of their dispute because they now have a common enemy," Ely remarked.

"You mean Spain? It seems there is conflict everywhere all the time. If it isn't France, then it is control over Munster in Ireland, then 'tis Scotland, and the Netherlands. It is nearly more than I can keep track of. Just be happy we are women when it comes to war."

This political intrigue was fascinating to Ely, especially if a war should break out between England and Spain, but it was the intrigue surrounding the liaison between Anne Vavasour and Edward Vere that interested Ely more. She still had not seen Anne; she shared a room with Elizabeth Knollys in the same wing of the palace where most of the queen's ladies lived, but Ely had yet to see Anne at any of the meals or palace functions.

It had been three months since Ely had overheard Anne and Edward Vere's conversation in the gardens of Bradwell Hall and she thought perhaps Anne had already been delivered of her child and no longer lived in the palace. She learned later this was incorrect.

~ * ~

It was quite by accident that Ely found an opportunity to meet Anne Vavasour. It was when she was walking toward the common room for her evening meal that Ely noted an open doorway. Inside she saw Anne Vavasour and Elizabeth Knollys in deep discussion. It appeared Mistress Knollys had brought in a tray of food to Anne. Ely stopped, not sure if she should interfere with the two women's conversation, deciding now was not the best of times. She continued her walk down the hall. Hearing footsteps behind her, she turned around to see Elizabeth walking toward her. The woman brushed past her without a greeting. Realizing Anne was alone, Ely changed her mind and turned around, going back to Anne's door—which was tightly closed.

Knocking, she heard Anne's quiet voice. "Who is it?" Without answering, Ely opened the door. "What do you want?" Anne sprung to her feet from the small table that held her dinner. She held a napkin in front of her stomach in a fruitless gesture of hiding her swollen belly.

"I am very sorry," Ely said, closing the door softly behind her. "I do not wish to disturb your meal, but I have been waiting for an opportunity to meet you and extend my hand in friendship." Ely slowly advanced into the room with her arm outstretched.

"Get out! Leave me at once. I do not desire your friendship."

"Please, do not send me away. Perhaps I know more about you then you would wish, but I only want to help."

"What do you know?" Anne nearly shouted at her. "Who are you?"

"Perhaps you do not remember. My name is Elizabeth Trentham. We met at my Uncle Ralph Sneyd's home...Bradwell Hall in Staffordshire. I was being interviewed by the queen to be..."

"Yes, I remember. What do you want?"

"Please, may we be seated so I may tell you why I wanted to meet you?" Anne appeared in genuine shock but eventually plopped back down in her chair. Her face was very pale, in direct contrast to her coal-black hair. She wore a loose-fitting gown of black muslin, putting Ely in mind of a very pregnant nun.

"Just what do you know? And what business do you think it is of yours?" Anne crossed her arms and rested them on her extended midriff.

"I know you are carrying Edward Vere's child." Anne stiffened her back, tears springing to her eyes.

"How did you...? I mean, what right do you have to infer such an insult?" Just then, Anne gripped the arms of her chair and leaned back in the throes of a labor contraction.

"My God, Anne. Are you in labor?" Ely stood up from her chair and approached her, putting her hand on Anne's hardened belly.

"No, no. 'Tis only indigestion...from the fish," she said, pushing her dinner away. Her breathing was becoming fast and shallow. A few seconds later, Anne said, "There, I am fine now. The pain has eased."

"Anne, whether you want to admit it or not, you are in labor."

"No, I cannot be. I have a fortnight before it is due."

"Babies are known to come early."

"What do you know about it? I tell you I am fine—now get out!"

"I dare not, unless you want to deliver this child by yourself." Ely pulled her chair closer to Anne and sat back down. She picked up Anne's hand into both of her own. "I am from the country and assisted the midwife when my mother delivered my brother, Tommy. Maybe I can help you, Anne, if you would let me."

"Will you tell the queen?"

"No, I will not, but she is bound to find out. Who already knows about you?"

"Only Elizabeth."

"And Lord Oxford," Ely said.

"And you—and Blanche by now, I should not wonder."

"No, I have not confided in anyone since I learned of your pregnancy, especially not Blanche. Had I done so it would have been spread all over the palace by now." Anne laughed at that comment and the two women looked into each other's eyes. Ely felt relief that perhaps Anne was beginning to trust her.

"Just how did you find out? Did Edward tell you? Perhaps he sent you to me...is that how you know?"

"No, not at all. I cannot abide the man—especially since he did this to you and then refused to divorce his wife so you could be married."

"I begged him so, but he is bound to that simpering woman just because she is Lord Burghley's daughter."

"Even so, he had no right to put you into this compromising position." Ely squeezed Anne's hand and then released it. "I was walking in the gardens of Bradwell Hall when I heard you and Edward talking. I was on the other side of the hedge and honestly did not wish to eavesdrop but was afraid to reveal myself."

"So that was it. You overheard us."

"Yes, it was quite by accident. But I decided when I came to court that I would offer my friendship and see if there was anything I could do to help. In my opinion, Edward Vere is no gentleman. He obviously took advantage of you. I know this to be true because he made an indecent advance to me three years ago, and I never forgot it."

Anne looked into Ely's eyes and said, "Perhaps you are in love with him."

"Me! Do not be ridiculous. Like I said, I cannot abide him. I have had many offers of marriage and have refused them all. I would have married any one of those detestable men over Edward Vere."

"Poof, I do not believe you. There is not a well-born lady in this country who would refuse Lord Oxford, the queen's lord great chamberlain. Even I have achieved a certain amount of respect as his mistress." With that comment, Anne broke down in tears. Her sobbing was interrupted when another contraction gripped her.

When the pain had abated, Ely helped Anne stand up. "Here, to bed with you." As Ely turned back the covers on the canopied bed, she asked, "How long have you been having these pains?"

"Not long. They began shortly before Elizabeth brought me my dinner. They were not this painful, though."

"Is this your first child?"

"Of course, you dolt. What do you take me for?"

"I was told the first takes longer to deliver. Someone should examine you to determine how far you are advanced. Shall I send for someone? Surely you have made arrangements with a physician or midwife?"

"Edward said he would arrange for me to be taken to a midwife's home when the time came."

"Shall I send for Lord Oxford?"

Ely knew the situation was desperate, and for the first time in her life she felt inadequate and unprepared. She had to find someone to help Anne besides herself, but this was only her first month in the palace and she only knew the ladies with whom she had sailed. She considered asking Blanche or Bess—but her maid Harriet would be better.

"Yes, yes. Please. I must see him. I cannot be in the palace when the baby comes. The queen will find out. Please keep this a secret—she must not know."

"You must realize that even if we can locate him, there may not be time to take you elsewhere. I remember when my mother was in labor, the midwife looked to see if she could see the baby's head. Maybe if I examine you, I can see how far you have widened." Ely patted Anne's hand. "It would give us a clue how much time we have before the baby is born."

"Are you sure you know what you are doing?"

"My mother did teach me many healing ways, and I did help when my baby brother was being born."

Anne finally relented and gave Ely permission. After Ely had Anne in the proper position, she tried to reassure her.

"You have widened some, but I think you are still too small..." Just then, Anne had another contraction and Ely could see the baby's head trying to be pushed through. "No, methinks you are advanced. The baby may be born soon. It is difficult for me to tell."

"Oh my God. You said..."

"I must find someone to help. We need water and clean linen—a piece of string. Anne, I must leave you now. I will fetch my maid and your friend Elizabeth."

Anne began to cry. "She would never. Oh my God, what am I to do...Elizabeth faints at the sight of blood. I am going to die. I just know I am."

"No, you are not. You are a healthy woman and I am sure your baby will be born normally," Ely said, wiping her hands. "I have to find someone to help. Will you trust me to do what is best for you and the baby?"

"You are going to leave me? I don't want to be left alone. Please, don't go." She grabbed Ely's skirt in desperation.

"Anne, be brave. I think the pains must come closer before the baby is born. Perhaps we have time to prepare, but we may not have time to move you. The baby will have to be born in this bed. Let me go now. I will make haste."

After Ely left Anne's room, she ran down the hall and up the stairs to the servant's quarters. She flung open the door, but the room only contained a man and a young girl. She asked the girl if she knew where Harriet was. She shrugged. Where is everyone? Of course, Harriet is probably having her own dinner in the palace scullery. Oh God, I do not know where their scullery is located! She ran across the room and down a different flight of stairs, hoping to find Harriet. She ran down a strange hall, not recognizing anything or anybody. My God, what am I to do? I'll have to tell Blanche. In a panic, she retraced her steps, ran back up the stairs into the servant quarters, and down a different flight of stairs, and dashed down the hall to the common room.

She saw Blanche along with several other ladies Ely had only met casually. She looked around frantically at the two girls serving the ladies, but she didn't know either of them. Ely had no other alternative but to tell Blanche and Elizabeth.

Blanche stopped her conversation with another of the elderly ladies to look up and smile. "Come here, Elizabeth. I have saved a place for you," Blanche said, indicating an empty chair alongside of her.

Ely bent over Blanche's back and whispered in her ear. "Please come with me. I need your help with something."

"Need my help? Whatever is wrong?" Blanche had spoken so loudly all the other women stopped talking.

"Please come. I need to talk to you in private." Ely looked around the table to see everyone focusing at her. She pulled at Blanche's hand. Blanche put her napkin on the table but had difficulty standing. Ely felt panicky, feeling all eyes upon her. She must look a sight, her hair and clothing in disarray from her flight throughout the palace.

Thinking quickly, she decided it may be safer to simply make a general announcement about Anne's condition and let the feathers fall where they may. The safety of the pregnant woman was more important than keeping secrets. Making a quick decision, she placed her hand on Blanche's shoulder, indicating for her to sit back down. Putting both of her hands on the table and leaning forward, she said, "Perhaps you should all know what is happening. After all, are we not all sisters here in service of the queen and each other?"

There was only silence in response to her question until Bess Hardwick, the self-appointed leader of the queen's ladies, spoke.

"Whatever are you referring to, Mistress Elizabeth?" she said in an authoritative manner. "Tell us immediately."

Ignoring the woman, Ely glanced at Elizabeth Knollys. She had such a haughty demeanor, Ely decided it was about time Elizabeth took responsibility toward her friend and roommate. "Elizabeth, if you care anything for your friend, Anne Vavasour, I suggest you find Lord Oxford immediately."

Elizabeth quickly stood. "What—whatever do you mean? I know nothing of—"

"You know exactly what I mean. I stopped at Anne's room to offer my friendship and found her nearly ready to deliver his child." Ely knew she had over-exaggerated, but she figured it was the best way to spur the ladies into action.

There was an immediate clamor of the other women. Chairs scraped across the stone floor with everyone asking questions at the same time. "Elizabeth, please find the earl, and if any of you women know of a midwife in the palace, you need to fetch her— right now!"

Twenty-four

Nor stony tower, nor walls of beaten brass,
Nor airless dungeon, nor strong links of iron
Can be retentive to the strength of spirit.
—*Julius Caesar*, Act 1, Scene 3

Ely did not seek her bed with Blanche until the gray dawn had shown through the window of their room. She stripped off her soiled gown and crawled into bed in just her underclothing. The slight wobbling of the bed and rustle of the mattress stirred Blanche into wakefulness. She turned over to face Ely.

"Elizabeth, is that you?"

"Who else but me, pray tell?" Ely's giggle was cut short by a yawn of tiredness.

"Did Anne have her babe?" Blanche asked.

"Yes, a robust boy. She plans to name him Edward. May we wait until the morn to talk about it? I am very tired."

Blanche sat up and tried to light a candle. "I am sorry to tell you, my dear, but the queen has summoned you to her quarters."

Ely propped herself up on her elbow. "At this hour? Surely not."

"What is the time?"

"'twill soon be light," Ely said.

"That late? I did not know. Perhaps it is best not to waken her. She is already enraged. She was ranting, issuing orders right and left, even sending the Earl of Essex in search of Lord Oxford. She is so angry with him for his duplicity, him married to Lord Burghley's daughter and all. I would not be surprised if she sent him to the block—along with Anne."

Ely was once again wide awake. "But why should she want to see me?"

"Someone told her you knew Anne was carrying Lord Oxford's child. She is quite put out you did not tell her."

"How did she know? Only Anne..." Ely glared at Blanche in the dim light. "Blanche! Surely you did not betray me?"

"No, no. I did not tell the queen...it must have been Bess."

"Bess? How?" By then, Ely was on her knees facing Blanche. She paused, thinking. "Of course. When you asked how I knew it was Edward's child, I made the mistake of telling you how I accidentally overheard them talking...I assumed you would know I did not want it repeated."

"I am sorry, Elizabeth. You did not tell me you...I mean... I did not mean you harm."

Blanche looked so downcast that Ely did not berate her any further. She knew she had made a mistake when she confided in Blanche, knowing full well the older woman's appetite for gossip.

"Do not let it concern you further. Surely I will be able to explain the circumstances to the queen. Perhaps she will understand."

~ * ~

Later that morning, Ely was led through the palace by one of the queen's pages until they reached an antechamber to the queen's private office. Ely was told to wait until she was summoned. A short time later, Ely was amazed to see Edward Vere being escorted between two red-coated soldiers. She rose, feeling unsteady. Even though his demeanor revealed the same proud man, she saw unease in his eyes.

"Mistress Ely. Have you seen Anne Vavasour?" Even though Ely felt repulsed by Anne's paramour, she couldn't help but feel a bit of sympathy for him, since it was obvious he was in deep trouble with the queen, and he did seem concerned about Anne.

One of the soldiers gave Edward's shoulder a nudge, forcing him to proceed down the hallway. "You have a fine son, sir," Ely called as he was being marched away.

"Thank you," he said over his shoulder.

A different page appeared to tell Ely the queen was ready to receive her. As they walked down the dark hallway toward a heavy door, she whispered, "Is the queen alone, or is she...?"

The page whispered in return. "No, Lord Burghley is with her." With that, he opened the heavy door into the office.

The queen was seated in a low chair, attired in a dress of silver gauze with slashed sleeves lined with green taffeta. Her dress was covered with a floor-length gold robe with a high collar. Lord Burghley arose from a chair situated in front and to the right of the queen's and bowed his head in a somber greeting. He was equally clad in exquisite clothing. Ely advanced a couple of steps and swept herself into a low curtsy, staying in that position until the queen told her to rise. She was not offered a chair.

When the queen threw open her robe, Ely could see the lining of pale green adorned with small ornaments of rubies and pearls. She wore a chain of rubies and pearls about her neck. On her head she wore a garland of the same gold material and beneath it, a reddish-colored wig with pearls hanging down over her forehead. Her white face powder made it appear she had no eyebrows.

"I have been led to believe you have involved yourself in an affair—and only on your first month at the palace. Is that not so, Miss?"

"Affair? Your Majesty?" Ely, in her tiredness, did not know what the queen meant. Did she want to know something unrelated to the birth of the babe? "No, I am not involved in an affair..."

The queen started to rise and then sat back down. "Have I thought you more intelligent than you are?" she shrieked. The queen looked toward Lord Burghley and he shrugged. "Not your affair, you dunce—I am referring to the affair of Edward Vere and Anne Vavasour. Are you or are you not involved in that liaison?" Ely could see the queen's face becoming quite flushed under the heavy makeup. "Answer me truthfully, or I will send you to the Tower too!"

"No, no, Your Majesty. I felt confused for a moment." Ely took a deep breath, trying to regain her composure, but she was furious Bess had put her into this untenable position. What had she told the queen?

"My involvement has been accidental." She looked into the queen's eyes, realizing she expected Ely to continue. "May I explain how I found out about... about Anne's being with child?" The queen remained silent, but her eyes narrowed, staring into hers.

Ely took a deep breath and began to tell her about overhearing Edward and Anne's conversation at Bradwell Hall, leaving out the details other than to say she was able to surmise Anne was pregnant. "I couldn't help but feel sympathy for Anne as I remembered a young girl in our shire who had...had a babe out of wedlock, and how she was treated so abysmally by everyone." Ely saw the queen begin to drum her fingers on the arm of her chair. "I made the decision to befriend Anne when I arrived at the palace," Ely concluded in a rush.

"How noble," the queen said with disdain. "Did it not occur to you to mention what you had overheard to your queen?" Her voice had become so strident she was nearly screeching.

Ely hated the feeling of being on the defensive, but she had no choice in the matter. She straightened her shoulders and said, "'Twas no concern of mine, Your Majesty." She suddenly realized she had inadvertently implied it was none of the queen's business either. "I meant to say I have never been prone to gossip and...I felt, I mean..." The queen continued to stare at her. Ely again sunk down into a deep curtsy, mumbling under her breath, "I am sorry, Your Majesty. It did not occur to me to say anything to anyone."

"Stand up, girl." The queen glanced at Lord Burghley. He harrumphed, as if he were about to say something, but the queen interrupted, looking back at Ely. "I welcome the fact you do not gossip. We could use more women of that sort in this court." She closed her robe around herself as if she felt a draft. "I understand you assisted in the birth of the child, is that correct?"

"Yes, Your Majesty. When I met Mistress Vavasour, she was in the final stages of labor. She needed help. One of the servants had experience as a midwife. I assisted."

"She had the child?" Lord Burghley asked.

"Yes, sir. Early this morning. A boy."

"So he has a bastard son. Born in this palace."

The queen stood and began to pace, coming to a stop in front of Ely. "Go fetch the guards and be quick about it." Much to Ely's surprise, the queen followed her. When Ely opened the door, the queen elbowed her aside, issuing an order to the guards. "Find Anne Vavasour and have her immediately taken to the Tower along with her lover."

"But what of the babe, Your Majesty?"

The queen crossed her arms and glared at Ely. "Since you are so resourceful, it will be your responsibility to care for it. Vavasour will not have access to the babe."

Ely's first reaction was to argue with the queen that it wasn't right to separate a newborn from its mother, but she had the good sense to keep her mouth shut. She'd think of something.

Twenty-five

I am a bastard, too; I love bastards:
I am bastard begot, bastard instructed,
bastard in mind, bastard in valor,
in every thing illegitimate.
—*Troilus and Cressida*, Act 5, Scene 7

"Here, let me have the baby," Ely said to the wet nurse. "He has had his fill." She took the sleeping baby from her arms and laid him in his cradle.

"'Tis a sweet one, this," the wet nurse said as she refastened the bodice over her ample bosom. "I have a bed in the servants' hall with my own wee one. Send for me should the babe give you unease," she said in her deep Scottish accent. She curtsied before leaving the room.

"For a bastard, this baby is beautiful. Black hair like his mother," Blanche said.

Ely used Vavasour's room, so caring for the baby would not disturb Blanche. She hoped to keep the room once the baby was no longer her responsibility. "'Tis not this little one's fault for the manner he was brought into the world." She gently wiped a dribble of milk from his chin.

"What are your plans? Surely you cannot continue to care for him." Blanche plopped herself down in the rocking chair the midwife had vacated.

"No. I cannot, but I must until someone from Anne's family comes for him. It is the punishment the queen has given me for keeping his parents' secret. I think the queen has had a change of heart—toward me, at least. She sent word to Sir Thomas Knyvett of the birth of the baby. He is Anne's uncle, who I understand was responsible for securing Anne a place here at court. He, or someone from his family, is due to arrive from Shropshire anon. I assume he will take Anne and the baby home—once the queen decides to release her from the Tower." Ely covered the baby with a blanket and sat down on the bed facing Blanche. "I am curious how Edward came to know Anne. I heard he met her before she arrived at court last year."

Blanche settled herself deep into the chair, ready to share gossip. "He met her in Yorkshire while on a trip to the northern shires for the queen—two years ago, I believe. Even though her uncle was her sponsor, I would not be surprised if Edward had something to do with securing her a position as one of the queen's maids."

"It is difficult for me to understand how...I mean, the earl is married to Lord Burghley's daughter. They must have been able to be somewhat discreet, or else the queen surely would have heard about their affair before now."

"Are you aware Edward would not have anything to do with Anne Cecil for these past five years?"

"I did know they were separated, but not for that long. You mentioned previously Anne had a daughter he claimed not his own."

"Yes. Her name is Elizabeth, too. She is now five. She lives in the Cecil household with her mother. I heard a few days ago she will soon be coming to court for her education."

~ * ~

A week later Ely was to meet Anne Cecil Vere and her daughter for the first time. It was a beautiful fall day and Ely had taken the baby into a garden near the women's quarters. She lowered a book to her lap when she saw Bess Hardwick lead a woman and a small girl toward her.

"Mistress Trentham, this is Countess Anne Cecil Vere. The queen has told us you will be tutor to her daughter while she is here at the palace." Bess put her arm around Anne's shoulders. "They wanted to meet you."

Ely was already aware Anne had served the queen, first as a maid of honor, and following her marriage, as a lady-in-waiting. After introductions, the three of them sat on a bench opposite Ely's chair.

"And your name is?" Ely turned toward the girl.

"Elizabeth," she piped up. "But I'm called Beth."

"I am an Elizabeth as well. You may call me Ely, as do my sisters at home." She smiled warmly at the girl. "That way we won't be confused with our queen." The small girl giggled. Ely turned her gaze toward Anne. "You have a lovely daughter."

Anne appeared too young to have a daughter of five. Tiny in stature and demeanour, she was not a haughty countess as were most of the other titled women Ely had met so far—especially Bess. Anne had blonde hair that hung in curls reaching below her shoulders, large hazel eyes set in a small face, and a bow-shaped mouth. She was pretty, whereas Anne Vavasour's beauty was stunning. Her daughter must have inherited the same green eyes as her father's, along with his brown hair and his taller stature. How he could refuse to accept this child as his own is shameful, Ely thought.

"Will Beth be your only student?" All three seemed unable to keep their eyes from straying to the sleeping baby. The little girl fidgeted, causing her mother to nudge her shoulder. It was obvious they had come to see the baby.

"It is my understanding there are to be other maids who will join your daughter. The queen wants the girls to receive lessons in history and languages in the morning. Others will be responsible for teaching them fine arts and dancing."

"The queen mentioned you are caring for—this babe," Anne said.

"Only until someone from his mother's family comes for him." By then, the little girl had stood and was inching her way toward the baby. "Would you like to hold him?"

Bess stood abruptly. "How dare you be impertinent to the countess!" Bess started to take hold of the girl's arm when Anne stopped her.

"My daughter is only curious."

"Mother, may I hold him?" Anne paused for a second and then gave her permission.

"Here, Beth. You sit in this chair." Ely instructed the girl. She then picked up the sleeping baby and placed him on her lap.

Anne approached the baby and looked down upon him. Tears began to course down her cheeks. Bess put her arms around Anne, pulling her in close as she wept.

"Perhaps the countess would prefer to leave," Ely said.

"May I stay awhile longer?" Beth asked. Her mother waved her hand in agreement as Bess led Anne back into the palace.

"Is he really my brother?" the girl asked as she nuzzled his cheek.

"Yes. You have the same father," Ely said, sitting on the ground next to the girl.

"Grandfather said he is Edward's bastard. What does that mean?"

"It means the baby's mother was not married to your father. 'Tis not a good name to call a tiny baby."

"Why does my father not come to see me? I would so like him to." She looked down at the baby. "If I had been born a boy, maybe my father would like me." The girl looked into Ely's eyes with such sadness, Ely's dislike of Edward increased measurably.

"I am sure your father likes you too, Beth." She patted the little girl's hair.

"Do you think so—Ely?"

"I will make you a promise. I will visit your father and tell him what a wonderful daughter he has. Perhaps then he will want to be with you."

"Will you? But Mother said the queen sent him to the Tower. How can you see him there?"

"Don't you fret. I will find a way." Ely said as she took the baby from the girl. "I think perhaps you need to join your mother now."

~ * ~

Ely did have an opportunity to visit the Tower of London the following week, as she was ordered to take the babe to Anne Vavasour. Whoever had persuaded the queen to relent and allow the child to be with its mother, Ely didn't know, unless someone from her family had arrived.

Ely held the baby boy close as she stood at the massive gates to the Tower along with one of the palace guards who had accompanied her from Whitehall. After removing a cradle filled with the baby's layette from behind his saddle, he handed off the reins of both horses to a blue-uniformed Yeoman Warder.

After they were led to Anne's cell, the guard unlocked the door. Anne and her maid stood in the center of the room. With a little scream of excitement, Anne rushed to Ely. Her smile of happiness was genuine.

A few minutes later, after the mother and child had been reacquainted, Anne sat in a chair with the baby cuddled in her arms. Anne's maid had been excused with the order to wait in the hallway with the guard.

"How can I ever thank you for persuading Her Highness to allow me to keep the baby?"

"'Twas not me," Ely said, "but I am happy you are now together. I've become quite fond of him. He is a very sweet child. Little Edward has brought back memories of when my brother Tommy was born."

The baby started to fuss, and Ely automatically stood, intending to take care of him. "I believe he may need to be changed.

He was fed before I left the palace, but it won't be long before he'll want to nurse again. Shall I ask your maid to secure a wet nurse?"

"No, I have milk for my child," she said.

"You intend to nurse your own child? But ladies of the court would never..." Ely said as she changed the baby's diaper.

"Yes, I know. My maid told me my baby would have a better chance to survive with his own mother's milk, and that is what I intend. She has shown me how to release the pressure in my breasts so the milk will continue to flow. I am anxious to have him do it for me." She started to untie her bodice.

"I think you should wait until he is hungry. I am sure your maid will assist you."

"I do want this baby to be healthy. Now that Edward has a son, I feel certain he will divorce his wife and marry me. I am going to do whatever is in my power to have my baby inherit his father's name and title."

"I must depart now. May I be permitted to visit you and the baby again soon? I have become quite fond of him."

"I suppose so," Anne said. "Do you have any information as to when I will be released from here?"

"I only know that your uncle has been summoned and will take you back with him to Yorkshire. I suspect he may have already arrived. Why else would I be ordered to bring the baby to you?"

"No, I cannot go with my uncle...not until I convince Edward. No, this does not fit into my plans at all. I must see Edward."

"You have not seen him since you've been here?" Ely asked.

"No. If I had money to bribe the guard, perhaps it could have been arranged." Anne looked at Ely with such anguish, she felt pity for the naivety of the girl.

"I intended to talk to his lordship today on another matter. Perhaps he could arrange something."

"You do? I shall be forever in your debt if you tell him about his wonderful son. Also tell him I love him and that..."

"I understand, but I am not sure what I can do." Anne was pulling at her sleeve with such force, Ely had difficulty removing the material from her grasp. After she was free, she said, "I will tell him about the baby and that you wish to see him."

A few minutes later, Ely stood at the open door to the apartment the earl had been assigned. Even though he was a prisoner, his high title and standing in court gave him special privileges. His quarters may not have been quite as luxurious as those he enjoyed in the many palaces throughout England, but these seemed comfortable. It had a canopied bed, tapestries on the stone walls, and a large rug covering the floor along with a separate alcove where his valet slept. The guard remained at the doorway as Ely entered.

Edward stood near the fireplace, looking fit despite his confinement. "Well, well. If it isn't Mistress Goodfellow. Whatever brings you to my humble abode?" Ely didn't curtsy as she normally would, had he not immediately started to tease her about her past escapade.

Edward turned toward his valet and ordered him to remain in the hallway with the guard. "And close the door when you leave." When the two men left, Edward pulled another chair near the warmth of the fireplace and gestured for her to sit. He pulled his chair near hers.

"Now tell me why you are here. I was under the impression you detested my company."

"Yes, I...that is true."

Edward stiffened and then laughed aloud. "Never in my life have I met a girl quite so..."

"Honest?" Ely offered.

"Honesty. From you? 'Twas it not you who paraded herself about as a boy? How is that honest, pray tell?"

"And you, are you so stuffed with honorable virtues? Methinks you are no less than a stuffed man."

Edward sputtered and stared at her. "And you, my Lady Disdain. Wait, wait. Do not say another word until I have..." With that, he stood and approached a table covered with paper. "I must remember what you called me." He sat himself down, dipped his feathered pen in an inkwell, and scribbled something. "Being incarcerated as I am gives me time to write," he said. "Methinks what you said will fit nicely into my play."

Ely was quite at a loss as to how to deal with this man, not knowing if he took offense at her insults or if he quite enjoyed their repartee. Since they shared writing in common, her curiosity took hold. She stood and approached the table, looking over his shoulder to see what he had written.

"You are composing a play?"

"Only a bit of much ado about nothing."

"That is odd. I never figured you for...but of course, you do write poetry."

"Yes, from time to time. How do you know that?" Not willing to tell him she had overheard the sonnet he had composed and read aloud to Anne Vavasour, she did not respond.

"No matter. Shall I write a poem of you? Perhaps about a dame who wishes she were born a boy? But no, that would be a waste, since you were born so blithe and bonny."

"And a hey, nonny nonny." She turned away.

"Damn, you are good." He then scribbled something else down. Without looking up, he said, "What say we discontinue our skirmish and form a truce?" Looking sideways at her, he must have seen her scowl, her arms crossed before her bosom. "If not forever, at least today. You still haven't told me why you are here."

Ely realized her behavior left much to be desired. To subdue her contempt would require her to overlook his shameful disregard for his wife, daughter, and yes, even his mistress. It really was none of her business, but the queen did bring her into his affairs, and he had a right to know.

"Yes, you are right. But it is difficult to overlook your disdain..." Ely bit her tongue, willing it to curb her insults.

"My disdain? Toward what...and whom? I have no disdain—except perhaps toward the queen—for this," he said, swinging his arm to indicate his prison quarters.

"Exactly. Even now you fail to see what damage your actions have done to the women in your life."

"And what is that to you? What have I possibly done to you? I barely know you."

"The queen has seen fit to bring me into your...affair. After she sent you and Anne Vavasour here, she ordered me to take care of your baby son."

"Ordered you. But why? Why should she do that?"

"Because I failed to tell her I knew of Anne's, er...difficulties, and that you were the one who..."

"And how did you discover this? I suppose Anne tattled it to the ladies of the court."

"No, that is not the case. I do not know who Anne told. I never ever talked with her until she was in labor with your baby."

Ely noted his puzzled expression and realized she must admit how she found out. "I overheard your conversation with Anne in the gardens of my uncle's estate during the queen's visit there. You read a sonnet to her."

"So that's how you know I write poetry."

"Yes. You are a skillful compositionist." Wanting to make peace with him, she smiled briefly. "I also write...I love to write. 'Tis my passion, but nothing will ever come of it."

"Howsoever did you learn to...? Tell me about yourself, Ely. You interest me."

"My father allowed his daughters to be tutored alongside his son."

A knock sounded at the door. "Enter." Edward's valet opened the door.

"The lady's carriage has arrived."

"Tell them to wait. We have not yet finished our conversation."

"No, not this lady, milord. Mistress Anne's uncle is here to fetch her and the baby. Her majesty has signed her release papers."

"Oh, that is it, is it? What about my release?"

"The guard said only the lady was to be pardoned."

Edward stomped his foot and would have thrown something at his valet if he could have found something to throw. Instead, he reverted to cursing the queen. "She's a waggish, horn-mad dogfish. A hideous, eye-offending hedge-pig...!"

Before Edward finished cursing, the valet, using good judgment, closed the door against his master's ranting. The earl must have quite forgotten Ely was still in the room.

"If she could hear you now, your neck would be under the axe instead of your being imprisoned."

"And I am certain you will go out of your way to tell her." He sneered.

"I am not a teller of tales, my lord. I don't blame you for wanting your freedom." Ely looked at him and realized perhaps there was a solution that would be in everyone's best interest. "Did you ever consider there is someone who has the queen's ear, someone who wants you to remain here?"

"An enemy of mine?" He fingered his beard. "You must have someone in mind."

"Your father-in-law, William Cecil, Lord Burghley. He was furious you had sired another woman's son while his daughter remained faithful."

He turned to her suddenly. "Faithful! Faithful, you say, when she had a child from another man."

"Have you looked upon this little girl?" He shrugged. "Well, you should."

"What is this to you?"

Her face flushed in anger. "Your daughter has many of your same features. Your same color of eyes and hair. She is tall for her age. I am sure her height was inherited from you." His eyes told Ely she had his interest, but he said nothing. "Whatever gave you the notion she was not your daughter?"

"A friend told me of my wife's infidelity. There is a question of when the child was born. It was when I was in Italy. My friend said Anne falsified the date of the baby's birth to convince me I had sired her." Ely had assumed correctly that this friend did not want the earl tied down to family life for reasons of his own.

"And you chose to believe him instead of discussing this with your wife? Who was this friend? What was his motivation for wanting you to distrust her?"

The earl pondered her question, pulling at his beard. "I did believe him—at the time."

"If you agreed to return to your wife, perhaps you could be released from here. Little Beth desires to know her father. She is a sad tyke, but very sweet. She thinks you don't like her. I am sure you could learn to love her."

Edward turned away and sat at the table. He picked up the quill and twirled it in his fingers. Ely felt fearful that she had overstepped her position as the earl's inferior, especially as a woman. Knowing the time was right for her to exit, she said, "I am sorry if I offended you, milord. But I did promise your daughter I would speak to you on her behalf." He continued to look down at his papers. She opened the door and told the guard she was ready to leave. She looked back at Edward. He continued either to ignore her or, she hoped, he was thinking upon what she had said.

~ * ~

Ely's life had taken on a satisfying routine of working with four girls, ranging in age from five to ten. In the mornings, she taught them Latin, Greek, and history six days a week. After their noonday meal, she turned them over to other women for lessons in music, dance, and needlepoint. This left the afternoon hours for Ely to pursue her own interests, which included exploring the queen's various libraries and sitting in with others of the court learning about the workings of the palace. She spent additional time writing letters to her family and to John Overall. Her father had given her the other volumes of the *Complutensian Polyglot Bible* and she had sent them to John in appreciation for his kindness on their journey to Chester. Through their correspondence, she was entertaining the notion of marriage to the good pastor, should he ask her.

She had learned through the ever-present court gossip that Edward had been released from prison on the proviso of re-establishing a relationship with his wife. Anne Vavasour was not yet completely out of the picture because she had put up such a fuss with her uncle about not leaving London until she met with Edward. A few days later, he did manage to arrange an assignation between the two former lovers.

According to the Earl of Essex, Ely learned that Edward told Anne there was no hope of ever becoming involved with her or her child again and that it was best she forget all about him. When her uncle heard of the manner in which the earl had treated his favorite niece, he challenged him to a duel. The result was a furious sword fight starting in a courtyard and ending up in the street. The uncle received various non-life-threatening wounds from Edward's sword, but the earl was more badly injured when he fell backward from a ledge and received compound fractures to his ankle and foot. The palace surgeon was able to set the bones as best he could, but Edward's foot became inflamed. The surgeon wanted to amputate, but Edward raised an uproar and ordered the surgeon from his sight.

The queen became involved when she visited the ailing courtier and decided what the earl needed was a skilled nurse. She must have remembered Ely's nursing skill from when she had helped Blanche on their voyage from the North. The queen ordered Ely to assist the surgeon in whatever capacity Edward needed. Ely wanted nothing more to do with him, but had no choice but to visit him.

When Ely entered Edward's apartment, she found a man so wracked with fever he had no consciousness of her ministrations. When she removed the rags from his foot, she noticed his skin was still dirty, and she cursed the surgeon for not cleaning him before he applied the splints. There was a two-inch wound that had been stitched just below his ankle. It had not yet developed the dreaded gangrene, but it was badly swollen and hot to touch. He needed special herbs to keep it from festering. She gave a list to Edward's valet to take to an apothecary.

"Who is here? Anne?" Edward turned and looked at Ely through bleary eyes.

"No, milord."

"Oh, it's you. Lady Disdain. Come to see me at my worst?"

"Not at all. I am sending your man to fetch medicines that may help heal your foot." Edward tried to sit but fell back against his pillow.

"What do you know?"

"My mother is a healer. I have learned from her." She put her arm under his shoulders and turned his damp pillow over to the other side. "It will be your own body that will cause you to heal. There are simples that can prevent infection and reduce your fever. I pray the apothecary has these herbs."

"They want to saw off my foot. Don't let them." Ely saw tears form at his eyes. "Don't let them."

Notwithstanding her own bias against the pompous earl, she felt sympathy for him. "It is too early to..." Edward turned his head from side to side. Ely took hold of his hand. "Please relax. It is best to trust me. You must believe you will get well." He whimpered and squeezed her hand. She looked upon the suffering man, who reminded her of her little brother Tommy when he'd had the measles.

"Are you in pain? Do you need more laudanum?"

He shook his head. "Makes me dream—terrible dreams."

"You are fortunate we have such a strong pain treatment on hand. It was only brought to England a short time ago." She patted his arm. "Willow bark will help with pain and fever. Fortunately, I have a small amount in my medicinal reticule. I will prepare a tea for you."

Ely motioned to a servant standing just at the door. "Bring me a pot of boiling water. Also, I will need a basin and clean cloths." She turned back to Edward. "I will need to wash your foot and bandage it with herbs that will not only ease the pain but also lessen the swelling. The splint will have to be removed, but just long enough to wash and dress your leg. We will need to be careful not to displace the bones. Can you withstand the pain while I try to help you?"

He closed his eyes. "Your voice is soothing."

Ely smiled. "Why don't you try to sleep until your valet returns?"

Later, she insisted Edward take more laudanum before she worked on his leg. When he was snoring softly, she asked his valet to assist her. After she had finished bandaging his foot and reapplying the splints, she heard someone softly tapping on the door. The valet admitted Edward's wife, Anne.

Ely smiled her welcome.

"My father said you were also a healer. I envy your ability. Thank you for trying to help him," Anne whispered. "How is he?"

"He's asleep." She took Anne's arm. "We should let him sleep." She motioned to the valet to stay near his master.

After the two women were outside the door, Ely briefly told Anne of her husband's condition. "I think he is resting more comfortably now. I have a container of willow bark tea that should help reduce his fever. We will need to wait and see."

Anne's hands shook as she raised them to her lips. "Will he lose his foot?"

"I don't know. It depends on..."

Tears began to course down Anne's face. "He cannot." She grabbed Ely's arm. "He would never be able to bear being a cripple."

"How about you? Could you?"

"It would never matter to me. I love him—I always have."

"Always?"

"Since we were children." Ely led her to a bench in the hallway. "Did you know Edward was a ward of my father after his father died?"

"How old was he?"

"About twelve, I believe. I was still a small girl. He had been there as long as I can remember."

"I see. What happened to his mother?"

"She was there for a short while, but she remarried and moved away."

"And she did not take him with her?"

Anne straightened her shoulders. "She was not allowed, even if she wanted to."

"Not allowed?"

"Of course not. He is the seventeenth Earl of Oxford. He needed to receive the proper education and training that befits his title."

"I see." Ely thought of herself and the love and attention she had received from her family.

The valet came into the hallway and the women stood and went to him. "His lordship is awake and is asking for you, miss."

Ely turned to Anne. "I have done what I can do for him. He just needs someone to sit with him for now." She put her hand on Anne's shoulder. "I am sure he would rather have you by his side."

"Could that be so?"

"I am sure of it. Tell him I will check his bandage in the morning. Try to get him to drink some of the tea."

~ * ~

Edward kept his foot, but the bones did not heal properly, which left him with a limp and needing a cane. During his recovery, the relationship between him and Ely improved so they were no longer adversaries, realizing they had much in common—not just their intellect but their love of writing, reading, and the plays. Ely could not remember when her feelings toward him changed from dislike to affection, but she was careful to keep it hidden from everyone, especially his wife.

As the months passed, Ely became close friends with Anne, Beth, and Edward, too. She enjoyed her intellectual conversations with Edward. It was apparent he now cared for his wife.

Ely's notion of marrying John Overall vanished soon after caring for the earl, but John and she remained friends, and the two continued their correspondence even after John married another woman. Ely developed a close relationship with the queen and she soon became one of her favorite ladies. Even though Ely was openly courted by many titled men, she did not encourage them. Her kinship with her queen, and being independent, meant more to her than marriage.

Twenty-six

Clay was true to his word and called me every Friday around five in the afternoon. We'd start each conversation with whatever information I'd learned to prove Elizabeth Trentham was Shakespeare. I'd fill him in and then he'd end the call. When he called me the day after Christmas, he was much friendlier than previously.

"Merry Christmas, Cynthia. Did you have a nice holiday?"

"Yes, I did. Quiet, but nice. The inn where I'm staying made me feel quite at home. How about you? Did you have friends who...?"

"My daughter came home from her school in Paris and we celebrated with my in-laws. Colleen and I are just about ready to leave for Sunriver. We're spending a week there, skiing Mount Bachelor."

"That does sound fun. I remember skiing Bachelor way back when. That may be the only thing I miss from my marriage." I'd never shared my personal life with him, so why was I now?

"I never knew you were married. How long ago?'

"I've been divorced for nearly twenty years. I have a son, Mark. He's in the Air Force. Stationed in Germany. He came home in September for my mother's funeral, so coming again for Christmas was out of the question."

"You have a son. I never knew. I should have asked about your personal life before this. No excuse for my being rude."

"You haven't been rude. Not at all. I know you're a busy attorney with a lot on your mind."

"Sudie spoke highly of you. When I return, we'll have to get together. Since we have joint ownership of the Shakespeare page, we really should get to know each other."

"I'd like that, too. By the way, I've found something very interesting I'm anxious to show you. It at least proves Elizabeth Trentham was educated and wrote poetry."

"Wow. I'm surprised..." He paused for a minute. "I admit I've been doubtful you could find anything much about the woman. Hold on a sec." I could hear him talking to someone who must have been in the room with him. "My daughter just told me our ride is here to pick us up. I'll be back after the New Year. I'll call for a date."

After we hung up, I wondered what he'd meant about a date. A real date or just setting up a time to meet? Probably for an appointment in his office, I supposed.

~ * ~

I was surprised when Clay called just a week later, on another Friday, the second of January.

"Hello, Cynthia. Did I catch you at a bad time?"

"No, not at all. I just returned from house hunting—condo hunting, to be exact." I paused for a second to sit near the fireplace in the common room. "Did you have a good time skiing?"

"For only two days. I've been back for three days, confined to my condo."

"Oh no. What happened?"

"Colleen and another woman in our party were standing on a slope taking pictures of the view when a snowboarder—totally out of control—came down and wiped me out. He knocked me into both women. My back is pretty sore. Fortunately, Colleen wasn't hurt at all, but the other woman broke her ankle when our skis tangled together."

"I'm sorry to hear that. How are you now?"

"I'll be fine. I was in the hospital overnight in Bend, and then I was able to take a flight back to Portland. I'll be confined to my place for a few more days. Colleen was here, but left this morning to catch her flight."

"Is there anything I can do to help?"

"No—I appreciate the offer, though. The reason I called is...I'd like to see you." He paused. "Not that I need any help. I'm managing on my own, but I'm not yet ready to drive anywhere. I thought, if you wouldn't mind coming here, we could discuss your—I mean, our project. You said you have something to show me. However, if you'd rather not..."

He seemed nervous. So out of character. I smiled, realizing he actually wanted us to get together.

"No trouble at all. I don't mind coming to your place. When?"

"That's great," he said. "How about tomorrow...it's Saturday and I hope it..."

"Tomorrow is fine. Just tell me where you live and...Why don't I bring lunch?"

~ * ~

When I told Lisa about my date with Clay, she insisted on preparing the lunch. Since her cooking was superb, I readily accepted. I offered to pay her, but she refused.

Clay owned a condo overlooking the Willamette River just off Macadam Avenue not too far from Portland's city center. In the entryway, I pushed a button opposite his name. He buzzed me in, then I rode an elevator to the top floor. I had looked at several condos in the Portland area, but had never seen these for the good reason that they were priced way beyond what I could afford.

He met me at the door dressed in gray sweatpants, shirt and sheepskin-lined slippers. A back brace was fastened around his waist. The casualness of his appearance seemed to make him more approachable, but still handsome, as he'd shaved and combed his hair. He was using a walker with a seat. "Come on in. It's good to see you, Cynthia. I feel absolutely elderly using this thing," he said. "Fortunately, it's only temporary."

"I'm sorry you're having problems." It was impossible to shake hands with a picnic basket in one hand, my briefcase in the other, and my purse slung around my shoulders. "My landlady was great about fixing us a lunch." I held up the heavy basket.

"Here, put that on the seat and I'll wheel it into the kitchen," he said. I followed him through the foyer and across a wide living room into a kitchen area separated by an open counter. "Excuse how I'm dressed. It's about all I can put on without help."

"Here, let me lift that." I picked up the basket and put it on the table. "Are you hungry? We have sandwiches and homemade soup which I can heat in your microwave."

"Not yet. Why don't we relax first and talk? Would you like coffee, tea...?"

"Tea would be nice," I said. "How about you?"

"Sure, tea's fine." He started to push the walker into the kitchen, but I stopped him.

"Let me do that. Just tell me where everything is."

"Okay." He sat on the walker and gave me directions. After I had the water boiling, I put a teapot, cups, etc. on a tray and carried it toward a sofa, where I could tell he had been lying. A bed pillow and a fuzzy blue afghan had been thrown off to the side. The sofa was placed in a position to give him a view of the river through a big bay window. He could also watch the television, which had been mounted on the wall over the fireplace. I put the tray on the coffee table and sat in a wingback chair near him. I picked up a large flat ice pack from the table. It still felt frozen, icy.

"Why don't you sit back down. I'm sure you're supposed to keep this on your back." It was obvious he was in pain, as there was perspiration on his forehead. After he was seated with his back against the pillow, he leaned forward and I placed the ice pack on his back.

After I poured each of us a cup of tea, his with a bit of sugar, I wasn't nervous at all; it was so much different from when I had been in his office.

"So, Cynthia. Tell me about yourself. You said you're divorced."

I nodded after taking a sip of tea. "I was married a year after graduating from high school—in St. Helens. I'd been dating Alan since I was fifteen. He was two years older. We got married when he was a sophomore in college—I was pregnant. I moved to Eugene so he could finish school, and had Mark there. His parents were well off. His dad owned his own business—they supported us until after Mark was born." I went on to tell him the same story I had given Sudie, finishing up with how I went to college with the babysitting help from my mother.

"You were both so young. Those marriages seldom work out, but look what you've done with your life. Did your son, Mark, go into the military right out of high school?"

"He was accepted into the Air Force Academy. He's a captain now. Flies all types of helicopters. He's engaged to a German girl. Not sure if they've decided to be married there or come back to the states for the ceremony. I'm anxious to meet her."

"Did Mark see much of his father after the divorce?"

"At first he did, until Alan moved to San Francisco. The first summer he spent a few weeks with Alan and his stepmother. By then she already had a child of her own and I think she resented Mark being in their lives. Anyway, he refused to go back there after that first year and Alan didn't make a fuss about it. Mark does have a good relationship with Alan's parents, though. They still live in St. Helens."

Clay lifted his legs off the sofa and onto the floor. He put the ice pack back on the table.

"Can I put that in the freezer for you?"

"Would you mind? I've had it on long enough."

After I returned to the living room and sat, I tried to shift the conversation to him. "You have a daughter. Colleen, is that right?"

"Yes, but she's my stepdaughter. She's twenty-two now—wants to be an artist. Studying in a Paris academy."

"That's impressive," I said.

"Impressive and expensive." He laughed. "Fortunately, her mother left her a sizable trust fund; otherwise, she'd be studying here in the states somewhere."

Smiling, I urged him to continue.

"I didn't marry until I'd already been in practice for a few years. Margaret was also an attorney, a few years older than I, but we fell in love. She'd been married previously and Colleen was about ten when I met her. We'd only been married for about a year when Margaret was diagnosed with MS. Some patients are lucky and can live a full life with occasional setbacks, but for some reason, Margaret's condition deteriorated quickly. I don't know for sure, but I suspect she had an underlying condition of some sort. We were married for five years before she died. It's been seven years now..." Clay looked down.

"And no one since...?"

"I'm not a monk, if that's what you mean." He grinned. "I've dated some, but nothing serious. How about you?"

"Not me either. There's something very true about old maid school teachers. You meet so few men, let alone eligible men. Then when you're my age..." I looked at him. "I'll be forty-eight in March."

"In March? When?"

"On the fifteenth—beware the Ides of March."

"That's unreal. My birthday's the fourteenth. I'll be fifty-one. Let's celebrate together. Shall we?"

"Let's! It's a date," I said. "Are you about ready for lunch?"

"Sure. Let's do it." He started to stand and I held up my hand.

"Why don't you sit still? If you don't mind me taking over the kitchen, I'll set out Lisa's lunch on your table."

"Be my guest," he said.

~ * ~

We'd finished eating clam chowder we both agreed was the best we'd ever had. Lisa had also fixed an assortment of sandwiches cut in fourths with pickles and olives. There was also a coleslaw salad made with broccoli and other veggies. She included baked items she had left over from her breakfast board: scones, muffins, plus a small coconut cake. I had included a bottle of pinot noir wine, Oregon's best seller.

"My God. Your landlady must have thought she was feeding a crowd. Can you believe this spread?"

"She has gone out of her way to impress," I said. "I must confess, though. I told her you were laid up and I'm sure she wanted you to have leftovers."

"As soon as I'm able to drive, I'll come out your way and thank her personally."

"She'll love that, I'm sure."

Clay's phone rang, and he took the call in his bedroom while I cleaned up the kitchen. After I put the leftovers in the refrigerator and repacked Lisa's basket with her dishes, I was sitting at the table finishing my wine when Clay came back. He sat in his walker and scooted his legs under the table.

"Sorry, that was my secretary—just checking up on me."

"Jenna Brooks. Isn't that her name?"

"Yes, it is. How did you know?"

"She located my address for Sudie."

"That's right. I had forgotten." He smiled. "She has been with me since I first joined the firm. My right arm." I was curious about just how close their relationship was, when Clay said, "She's married with five children and two grandchildren. She makes me feel like I'm one of her kids, too. I'll hate it when she retires."

"Would you like more wine?"

"Love some, but better not. May need a pain pill later." He picked up the book I'd brought with me.

I pulled out the copy of the Avisa poem I had placed inside the cover.

"We don't know for sure Elizabeth wrote this poem, but it tells of where she lived as a child. It's in a small village of Rocester in Staffordshire. That's in England's midlands. Shall I read it to you?"

"Please."

After I finished reading, I gave him a history of Rocester Hall's having been a Catholic abbey, and how the Trenthams came into possession of the land. "Originally, it was a Roman fort because of its logistical advantage of being between two rivers. We think there is a real possibility this poem was written by Elizabeth as sort of an autobiographical piece."

I picked up the book. "Now let me show you this poem which I think was definitely written by her." I opened the book to the page and pointed.

Clay began to read:

When I was fair and young then favor graced me.
Of many was I sought their mistress for to be.
But I did scorn them all and answered them therefore:
Go, go, go, seek some other where, importune me no more.
How many weeping eyes I made to pine in woe,
How many sighing hearts I have not skill to show,
But I the prouder grew, and still this spake therefore:
Go, go, go, seek some other where, importune me no more.
Then spake fair Venus' son, that proud victorious boy,
Saying: You dainty dame, for that you be so coy,
I will so pluck your plumes as you shall say no more:
Go, go, go, seek some other where, importune me no more.
As soon as he had said, such change grew in my breast
That neither night nor day I could take any rest.
Wherefore I did repent that I had said before:
Go, go, go, seek some other where, importune me no more.
Finis ELY.

"What does 'importune' mean?"

"Urge. See, it's signed Ely. It has the same Ely signature as on the *Midsummer* page. It's a derivative of Elizabeth. My friend Josie thinks it's the breakthrough we've been looking for."

"Hmm, I don't know."

"Let me explain. This historian must have felt the queen wrote it to Edward de Vere, which is why it's included in her biography. Ely could be a nickname for Queen Elizabeth, but it makes more sense that the poem was written by his second wife, Elizabeth Trentham, not the queen. Besides, I could find no reference whatsoever indicating the queen ever used Ely as a nickname or in her signature. Since everyone else is making assumptions, I think we can safely assume Elizabeth Trentham was Ely—the same Ely written at the bottom of Sudie's page."

I continued with my argument. "Also, I read in a biography of Edward de Vere that Elizabeth Trentham, his second wife, was quite pretty but refused many offers of marriage throughout her life. She seemed to prefer to be one of the queen's maids. Elizabeth Trentham stayed with the queen for ten years before marrying de Vere. This poem fits directly into her refusals of marriage." I pointed to "1: of Oxford" written at the end of the poem. "That alone proves it was written to Lord Oxford, the fair Venus' son."

Clay listened intently to my theory, but still displayed that bland lawyer expression. "What do you think? Would something like this hang together in court to prove Elizabeth Trentham was Shakespeare?"

"You make a strong argument. You're probably correct in assuming it's a love poem written to Lord Oxford. It makes perfect sense his second wife would have been his lover." Without warning, he put his arm around me. "Great job finding it." He handed the book back to me.

"Do you think this could be considered convincing evidence?"

"In court, I would offer it as an exhibit, but it probably wouldn't stand on its own without corroborating evidence." He removed his arm from around me. "I suppose there are those who'd want to discount it, saying the two Ely signatures were just a coincidence. But you should definitely include it when you write your report."

"That's what I thought, too. Also, this poem proves she wrote poetry. I'm not an expert, but I think it could be comparable to the sonnets. But it's a rhyming poem, not iambic pentameter like most of Shakespeare's writing. I don't know if that matters much." Saying that brought Sudie back into my thoughts.

"Sudie was reading the sonnets the day before her heart attack. She was looking for hidden clues. I wish I could share my progress with her. She would have been so excited to see both of the poems."

"Please consider me a substitute for my aunt," Clay said. "Sudie was very fond of you. I can now understand why."

Twenty-seven

Fridays were special, but Clay called me other days, too. Our conversations became longer and were not always about my research. When he was able to drive, we made a date for him to come to White Dove Inn. First, we met with Lisa and Karen, and then had lunch at his favorite winery. Next, I had him look at a condo I was interested in. When he drove me back to the inn, we continued to sit in his car for several minutes just talking. I had already unhooked my seatbelt.

"I know it's none of my business," he said, "but since I am an attorney, it's difficult not to give you my opinion about your buying a condo."

"As long as you don't charge me." I laughed, but he seemed serious.

"You've been open with me concerning your financial assets, needing to use all of the money from the sale of your mother's house as a down payment. Forgive me, but I think you're spreading yourself a bit thin."

"I know why you'd say that, but I have a budget. Most of what Sudie left me is still in the bank—plenty enough for that trip to England. My substitute teaching brings in enough for me to pay my bills. But you're right. I do need to find a permanent teaching position. Not just for the salary, but at my age, I should have good health insurance."

"Don't forget, your car isn't exactly reliable."

"Yes. That's true. I've had my Volvo for nearly ten years, and it was used when I bought it."

"What I'm getting at—Cindy. Do you mind me calling you Cindy?"

"Only my mother called me that...but you can if you want to."

"No, Cynthia it is." He cleared his throat, unhooked his seat belt and put his arm around me. "Would you consider moving in with me?"

I couldn't have been more surprised. I just sat there and stared at him with my mouth wide open.

"We have a lot in common—in fact, we're very good for each other. I think of you at the strangest times, when I'm dictating and even in court." I was still staring at him, not knowing what to say. "I find myself worrying about you, too." He leaned forward and I knew he intended to kiss me.

"Wait a minute, Clay." I swallowed and shifted from him. "I know this sounds cliché, but we hardly know each other. At our age, and living alone, we've become set in our ways and having us together, living together, may be difficult. I do value my independence."

"You'd still be independent. I'd make no demands on you—well, I take that back. I don't mean our relationship would be platonic. I wouldn't be able to keep my hands off you, but you could still be independent."

"I like you very much; in fact, the way I feel goes beyond liking, but can we give it more time? Continue to see each other? I do look forward to your phone calls."

With that, he pulled me to him and kissed me. Wow. It had been a very long time since I'd been kissed like that. It didn't stop with one kiss either. Breathlessly, I finally broke away. I think I said I wanted to think about it, but I'm not sure exactly what I did say. After opening the car door, I stumbled up the stairs into the inn.

~ * ~

In February, I moved into my one-bedroom condo in the west hills of Portland. I had mixed emotions when I left my comfortable lodgings provided by Lisa Nyberg, but felt reassured in knowing I had made good friends with her and her daughter. To say I hadn't given any thought to moving in with Clay would be ridiculous. I thought of little else. On the other hand, I was excited to finally have a place of my own, but the days I spent with Clay were heady business.

I made the decision to buy the condo, notwithstanding Clay's offer. I'm old fashioned enough to want marriage with a live-in arrangement and told him words to that effect—quickly to include I wasn't hinting at wanting to be married. Just the opposite. I wanted a place of my own, something I'd never had. I had moved directly from my parents' home into a marriage and a tiny apartment. Then following our divorce, back to my mom with my little boy. I stayed there until I had a full-time teaching position. We left my mother's home and moved into an apartment in Portland. When Mark left for the Air Force Academy, I rented a room from Josie for a year, and then moved back home to take care of my mother. Finally, after thirty years, I owned my own place.

My condo was set in a woodsy area in the west hills of Portland, an easy commute to both downtown and into the suburb of Beaverton. By early March, I was finally settled in. Fortunately, my bedroom was large enough to double as an office. I kept my mother's furnishings with the hope I'd inherited some of her good taste in interior design. Before she became so sick, we had visited an art gallery on the coast and we both fell in love with an original painting of water lilies, which neither of us could afford. "It reminds me of a Monet," she had said.

"I agree. Let's get it." We'd shared the expense. Since I had become her caregiver within the year, we both enjoyed it until her death. Now it was mine. The painting on the wall above the fireplace gave me pleasure, thinking of my mom.

By the following Friday, Josie called to tell me she had found something that would interest me. I wasn't sure if she'd managed to do any research, considering her busy work schedule, plus putting up with Frank. It was Friday and I invited her to come see my new place. Clay was due to come, but so much the better. I'd been wanting them to meet.

When I let her in, she had on a big smile. "It's been a while," I said as we hugged.

"Too long." She shrugged out of her coat. "I'm anxious to show you what I've found." She pulled a large Bible from her book bag.

"Great. You'll stay and have dinner with me, I hope. I bought salmon at a seafood market. There's plenty."

"Thanks. It's Frank's poker night. I have the evening to myself."

"How are things with you and Frank?" I turned on the gas fireplace and we sat together on the sofa. She placed the Bible on the coffee table.

"We were good—for a while. His parents must have given him money when he saw them over Thanksgiving. It must have been enough to help with his debts—but now we're back where we were. I just wish he'd stop gambling."

"That's got to be rough on you. Is he still insisting you sell the house?"

"His pressure has been intense. As a compromise, I took out a letter of credit. He said he'd make the payments." I had my doubts about that, but kept my mouth shut.

When the doorbell rang, I let Clay in and he gave me a quick kiss. I took his hand and whispered we had company.

"Josie, this is Clay. I've been wanting you two to meet." Josie tried to stand, but Clay held up his hand.

"No need to stand. I'm very happy to meet you." He held her hand in both of his. "Aren't you Cynthia's librarian friend who's helping with my Aunt Sudie's project?"

"Yes. I am. She's mentioned you, too," Josie said, looking at me. She seemed shy all of a sudden and then I remembered I'd been intimidated by him too at first. The overhead lighting caused the silver in his hair to shine, but it was his eyes—a piercing blue. I was sure it was this quality that gave him the reputation of being a hard-nosed attorney. I'd heard not many witnesses could withstand his cross-examination scrutiny.

"Speaking of Sudie's project, Josie was just about to show me something she's discovered. But first, something to drink?" I started toward the kitchen. "I have scotch or wine."

"Scotch and soda, if you have it." Knowing Clay drank Scotch, I made sure I had it on hand.

"How about you, Josie. A glass of wine?"

"No thanks, just a soda and lime for me," she said.

I poured myself a glass of white wine and Josie's drink from the refrigerator. By then, Clay had sat beside Josie. After handing out the drinks, I sat on her other side.

"Now you can show us together. Something to do with this Bible?"

"Yes. What I want you both to see," she glanced at Clay, "can only be found in the King James Version of the Bible. Are you familiar with the history?"

"Yes," I said. "King James came to the throne after Queen Elizabeth. The translation also occurred during Shakespeare's time."

"The king wanted the new translation made available to everyone, not to just the priests. It came about because of pressure from the Puritans, if I'm not mistaken," Clay said. We both looked at him with surprise. "Don't looked so shocked, you two. Besides law, I was a history major." I patted him on the arm.

"That's right," Josie said. "King James brought together fifty-some transcribers in 1604. Finally published in 1611." She paused and took a drink from her soda. "Today, one of the students turned in a small book about little-known facts in history. I was flipping through it and saw a reference made to a verse in Psalms that relates to Shakespeare. Here, let me show you." She opened the

Bible to Psalm forty-six and showed us. "Count the words from the beginning until you reach forty-six."

I did as she instructed. "Shake." I showed it to Clay.

"Now count forty-six words from the end."

"Spear. For heaven's sake." I looked up at her. "Forty-sixth chapter and forty-six words. That's no coincidence."

"It sure isn't. What do you suppose it means?" she asked.

"I don't know. What do you think, Clay?"

"A tribute to Shakespeare, that's for sure. Maybe he was forty-six when this verse was translated."

"Or she," I said.

"Touché."

"That's what I thought," Josie said. "I figured out Will Shakespeare would have been forty-six in 1610. Whereas Elizabeth Trentham was four or five years older than he. If forty-six is based on age, Elizabeth seems the most likely candidate."

"Perhaps," I said. "It's a puzzle, that's for sure." I looked down at the Bible verse again. "It would be helpful if we knew the name of the men who actually translated the Bible. If we could find a correlation between one of the translators and Elizabeth—or Edward de Vere—that could be very revealing." I looked at her. "Do you know who they were?"

"Not yet. I only discovered this today."

"Let's look now. Wait a second." I went into the bedroom and brought out my laptop. I powered it up and when I had a list of the transcribers before me, the name John Overall stood out. "I can't believe it."

"What?" she said.

"John Overall." I looked at her.

"So—besides being a translator, who was John Overall?" Clay asked.

I thought about the woman's voice that had come to me right after Sudie died. I was ready to give up the project when she said look to the Psalms, overall. She was referring to a name—not all of the Psalms. Should I tell them about my ghostly experiences? No, I didn't think so...

"I'm not sure," I said. "Maybe it's a name I ran across during my research. I'll have to look through my notes." I turned off the computer. "Let's see about grilling that salmon. Would you two prefer rice or potatoes?"

Twenty-eight

Our battle is more full of names than yours,
Our men more perfect in the use of arms,
Our armor all as strong, our cause the best;
Then reason will our hearts should be as good.
                    —*King Henry IV*, Part 2, Act 4, Scene 1

1587

During the next six years, Ely's life was full. She was the tutor to five titled girls of the court, while continuing to pursue her passion for writing poetry. She accompanied the queen to her various palaces and was in high demand for evening entertainment.

One area of great fun for Ely was working with the court jesters, especially William Kempe, a merry juxtapose for Ely's more stoic behavior. It was not that she didn't have a sense of humor; her reticence was due to her queen's stern expectation that her ladies be simply decorous when men were present. Will, in contrast, seemed totally uninhibited, making light of any serious nature; he even used Lord Burghley as a target for his humor. Even though the man took umbrage to Will's banter, the queen laughed uproariously at his quick wit, which gave him permission to continue with the mockery.

Court jesters also appeared in plays, with Richard Tarleton being one of the most popular with the queen and her subjects. It was not well known by anyone that Tarleton was a favorite of Edward Vere, who used him as a front for his own plays. Ely learned of his deception from Edward himself. When she questioned him as to why he did not want his own name on the plays, he told her in no uncertain terms that it would have been unseemly for a titled man to lower himself to the occupation of a playwright. The only reason he wrote plays was his dissatisfaction with the quality of some of the plays available for his own troupe of players.

Having access to the various palace archives, Ely became an authority on British and European history, developing her own lesson plans for her students. At the time, Spain was the foremost power under the leadership of King Philip II. Ely, due to her curious nature, wanted to know the relationship between him and her queen. She knew Philip had been married to Queen Elizabeth's elder half-sister Mary Tudor, both being staunch Catholics. They had overruled King Henry VIII's edict of Protestantism for the British. It was during Queen Mary's five-year reign that over three hundred people were executed—often being burned at the stake for heresy. This zeal for religious persecution resulted in her being called "Bloody Mary."

After her death, Philip, among others, tried to promote Mary Stuart, Queen of Scots, to the throne, believing Elizabeth unfit to rule due to her "illegitimate" birth as well as her Protestant beliefs. Ely's father and John Stanhope, Kate's husband, among others, were involved in the imprisonment of the Scottish queen in various castles and manors in the north to keep her from claiming the throne of England. Ely was unaware of the activities of her father in this regard. It was only after she was firmly installed in the court that Queen Elizabeth herself revealed the secret of Ely's family's involvement, and only after Mary Stuart was executed.

During the years Ely served the queen, she was often allowed access to her bedchambers. It was one winter evening when Ely was assisting with the queen's preparations for bed that she learned of the deep worry that beset her.

"I am positive a sea war is imminent with Spain, and their vessels are superior to ours." The queen was seated on the edge of the bed while Ely assisted in removing her leggings and putting her feet into wooly slippers.

"I have heard of their great armada," Ely responded.

"I have more ships under construction, but we lack the manpower and supplies necessary to have them ready by spring." The queen swung her legs under the counterpane and Ely propped pillows behind her back, as it was apparent she wanted to continue their conversation. "Preparing for war is expensive, and Cecil, Lord Burghley, has had to increase taxes. I am fearful this has caused a hardship for my people. There may soon be repercussions from those who do not support my action against Spain." Ely was deep in thought as she folded the queen's undergarments and hung her heavy dress. She picked up a fire iron to stir the embers in the massive fireplace, when the queen spoke.

"You are unduly quiet, my dear."

"I am pondering something that may gain the support of your people," Ely said.

The queen shifted in bed. "What are you thinking?"

"*Propogare.*" Ely used the Latin pronunciation.

"Propaganda? How so?"

"The plays, Your Grace." The queen's quizzical expression prompted Ely to continue. "Since the opening of the Theater, the crowds trying to see performances are astonishing. They stand before the stage for hours, even in the rain, to witness the plays."

"I have heard this is so. Lord Chamberlain's players are said to be very popular. I must make it a point to visit the Theater."

"I would not recommend it, Your Majesty; 'tis a place of great crowds, dirt, and noise."

"What do you know of this?"

Ely shifted from one foot to the other, not willing to tell the queen of her visits to playhouses—indeed, that she had on more than one occasion sneaked from the palace dressed as a street urchin along with one of the burly guards whom she paid to follow close behind. "I know only what I have been told, Your Majesty," she said, stirring the embers and putting on another log.

"What do you have in mind to influence my people?"

Ely brushed dust from her hands and turned around. "I have read of the lives of the kings before your reign, Your Majesty." Ely seated herself on a stool close to the queen. "Even after two hundred years, King Henry the Fifth is especially well loved due to his victories in France. If a play could be written of him, perhaps that would influence the attitude of the people—to show a pride in their country."

"Yes, I hear what you are saying. Perhaps you are correct. The way King Hal's army captured so many French cities is inspiring." The queen shifted in bed and reached under her nightcap to scratch her head. "Perhaps the story of Henry the Sixth would be more... interesting."

"But it was under his reign the French recaptured those towns. Why do you think that story would be more effective?"

"It does depend upon how well the story is portrayed on the stage. It does not have to be totally authentic. A good playwright could make it exciting...and I like the fact that two strong women influenced the outcome."

"Oh, I see. A comparison to Jeanne d'Arc's exploits could be made of your strong leadership. It would show that a woman is as capable as a man—maybe more so."

"Exactly." She paused deep in thought. "The problem is Jeanne was French. Should such a play be written, her heroic achievements should be underscored. She was strong—that cannot be denied."

"In contrast, the role Queen Margaret played could be emphasized. As Henry's wife, she was the real power." Ely paused. "There should be more roles that depict strong women—and they should be played by women," Ely commented.

"Please, one battle at a time." Queen Elizabeth laughed. "Your queen is a woman. That will have to suffice."

The more the two women discussed the history of the kings, the more animated they became, to the point where the queen got out of bed to warm herself by the fireplace. She picked up a fire iron to push a log closer to the flame. "My biggest fear is that events may take place next year before the play could be written and performed. Should we enter war with Spain, methinks it will be of a long duration. Many plays could be performed during that time showing the history of our great island country and thus create national support. Even more taxes will need to be raised for our military."

Ely admired how the queen was considering the long-term consequences, not just the immediate crisis.

"I could discuss this first play with Lord Oxford. His players are currently at the Curtain playhouse." She bit her tongue, afraid the queen would begin to question her on her knowledge of the theater world.

"We need to find someone to write the play of Henry the Sixth," the queen said. "What was the name of that man who wrote *Dido, Queen of Carthage*? Didn't we rescue him from the university in France when he was suspected of being a spy?"

"Yes, Christopher Marlowe. I remember fondly when the play was performed at Windsor."

"I too enjoyed it," the queen said. "I remember you recited the Ovid poem for me when we first met." The queen stifled a yawn behind her hand. "It grows late." She let Ely help her get back into bed. "First thing in the morning, I want you to send someone to fetch Christopher Marlowe."

"Yes, Your Majesty. May I also ask Edward—I mean, Lord Oxford—to be in audience when you discuss the play?"

"Of course." The queen smiled and patted Ely's hand. "And before you ask, you may also attend, since *propagare* was your idea—you may be needed."

~ * ~

Many events had taken place during the following week, including news from Ely's mother that her father had taken ill and had sent a messenger to summon her to Rocester. Her departure was delayed because of stormy weather, but she hoped to be home to celebrate Christmas with her family. While she waited for conditions to improve, Ely sent word to Edward. She needed to meet with him.

Their meeting took place in a room adjacent to his apartment in Windsor Palace. They sat before a fireplace as sleet peppered the mullioned windows. After she explained the queen's rationale for wanting a production of a historical play regarding the life of King Henry VI, Edward smiled.

"Methinks you have had a hand in the plan. Is that correct, mistress?"

"The queen made the selection, but I did suggest a play could have a positive role in gaining patriotic support," Ely said. Edward stood from his chair and began to pace. "She asked for Christopher Marlowe to be summoned."

"Marlowe! That rum pot! Better you than him!"

She knew Edward said this in jest, but she privately agreed with the notion. She was up to the challenge and itched to write the play. An outline as to how the play should be written was already on paper.

"Edward, I am surprised. Isn't Marlowe recognized as one of England's foremost playwrights?"

"Yes, 'tis true—when you can get him to settle down long enough to actually produce something my players can perform. With the hostile political scene now developing, I assume this play should be written post-haste." Edward stood with his back to the roaring fire.

"True. Do you have the inclination to put pen to paper? I mean, perhaps I could assist."

"The thought did cross my mind, but I have other obligations the queen has given me—and time is a factor." Ely watched as he continued to pace across the room, his cane clicking in cadence to his thoughts. "I could never admit to authorship. It is bad enough I have my own troupe, but to claim to have written...however, I have used others to take credit for my work."

"Milord, perhaps I have a solution." Edward stopped pacing to look at her. "My father is very ill, and I will be leaving for Staffordshire as soon as this weather lets up. I expect to be gone for several weeks with nothing but time on my hands." Edward sat and waved his hand for her to continue. "I believe I mentioned in our previous conversations I've enjoyed reading of the past exploits of our former rulers...both in England and other countries."

"Are you suggesting you write the stage play?" He laughed out loud. "My God, woman! 'Twould be bad enough for me to take credit, but a woman...'tis ridiculous. No one would believe it, let alone accept the notion."

"You mentioned you have used others to front for you."

"True." Edward stifled a laugh. "There is a new actor recently on the scene from Stratford-upon-Avon. I hired him to hold horses during the plays and have allowed him to have small parts." He shifted his gaze to Ely. "But how important is it that someone be named at all?" Edward grunted. "Whether it is anonymous or not is the least of our problems. It's more important we get the damn thing written and worry about authorship later." Edward moved his chair closer to hers and propped his bad foot upon a stool.

"This is what we will do. You pen your ideas for a play while you are away, and I will try to do the same whilst in the Netherlands. When we return, we can put our brains together to construct the thing."

Ely was willing to have him make the arrangements. She was overjoyed she could fulfill a dream she had had since she was a child. To prepare a play that could be seen by the general public and to receive credit was not as important. To assist the queen was far more essential. Edward was not to know she had no intention of only writing ideas. She would write the whole damn play. She would need to give Joan of Arc, and especially Queen Margaret, more emphasis to show the comparison between the strong female leaders and her own beloved queen—something she was sure no male writer would consider.

"If we are diligent, perhaps we will have the first performance ready by early summer," Ely said. "That would please the queen."

"You are an ambitious thinker, Ely. By the by, would you visit Anne before you leave? She is in poor health since the birth of our last child, and this foul weather has influenced her melancholy."

Ely had planned to do this even without his suggestion. She and Anne had become friends since Edward's injury. She knew the primary reason for Anne's poor health was three births in the past five years, especially since her baby boy died shortly after birth. Anne's sorrow at losing the baby had caused much sadness for the young woman. Then to have her give birth to another female child less than a year later...Ely was gravely concerned for her.

Twenty-nine

Thou know'st 'tis common. All that lives must die,
Passing through nature to eternity.
— *Hamlet*, Act 1, Scene 2

1588

"What do you know of your birth?" Thomas Trentham surprised Ely with this question; she was unsure how she should respond. He lay in his sick bed, surround by pillows and a heavy counterpane. His wife, Jane, sat on the opposite side of his bed.

Jane responded. "Remember, I told you of Aunt Dorothy's and my conversation..."

"Yes, yes, I know." He shifted in bed. "I want to know what the queen told her. Does she know the truth yet?"

"The truth? What do you mean?" Ely took hold of her father's hand. It felt warm and smooth, not like the calloused hand she remembered from her visit just a year ago. She hated to see him so ill, but was relieved he did not seem to be in pain. She suspected Thomas' liver was failing; his eyes and skin had a yellowish tinge. She also knew there was nothing they could do to prolong his life.

"Perhaps the queen herself does not know," Jane said. "After all, she was so young when..."

"Poppycock," Thomas said. "Of course she knows."

"Wait. What are you both saying? I know King Henry the Eighth was my grandfather...and that he had, er, an affair with Aunt Dorothy when she was lady-in-waiting to Catherine Parr. Dorothy gave birth to my mother, Ann, and was sent to live with her brother in Chester."

"That is only partially true. King Henry is truly your grandfather, but he had been dead two years before your mother was born."

"Thomas, no! If the queen and Dorothy did not see fit to tell Elizabeth, then do we dare?"

"What are you both saying?"

"She needs to know, Jane. The queen is getting old and must name her successor. Her own granddaughter should be next in line, legitimate or no."

Ely dropped Thomas' hand and jumped up from her chair, nearly knocking it over in her haste. "What are you both telling me?"

"Elizabeth, please sit. I am surprised you have not already reasoned it out. You must have noticed the strong resemblance between the queen and yourself. The same color of hair and eyes. You both having high intellect and..."

"Yes, yes, as my kinswoman..." Ely sat back down and looked at Jane. "My mother was not Dorothy's daughter?"

"Ann was as much her daughter as you are my daughter." Ely could not sit still. She stood, walked around the room and looked out the window. Turning around, she moved to sit on the edge of the bed near Jane.

"Is the queen truly my grandmother?"

"Yes, Ann was the queen's daughter." Jane's hand came to rest on Ely's knee. "No one, and I mean no one, must ever know the truth of Ann's birth. If the truth ever came to light, it could destroy the queen. Even Ann, her own daughter, did not know the truth of her birth. Dorothy was willing to accept the blame to protect the young princess. She sacrificed her own reputation and future to protect her. Even on her deathbed last year, Dorothy felt it best that you did not know."

"She was wrong," Thomas said, looking at Ely. "There is succession to think of, and you must be in consideration for the crown when she dies. And when you marry and have a son, he would succeed you."

"Never!" Ely jumped from the edge of the bed. "I realized years ago I could be in line as King Henry's granddaughter, but never this. I have observed the toll the queen has had to pay, and understand full well why she never married, even though she shared her remorse of never having a family of her own." Ely sat back down on the bed. "As far as my having a son, I doubt I will ever marry, let alone have a child. My desire is to remain with the queen. Knowing now of our even closer relationship, I will remain at her side."

"You are being foolish," Thomas protested. "Your duty is to—"

"No, Father. My duty is to my queen...and to myself. As long as no one knows the truth, then so be it."

"What is your plan? Are you going to mention anything to the queen?" Jane asked.

"How can I? I still don't know the whole story. Who was the father of Ann?"

"It was Thomas Seymour, the bounder," Thomas replied. "After the king died, Catherine Parr married Seymour, and Princess Elizabeth came under her care."

"She was barely thirteen at the time," Jane said. "Rumor was strong that Seymour was behaving in an inappropriate manner toward Elizabeth. Catherine learned of this and sent Elizabeth away to Hatfield for her own protection. Catherine also sent Aunt Dorothy to be with her. They both retreated to a midwife's farmhouse on the estate for the last three months of the princess' pregnancy. According to Dorothy, the princess had a difficult delivery, her being so young and all. The midwife told Dorothy there was extensive injury while giving birth and it was doubtful Elizabeth would ever have another child. It was a miracle she did not bleed to death. She named the baby girl after her own mother, Anne Boleyn."

"But how could anyone be assured the midwife would not reveal Princess Elizabeth's identity?"

"According to Dorothy, the midwife did not know. She thought the princess was a servant girl from the estate."

"How did Elizabeth feel about it? I mean, not being able to keep the baby?"

"She respected her lineage and that of Queen Catherine's reputation. The scandal of the pregnancy, notwithstanding, how Seymour had...well. She could not possibly keep the baby. That is the reason Dorothy accepted baby Ann as her own, promising Elizabeth to keep her informed of the child's development. Seymour got his just deserts when he was beheaded."

"Princess Elizabeth became godmother to both Ann and you, knowing she could not have a closer relationship than that," Thomas said.

"Until you became part of her court," Jane said.

"'Twas a good thing I escaped from your arranged marriage notion to that loathsome duke; otherwise..." Ely stopped short, feeling immediately sorry she had mentioned it, as Thomas' eyes clouded over.

"I should have shot the cad when he tried running off with Dorothy. Thank God she is now married to William Cooper."

"Do not let us remember that dreadful duke," Jane said as she patted her husband's shoulder. "'Tis in the past and he is dead... earning his due from the plague."

Ely was happy her sister had fallen in love with a good man—even if he was a commoner. She could only imagine the heartache the queen must have suffered delivering a baby at such a young age and never being allowed to know her. Ely realized how fortunate she was to have been raised by Jane and Thomas, receiving as much love as their natural children. For most of her life she had thought them her true parents, and her siblings her own brothers and sisters. That mattered little now. She would always love them, even though their blood relationship was different.

"Do Kate, Francis, and the others know the truth of my birth?"

Jane and Thomas looked at each other; a question was in her father's eyes. Jane allowed Thomas to take the lead.

"No, they do not. Francis will soon be head of the family, and he should be told." He looked toward Jane. "Dorothy only told Jane because she realized she was dying. The only other person who knew was William Sneyd, and he is dead, too. There is no one else that knows—except the queen herself. It should be your decision whether your sisters and Tommy are told."

Ely walked to the window to consider the ramifications of allowing others to know. "No, it would be best if it goes no further. Not just for my sake, as I do not desire to be in consideration for any succession, but for the queen's as well. She must be protected. Should this information leak out, the scandal would be disastrous. War with Spain may be inevitable, and the queen must continue as our ruler to avoid chaos." Ely continued to think about what she knew. However, for her own well-being, it would be good to have someone to confide in. She looked back at her mother. No, Jane's first obligation was to her husband during these last difficult days. She thought of Edward, and immediately put the thought out of her head. He was too close to all of the queen's courtiers. If she did have a confidante, it should be someone far removed from the queen. Perhaps Kate. They had always been close. She planned to visit Kate on the morrow and would make her decision then.

She extended her stay in Rocester until March, when her father died in his sleep. She learned from Francis that their father had designated her as the executrix of his substantial estate.

"With your legal background, Father felt you were the better choice to execute his will." Ely and Francis' conversation began in the barn as they saddled horses to take advantage of warmer weather with a morning ride. "I would do it, but with Father gone, plus my own responsibilities…"

"Yes, I know how busy you've been. Have you had a chance to interview men from Oxford to assist you?" They both mounted their horses.

Their uncle, Ralph Sneyd, having no children, had designated Francis as his heir. Francis had worked under Ralph's tutelage since finishing his Oxford education and had become an expert in financial dealings. Since their father had become ill, he also handled most of Rocester's land management business. With the responsibilities of both estates, he had many tenant farmers sharing their crops with him, as well as administrative duties in Derbyshire.

"I've had some success finding two young men to work with me. I expect to be extremely busy getting them trained. You cannot believe how much still needs to be done." They spurred their horses to a gallop. It felt good to Ely to have the wind in her hair and to see the countryside of rolling hills, green grass, and trees. As they rode through a circle of trees, Ely looked around for the fairies and then laughed at herself. An hour later they dismounted, handing the reins of their horses to a stable boy.

"I hope you are able to extend your stay a bit longer to work on how best to handle Father's estate—and yours too, for that matter," Francis said, taking her arm as they bypassed a mud hole on their way back to the manor house. "Are you aware of the fortune you are to receive?"

"Yes. I reviewed his will last evening."

Francis opened the door to the kitchen, where they entered to the smell of a roasting ham in the massive fireplace. The cook was preparing vegetables in a basin near the door. "Marie, please fill plates of ham, eggs, and bread. We're starved."

They entered the dining room and sat, waiting for their meal to be served. "He has left me a thousand pounds a year, with a percentage of dividends received from his renters," Ely said. "I know Tommy is well provided for, but what of Kate and Dorothy? They are not mentioned."

"Dorothy has a husband and he will look after her, and the same with Kate. She and her children have been provided for by Sir John. He has been equally successful in business."

"Amazing," she murmured, then sipped the tankard of ale before her.

His voice dropped to a whisper. "I am happy you were not overlooked, considering..."

"Considering I am not of his blood?" She grabbed Francis' arm. "Please do not share this knowledge with anyone. Not just for me; our queen and our entire country could be affected." Ely looked toward the kitchen door to be assured no one could hear them.

"I won't. Nor will I tell a soul. Are you sure you have no desire to...?"

"Absolutely sure. I'd rather die." Their conversation was cut short when the cook entered with two plates loaded with food. "I hope you will give me wise counsel on how best to handle my inheritance, plus the money Aunt Dorothy left me."

Ely was relieved she hadn't confided in Kate regarding her mother's birth. She now had her brother as a confidante, and that was enough. Perhaps she would tell Kate later, after the queen selected her successor and the knowledge of her birth no longer mattered.

"I will." Francis took a large bite of meat. "Providing you use your influence with the queen considering matters in the North Country."

"We will have to see about that." She laughed.

"What is all the scribbling you've been doing of late? And the heavy books of England's kings you brought with you?"

Ely realized there could be no secrets between her and her brother. Gone were the squabbles they had as children, and in their place was a common respect for each other.

"That concerns another confidence I must ask you to keep," she said. She then told him of her conversation with the queen and of her own future desire to write plays for the stage in London.

"I am aware of your talent, Ely, but how on earth did you convince the queen?"

Ely gave him a sidelong glance. "To be honest, she did mention a man who has an association with the stage, but I suggested I could assist because of my knowledge of England's history. She has agreed to my involvement."

"Knowing you, I am sure your role will be more than mere assisting."

"You know me too well. Howsoever, to write a play for the London stage will fulfill a lifelong dream of mine. I am aware I cannot possibly take credit for my work. Not only would no one believe a woman capable, but should I be found out, it would cause a scandal at court. I will have to be mindful. Lord Oxford, his daughters, and his wife have become good friends. He has a troop of players and mentioned he used someone else's name for his playwriting. I believe I could do the same."

"Yes. I understand the risk, but what of marriage? I know you have resisted suitors in the past. Do you not desire to have a family of your own?"

"I am happy as a spinster. I have no desire to be subservient to a husband. You should know better than anyone my desire for independence. I will not place my hands below my husband's foot."

"Even if it brings your husband ease?" Francis said.

"Pooh! He has servants for that duty."

~ * ~

Spring arrived before Ely was able to return to London. War with Spain had never been declared, but there had been recent conflicts in the Netherlands as well as Drake's raid on Cádiz last year. The queen's spies had told her the King of Spain had made plans to retaliate.

This was the queen's largest challenge. Many of her courtiers and advisers offered to take the lead in England's defense. The queen was not about to relinquish power to any of the men, knowing full well that if she were to do so, she could ultimately lose the throne in the bargain. This was not the only worry that plagued her. If Spain were successful in defeating her navy, it could well mean Philip would take rule over England and put Elizabeth's head on the block. Nevertheless, even with all of this weighing on her shoulders, she seemed pleased to receive word of Ely's return.

When the guards opened the doors into the queen's bedchamber, Ely was apprehensive to again see the woman whom she now knew to be her grandmother. She was undecided whether to mention that she knew the truth of their close kinship. Upon observing the queen, Ely saw she had changed much since their last meeting six months earlier. She had lost weight, and the purple circles under her eyes could not be hidden even with the white makeup. Ely knew this was not the time to discuss personal relationships.

"It is good to see you again. How are affairs in the North Country? Is your mother well?" The queen stood from her chair and motioned for Ely to stand from her curtsy.

"As well as can be expected," Ely replied. "She has my brother and sister close by. Thank you for asking."

"You may assist as I prepare for bed." Ely untied the many ribbons at the queen's back, and setting her ruff aside, she let the heavy dress fall to the floor. She picked it up, laid it across a chair and went about removing her undergarments. "I am most concerned with happenings here, Your Majesty. How may I be of service?"

"I have more advice than I care for, but it is good to see you again. I've missed our conversations."

"Would it help if you told me of your worries? You know I am a sympathetic listener, and you have my true loyalty never to reveal anything you choose to tell me."

The queen gazed at her with such tenderness that for the first time Ely realized this woman—her grandmother—truly loved her. The feeling was mutual. Gone were the trappings of leadership that so revealed the outward strength of the woman, the conduct she wore with pride and determination. Perhaps only with Ely was she able to reveal any vulnerability.

The queen remained quiet while Ely helped her into her nightdress. She appeared to be deep in thought as Ely removed the wig from her head. She then gently brushed her sparse hair, now nearly white.

"I am sorry we were unable to produce a play before hostilities began. I was unable to meet with Marlowe before I left, and then with Edward in the Netherlands..."

"I had quite forgotten about the play, but don't give up on the plan. Even if we are successful in defeating Spain's Armada, the conflict could continue for years." Ely finished with her brushing and then helped the queen into bed, all the while thinking of the play and the role Joan of Arc had in helping France take back the cities overthrown by the English.

"I've been thinking of Jeanne d'Arc, Your Majesty."

"Yes, what of her?" the queen asked as she placed a nightcap on her head.

"Can you imagine the painting of her dressed in armor and wielding a banner while she confronted soldiers in the field, urging them on to victory?"

"Yes, I do remember the painting. What of it?"

Ely sat down on a stool close to the queen's bedside. "If it worked for her, why not you?"

Elizabeth lay still, staring at the canopy over her bed for several minutes. With a sudden intake of breath, she sat up. "What an idea! Yes—it may work!" Gone was the downtrodden demeanor of her queen, replaced with an excitement rarely seen on her face.

~ * ~

It was a month later before Ely saw Edward Vere. She hadn't heard he had returned from the Netherlands, and was surprised to see him.

"My lord, it is good to see you. When did you return?"

"Two days ago. Lord Burghley summoned me. Anne is much worse, so I hastened home. She is asking for you. I have a carriage waiting."

"Of course. I shall get my cloak."

On the ride to the Burghley estate, Edward asked her questions about affairs of state. "I haven't had an opportunity to discuss this with Lord Burghley at length yet, but I hear the queen plans to address the troops at Tilbury."

"Yes, 'tis quite true," Ely replied. "She has even commissioned breastplate armor to be fashioned for her." She didn't mention that she had been advising the queen to admit she had the body of a weak, feeble woman, but the heart of a king. She would announce that she was ready to take up arms along with her troops, if necessary. The queen quite agreed this was not only good strategy, but factual as well. She truly loved her country and its people.

"Who does she think she is? Jeanne d'Arc?" He sniggered.

"I do believe the thought did cross her mind." They reached the Burghley's palace and agreed they would talk more of this later.

The Burghley estate was massive, and Ely could understand why Edward and Anne had continued to stay there after their reconciliation—of course Edward's shortage of funds was a factor as well. Edward went his separate way as Ely was led to Anne's bedside. Anne's mother, Mildred, and her daughter Beth were with her. Beth was now thirteen; Anne's other daughters were too young to understand what was happening to their mother. Bridget was four, and the baby Susan had been born less than a year ago. Anne still deeply grieved the baby boy who died in infancy shortly before Susan was conceived. These pregnancies so close to each other had left Anne so fragile there was little chance she would recover.

"Anne's fever has not abated, and I fear the worst," Mildred said. "She has been asking for you. She is worried about what will become of her daughters when she is gone." Anne appeared to be sleeping; her pillows kept her head raised to aid her breathing.

"I will help care for them," young Beth said.

"'Tis too much to ask of you. Don't forget, you have your duties to the queen as one of her maids," Mildred said. "I am too old to be of much assistance, but they have an excellent nanny."

"Your grandmother is right...you will need help." Ely put her arm around Beth's shoulders. They had become close since Ely had become her tutor seven years earlier. She knew it was not practical to be responsible for the day-to-day care of the three girls, but she promised Anne and Mildred she would always take an active role in their education and make sure they made good marriages. Mildred interrupted, saying it was Lord Burghley's responsibility to decide who the girls would wed. But what of their father? She knew it was not wise to voice her opinion. Obviously, the dominance of the girl's grandfather ruled the household, and perhaps Edward as well. Only a short time later, Anne seemed to fade away and eventually simply ceased to breathe.

Thirty

Men are April when they woo,
December when they wed.
Maids are May when they are maids,
but the sky changes when they are wives.
—*As You Like It*, Act 4, Scene 1

Ely had an opportunity to keep the deathbed promise she had made to Anne Vere to assure Edward's daughters made good marriages. When Beth turned fifteen, Lord Burghley arranged a marriage to Henry Wriothesley, the third Earl of Southampton. Since Edward's three daughters still lived in the Burghley household, William Cecil saw fit to arrange her marriage, especially since Edward did not have the funds to provide a suitable dowry.

Henry Wriothesley's father had died when he was eight and the queen had made him a ward of William Cecil. This was the exact same arrangement she had made following Edward's father's death twenty years earlier. The marriage arrangement between Beth and Henry was also the same arrangement Cecil had made for Edward to marry his daughter Anne.

Edward and Anne and their daughters had lived in the Burghley household along with Henry. Edward considered Henry to be more like a son, with a fondness that overshadowed that of his own daughters. Their relationship blossomed as Henry toured with Edward and his acting troupe. Edward would have liked to have groomed Henry as an actor, since he had feminine looks and attributes and would play the part of women with much believability. Even though Henry was not averse to the idea, they ultimately decided it was too risky. If the queen ever got word that the young earl acted on the stage, especially as a woman, they both could have been sent to the Tower.

Henry's path continued to follow that of Edward's when he chose to attend St. John's College at Cambridge. Because of his close association with Edward, Henry's love of literature and the stage blossomed at Cambridge. He graduated when he was sixteen, and when he returned home, Edward and he often frequented the same haunts as the poets and authors they admired.

When Ely heard from Beth about the nuptial arrangements, she at first was pleased, since Henry was so close to Beth's own age and the queen was very fond of Henry. But she changed her mind when Beth came running to her in tears.

"How can I possibly marry Henry? It would be like marrying my own brother," she sobbed, and Ely held her close. "Now I know how my mother must have felt when she was forced to marry my father."

"Now, now, Beth." Ely patted her back. "I knew your mother well, and she loved your father very much. She told me she had been in love with him since they were children."

Beth excelled in her scholastic endeavors and sought to emulate Ely's life of independence. Since Beth was also a maid of honor, she shared Ely's rooms whenever her presence was needed by the queen. Beth also accompanied Ely to her home in Staffordshire on one occasion. Ely thought of Beth with the same sisterly love she felt toward Kate.

"I like Henry, but I don't want to marry him. He told me that he does not want to marry me either. He is wealthy in his own right and has no need of my dowry."

Ely wasn't surprised Henry did not wish to marry, especially at the age of seventeen. She wondered if Edward had counseled Henry on the folly of marrying so young. Just as she was thinking about him, Edward walked into her rooms without knocking.

"Beth, what are you doing here?"

Ely put herself in front of the girl. "Why do you ask? Who else would she want to see but her longtime friend during a time of distress?"

"What kind of distress, pray tell?"

Ely turned and put her arm around Beth's shoulders.

"She doesn't want to marry Lord Southampton. She sees him more as a brother than suitor."

"She has no say in the matter, as you well know. Henry is very wealthy, and she could do no better."

"She does have a say," Ely said.

"And what shall she do? Cut her hair, put on boys' clothes, and run away into the forest?"

Ely smiled at Edward. "Yes, if that is what it takes. It worked for me."

Beth looked from her father to Ely. "What are you talking about? Did you do that?" She shrugged away from Ely's arm, looking into her eyes.

"She did," Edward said. "I am surprised you have not heard her story."

"Don't change the subject. As her father, surely you can convince Lord Burghley of the foolishness of having Beth marry Henry. They are too young."

Edward laughed and pulled Beth into his embrace. "You don't have to worry about it, my girl. Henry has refused William's offer of five thousand pounds."

"Thank God." Ely put her arm around Beth's waist, and the three of them stood close together. "There is nothing to worry about now, my sweet girl. Henry at least showed good sense." Ely looked into Edward's eyes. "I suspect you had something to do with it. Am I correct?"

"Perhaps." He stood back from both Beth and Ely. "Henry has followed my path so far, but marrying a girl he grew up with is a bit much. He needs to mature before making a decision as important as marriage." He turned to Beth. "I am surprised you did not wish to marry Henry. He is a good catch."

Beth turned toward Ely as if she were afraid to answer her father. "Beth has a keen mind and can think for herself."

"It is obvious you have had a huge influence upon my daughter. I suppose she desires to be a spinster such as you."

"Whatever will make her happy is what I desire for her. If she had the privilege of being allowed to attend college, her future could be amazing."

"Now you are being ridiculous. Married to the right man is what would be amazing for her." He took Beth's arm. "You have your problem solved. I saw your horse in the stable and knew you would be here. Come, I will ride home with you. I must talk to your grandfather about this matter."

~ * ~

Eighteen months later, *King Henry VI, Part 1* was performed at court for Queen Elizabeth's enjoyment. Edward was impressed with Ely's version of the play. He used what she had done, adding humor he knew drew in large audiences. Many royals were in attendance, eager to see the possible portrayal of their ancestors, who'd had influence over the ineffectual king.

When the play was performed at the Theater, it was the first lesson in English history for many, especially the groundlings who stood in the yard to watch the play. It did much to improve the patriotic feelings of the populace, which was the intent of the queen. It was important to her that the people would see the strong comparison among her, Joan of Arc, and Queen Margaret, the wife of Henry VI.

The conflict with Spain was in full force, which prompted the urgency for the completion of the first *Henry VI*. So great was the task of creating a reenactment of the War of the Roses, and the impatience of the queen to complete the full history in the plays, that Edward considered adding another playwright to their efforts if they were expected to finish as the queen ordered. But there was a problem Ely considered more critical than the rush to write the second and third parts to *Henry VI*.

The problem facing Ely was her old enemy—gossip. She had learned of it from the queen just this morning. "Are you not aware that you are being named Lord Oxford's paramour? To marry him is the only logical solution."

Ely was surprised the queen would tell her to marry, something Ely had resisted all her life. After giving it some thought, she realized with pleasure the queen's advice was as her grandmother. On the other hand, Ely was furious to be the topic of such slanderous gossip and immediately marched to the earl's apartment in the palace.

"Gossip is spreading that I am your mistress. Working with you is causing the rumors."

"'Twas bound to happen, but I fail to understand why you would object."

"Do you not understand? You are dastardly and a pompous ass!" The veins in her forehead stood out, so great was her anger.

"My Lady Disdain has returned." He laughed. "Perhaps you'd rather be known as my countess."

"I made it perfectly clear I have no desire to wed. My service to the queen must come first."

"Why don't you admit you do not want to be subservient to a husband?" Edward sat before his fire with his feet upon a stool, smoking a long-stemmed pipe. "Am I not correct?"

Ely flopped herself down on a chair near him, most unladylike for one of the queen's maids. "Yes, that is quite true. I am relieved I am now twenty and eight, much too old for eligible men to be interested any longer." Of all the men who had courted her before coming to court and even more since then, she could not imagine any man she would want to marry—except perhaps Edward. He at least seemed to respect her intellect.

"That is not necessarily true." Smoke rose above his brown hair, now turned gray at the temples. "Much to my dismay, I have considered courtship, but unfortunately I must seek a young wife who would bear me a son and have a substantial dowry as well as a father willing to trade his daughter for a title of countess."

Ely bit her tongue to keep from responding that she had more than enough assets to get him out of debt and she was still able to have children, but she did not want him to know either. Their working relationship satisfied her, providing they could find somewhere else to meet.

"I am content to know you do not consider me marriage material. I do, however, wish to continue our work together. Our first play of the early years of King Henry the Sixth went over quite well, do you not agree?"

"Yes, I suppose so, but I hope the next two parts will show improvement. We have created a good partnership. Your wealth of knowledge of England's history has been invaluable."

"And I could not have accomplished anything without your knowledge of how to write a play, not to mention your ability to work with actors and directors."

Edward relit his pipe. "It would be a good idea to add another person for our collaboration. I happened to see Marlowe at the Theater this morning, and he agrees; not to mention there is his need of funds."

"That will add another worry for me." Ely stood and looked out of one of the mullioned windows. "Do we dare let Marlowe know we are working together? Kit is an educated man and I enjoy talking to him whenever we have a chance to meet, but he drinks too much."

"Yes, I see what you mean." He shifted in his seat. "We will have to keep our liaison a secret from him. Let me think how we can achieve this." He reached for his cane, stood, and joined her at the window. "I will have to work with you both at separate times. It will be cumbersome but necessary. Unless...yes. I think I know a way. A scribe is necessary to make copies for the players. Since you have already met Kit, I will tell him that you have offered to be our scribe. That way I may ask for advice on certain passages if it becomes necessary without revealing we are collaborating."

"If he becomes suspicious, we will have to make other arrangements." She turned toward him. "You and I must meet elsewhere beyond curious noses."

"Do you have a place in mind?" He left her side and walked to a table, where he filled a flagon with ale.

"I do, which is what I wanted to tell you when I first arrived." She also helped herself to a cup of ale and sat back down in her chair. "The queen has given me permission to take residence outside the palace. She is adamant for me to remain anonymous when it comes to writing plays."

"She also warned me years ago, feeling it unseemly for her lord great chamberlain to write plays. It was permissible for me to have my troupes of players and write poetry, but I could not lower myself to associate with the lower classes of the stage."

Ely nodded in response. "She recognizes the importance of her courtiers and ladies' having a certain amount of decorum in those with whom they associate. She feels she is making an exception regarding our efforts. It was necessary, as no one else associated with the stage would have access to the historical records I have had."

"You have shown a remarkable talent for study."

"Thank you, my lord, but back to the subject at hand. My brother Francis is looking for a house to buy, a place to stay whilst in London. He has been coming often since taking on partners.

They have expanded their business interests into buying income-producing property throughout the city."

"That is very interesting." Edward returned to his seat in the chair he had vacated. "I have property in Great Garden at Aldgate I would be willing to sell."

"You did mention that several days ago. I had an opportunity to see the house, and it is exactly what I have in mind. I talked it over with Francis and he has asked me to set up an appointment with you to look over the property and make an offer. He said I would have *carte blanche* permission to live there." Ely would have preferred to own the house on her own, but women were not allowed to own property except through inheritance.

"Good. When does he plan to be back in London?"

"He is here now. You may meet with him whenever it is convenient for you."

"Send word for him to meet me at the house on the morrow."

~ * ~

The next day, Edward's valet opened the door to Francis. After the two men met and toured the house, Edward led Francis into the parlor and ordered his servant to bring ale.

"Where is Ely? I thought she would be coming with you."

"She opted not to come, fearful of causing more gossip."

"You must know of our activities, then?" Edward sat and motioned for Francis to take a seat as well. Edward proceeded to light his long-stemmed clay pipe.

"Oh yes, for quite some time. I saw the play a few days ago and must say I was impressed. I have known of Ely's advanced intellect since we were children, but the two of you working together is an amazing collaboration."

"You are close, then, as brother and sister?"

"Very. I handle all her financial holdings. She wanted to buy this house, but since I have a need of somewhere to live whilst in London, I said I would purchase it in my name with the understanding she would live here."

"That is my understanding also, but—" Just then the valet interrupted them, bearing a tray with two steins of ale and sweetmeats. After the servant left, Edward continued. "Does Ely have the assets to purchase a house?"

Francis laughed after he took a swallow of his drink. "Excuse me, your lordship." He wiped his chin with his sleeve. "You must not know of Ely's inheritances."

"No. Tell me." Edward leaned forward, his eyes on Francis' face.

"I am not permitted to give you an exact amount except to say it is substantial. Plus, we have both invested smartly and see good return."

"Holy Jehovah," Edward said. "I had no idea...she never said a word." He smiled broadly and took a large drink of his ale, then popped a candied walnut into his mouth. "Too bad she doesn't have royal blood. Otherwise, I would court her."

"Not royalty. That is very amusing."

"Is there something else I do not know about my writing partner?"

"I am surprised Ely has not already told you. Are you not paramours?"

"No! Not you, too?" Edward hooted his laugher. "You must not know your sister as well as I thought. Ely is not one to enter a romantic liaison. I assure you she is quite chaste, which is nearly unheard of for one of the queen's ladies." Edward laughed again. "Many have tried to get her under the covers, so to speak, but to no avail. Tell me, do you and your family have royal connections?"

"My family? My grandfather was a knight, but that is as close as it comes. Ely is a different story."

"How so?"

"Ely was adopted by my father and mother right after she was born. I learned of this when my father was on his deathbed. Only Ely, my mother, and the queen know this, and it was our father's wish no one else in our family was ever to know she is not of our blood."

"Ely has royalty in her lineage?"

"You might say so. She is King Henry's granddaughter. Ely's mother was one of the king's bastards."

"You surprise me to no end!" Edward stood, nearly overturning his ale. "That explains why our queen would invite a commoner to be part of her court—and a favorite, no less."

~ * ~

That same afternoon, Francis sought Ely's company to tell her of the purchase of the house, confessing he had told Edward of her wealth and birth.

"Francis! I thought I could trust you!" They were sitting in a small private garden outside Windsor Castle. She stood, so angry her face turned red, but before she could move, he stood and tried to put his arm around her shoulders.

"I am sorry you feel you cannot trust me. The opposite is quite true."

She jerked away from him. "How can you say that after what you did?"

"Hear me out. I told him for your own good." She harrumphed. "No, 'tis true. He told me he could not court you because you were not wealthy or titled. I felt he needed to hear the truth about you."

"You told him I was the queen's..."

"I told him your grandfather was King Henry—that your mother was one of his bastards."

"Aunt Dorothy's version of my mother's birth?"

"Yes. If you want him to know the real truth, that is your decision."

"What right did you have to tell him anything about me?"

"So that you and he can marry. No other reason." He pulled her down to sit beside him on a stone bench set among flowering shrubs. "It is obvious you both love each other, and the gossip being told about you two is correct, except for the fact you have not slept together." He patted her hand. "This is something I am at a loss to understand."

Later the same day, Edward proposed they marry.

Even with the queen's support, Ely was at first enraged with the notion of Edward wanting to marry her because of her wealth. They had so much in common, and to marry Edward was not as dreadful as she would have had others believe—including Edward—but to do so for mercenary reasons was insulting.

~ * ~

Several weeks later, Ely had not yet given Edward her answer, nor would she until she had secured certain agreements with him. Except for the thousand-pound a year dowry provided from her inheritance from Thomas Trentham, she and Francis agreed no other money would be given to purchase property previously owned by Edward. To do so would put the property at risk of being procured by his debtors.

Ely also wanted Edward to agree she would continue to write poetry and plays with or without his collaboration. She would remain a lady-in-waiting whenever the queen had need of her. Finally, she would be considered his equal and not subservient to him in any way. Edward finally agreed.

Ely also chose not to be married until after they had finished writing both remaining parts of *Henry VI*. They did collaborate with Christopher Marlowe in writing the two plays, and if Kit knew Ely played a more important role than mere scribe, he said nothing to anyone. To ensure his silence, unbeknownst to Edward, Ely arranged through Francis to pay him five pounds a month for the nine months it took them to write the plays.

They were finally married in late 1591, when Ely was twenty-nine years old and Edward forty-one. The wedding gifts Ely valued most were the silver bowl from Queen Elizabeth and the Geneva Bible emblazoned with the Vere crest given to them by John Overall.

Edward had one remaining property, a house at Stoke Newington left over from his once vast holdings. It was strategically located near the Theater, a perfect place to live and to conduct their playwriting subterfuge.

Thirty-one

Small cheer and great welcome makes
a merry feast.
        —*The Comedy of Errors*, Act 3, Scene 1

Six months after Edward and Ely were married and after they had completed the plays ordered by the queen, they traveled to the North Country to give Edward the opportunity to meet Ely's family and attend Francis' marriage to Katherine Sheldon. Dorothy and her brood of three children came from Thurgarton to the wedding, which gave Edward a chance to meet her as well. Her husband, William Cooper, opted not to accompany her.

The marriage ceremony took place in the Sheldon home church in Beoley. The following day, the Trentham families returned to Rocester. The weather was so idyllic that a picnic by the River Churnet was planned. Two days later, servants brought baskets of food, ale, and wine and laid the feast out on blankets. Kate and Dorothy's older children played at the riverbank, watched closely by their nannies. Ely's mother Jane dozed under the shade of a tree along with Kate's twin baby girls. The three sisters, Kate's husband John Stanhope, Francis, and Tommy regaled Edward with their stories of how Ely had rebelled against their father's authority. He was greatly entertained hearing the siblings' side of the stories...especially when he heard their side of how Ely stole some of Francis' clothes and forced Kate to cut her hair.

"You have to understand Father," Dorothy said. "He would not permit either me or Kate to marry until Ely had a husband."

"To marry an odious duke that smelled like he hadn't bathed in years," Ely said. She was lying beside Edward. She picked a sprig of rue and was rolling it around in her fingers.

"Dorothy quite liked the odious duke." Kate playfully nudged Dorothy.

"I didn't like the man; it was his title I desired." Dorothy was anxious to change the subject. "Our parents were in a frantic state when they discovered Ely had run away dressed as a boy. They were certain she would be beset by rogues."

"The only rogue Elijah Goodfellow met was me!" Edward proceeded to tell his side of the story and how he'd seen through her disguise almost immediately. Ely put the rue in Edward's hair.

"What's this?" He removed the flower.

"Put it back. It will ward off pixies." She turned on her back and looked at the sky. She then proceeded to tell them about the landlord stealing her purse and her ride to Chester with John Overall, which Edward had not heard until then. "Now I know why you have remained friends with the good priest."

"It was generous of him to give us the Geneva Bible. I find much comfort reading the Psalms."

"Why do you bother to read them?" Francis said. "Surely you have them memorized by now." Turning toward Edward, he said, "Did you know our tutor would have Ely translate the Psalms from our Polyglot Bible to English as punishment for belittling him?"

Ely smiled at the memory. "What he didn't know was that I quite enjoyed the work."

After Ely and Edward had retired to their rooms, they were still laughing about her escapades. "It appears to me, my dear wife, your childhood adventures would make the basis for many plays."

"The thought occurred to me as well, especially after hearing Kate's and Dorothy's versions of the events. At the time it seemed my only solution to keep from being forced to marry the man, but in hindsight, avoiding the problem was foolish on my part. I may have found a different solution without running away. I remember how frightened I was when I got lost in the woods, and when that innkeeper stole my money."

"I can understand why, but it is also entertaining. Since we will be here for most of the summer with idle time on our hands, why don't we prepare ideas for future plays? These types of plays would be well received, and there are actors I know who excel in comedy."

"Methinks it is you that would excel in writing comedy." Ely sat up in bed, putting a pillow at her back. "Yes, I like the idea. I shall write the stories, which we can later adapt to plays. If you would do the same with your past, especially the time you spent abroad, we could somehow bring our experiences together."

"An excellent idea. I would like to first finish a long poem I have been writing." Edward finished undressing and climbed into bed alongside her. "I have been thinking about my poem..."

"What is the title?" Ely snuggled against his side.

"'A Lover's Complaint.'"

Ely smiled. "Do you have a complaint, my lord?"

"No, never with you—except perhaps when you refused to be my mistress." She playfully pulled his hair. "No, it is more about Henry Wriothesley and his relationship with women. He is a very romantic man."

"Not according to Beth." Ely smiled. "I know how close you are to Henry. He will be pleased you are using him for inspiration."

"I hope so, as I plan to dedicate some of my poems to him. He has been known to pay generously for dedications, and I could use the money." He turned over and began to gently rub her hip. "You have been my inspiration, perhaps even more so than Henry. I was quite taken with your looks on our long trip here. I fell more in love with you with each passing day. I particularly enjoyed watching you in the fields, wearing straw on your head to protect you from the sun."

"I will be anxious to read your poems." She turned over in bed. "Do you plan to use your own name if it is published?"

"I haven't given it much thought. Perhaps I should consider using a pseudonym to avoid bringing attention to you through me."

"Yes, I think that would be wise. Have you come up with one?"

"No, I have not."

"I believe I have. You mentioned the name of a man who joined your Oxford Men in Stratford-upon-Avon. You said he might be willing to be our liaison with the theater."

"Yes. Will Shaksper."

"His name brought to mind one of the Psalms wherein God ends all wars by making the mountains shake and splitting the spear." Ely quietly quoted the verse in its entirety. "Shake-spear and his name sound much the same."

"Shake-spear. I quite like the sound. Your ability to memorize still astounds me. If only we could allow you to appear on stage."

"Tell me about the man. Would he suit?"

"He has limited education, which is a concern of mine, but with some coaching, perhaps he could pass as someone with intellect." He turned over in bed and faced Ely. "He was given a few minor roles, but he has much to learn as an actor."

"There was a time I too had a desire to act, but now I am content to write plays for others. You have no idea how I have dreamed of seeing my plays performed."

"When we return to London, I shall have a talk with Will. I do have a concern. He is a shrewd man and not above blackmail. He may have to be paid to keep our identities concealed."

"He sounds like a disreputable character. Yet you would assume he would be happy to work with us. Are we sure we want to do business with him?"

"I will meet with him as soon as we return and make our proposal. I want you to meet him and give me your impression before we make such an arrangement."

"Even if we don't need him, perhaps we could use shake-spear as a pseudonym." She pondered this thought for a few minutes and, hearing Edward yawn, she quickly added, "If he is suitable, financial arrangements should be made by someone else. We don't want him to expect to deal with either of us directly."

He nuzzled her neck with a playful nip of her ear. "Francis would be a perfect choice."

"That is what I was thinking," she said as she responded to his attentions.

~ * ~

Ely became pregnant in June, and the months following were the happiest she could ever remember. She prayed it would be the boy Edward longed for. After Anne Cecil's son had died shortly after birth, Edward considered naming his son by Anne Vavasour as the next Earl of Oxford. Even though Ely would have been happy to have a girl, she did long for a boy for Edward's sake.

Her prayer was answered when she delivered their son on February 24, 1593. Henry's half-sisters arrived at the Vere home in Stoke Newington bearing gifts for their new brother.

"He is truly a beautiful baby," Beth said, rubbing the baby's fuzzy hair. The picture of Beth holding her baby put Ely in mind of when she had first met Beth after Anne Vavasour's son Edward was born. "What will you name him?"

"Edward wishes to call him Henry, in honor of Henry Wriothesley. He will be christened next Sunday at the Church of St. Augustine in Hackney. Because of the sickness that is spreading in our city, I have asked for a simple ceremony to avoid crowds, but I do hope you girls will be able to come. We will have a feast to celebrate his birth afterward here in our home."

"We were nearly not allowed to come today for fear of coming in contact with someone who is sick," Susan said. "Grandfather is having us move from the city. The black plague is fearsome." Beth handed the baby to Bridget. "We are to leave in two days, and we will be unable to be at the christening. That is why we brought our gifts today." The girls each had an opportunity to cuddle the baby.

"I had not heard of the sickness until one of the servants told me a few days ago. I've been confined to this house during these past two months." Ely took the crying baby from Bridget and handed him to the nurse who was standing by. "Come. A friend of mine at the palace sent me a packet of an herb they call tea. It's newly arrived from the East. I'm anxious to try some and have been waiting until you girls arrived to sample it."

~ * ~

After the girls left with their carriage driver, Ely returned to the nursery to check on her son. She felt pressure in her breasts, and knew the baby must be hungry. Even without this reminder, it was all she could do not to hold him constantly.

"Here, I will feed him now." The nurse handed the fussy baby to her. Ely sat in her favorite rocking chair near the cradle and opened her dress. She insisted on nursing her own baby, much to the chagrin of Edward. He was vocal in his opposition when she was constantly getting up whenever he cried.

"'Tis not fitting for a countess to be nursing," he had said, but she did not care. She would do as she desired. Edward had slept in his own rooms since then, stating he needed his rest. Ely knew this was true as his injured foot had been giving him distress. Ely had diagnosed his inflamed and swollen foot as gout. She had prescribed certain herbs to be applied, which had helped enough such that he was now able to walk.

Ely could hear Edward's cane on the stone floor, before he opened the door to a small room that led into Ely's bedroom.

"How now, is that my lord cometh?"

"'Tis me, my sweeting." He leaned over Ely and the suckling baby, kissing them both on their heads.

"How is our Henry?"

"Perfect and getting fat on his mother's milk." She touched the baby's delicate cheek. "Isn't he the most beautiful baby you have ever seen?"

"I do believe you are correct, but all my children were beautiful."

"And just how many were there?" She loved to tease him, knowing perfectly well of Edward's former indiscretions.

"Let us not discuss the matter. You know you are my only love." He squeezed her shoulder. "However, I am getting too old to be much good to anyone." Edward was forty-three years and Ely knew his health had begun to wane. Along with the constant pain in his foot, his lifestyle had changed remarkably.

"Not so. You are good for me." She pulled the baby from one breast and shifted him to the other. "Where have you been?"

"I went to Gray's Inn to meet with Henry W. I told him about the christening. He is anxious to see his godson." He pulled up a padded bench near them and sat, putting his leg straight in front of him. "There is news of the sickness spreading in London, and Henry said the queen is considering closing the theaters. The groundlings in the theater are so jammed together, there is fear of spreading contagion."

"How bad is it?"

"Only a few cases so far, but it is sure to get worse. The black plague is not to be ignored."

"Lord Burghley has plans to send your daughters from the city. They didn't know where yet."

"Probably near the sea. Cornwall would be my surmise. Methinks it would be good for you and the baby to go with them."

"They leave in two days. I could never be ready in time. I would much prefer to go to my mother. I hope she has received the message of Henry's birth by now, and she will be anxious to see our baby. The future Earl of Oxford, no less! We had such a wonderful time there last summer."

"It is an exceedingly long trip, and the weather in March is unsettling. The roads will be a sea of mud. If you went to Cornwall, you could travel by water."

"If we stay confined to the house, we should be fine. The baby is still tiny and should not be exposed to the cold weather. I believe we can wait for two or three months before we leave."

"If you say so, my dear. A delay will allow me to settle my affairs and find accommodations for my Oxford Players. I will try to travel with you."

~ * ~

The day of the christening had arrived, and the queen sat next to Henry W. She was dressed in her riding costume and accompanied by a single guard also dressed in simple attire. Ely knew the man was someone the queen trusted. She was not wearing her usual white makeup, and her wig was replaced by a hat that shaded her face. They had come on horseback.

Ely was concerned the queen would still be identified by someone, but she need not have worried. It was obvious she had taken extra precautions to come secretly. The only personage present in the church at the time was the parish priest, whom Ely had warned not to say a word about the queen's presence. Edward had made the cautionary imperative to Henry W.

The ceremony was brief: the priest read a Bible verse and said a prayer, and giving the baby's name in full, he poured water over his head, baptizing him. The baby cried loudly, bringing smiles to everyone there.

After the ceremony, they returned to the Vere home. The queen seemed content to relax in the company of friends and enjoy a good meal with excellent wine. When it was time to feed the baby, the queen accompanied Ely into the nursery.

After Ely dismissed the nanny, the queen made sure the door was firmly closed and sat while Ely prepared to nurse her son. "It does seem strange to see one of my ladies nursing a baby. You truly are a country girl at heart."

"I don't feel like a countess. This is quite beyond all I could have imagined." She smiled at the queen, who seemed happy perched on the wide padded bench. "I am so happy you were able to attend the christening, Your Majesty. It meant a great deal for me to have you there."

"I have wanted to talk to you for some days now, my dear. I have much to say." She paused to watch the scene in front of her. "Do your breasts hurt when they are full of milk? I can remember when..." Tears came to the queen's eyes.

Ely stood with the baby still latched to her breast so she could sit near the queen. "I know you were referring to after my mother was born." The queen nodded, not looking at Ely. "I have known for several years. My father...Thomas Trentham...if he had not told me, I would have continued to believe Aunt Dorothy gave birth to my mother. Your secret would have died with her if she had not told my mother...my adopted mother."

The queen's face took on such sadness it reminded Ely of what they most had in common. "I wish I could have known my birth mother."

"And I as well. This is why I named my baby Ann." She continued to look at the nursing baby. "A wonderful, devoted friend was Dorothy Sneyd. She gave up much to take the blame for my misadventure. I am sorry we were not able to be with Dorothy when she died." The women looked down on the sleeping baby, still suckling. "Pray tell, who else knows?"

"My brother Francis, but you need not worry about him. He is loyal to you, and we made a pact never to tell anyone. I have told no one, not even Edward, and have no intention of doing so."

The queen sighed. "I am getting old, and Lord Burghley is insisting I name someone as my successor. Since I had a child with Thomas Seymore, even though I was barely fourteen at the time, 'twould be a great embarrassment for me, and possibly weaken my leadership. But, since I had a daughter and Ann also had a daughter, succession was not an issue. With the birth of a boy who is my direct descendant, I have been forced to give it consideration. Baby Henry would be a natural successor to the throne."

Ely put the baby onto her shoulder to elicit a burp. The queen reached for him. "May I hold my great-grandson?" After Ely positioned the baby on the queen's shoulder, she answered.

"I have thought long and hard about the possibility you might ask this of me. I love you dearly, and I know your duties have been a dreadful strain on you."

The queen squared her shoulders and handed the baby back to Ely. "Are you accusing me of not being able to rule?"

"No, no—not at all. You have been a tower of strength. I meant emotionally, with everything you have had to give up. I would never wish this upon myself, nor on my son, even though he may at some time wish it himself." Ely laid the sleeping baby back into his cradle. "I don't believe I will ever tell him of our close relationship. The eighteenth Earl of Oxford is quite enough recognition for my baby."

"If you are certain of this, my dear, I will pursue it no further." Ely put her dress to rights and started to step away, but the queen pulled her into a long embrace. "In all honesty, even if you had wanted to make a claim for your son, I would have had to deny you."

"I am relieved to be spared that decision." The queen released Ely but continued to hold her hand.

"I hear from Edward you two will continue to write plays."

"I truly hope you do not object. We will take the utmost safeguard not to be identified. In fact, we are meeting with a man by the name of Shaksper who we may use as a stand-in for us. To be assured of his silence, I have arranged for my brother Francis to make financial arrangements with the man."

"Good. Make sure he remains a dumb man." She squeezed Ely's hand. "I do not want Edward's name demeaned as a writer of plays, but for you it is far more distasteful, as one of my ladies, to be lowered to that level. I do not wish for you to gain any negative recognition for involvement with the lower classes of people. If this Shaksper person ever reveals your name, I will throw him in the Tower and have his head."

Ely knew this was not said in jest. Had she not had total devotion to the queen, it would have mattered little to her to be recognized as a playwright, but if it brought humiliation to the queen, she would take every precaution not to be identified. Shaksper would be told of the queen's warning.

They returned to the library, where they overheard Edward and Henry W. talking while they smoked pipes and drank their ale. "Did you hear about Kit Marlowe being killed in a barroom brawl?" Henry asked.

"Yes, his hot temper was finally his undoing. Howsoever, 'twas far better than dying due to the plague."

"I agree," replied Henry. "It is fearsome to even venture toward the houses labelled with the black cross."

The queen overheard the last comment and replied, "I plan to close the theaters and other locations if the plague continues to curse London." The queen stood in the entryway. She turned to Ely. "I am ready to depart. Fetch my man." Ely left the room to find a servant.

"Will you leave London to avoid the sickness?" Henry asked.

"I am anxious to get away from this smelly city with its rats and vermin as much as anyone else. We must do something. I assume you two know I have ordered the lords to meet with me tomorrow to discuss the best way to clean up the sewage? I hope most of them have not already fled."

"We were discussing that earlier. We will be at the meeting."

~ * ~

Ely preceded Edward to Rocester by several months due to Edward's having not only to try to find housing for some of his Oxford Players, but he had other legal difficulties surrounding the small theater of Blackfriars. Finally, with Francis' help, Edward was able to purchase a sublease. Since Blackfriars was an indoor theater, winter performances were possible with higher admission fees. After Edward was assured everything was moving forward as he desired, he gave the lease to his secretary, John Lyly, to manage whilst he was in the North.

Thirty-two

You speak an infinite deal of nothing.
　　—*The Merchant of Venice*, Act 1, Scene 1

Edward, Ely, and the baby remained in the North Country in a house they had rented in Derbyshire not far from the Stanhope estate. The following spring, Ely received word from the queen that she was needed. Edward had been restless and desired to return to London now that the plague had abated. He especially missed the comradeship of his friends at Gray's Inn and Blackfriars, where some of his players had taken residence.

While he was away, Edward finished a long poem he titled "Venus and Adonis" describing sensual affairs. "How can you write of our personal lovemaking? It would be an embarrassment to me as it should be to you," Ely said. "I would be ashamed if the queen should ever read it!"

"The queen would be envious she had never felt such strong desire. Howsoever, why would anyone make the association with our relationship? If anything, it is the reverse to what we have, a Roman goddess pursuing a Greek god. I felt so strongly of what we mean to each other, I desired to write of it." He put his arm about her shoulders and whispered, "I had every intention of giving you the poem, my darling. Whatever you desire to do with it is your decision."

"It is beautiful poetry; I will keep it always."

"I have written two longer poems I have dedicated to Henry W. It will be important to explain why it was necessary to use Shake-spear as my pseudonym. We need to make plans to return to London. What are your plans for the baby?"

"Little Henry and his nanny will stay with my mother until we are sure the plague is over. I hate to think of leaving him behind, but will feel safer if he remains here."

"With such good weather, we must not delay our return. Francis has asked to accompany us. I am glad, as we may need him when we meet with Will Shaksper."

~ * ~

Ely missed her baby and was anxious to tend to her business affairs so she could return to the North. Her first task was to meet with the queen.

"It is good to see you again, Your Majesty," Ely said after she was admitted to the queen's quarters. She noted the queen had aged since she had last seen her. "Are you well?"

"As well as you can expect a woman of sixty and one." The queen was sitting in a large, padded chair; symbols of her reign had been carved into its arms and legs. "Sit here by me." She motioned toward a chair much smaller than the one she was sitting on. "How is baby Henry?"

"He is well." Ely picked up the chair and moved it nearer the queen. "A chubby little boy, fair hair and blue eyes. I was hoping he would have the same hair color as ours, but it is not to be. He is walking now and getting into all kinds of mischief. Very much his father's son."

"I should like to see him."

"I felt it safer to leave him with my mother until we are sure the plague has ended. I will return to fetch him after I have finished with my tasks."

"What tasks are those?"

"To meet with you, of course, and I will also be meeting this Shaksper man this evening. We plan to hire him to be our broker to take our plays to the various theater managers. Edward has written two long poems using the pseudonym Shake-Spear. If the managers insist on knowing who authored the plays, we will have to allow Shaksper to take credit. My strong desire is that the time never arrives, but we must be prepared just in case."

"Is it necessary for you to meet this man? Surely Edward can talk to him without you."

"Edward and I discussed this at length. We were fearful he would not see the urgency to keep Edward's involvement secret, since there has been no need in the past. A woman's involvement would heighten the need for confidentiality." Ely shifted in her chair. "He needs to know with whom he is dealing."

"I suspect what you actually want is not to be left behind when arrangements are made."

"You know me well, Your Majesty. I also have every intention of giving him your warning."

"See to it you do. I do not want your good reputation tarnished." The queen leaned forward in her chair. "That brings up what I wanted to see you about. Our conflict with Spain continues, and our tax coffers are growing low. It is time we had more plays of England's history to make sure the morale of the people is kept high."

"Do you have a preference, Your Grace?"

"Your Richard the Third was successful before the plague struck. Now methinks King Richard the Second should follow. I enjoy these performances. They increase my morale as well as that of my people, and God only knows I need enjoyment and laughter in my life."

"Methinks you would enjoy the play I have been writing. I expect to have it finished while here. This is the first play to be produced written solely by me. Edward gave me suggestions, but I wrote it."

"What is its title?"

"I call it *The Comedy of Errors*. It came to mind after being with my sister Kate's twin girls; they are identical in every way. This play is about mistaken identity between two sets of identical twins: men of royalty and men of servitude. Both had been separated during their youths. All four of the men end up in the same city at the same time. Comical events take place when the wife of one royal twin mistakes the newly arrived twin as her husband. The same occurs with the wife of his servant."

"Marvelous, when can it be performed?"

"If I make it a shorter play, we can bring it about sooner. I have highlighted the legal profession in the play, and Edward wants it first shown during Christmas season at Gray's Inn. I will work closely with Edward so other details may be worked out."

"Please keep me informed. I may want it performed at the palace as well."

~ * ~

Edward and Francis talked to Shaksper about using him as a broker and secured his agreement before bringing him to meet Ely. It was decided the best place to meet would be Francis' house at Great Garden, with Francis taking the lead in the conversation. Ely knew the men would be hungry, so she had a table with ale, bread and honey, and slices of beef. She sent the servant and cook away with instructions to return at dusk. A longer table had been set with four straight-back chairs. Ely set the penner the queen had given her so many years ago on the table. She removed paper, a quill, and ink and placed them near where she would be sitting.

When Ely first saw Will, as he preferred being called, she was surprised he was younger than she, guessing him to be in his mid-twenties. He had a dark, receding hairline, slightly protruding hazel eyes, chin whiskers, and mustache. He was dressed in a brown worsted suit of the style of others of his class.

"This is my wife, the Countess of Oxford." Will stared at her. Ely stared back until he lowered his eyes.

"We need to have someone broker for us, to make sure our plays are performed to our satisfaction," Ely said.

"Your man told me so. I said I would be willing, but I need to know more about my duties—and what of money, my payment?" Will looked from Edward to Ely and then to Francis.

"Do not be impertinent," Francis said. "You are in the presence of the countess. Bow to the lady." Will gave a quick bow, his face taking on a red tinge.

"There are refreshments." Ely nodded toward the side table. "Help yourself and then let us sit and have a meeting of the minds." She was not repelled by Will, but neither was she impressed. Perhaps that would change in time.

Ely sat at the table and waited for the men to join her. Will stood back while Edward and Francis filled plates, poured themselves flagons of ale, and came to join Ely. Edward nodded toward Will, indicating he could eat as well.

While the men ate and drank, Ely sat quietly, idly using a quill to write on a piece of paper. "Shall we begin, my husband?"

"Yes, go ahead, my dear," Edward said as he munched on a tough piece of meat.

"My husband has been using a pseudonym for some of his poetry. It is similar to your name. Shake-spear." Will appeared confused. "Mr. Shaksper, do you know what pseudonym means?"

"Call me Will." He scratched the stubble on his chin. "Lord Oxford is using a pretend name?"

Francis looked toward Ely and Edward. "Would you be willing to change how you pronounce your name?" He looked confused again, and Francis continued, "There may come a time when others will want to know the identity of the person who wrote these plays. We hope that time never arrives, but should it, we want you to admit you are Shake-spear."

"I do not understand. Why would you want me to take credit for work done by others?"

"You are a member of my Oxford Men. Surely you understand I have sponsored this troupe all my life, and my father before me. I am the Earl of Oxford, the queen's lord great chamberlain, and as such it is unseemly for me to be identified with anything of a lesser class. Is that understood?"

Will nodded.

"My wife, the Countess of Oxford, is a special woman. Before our marriage she was with Queen Elizabeth for ten years as a maid of honor. My lady knows the queen well and is one of her dearest friends. Is that understood?"

"Yes sir, but..."

"Let me explain," Francis interjected. "My sister too writes plays and poetry—she has for nearly all her life. The queen knows this and enjoys her writing. The queen has given permission for them to write plays with the understanding no one knows. If no one is curious who wrote the plays, they can continue to be anonymous. However, there may come a time the author will need to be identified. If that time comes, and since Lord Oxford has used the name of Shake-spear on his poetry, we will need you to accept that name as your own."

"It seems to me no one would believe a woman capable of writing; me wife cannot even write her name," Will sniffed.

"This woman is scholarly. The queen would never allow a maid of hers to be uneducated," Francis said.

"Until it becomes necessary for you to assume the name Shake-spear, we will use you to broker the plays for us. That way the transition will be natural," Edward said. "Before you begin to assume to be our broker, you need to leave the Oxford Men and meet with James Burbage of Lord Chamberlain's Men. Your desire to be an actor may end and you will instead become a broker of plays to him."

"What are the duties of a broker? And why is it not possible to be an actor as well?" Will stood and refilled his cup with more ale.

"I will give you a play and you bring it to Burbage. Methinks Burbage may not want to hire you as both an actor and broker. But you never know. He could. Should he ask for the name of the author, refuse to answer, saying the author does not wish to be identified. Eventually, when he is used to accepting plays from you, you may have to admit it is you who is the author. Before you admit to authorship, you must get permission from me." Ely touched Edward's hand and he leaned toward her. She whispered something into his ear and tapped the quill on the table for emphasis.

"If you agree to this arrangement, you will need me to coach you on what being a broker means and how to conduct yourself. You must learn much to convince people you are the writer. It may be difficult to pull this off without your learning much from me."

"How long will I need to pretend to be this Shake-spear?"

"As long as we are alive, or until you are dead, whichever comes first." Edward turned to Ely and she nodded.

"One more detail," Francis said to Edward. "Since Will spent this past winter with his family in Stratford instead of at Blackfriars, it is best for him to continue to live at his home except during the times we are working with him and he is ready to present himself to Burbage. I fear too much socializing will lead to loose lips. I do not want him to live or drink with the actors."

Will raised his arm as if to object, when Edward said, "You have a home, wife, and children in Stratford. You will return to them until either I or my brother-in-law summons you."

"But what am I to live on before you feel I am ready to assume the role of broker? And after a play is sold, will I be able to keep the money, or shall I be expected to turn the money over to you?"

Edward nodded to Francis. "My brother-in-law will explain the financial arrangements. You will receive money from him, and we are not to be approached directly concerning matters of recompense. Be assured from this day forward you will be paid well to keep your mouth shut. You are a dumb man. You cannot talk. Is that clearly understood?" Edward drew his thumb across his throat. Will swallowed noisily, then nodded.

Ely looked out the window and saw dusk was at hand. "The servants will be back soon." Ely put her notes into the penner along with the quill and ink. She closed the leather case and stood from her chair. "We should be on our way." Turning to Francis, she asked, "Do you need anything from us before we leave?" Edward left the room to fetch his driver.

"No, I will take it from here." Francis reached inside his purse and gave Will a few coins. "Come to the stable with me. You may have one of my horses. We want you to return to your home in Stratford immediately. Stay there until you hear from me."

"Will, I will be leaving for the North Country," Ely said. "I may not see you again for quite some time." Will stood from his chair and bowed. "Just one more thing—and you may consider this a warning. The queen knows of our arrangement, and should she receive word my identity as a playwright is known by anyone outside of this room, you will be sent to the Tower to never again see the light of day."

Will swallowed noisily again and nodded. He put on his hat and followed Francis to the stable.

Thirty-three

Get thee a good husband, and use him
as he uses thee.
—*All's Well That Ends Well*, Act 1, Scene 1

Ely received a message from Beth asking to meet her at the palace in the queen's ladies' quarters. Ely was anxious to return north to her son, but delayed her trip by one day to meet with Beth.

After dismissing Edward's valet, her escort to the palace, Ely and Beth walked the familiar route they had trod for over ten years.

"Grandfather has me betrothed to William Stanley, Sixth Earl of Derby," Beth said after they both sat on the same bench where they had first met.

"I know, Edward told me. How do you feel about him? Does he meet with your approval?"

"I suppose so. He is older than I by fourteen years and not handsome at all, but he has an interesting background, which is appealing."

"I have met the earl several times and heard many of his experiences whilst abroad. A background not unlike your father's. Is that what attracts you?"

"Yes, and he pens plays—not nearly as good as yours, though."

"What do you know of me, pray tell?"

"One learns many things at court with our queen—such as your many meetings with my father before your marriage. I discovered you were writing the Henry the Sixth plays."

"How well known is this? The queen will be disturbed if anyone else finds out."

"I know, she told me. When I broached the subject with Queen Elizabeth, she confirmed she had asked you and my father to collaborate." Beth patted Ely's hand. "Never fear, your secret is safe with me." She laughed quietly. "I do not relish the thought of spending time in the Tower should I be blamed for spreading the word."

"That is a relief. I must say, I am happy to have another woman with whom I can converse openly."

"Speaking of other women to talk to, I have a new friend. She was mistress to Henry Carey, Lord Hunsdon. Her name is Emilia. She writes quite good poetry, considering her background."

"Yes, I met her years ago. She was with Lord Hunsdon at the Theater during a rehearsal of...oh, I can't remember. Edward and I had a long conversation with her. Her family is Italian—Bassano is their name. Edward still remembers his travels, his time in Italy being his favorite. But she was born in London, so her only knowledge of Italy is through her parents. She seemed unhappy to be with a man so much older than she, but I understand he took good care of her. In fact, I used her name in one of my plays, *The Comedy of Errors*."

"Yes, I remember the play. Lord Hunsdon got her pregnant and she was quickly married off to a man named Lanier, one of the court musicians. That was about a year ago. She has a son she also named Henry."

"I hope she is happy now."

"I don't believe so. The money and jewels Lord Hunsdon left her are nearly gone, and her husband is quite violent. I would never allow a man to hit me."

"You won't need to take that kind of treatment since you aren't marrying for security, as she was probably forced to do."

"That is why I wanted to see you today. I would like to discuss my wedding."

"When will it take place?"

"In January at Greenwich Palace. The queen will be present, and I want it to be a special occasion. Will you write a play for me?"

"It's an honor that you ask this of me. A compliment indeed. Do you have a theme in mind?"

"A play that is gay and lighthearted. I want it performed during my wedding festival."

Ely pondered the occasion. "Many years ago, when I was only a child, I had a very real dream I have never forgotten. It occurred on a midsummer's eve when I stole out of the manor to see the fairies. I fell asleep in a meadow surrounded by trees. I never knew if what I saw was real or a dream. A play would be like my dream, fanciful with fairies, a unicorn, and strange characters. It would be better to have the play outside in the summer, but I believe we could decorate the great hall at Greenwich with greenery to depict a wooded area."

"That sounds perfect. What fun! But what if someone asks who wrote it? What will I tell them?"

"Your father and I have foreseen that possibility and have made arrangements." Ely went on to tell Beth of the agreement they had made with Will. "I will be leaving for Staffordshire tomorrow to be with my little Henry. I will spend the summer with my family and work on the play then."

"Wonderful. Please send me a message when you return. I promise you no one will know I asked you to do this for me. I am happy to have you for my stepmother—someone to whom I can confide my sins!" She laughed heartily.

"I will always look forward to our meetings and hope there are not too many sins." Ely laughed along with Beth, giving her a warm embrace.

~ * ~

Ely traveled with Francis on their way north, staying at homes where Francis had been welcomed on his many trips to and from London. During the time they were together, Francis spoke of the financial arrangements he had made with Will. Will would receive twenty pounds a year, paid in four installments from Ely's account. Will would be allowed to do his own negotiating for brokering the plays. Any money he received he would keep. Will had asked Francis to give him financial advice, and Francis agreed. Ely asked about her investments and was pleased to learn her fortune had increased substantially. She told Francis she wanted to buy back Edward's ancestral home of Hedingham Castle in Essex. Lord Burghley had purchased the castle from Edward and held it in trust for Edward's daughters. Since Edward now had a son who would be named the eighteenth Earl of Oxford, Ely wanted the property for him.

When they arrived in Derbyshire, Ely found her baby in the capable hands of Kate and her brood. She was told little Henry was happier when he was around other children, and having one more caused no problem for Kate. While there, Ely confided in Kate about her promise to write a play in honor of Beth's marriage. Ely was installed in her own bedroom, but when she worked on the play, she would be able to use John's library whenever he did not need it. Kate had told her it was the only room the children were not permitted to enter.

Jane Trentham alternated living with both Francis and Kate. She loved being with her grandchildren, but there were times when she sought quieter surroundings in Rocester.

During her time in Kate's home, Ely enjoyed playing with her son, always settling disputes between the children in Henry's favor, as befitting the next Earl of Oxford. In addition to writing the play she had titled *A Midsummer Night's Dream*, she wrote sonnets to her fair young son. Her favorite was composed when she took Henry on a picnic near the River Dove, where as a child she had dreamed alone and written poetry. While her baby napped, she wrote:

> Shall I compare thee to a summer's day?
> Thou art more lovely and more temperate.
> Rough winds do shake the darling buds of May,
> And summer's lease hath all too short a date.
> Sometime too hot the eye of heaven shines,
> And often is his gold complexion dimm'd;
> And every fair from fair sometime declines,
> By chance, or nature's changing course, untrimm'd;
> But thy eternal summer shall not fade,
> Nor lose possession of that fair thou ow'st,
> Nor shall death brag thou wand'rest in his shade
> When in eternal lines to time thou grow'st.
> So long as men can breathe, or eyes can see,
> So long lives this, and this gives life to thee.

Thirty-four

It was April and I had narrowed my research to Queen Elizabeth's reign and the role Ely could have played as one of her close confidants. I also read everything I could find on the life of Edward de Vere. I figured this was about the only way I could trace the life of his second wife. I admit, I made a great many assumptions, but isn't that exactly what other historians do? Of course, I had the advantage of Emma's journal and the signature on the bottom of the *Midsummer* page—and, my ghostly visits, which no one was to know about. During my most recent phone conversation with Clay, he asked me the sixty-four-dollar question.

"You've been working on your research now for five months. Besides the two poems, do you expect to uncover more data proving the Ely hypothesis?"

"I have no idea, Clay. We could still discover leads and solid clues."

"I realize that, Cynthia. I was only wondering how much more time we should give this search before we call it a day and make the page public."

"How about coming here Saturday afternoon—we can discuss the project and then have dinner? In the meantime, I'll prepare my argument as to why we need to give it more time."

"A home-cooked meal sounds really good. I'll bring the wine."

That conversation had taken place on Wednesday, and since then I had worked steadily preparing my notes. When Saturday arrived, I was ready with my argument and then concentrated on dinner. I'd made it simple, deciding on chicken and dumplings, a dish I'd made so often, I hadn't needed a recipe for years. I made an apple pie, too, remembering my grandmother's old adage about the quickest way to a man's heart being through his stomach.

Clay arrived at four that afternoon armed with a bottle of white wine. "I know this is your favorite." He showed me the label. "Wow, what's this?" He picked up the pie I had cooling on the counter.

"Apple pie. For dessert," I said, receiving his kiss on my cheek.

"How did you know that's my favorite?"

"And every other man's I know, too," I said with a smile. "Have a seat at the table. I have my evidence ready."

"Okay," he said, looking through some of my notes.

"While I was getting ready for our meeting, I felt what being a lawyer is all about. I'm going to try to persuade you to rule my way—you be the judge and make the decision as to whether I continue the project." I patted him on the shoulder. "Would you like coffee—or something stronger?"

He looked at his watch. "Hum, happy hour. How about scotch? Make it light, though." I did as he asked, and poured myself one that was mostly ice and soda.

"Speaking of a judge, that is something I was going to tell you," he said. I pulled out a chair on the opposite side of the table and sat. "I've been asked to run for a seat in Oregon's circuit court. There's a vacancy and I've been recommended."

"Aren't judges in Oregon elected?"

"Yes, all judges are chosen in nonpartisan elections to serve six-year terms."

"Are you going to? I mean, you're such a successful trial attorney, are you ready for a change?"

"Hell yes, and being a judge really interests me—to weigh both sides of a question." He took a sip of his drink. "Did you know my Uncle Paul, Sudie's husband, was a judge? I admired him so much and he loved the job. I think I will, too."

"Won't you have to campaign?"

"I'd be unopposed...so far. A few speeches maybe. I'd be interested in vying for the appellate level after the term is over."

"That's wonderful. I'd be so proud of you—not that I'm not already." I reached across the table and squeezed his hand.

"Well, enough of that. Let's discuss the project," he said.

"According to historians, Will Shaksper didn't arrive in London until 1588. He was born in 1564, so he was still very young. The research is a bit contradictory, but it seems the first plays were the histories, anonymously written. I think they were first performed in the early 1590s. Shakespeare was not given credit until 1598, I think it was. Why wouldn't he want credit right off the bat? Of course, another plague epidemic took place in the early '90s, and that could have been the reason. But even so—"

"I can see why dates are important in your research," Clay said. "It doesn't make sense Shakespeare would wait to take credit as the true playwright until many years later. More proof he wasn't the true bard?"

"That's right! Besides that, I think the name Shake-Spear, with a hyphen, was originally a pseudonym. The name first appeared in the early 1590s with two long poems. They were dedicated to Henry Wriothesley, the third Earl of Southampton. The name Shakespeare must have evolved from that—a name Will took when he was allowed to take credit for the plays, about eight years later. Any questions so far?"

"Not yet. Go ahead."

"I remember my Shakespeare professor remarking most recent historians believe the plays were a collaboration of several playwrights of the era. But I've concluded the collaboration was with Ely and Edward. Since he had his own troupe of players and knew the industry, so to speak, it makes sense he would try his hand at writing plays. However, Ely could have been the chief writer of those plays that depict strong female roles."

"That makes sense," Clay said.

"Those long poems were written at about the time Edward and Ely would have married. Because of the nature of the long poems, especially *Venus and Adonis*, I think Edward was probably the sole writer. The sonnets were another matter. The two most noteworthy themes occurring in the sonnets were those of the dark lady and the fair young man. I read the differing comments made by historians. Some of Edward de Vere's proponents believed the dark lady poems were written to Anne Vavasour, his mistress, who had borne him a son while he was still separated from his first wife, Anne Cecil. Will Shakespeare proponents opined Will had a homosexual relationship with Henry Wriothesley, since he dedicated the two long poems to him, plus the sonnets of the fair young man. They also believed Will learned to write of court activities through this relationship with the young earl. I think they're way off track there."

"Why?" Clay asked.

"If you read the sonnets of the fair young man, or boy even, it makes more sense they were written by Ely. She had a son, her only child, born when she was probably thirty. I can imagine she would write these sonnets to show the love of her son."

"That does make sense. Did you ever see the movie, *Shakespeare in Love*? Can you imagine that Shakespeare as being gay?" We both laughed.

"I love that movie—even though I think it's full of historic holes."

"The history of Henry Wriothesley is practically the same as Edward de Vere twenty or more years earlier. Both of their fathers were earls, and when they died, Edward and Henry were made wards of William Cecil, Lord Burghley. After Edward reconciled with his wife, they had two more daughters and continued to live in the Burghley home. Henry would have been raised alongside Edward's daughters. You have to wonder if Edward thought of Henry as his son." I went on to give him the history of Henry, and how it closely paralleled Edward's childhood.

We continued to talk until it was nearly six and I could hear Clay's stomach rumble. "Oh, my goodness, Clay. You're hungry." I pulled a relish tray of olives, cheese, and pickles from the fridge and added a few cocktail crackers off to the side. "Here, you can munch on this while I finish dinner. I'll have it ready in less than a half hour." I turned the heat on under the chicken stew.

"Thanks." He followed me into the kitchen and looked over my shoulder, munching on a cracker. "What are you making?" He nuzzled my cheek, setting off shiver bumps down my arms.

"If you start that, we won't be having any dinner."

"Um, you're good enough to eat."

"Clay, stop. Look what you're doing to me." I showed him my arms. "You can help by setting the table."

"Okay...reluctantly," he said, popping an olive into his mouth.

"I'm making chicken and dumplings. This is biscuit dough. When the stew is bubbling, I drop in spoonfuls. Twenty minutes with the lid on, then we eat."

During dinner, we discussed the project more. "Even with no actual proof of authorship, I think you have enough material to write a book, with or without Sudie's page," he said. "Have you given any thought to that?"

"Yes, I've had that thought ever since I came up with the theory when I was in college."

"What gave you the notion in the first place?" he asked, forking another helping of chicken into his mouth.

"It was the nature of some of the plays. It seemed odd to me a man would write plays with such strong women, considering the culture of the time when women were treated as subservient to men." I wiped my mouth on a napkin and gave him more of my thoughts on the subject.

After we finished our meal, Clay was effusive with his compliments, and they must have been true because he had two large helpings. We both decided we were too full for dessert. He refused coffee but did refill both our wine glasses. As he helped me load the dishwasher, our conversation returned to research once more.

"Oh, did I mention? I've been doing research regarding our 'project,' as Sudie called it." He smiled. "I guess she isn't far from our minds, is she?"

"Sudie is the first person I think of whenever I uncover a new clue." I touched his arm. "I often talk to her. I so wish she could have lived long enough to see this through." I couldn't stop a few tears from forming.

He put his arm around my shoulder, and I leaned into him. His musky, clean smell caused me to catch my breath. "I'm sorry, I'm too sentimental." I leaned back from his arm. "You were saying you've been doing research, too?"

He carried both glasses to the coffee table and sat on the sofa, patting the seat next to him. "I've always been interested in history. I guess I already told you, it was my undergraduate major before I switched to law." He picked up his wine and took a sip. "While I was laid up with my back, I started reading Shakespeare's histories."

"Really? I haven't tackled those yet. They seem too boring for me. I'm more of a fiction fan."

"Actually, I think they are mostly fiction. Falstaff is introduced as a comic character in the first Henry the Sixth," Clay said. "Also, Joan of Arc wasn't depicted as a true heroine. That's understandable, I guess, considering Shakespeare wrote for an English audience." Clay turned and faced me, then leaned in. "It came to mind that there is a similarity between Queen Elizabeth and Joan of Arc."

I felt his breath against my ear, sending goosebumps up the back of my neck. "They were both strong female leaders. Is that what you mean?" I leaned away from his obvious attraction.

"That's not all. Have you seen the portrait of the queen giving a speech to the army before the Spanish Armada defeat? Doesn't that put you in mind of a similar painting of Joan of Arc in armor, holding a banner?"

"Are you inferring the queen was emulating Joan—that she was as capable of leading an army?"

"Yes, she must have felt vulnerable, which may be the reason why the play was written—perhaps propaganda for the general population of the English people. Obviously, taxes were a factor in supporting the war with Spain." He took a sip of wine. "Do you know the date of the Spanish Armada?"

"Let's Google it." I stood. "Also, the dates the plays were produced could be a clue." I pulled on Clay's hand. "My computer is in the bedroom."

While I powered up my computer, Clay brought a chair from the table to sit close beside me. "One of the other arguments against William Shakespeare is that he couldn't possibly have been able to write the histories because he didn't have access to records of prior English kings. Someone at court certainly would have."

"Like our Ely or her husband."

"Yep! Look, the Armada was in 1588." I typed another search into the computer. We both stared at the monitor as we read. "Look. Shakespeare's *Henry the Sixth, Part One* was the first—played in 1590, two years after the Armada. I think we may have figured it out. I bet the queen had something to do with having it written in the first place. That would support your notion of propaganda." Clay's face was just a couple of inches from mine, and as I turned our noses were nearly touching. He leaned closer and captured my lips in a kiss that shook me to my toes. He pulled me from the chair and onto his lap.

"I think we should talk about this later," he whispered as his hand rubbed the back of my neck, sending more trembles to my toes. He rose, setting me on my feet as my arms encircled his neck. He had my full cooperation as we kissed again.

Thirty-five

All the world's a stage,
And all the men and women merely players.
They have their exits and their entrances,
And one man in his time plays many parts.
—*As You Like It*, Act 2, Scene 7

In the following years, Edward, Ely, and their son Henry were firmly installed as a family with many servants as befitting the earl and his countess—thanks in no small part to the generosity of Ely, Francis, and Queen Elizabeth. The days of Edward spending money like it was shot out of a cannon were over. He had wisely deferred all expenditures to Ely and Francis.

By clearing legal matters concerning the previous owner, Queen Elizabeth helped Ely and Francis purchase King's Place in Hackney. The country manor included vast acreage, gardens, and orchards. Inside was a great hall, chapel, and what was most important to Ely and Edward: a proper library where they could collaborate.

Shaksper became installed as a broker of plays to James Burbage, and following James' death in 1597, to his son, Richard Burbage. The Oxford Men had merged with Lord Chamberlain's Men and Richard Burbage had become the lead actor and leader of the troupe of players.

Francis sent word that Will wanted to speak directly to Edward. He was granted an audience the following day.

Will was admitted into the library where both Edward and Ely were sitting at their respective desks. Will now had a tailor, who had provided him with fashionable clothing, which included gartered silk hose and a doublet of fine mustard-colored wool with puffed sleeves.

Ely thought about leaving the men alone, but decided to stay to see what Will had on his mind. She stood up to greet him, offering her hand after he had bowed to her.

"Please, let us sit over here." She pointed to a group of chairs situated in front of a blazing fire. After Edward dismissed the butler, they were seated. "We were sorry to hear of the death of your son. How old was he?"

"Hamnet was just eleven, Your Ladyship. Praise God his twin sister and my other daughter are in good health."

"Perhaps we could use his name in a future play. Would that please you?"

"Oh yes, Your Ladyship. 'Twould truly make me happy."

"What brings you to our home, my man? We have not yet finished a play for you to broker for us." Edward paused to light his pipe.

"That is not why I wanted to see you..." He looked at Ely and added, "...both." He went on to tell them of Burbage's difficulty in finding a suitable place to show the plays. "He desires to build a new theater. I have a copy of the construction plans. Would you care to see them?"

"I would be very interested," Edward said. Will unrolled an architect's drawing and placed it on his desk. It showed an auditorium with only the tiers and stage having a thatched roof, leaving the center exposed to the weather.

"Burbage calls this 'The Globe' due to its circular shape." Edward leaned heavily on his cane as he viewed the plans, asking Will many questions. "He calls this his second-best theater."

"How much will he spend on this new building?" Ely stood back as Will rerolled the plans.

"Around a thousand pounds, I should imagine," Edward said. "You desire to be one of Burbage's partners and want more money from us. Is that not the reason you are here today?"

"Not so, sir. I have enough saved to contribute, as have some of the other actors."

"This transaction smells of my brother, Francis. Did he advise you to make this investment?" Ely sat back down at her desk.

"Yes, he did advise me."

"I understand. Do you not see what is happening?" Ely turned to Edward. He shrugged and sat in his chair.

"Our Master Shakespeare has seen a way to profit not just from brokering our plays but also from their performance. So far Will has been able to bring our plays to Burbage as a broker with no one the wiser. But I suspect the time has come where Will wants to admit he is Shake-spear."

"Is this true, Will?" Edward asked.

Will's face took on a reddish hue. "Burbage is putting pressure on me to name the playwright."

"You could have arranged this without our consent. What is your problem?" Ely motioned for Will to sit. "Are you afraid he won't believe you capable of writing the plays?" Will shrugged.

"Even after all my coaching to turn you into a gentleman and your new clothes, you cannot convince them of your ability to write plays."

"Ben Johnson is another dramatist who has been selling plays to Burbage. He has been spreading it around that I have not the education or background to be a writer. Some of the others agree. Methinks there are others who know I have been brokering the plays for you—not you," he nodded toward Edward, "but a man of importance."

"Has my name been mentioned?" Ely crossed her arms.

"Oh, no, ma'am. No one would ever believe a woman—"

"Good." Ely turned toward Edward. "Who do you suppose could have said something?"

". I'm certain only Henry Wriothesley knows my pseudonym because of the poems I dedicated to him. If Burbage and Ben Johnson knew I was the playwright, perhaps nothing untoward would happen...especially if I warned them of dire consequences should they spread it around."

"You seem to have forgotten our queen is involved in our subterfuge." Ely put down the quill she had been twirling in her fingers. "I do believe Henry could help us. Please invite him to sup with us soon." She turned to Will. "It is your lack of both a university education and experience with travel abroad that is the problem. You must continue to stay away from the stage, especially from Ben Johnson. Limit your involvement with the actors and do not share your background with any of them...let them wonder. If need be, Edward or someone on his behalf can talk to Richard Burbage. He can be an asset in keeping your secret."

It was ultimately decided Henry would befriend Will, therefore giving Will the appearance of a man of quality. Since Henry was already acquainted with Richard Burbage, he would tell Burbage that Will had been fronting for someone of importance who was willing to allow Will to take credit. Shaksper would now be known as William Shakespeare, and he would say he was the playwright for all the plays Edward and Ely had written since the Henry VI plays were first produced. Edward also agreed Will could take credit for the two poems dedicated to Henry. That alone would give credence to a relationship Henry and Will had never had.

Thirty-six

When beggars die there are no comets seen.
The heavens themselves blaze forth
the death of princes.
                    —*Julius Caesar*, Act 2, Scene 2

Bells could be heard all over London tolling the death of Ely's beloved Queen Elizabeth on March 24, 1603, at Richmond Place. Ely had visited the queen many times during her final days, but her last meaningful conversation had been at Christmastime three months earlier.

Ely was allowed into the queen's bedchamber at Windsor, where she sat in a chair looking out a window watching the snow fall. A fire blazed in a huge fireplace. An unfinished bowl of soup sat on a small table near her. The queen had been in ill health for some days, and Ely was worried the end was near.

"Come in, my dear. I am happy to see you." Ely curtsied. The elderly woman touched Ely's hair and motioned her toward a stool. The action brought back memories of the many times Ely had sat at the queen's feet—some of them historic, when major decisions had been made. "Was the trip from your home difficult?"

"Not so much. We now have a carriage that makes winter trips more comfortable." Ely smoothed the velvet of her dark red dress. The queen's face had been powdered as usual with white makeup, and her attire was more sedate. "I am here to meet with Isaac Oliver to have my portrait painted."

"'Tis tedious sitting still for hours on end. I finally had a mask of my face worn by one of my ladies to sit for a portrait. Seems to work favorably well." The queen smiled. "I don't recall ever seeing a portrait of you. Why is that?"

"I was taught not to bring attention upon myself—or value it overmuch." Ely could still hear her father's harsh reprimand when she asked to be recognized the same as her brother. "Edward has asked for a portrait. When I showed reluctance, he said even Anne Vavasour has one. That convinced me that I should have it done." Ely joined the queen in soft laughter. She looked at the portrait of the queen on the wall next to the fireplace. "Did Oliver paint that one?" Ely pointed toward the painting.

"I really don't remember. There are so many. But I particularly like it." She shifted in her chair, trying to get into a more comfortable position. "When your portrait is finished, I want it to hang on the other side." She pointed to the left of the fireplace. "It is only fitting my daughter should be alongside of me. I want to gaze upon you before I sleep." Ely didn't respond, wondering if the queen's memory was slipping. Did she see Ely as her daughter, rather than granddaughter? Either way, it was proof of the love the queen had for her. "You can always have another one painted for Edward."

The queen started to stand, and Ely jumped up to assist her. "Help me to my bed. I am tired, but I do not want you to leave. I see you so rarely now, I want to prolong our visit."

After Ely loosened the queen's garments, she settled her on the canopied bed, putting several cushions at her back and under her knees. She spread a fur coverlet over her legs. When she was settled and comfortable, Ely pulled up a chair and sat near her.

"Tell me of your life, Ann." Ely was not too surprised she had called her by her mother's name. The queen had been calling her by that name off and on over the past few months. Ely surmised her mind must be dwelling more in the past lately.

Ely told her of Edward and the play he had been working on. Ely had assisted him only nominally, understanding that he seemed to need to write this play alone. She told the queen it would truly be one of Edward's best works; it included his own experiences of being beset by pirates while coming back from one of his trips abroad. The main story told of a Danish prince whose mother was a caricature of Edward's mother, who married too soon after his own father's death. "The girl in the play is called Ophelia. I am sure he was thinking of Anne Cecil when he wrote of her. The prince is called Hamlet, a tribute to Shakespeare's son, though the names were pronounced differently. Edward said that Shaksper would probably not even notice, since he could barely write his own name."

"What of your plays?"

"I believe you saw *The Merry Wives of Windsor* before it played at The Globe." The queen smiled. "*Twelfth Night* you may have seen. Its first playing was two years ago. It is one of my own favorites. Edward and I wrote *Othello* together. He patterned the villain, Iago, after his friend who convinced him Anne Cecil's daughter Elizabeth was fathered by a different man. A bit sad, but life can be sad. I am currently writing one I've titled *Measure for Measure*."

The queen motioned to Ely. "Sit closer. I want you to hold my hand." Ely continued to talk of the plays while holding the queen's soft white hand. When she saw her eyes begin to droop, she changed the subject to talk of her son, Henry.

"Henry is now ten years and progressing well in his studies."

"I should have insisted he be my successor."

"Please, no. I thought we had come to an agreement."

The queen squeezed Ely's hand. "Yes, I know and will keep my promise. Robert Cecil has been pressuring me to appoint James of Scotland, but I am not sure yet. I wish Robert's father were still alive. William gave me such wise counsel. Perhaps it should be James, as it will join Scotland and England closer as one country." Ely was saddened when she saw tears coursing down the queen's face. "All my favorites are dying afore me," she said. "Robin executed for treason. I loved him, but he should not have tried to have me overthrown. Mary executed, but I had nothing to do with that—they plotted her death behind my back. Now they want me to appoint her son as..." She wiped her eyes and turned her head toward Ely. "But I have you."

Ely noticed the queen's eyes closing. "My Robin, I miss him so...am sorry..."

Ely leaned over the queen and saw she was finally asleep. She softly kissed her forehead and tiptoed from the room.

When the queen moved from Windsor to her favorite residence in Richmond Castle, Ely knew it was because that is where she wanted to die. Ely took residence in rooms near the queen. She witnessed her bizarre behavior of standing upright for hours on end. Ely alone suspected the reason. Queen Elizabeth wanted to castigate herself for the lives taken so she could remain in power, especially those of Lord Essex and her cousin, Mary of Scotland. If England would not punish her, she would do it to herself.

~ * ~

A year later, Ely still mourned the queen's death and had turned the major responsibility of raising her son to Edward. She agreed it was time Henry learned what it meant to be the Earl of Oxford. Her son was nearing puberty and she feared he preferred being with his male friends, especially his second cousin, John Hunt. She voiced her concern to Edward, but he seemed to make light of her worry.

Edward had become good friends with King James, and he quite approved of Henry's spending time with the king's sons. Edward introduced the king to the stage, and he loved it. Eventually, he set up his own troupe of players, including Shakespeare, called the King's Men. It didn't take long for Edward to tell the king the true role of William Shakespeare—albeit excluding Ely's involvement. The king agreed to keep the same arrangement Edward had with Queen Elizabeth, even to the extent of continuing Edward's annual allowance of ten thousand pounds.

Just as Ely was beginning to adjust to the death of the queen, Edward became even more infirm. Despite his discomfort, he spent more and more time at the Globe Theater on the off chance the king would show. He even involved himself in the production of the "Shakespeare" plays.

The proximity of The Globe to the River Thames made rat infestation a major problem. Ely was sure this was why Edward had been stricken with the plague. Their son was banned from their home in Hackney and was given rooms at St. James' Palace during Edward's sickness. Edward was confined to his rooms, and Ely and her handmaiden, Marie, cared for him alone. Edward died of the disease on June 24, 1604.

Ely was still in deep mourning for the two people she loved most when Francis came to visit her at her home. He reported Shakespeare was concerned about the arrangement, since Edward was dead. He wanted to know if any more plays were to be written.

"You tell that jackanapes to go to hell!"

Francis consoled her the best he could. "Do you mean you don't intend to write anymore?"

She didn't know why she had showed such anger toward Will. He wasn't to blame for her sadness. But she still always felt an underlying resentment toward the man as he received recognition and wealth from her and Edward's talent and hard work.

"I'm sorry, Francis. All that cursed man thinks of is his purse." She pulled a handkerchief from the sleeve of her gown and wiped her face. "I don't know. I suppose I will in time, but right now I don't feel up to it." She stood from her seat near a window in their library. "I do have one play finished. It's called *Measure for Measure*. Edward and I discussed having it performed before court at Christmastime. Give it to Henry W. with those instructions." She stood up and found the manuscript in a trunk near her desk. "Tell Will to return to his family until he hears from me."

Ely realized she had become victim to melancholy, not only because of her grief but also due to the worry that her son was falling under the influence of John Hunt. She recognized she needed to pull herself to rights. What had always helped in the past was her preoccupation with writing, especially putting together stories that plagued her during her sleep—and now in the daytime as well. As such, her plays began to have a darker focus; gone were the days of the lighter comedies she and Edward so enjoyed writing, playing off each other with amusing quips. Her first play after his death was titled *King Lear*, and it reflected her preoccupation with anger, insanity, and vengeance. Even Will was surprised at the vehemence depicted in the drama.

Thirty-seven

Ignorance is the curse of God,
knowledge the wing wherewith we fly to heaven.
— *Henry VI*, Part 2, Act 4, Scene 7

1606

Ely was delighted when she received a message from her old friend, John Overall, to tell her that he was one of the transcribers of King James' new English language Bible. He was working at Westminster Abbey in London as well as serving his priesthood duties at St. Mary's Church in Hadleigh. She had seen him on occasion when in London, but not since Edward had died. Since moving into her estate in Hackney, she had become a regular member of the church and read her Geneva Bible every night before falling asleep. She looked forward to having conversations with John as they renewed their friendship.

On one spring day, they were having lunch in Ely's garden room. "Tell me more about King James' edict for a new Bible. He sounds determined to have it available for all his people," she said.

"Yes, much to the consternation of Rome. The pope and his bishops passionately believe they will lose control of the church and are in much opposition. There could be violence to curb the translation, but King James will not be deterred, and neither will any of the translators."

"Besides yourself, who else has been selected to make the translations?"

"We started at fifty-four, but now we are forty-seven. There are six companies, two each in Westminster, Oxford, and Cambridge. We have strict rules and work in teams of two. My partner is with the director of Westminster, Lancelot Andrewes. We are becoming good friends."

"Are you assigned certain books to translate?"

"Yes. Our company will be working on Genesis to Kings."

"I am most interested in whom has been selected to translate the Psalms. The poetry of King David must be preserved."

"I agree. It will take a man who has both musical and prose ability to preserve the works of King David. So far, we have not yet found someone suitable within our religious body."

"Will you have more wine, John?" Ely took a sip from her own glass. "Is there something I can do to assist? I have already translated many of the verses for my own benefit."

"I know you have. The Polyglot Bible you gave me years ago has many of your margin notes. Our rules state we are to use the Bishops' Bible as our guide as we translate from Hebrew and Greek."

"Do you have rules that preclude you from using sources outside the list of translators? As consultants?"

318

"I do not believe so, at least that is not in the list of printed rules...however, it would be a good idea to have that person approved by Richard Bancroft, our overseer. He is the Archbishop of Canterbury."

Ely nodded. "I do not expect he would approve of a woman as a translator."

"I suspected that was where your line of questioning was leading. You want to transcribe Psalms." Ely felt the palms of her hands perspire and she rubbed them on her dress. Her mind worked at high speed; she wanted to confide in John, but her instinct for years had been to remain quiet. This was not necessarily for her own sake, but because she would do nothing to besmirch the reputation of Queen Elizabeth. However, if you can't trust a priest...And the queen had been dead for three years.

"John, may I confide in you as a priest and not as my friend?"

"I believe I know what you are about to say." Ely shook her head, not believing he would ever come close to what she was about to tell him. "When I saw the plays *Twelfth Night* and *Measure for Measure*, I suspected I was not hearing the writing of a man, but that of a woman, and I wondered if it could possibly be that of my old acquaintance, Elijah Goodfellow. Your intellect and ability to write amazing poetry, coupled with your connection with the queen and your marriage to a man so closely associated with the stage...I knew it must be you." Ely was shocked at first, but then she couldn't help but laugh.

"You are wise to figure that out."

"No one else knows you quite like I do, either. One thing bothers me...I know it would be unseemly to admit you are the rightful playwright, but does it not make you uncomfortable to allow a man to take credit for your work?"

"Not just for my work, but that of Edward's, too. We have been in collaboration since before we were married. At first it was by order of the queen to write of England's history, but later, for me, it was for the pure enjoyment of working together. Edward's primary purpose was to see the plays performed. But it does gall me to see Will Shaksper take credit, as well as be paid for standing in our stead—the strutting jackass."

"I can well understand that, but have you thought of the outcry should the public find out?"

"Of course. That is the reason we had to keep my name quiet. Since Edward died, I am no longer able to watch rehearsals or have any association with the stage. If I desire to go to the Globe Theater to see my own plays, I must dress as a boy and stand with the other groundlings."

"Well, I'll be hanged. Not fair at all."

Ely finished her wine. "Enough of pitying myself. You have not seen my chapel. We should pray for the success of your translations."

"Yes, I would like to pray for you too, my friend." She hooked her arm into his as they left the room to walk down a long hallway toward her small chapel.

After their prayers, they sat back in one of the two pews before the altar of the Virgin Mother. Ely spoke quietly. "I am so used to working in secret, it would be possible to transcribe the Psalms without anyone being the wiser. I would love to be a part of your endeavor. I assure you this is not for my own glory. It is for that of the king and our Lord."

"I can think of no one who could do a better job, but I don't know. It will be necessary to get approval." John thought of this for a few minutes. "Has it occurred to you to ask King James yourself?"

"If our Queen Elizabeth were still in power, I would not hesitate. In fact, she would have come to me herself. But with King James—that is a different matter. I feel he is not as predisposed to knowledgeable women as was our queen. Edward told him of his arrangement with Will Shaksper, but did not mention me. Edward must have had a good reason not to tell the king, and methinks it was to protect me. No, I don't believe I shall ask him."

"Give me some time to think upon this. May we meet again later? Perhaps they have already found someone to transcribe the

Psalms and Proverbs. I hope not, but I must have time to ponder this."

Another year passed, and Ely heard nothing more from John. She concluded the committee must have found someone else to transcribe the Psalms. She was disappointed, but felt she must continue with her life and spend more time with her son. Henry was with the king's sons more than with her, and there were times she did not see him for days. She was worried when she heard rumors of debauchery with the king's sons and acquaintances. She was relieved when she learned John Hunt and his gang of friends were not permitted within the palace, but wondered if Henry still spent time with him anyway. When she questioned Henry, he laughed and told her she was an old woman for being concerned.

She discussed her worries with Robert Cecil. He advised her to send Henry to St. John's College at Cambridge. She agreed and arrangements were made. Henry did not object, since many of his older friends were already there and it was where his father had attended. Ely breathed easier knowing her son was out of the influence of John Hunt and the older boys of the palace.

It was in the spring when Ely received a message from John Overall to meet with him and the translation committee the following day. She was to bring evidence of her transcription of at least two of the Psalms. She was excited and had Marie assist her in donning her best frock, given to her by Edward as a wedding gift; its buttons were encrusted with jewels.

She was admitted to a meeting room at Westminster where John Overall, Lancelot Andrewes, Thomas Bilson, and Miles Smith waited for her. They greeted her with the deference deserved by a countess. She was seated in a chair across the table from the four men.

"John Overall has previously informed you of our difficulty in finding a suitable man, er, person to transcribe the Psalms." It was Andrewes who took on the role of interviewer while the others listened. "John has been very effusive in describing your ability—and we have reached a point where we are ready to consider you for the privilege of joining us."

"Thank you, sir." Ely bowed her head and crossed herself. "It is truly an honor for me."

Andrewes continued. "Before we make our final decision, we must be assured of your ability. You have brought such evidence with you?"

"Yes, sir." She took the translations from a leather case and pushed them across the table toward him. She had transcribed two of her favorite verses, Psalms 23 and 24. Even though translations had already been made in both the Geneva and Bishops' Bibles, Ely made her translations from the original Hebrew, making sure her version included the melodious singing style of King David. "May I cite them for you?"

Andrewes nodded his head in approval. Singing was not one of her talents, but she did have a steady contralto voice and led her recitation off with, "The Lord is my Shepherd..." She gave the verses the emotion of her own true belief. She must have been acceptable, because when she had finished, all four men stared at her in silence.

John looked from her to the other men. Andrewes cleared his throat. "We will discuss your application, and John Overall will let you know of our decision."

~ * ~

It was nearly a week later, and Ely was on tenterhooks waiting for the committee's answer. She had never wanted anything as much as this assignment. Tired of waiting, she decided to don her oldest wool gown to garden and try to soothe her anxiety. She was on her knees pulling grass from a bed of violets that had just peeked their blossoms through the damp earth when John came upon her without notice.

"Is this the Countess of Oxford I see on her hands and knees?" Ely stood up so hurriedly she nearly tripped on her long gown.

"Oh, John. Why did you not tell me you were...?" She saw he was smiling. "You have an answer." She removed her gloves and tossed them onto a bench nearby. "Tell me, what is it?"

"The answer is yes, but with many conditions."

"Oh, thank you, thank you!" She threw her arms around him and gave him a kiss on the cheek.

"Let us go inside and I'll explain further. It is chilly out here. This is still only April," he said, backing away from her arms. She pushed her long tawny hair, now streaked with gray, from her eyes. "I took the liberty of having your footman bring us a hot drink."

"That is good. I didn't realize...it is cold out here." She brushed grass and dirt from her dress and removed the shawl she had fastened around her shoulders and waist. John opened the door into her garden room.

When they were seated before the fire, Ely's housekeeper brought in hot tea and sweetmeats. "Have you met my waiting-woman and friend, Margery Flower?" John nodded and smiled. She curtsied in return and left the room.

"I love her name—Flower. That may be the reason I hired her after we moved to Hackney. She has served me well." Ely leaned forward and handed John his cup. "I have become very fond of this drink from the east." She took a sip. "Tell me. What are the conditions?"

John reached into a large leather case he had brought with him. "Here they are...these are the same rules every translator was given. I believe we discussed them during our meeting."

"Yes, and I agree with them for the most part. I suspect there are additional rules for me because I am a woman. Am I correct?"

"Of course. You must agree that a woman's place is to—"

"Please, John. Do not spout the same old rhetoric I have heard all my life. A woman's place is to serve her husband because her husband is her lord." She quoted Ephesians.

"For the husband is the head of the wife, even as Christ is the head of the church, and he is the savior of the body.

"Therefore, as the church is subject unto Christ, so let the wives be to their own husbands in everything."

"You did not quote the next verse," John said gently.

"Husbands, love your wives, even as Christ also loved the church, and gave himself for it."

"John, please look upon these verses from a woman's viewpoint. Cannot you see St. Paul was looking upon these matters based on the culture of the time, which has not changed? This gives the man total control over women. That is not right. I could agree with St. Paul if had he said, 'Husbands and wives, love each other as Christ loved the church, and treat each other with respect as equals in life.'"

"I see your point of view, but our laws..."

"Were written by men." She continued her argument until she saw John start to withdraw from her—not just physically, but emotionally as well. "I am sorry, John. You must think I am a heretic to say these things, but there comes a time when women must speak up for themselves without fear. I know for the most part, women, especially wives, have had to learn to be compliant or suffer the consequences. Why do you suppose I remained a spinster so long? Why do you think our queen never married?"

"You did not wish to give up your power."

"Yes, but only partially true. It is mostly based upon wanting to be treated as an equal, not as subservient." John remained quiet, and she felt she was losing a dear friend because of her outspokenness. She realized she needed to make amends if she wanted to salvage their friendship. "I am sorry I got off on a tangent, John. Sometimes my views are best kept quiet." She thought of the girls she had tutored under Queen Elizabeth's command. She had voiced her opinion openly to them; perhaps this was her only contribution for change. She was especially proud of Beth, Edward's eldest daughter. Even now Beth was making progress in establishing her own worth without opposition from her husband.

"Since the first time I met you, when I thought you were a boy, I have respected you. Have I not treated you as an equal?"

"John, you have. And just as all women are not the same, neither are men. It would be good if there were more men like you."

"And heaven help us if there are more women like you." They both laughed. "What about Edward? Did he not treat you well?"

"We had a special arrangement. Because he was much older than I, he had certain...limitations. We were more business partners than the traditional husband and wife, but that's another story I would rather not discuss."

"So be it," he said. "You have already figured out for yourself what you must do to be a transcriber of the Psalms."

Ely was relieved John had returned to the conversation at hand. "It is to remain a secret that I am transcribing." She saw John nod his head. "I am certainly an expert at keeping that secret."

"The committee has determined you will do your work here at your home. I will bring the necessary reference material for you to use as you transcribe, and every two weeks, I will come here to discuss what you have done. I will then deliver your work to the committee at Westminster for a decision."

"Who then will receive credit for transcribing the Psalms?"

"And Proverbs too will be included." He gazed at her. "Is that not understood?"

"Yes. That is proper." She nodded. "You have not answered my question. Who shall receive credit for my work?"

"I did bring that up to the committee. It was decided no one person will, but everyone. That is, it will be known as a combined effort."

"I see. That solution is much preferred over one man—as I have had to do with Will Shaksper. Good. That is acceptable."

"You surprise me, Ely. I thought you would be prepared to argue with the decision."

"What good would it do? I have strong opinions about certain subjects, John, but I am also a realist."

Thirty-eight

I turned over, finding myself snuggled against Clay. I opened my eyes to see dark blue eyes with long black lashes staring back at me.

"And she awakes."

"Um, yes, 'tis me. And thee...let me guess, Shakespeare in disguise?"

"Oh God, I hope not." Clay laughed, putting a lock of hair behind my ear. "Pictures of him are really weird."

"You are far from weird. Very handsome, even without your glasses." I caressed his whiskered cheek. "What time is it?"

Clay rose to look at the clock on my side of the bed. "Seven-thirty. Have any plans for the day?"

"Nope. What do you suggest?"

"I at least know how to start our day," he said as he began to nibble at my neck with his hand roaming over my body.

~ * ~

Waking up, I turned on my back, still in a rosy haze. I could hear my shower turn off. I stretched, grinning like a Cheshire cat. I couldn't remember ever being so happy. My clock said eight-twenty. I sat up and was putting on my robe when Clay came from the bathroom in jeans and undershirt, carrying a shaving kit. He was freshly shaven, with his damp dark hair combed straight back.

"I don't remember you bringing in a case last evening."

"I snuck out to my car this morning while you were sleeping." He unpinned a starched checkered shirt fresh from a laundry, shook it out, and sat on the bed alongside me while he put it on. He kissed me again, then nuzzled my neck. "Last night, was...terrific."

"The best." I leaned against him. "I see you came prepared to stay over."

"Wasn't sure, but I hoped." He laced his fingers through my hair. "I have a suggestion."

"What's that?" I asked, kissing his hand.

"I've been single for a long time, and even before that when... Anyway, I learned how to cook—breakfast is my specialty. If you'd prefer to go out, that's okay."

"No, my kitchen is yours. I love the thought of you making yourself at home."

"That's what I hoped you'd say. I even brought groceries, just in case."

"For heaven's sake. A man in a million."

"I doubt that." He laughed. "While you're showering, I'll surprise you with my expertise."

As I was donning jeans, t-shirt, and coral V-necked sweater, the wonderful smell of coffee and bacon hurried me along. I was putting on light makeup when I heard Clay yell from the doorway. "Breakfast's nearly ready—how about you?"

"On my way, Master Chef."

When I walked into the kitchen, I saw he had chopped fresh veggies, grated cheese, and whipped eggs. "Wow. Omelets." I poured myself a cup of coffee and looked at the mess he was creating.

I couldn't care less, and tried to swipe a strip of bacon. He playfully slapped my hand. I was about to go to the porch to pick up the Sunday *Oregonian*, but saw it was already on the table.

"Would you set the table? Plates are warming in the oven. There's both orange and grapefruit juice in the fridge," he said. I had the wonderful feeling of what being married to Clay would be like, and wondered if he felt the same.

"Look, Clay. We forgot about my pie," I said, picking it up from the counter.

"I saw that," he said. "I have to say, as much as I love apple pie, the dessert we had last night was much better." He ladled the first omelet onto a plate.

"Um, I agree." I put my arms around his waist. He turned, gave me a quick kiss and handed me the plate. Next he opened the oven and pulled out a plate of cinnamon rolls and handed me those, too.

"I suppose you made these too, in your spare time." I laughed.

"Not hardly. They looked good while I was grocery shopping."

For someone who usually ate light breakfasts, I somehow managed to do justice to his light and fluffy omelet. "You are a marvelous omelet maker. What's your secret?"

"Just my magic touch," he bragged. "No, I separate the eggs, whip the whites and yolks separately, then fold them in together. Something my mom showed me years ago."

"You never mentioned your parents. Where..."

"Just my mom. My dad died when I was in law school. He was Sudie's younger brother. My mom's remarried and lives in Phoenix in a retirement community from October to May. Her husband has a small condo in Cannon Beach where they spend their summer months. This year, they plan to take an ocean cruise to Rome and Athens in June. They sure know how to make the most of their retirement. I usually spend Christmas with them in Phoenix, but since Colleen was coming home, I decided to stay here and ski. You know how that ended up."

"It's my turn now," I said, refilling our coffee cups. "You sit here and read the paper and I'll do KP."

"It's a deal. By the way, did you know I have a cabin near Mount Hood?"

"No, I didn't. Tell me about it."

I continued to clean the kitchen as he talked. "I coerced my father into buying it when I was in high school. One weekend, a buddy of mine and I were out looking for a spot to go fishing. We had a rubber raft we hauled around in the back of his pickup. Anyway, we happened to stumble upon Hidden Lake. It was well named. Long story short, we saw a For Sale sign on an A-frame cabin on the far side of the lake and talked to the owner. I convinced my dad we should buy it for a fishing cabin. It's really off the grid. No electricity, and cell phone service is non-existent. But that's what I like about it. A place you can go to just get away from the maddening crowd."

I stopped cleaning for a minute to listen to him talk about his cabin. It was obvious he loved being there.

"Anyway, about a month ago, I heard the roads were open, so I spent the weekend there. I have it all set up now for the summer. I just need to go again with some supplies. I was planning to do that today. Want to ride along?"

"I'd love it. Shall I bring the pie?"

"Absolutely."

~ * ~

We were about a half hour from my apartment when I remembered my cell phone was still on the charger by my bed. I didn't want him to waste time returning for it, so I settled down to enjoy the trip. He was driving his SUV. "It must be nice to have two cars."

"I need it for my trips to the cabin. The elevation is over five thousand feet, and you never know when it may snow."

"Tell me more about the cabin."

"It's an A-frame about fifty feet above the lake. It has its own dock with a trail leading up to the cabin. There's about a dozen cabins scattered in the area. Mine is the last one at the end of a gravel road. When it was built, it was possible to get a ninety-nine-year lease from the forest service. That was years ago, and they no longer permit it, but we were lucky and got grandfathered in." Clay stopped at a red light in Sandy.

"It's close enough to Portland that we were able to go up almost every weekend. We enlarged the cabin by adding a bedroom and bathroom. Dad and I put a lot of work into it—even Uncle Paul came and helped one summer. You know, my aunt Sudie's husband."

"Did your mom or Sudie spend time there?"

"Just day trips. Mom did a few times after we had the bathroom put in." He stopped talking for a few minutes, and I sat back and enjoyed the scenery as we started our climb toward Mount Hood. It was a cloudy day, and we only had glimpses of the snowy mountain.

"I hope you like it. We never minded a few inconveniences."

"I'm sure I will. I've always been an outdoor girl. I went hunting and fishing with my dad lots of times. I tried to be the son my dad always wanted. I loved camping."

"My cabin is just a step above camping out. I haven't come here much after my dad died—just one or two times a year to keep the place from deteriorating. The squirrels take over if you don't keep it up."

As we got closer to the mountain, I saw several inches of snow still piled along the sides of the highway and in the woods, but the road was clear. Passing by Government Camp, we started downhill to where the accumulated snow wasn't as heavy. We turned off the highway at a sign that read "Hidden Lake Campground, 11 Miles." We drove down a narrow two-lane road for several minutes. Once we bypassed the campground, we turned onto a potholed gravel road marked "Dead End." Clay had to use the four-wheel drive to get through a few inches of fresh snow. We continued around the lake for about three miles until we came to a tiny community. A sign by the side of the road said "Wind-Up Trail."

"Strange name," I commented.

"It means what it says. The trail winds up here." We both laughed.

As Clay was unlocking the door, he said, "I'll start a fire to warm it up."

The cabin was as small as I'd imagined, but it looked comfortable. A wide wooden-framed couch with colorful cushions faced an open cast-iron stove with a mesh screen. A box full of firewood and newspapers sat next to it. While Clay was building a fire, I looked around. Along the side of the stove, a windowed sliding door led to a deck that overlooked the lake with Mount Hood off to the north. The room was both the kitchen and living room, separated by a butcher block island. Off to the side was a dining room table with six chairs. I saw a narrow loft above the kitchen.

"You must have a well for water," I said.

"Yes, but we did have to have the house plumbed after we bought it. The original owners just had a hand pump." He pointed to the loft. "My bedroom was up there."

I climbed up a wooden ladder and peeked at the tiny bedroom, which featured handmade twin cots and deflated air mattresses. I climbed down and went behind the ladder into a short hall. Behind a door on the left was a bathroom with a shower. Across the hall was a bedroom with a queen-sized bed and chest of drawers. A plastic sheet covered the bare mattress and box springs.

"There," Clay said, brushing off his hands. "It won't take long to heat up the place. We had the cabin piped for propane gas. All the light fixtures run off it. I've left strikers throughout the house, so no big deal in lighting them." He showed me how to do this. "That's a Coleman lantern on the table. The extra light is needed after dark." I saw a propane bottle screwed into the base of the lantern. "We also found a refrigerator, stove, and water heater that runs off propane, too. All the conveniences of home." He patted the stove.

"It's not nearly as rustic as I thought it would be. How do you get the propane?"

"We have to take the tanks into Sandy to fill them, but I had that done the last time I was here. There should be plenty of gas. Come with me and I'll show you."

He led me to a small shed attached to the back of the house. He unlocked it and showed me the two large propane tanks and how to turn them on and off. Cut firewood, a canoe, and patio furniture were stored inside.

We unloaded the car together. He had the staples of coffee, flour, sugar, etc. in plastic containers. "We need to do this in case a squirrel somehow makes its way in. Doesn't happen often, but you never know." He brought in two large plastic bins full of blankets, linen and towels.

"Why don't we put on a pot of coffee and have a piece of that pie?" he said.

After we finished eating, Clay put our dirty paper plates in the fire. I took my coffee onto the deck to look at the view. "It's absolutely gorgeous here."

Clay followed me. I stared down at the lake surrounded by evergreen trees. I breathed in deeply, the air so fresh it almost made me giddy. "So wonderful, I'd hate the thought it would ever be settled more than it is now." I sipped my coffee.

"Would you be willing to spend a weekend here?" Clay put his arm around my shoulder.

"Anytime. I was thinking...this place would make a perfect writer's retreat."

"You think you'll write a book?"

"Yes, I've decided that would be the best way to present my argument for authorship. I'm convinced Edward de Vere and Elizabeth Trentham were collaborators, and after he died, she continued to write. It makes sense that many of the later tragedies were written by her alone. She must have been in deep mourning after losing both her queen and husband so close together."

Clay changed the subject by asking, "Will you still be seeking a permanent position in a high school?"

"I have no choice. I stopped taking substitute jobs so I could work on our project. It's so close to the end of the school year, I'll try to line something up before fall term."

"Have you considered a change of profession?"

I looked at him and smiled. "To tell you the truth, I've enjoyed my research so much, the thought of becoming an historian would be my dream. But I have to be realistic..."

"Maybe not so farfetched as you may think." Clay moved behind me, pulled me against him, and held me close around the waist. We both faced the lake. "You already have degrees in history and education," he whispered in my ear. "Why not marry me? You could go back to school for a master's in English. Aren't those the credentials you'd need?"

I turned around and faced him. "Did I hear a proposal mixed in with...?"

"I love you, Cynthia. Would you become my wife?"

Thirty-nine

So we grew together, Like to a double cherry,
seeming parted, But yet an union in partition;
Two lovely berries moulded on one stem;
So, with two seeming bodies, but one heart,
Two of the first, like coats in heraldry.
—*A Midsummer Night's Dream*, Act 3, Scene 2

Ely worked under the translator committee's arrangement for several weeks. On her forty-sixth birthday, she happened to be transcribing Psalm 46, the verse from which she and Edward had selected the pseudonym Shake-Spear. Ely thought of that day. Margery and Marie were quietly cleaning the room when Marie, who was using a small metal shovel to remove the ashes from the fireplace, accidentally dropped her tool. The clattering stirred Ely from her work. She smiled and pushed the papers off to the side.

"Margery, Marie. I did not realize you two were in here. I am pleased you are. Please sit. I would like to discuss something with you both." The two women looked at each other, then at Ely. It was not unheard of for Ely to invite them to sit in her presence, but it did not happen often. Margery stuffed her dusting rag in the pocket of her smock and Marie brushed her hands on her dress and curtsied. "There," Ely said, pointing to a bench under a window that overlooked the apple orchard.

Ely stood and walked to a window near where the women sat. "The orchard is in full bloom. I had not noticed. 'Tis truly a sight to see. I love the smell of the blossoms. Springtime is best in England, do not you both agree?"

"Oh yes, ma'am. Shall we have branches cut to bring inside?"

"That would be nice. Put them in a container for the dining room table." Ely pulled a chair near the women and sat down. "Today is my birthday. Did you know?"

"Yes, I did remember. Happy returns of the day," Marie said.

"I am not surprised, given you have been with me for so many years—even when I was lady to our queen," I replied. Marie had a big smile on her face.

"You should have told me, Marie," Margery said. "Howsoever, I do know it is a special day when you have guests for dinner."

"Do not be concerned you did not know. We never have observed birthdays with fanfare." Ely sat back in her chair and crossed her ankles. "This one, however, will be a celebration. My brother Francis and his wife Katherine, the Earl of Southampton and his wife Elizabeth, and my Henry will be here from Cambridge for the weekend. But that is not what I want to discuss with you. I need to get your opinion about a matter that concerns only women, and I would expect you to keep it in strictest confidence."

Both women nodded their heads vigorously. "Yes, ma'am. Of course," Margery said.

"Marie, you have known me for over twenty years, and Margery for nearly ten. You must realize by now that even though you serve me, I consider you friends." Both women looked at each other, not sure what to say. "I know you have overheard conversations I have had with various people, both men and women, and I am not foolish to think you do not know what is going on around here. Let me ask you both—and I expect you to be honest with me."

"Yes, my lady. What is it you wish to know?" Margery asked.

"Are you aware of the work I am doing with John Overall?"

Marie squirmed, and Margery pushed an elbow into Marie's ribs. Marie was the first to speak. "My lady. You have taught me so much these past years, to read and write and to think for myself. I have always served you loyally and will continue to do so until the day I die." She paused and looked at Margery. "I believe Pastor Overall has asked you to transcribe a portion of the King's Bible."

"We also know you have written many of the plays for which Will Shakespeare takes credit. But never fear, no one will ever hear of this from either of us," Margery added.

"I have always suspected you knew and I appreciate your confessing as much. What I want to know is, do you know how I feel about the role women have been forced to play since—well, probably since the beginning of time?"

"'Tis the way it is," Margery said. "We must obey men to avoid punishment."

"That is true, but do you ever feel like rebelling at the notion?" Margery shrugged as if confused by Ely's statement. "How about you, Marie?"

"Well, ma'am. The way I look at it is a smart woman knows how to get around that—when my Archie was alive, God rest his soul, I would cook him a special treat, or tell him how handsome he was, or..."

"You learned the lesson of the golden rule: do unto others as they would do unto you." Ely smiled. "What you send out, you get back in return. Some may call it manipulation, but if you do it with a clean heart, it is not manipulation. I do not condemn you for doing what you needed to do."

"That is what I tried to do. I wanted to be treated the way I was treating him."

"The reason I wanted to talk to you is, I need your help. Marie, I have noticed your sketches over the years, and they show you have talent. Margery, I want you to give Marie ideas on what I want drawn."

"What is it you want me to draw?" Marie asked.

"It is a crest—a Vere crest." Ely stood and reached for her Geneva Bible. "I want you to draw a crest using Psalm forty-six as a guide."

"Is this crest for Henry?" Marie asked.

"No, there are already many Oxford crests and coats of arms. This will be a crest of my own—a woman's crest. That is the secret I want you to keep." She opened the Bible and read them the forty-sixth chapter.

"Many English crests and coats of arms depict a lion. Marie, since you worked at the palace, I know you have seen many coats of arms. Some may give you an idea. Just keep in mind, this is a woman's crest." Ely paused. "Margery, please watch what she is drawing and give her advice. Please come to me whenever you need my direction, but I know you will do well without me."

After she had given the women their task, they departed armed with a slate and chalk, paper, quills, and a small pot of ink. Ely knew they were pleased she had asked them to do her this favor.

Now to her task. As she transcribed Psalm 46, she put special attention to the placement of the words *shake* and *spear* in the verse. She knew she could not change the theme of the verse, and no one should discover it easily. She placed the hints exactly at the forty-sixth word from the beginning and forty-sixth word from the end. Next, she concentrated on verse five, because the use of the feminine *her* and *she* was already there, but she would include one more *her* to make sure it had even more emphasis. This is where she intended to leave the most important clue to her identity as Shakespeare. She then decided to use the words *right early*. "Early" she chose purposely, as it included the letters needed to show hers and Edward's collaboration: Earl and Ely. Like a double cherry on a stem, joined together with one heart.

The word *right* was to mean not only "correct," but "write" as well.

When she was finished, she read it again, satisfied the clues would not be easily discoverable and placement would not change the meaning of the verse.

~ * ~

Two days later, after Ely's guests had departed, the two servant women brought in their concept for Ely's crest.

"We have finished with the drawing. I hope you will approve," Marie said. Ely motioned them to come close to her.

"Let me see what you have." Marie carefully laid the picture in front of her. It depicted a lion standing on hind legs and holding a spear in both paws, just as Ely had instructed. "Yes, I like this. You have chosen a female lion. Especially the point of the spear being the nib of a pen. Very clever."

"'Twas my idea," Margery boasted.

"Why have you broken the spear?" Ely asked.

"We noticed in the ninth verse, God had cutteth the spear. That brings the crest back to Psalm forty-six."

"Brilliant! That is an important clue. Whose idea was that?"

The two servants looked at each other. "I think I saw it in the verse first, but we both came up with the idea," Marie said.

"The female lion does not have a mane. Why do you depict it in this way?"

Marie answered. "We did not know what a female lion looked like, but someone told us a male lion has hair surrounding its head and a female does not. We did not know what to do other than to make the hair look like yours when I finish brushing it."

"Very nice. Thank you."

Margery spoke up. "We were also inspired by another lion on a crest with its mouth open and tongue sticking out."

"I think you should have the lion's teeth against the tongue," Ely said.

"I know what you mean—so it can't talk," Marie said, making changes with Ely's quill. "Maybe the eyes need to be closed, too."

"Long eyelashes, I think," Margery said.

"That's taking shape nicely," Ely said. "The tail. It needs to be like this." Ely took the quill from Marie's hand and dipped it in the ink. "Shape it like an 'S.'" She started to say Shakespeare, but changed her mind and said, "Like a snake ready to strike. My drawing is poor, but you get the idea."

"What is it standing on?" Ely asked.

"'Tis a rope. I thought it would show how easily she could fall off," Marie said.

Ely laughed. "She is balanced upon a tightrope. A testament to my life. Very crafty, and so very true. Please make a clean drawing and I will send it in to register as another Oxford crest." She gazed at the drawing a bit longer. "I like it. Perfect. Thank you both for doing this for me."

Forty

Putting up a card table near my computer, I spread out my research notes and the books and papers I had accumulated over the past months. I was ready to begin to draft my book of the life of Elizabeth Trentham. Glancing through my notes, I again saw my scribbles about Psalm 26, realizing I hadn't yet done the research on John Overall. I pulled his name up on my computer. As I was reading his background, I saw he and his partner were assigned to translate Genesis through Kings—not Psalms. I could find no mention of who did the translating of Psalms and Proverbs.

Was there a chance it could have been Ely? That seemed doubtful, but what if? I squirmed in my chair. Could that be the reason the translator of those two books was not mentioned? I then remembered she would have been forty-six in 1608, a much more likely year for the translation to have taken place.

I then brought up the King James Version of the 46th chapter in my computer. In reading it slowly, I saw in the ninth verse the mention of God "cutteth the spear." Cutteth? What an odd word.

"Holy moly! I can't believe it, but maybe." I had remembered the Oxford coats of arms and crests. One of them was a lion holding a broken spear with a pen nib as its point. It was the same one the Oxfordians used as their logo, the proponents of Edward de Vere as Shakespeare.

I then brought up the pictures of the Oxford crests and stared at the lion. The spear was cut, not broken unevenly or shattered. By then my heart was beating so rapidly, I couldn't believe what I'd stumbled upon. If there were a direct correlation between the crest and the Bible verse, then the crest had to be designed during the translation—1604 to 1611. Edward died in 1604, so it couldn't have been his crest. Who else but Elizabeth Trentham, his wife? Was this proof Ely was the translator? If so, then could this be proof she was Shakespeare?

I was so excited, I immediately called Clay. Jenna, his secretary, told me he was in court. "He mentioned he wouldn't be coming back to the office today." I couldn't sit still. I called his cell phone and left a message that I had exciting news and would meet him at his condo. I proceeded to print out a copy of the lion crest and Psalm 46. I gathered up my laptop and notes.

Once Clay and I had become engaged—I loved that word *engaged*—we exchanged keys to our homes after deciding we'd continue to live separately until we were married. Afterward, we'd look for a house together.

As luck would have it, we both drove to his building at the same time. I threw myself into his arms, bubbling over with excitement. "I think I've found something that has been hidden for four-hundred years! I can't believe it."

"Simmer down, Cynthia. Let's go in and you can show me." I felt like a kid again, I was so excited.

After we went inside, I realized this was only the second time I'd been to Edward's condo. I looked around. So spacious compared to my place. Bay windows with a view of the Willamette River was the focal point.

"Do you mind if I have a scotch before you show me? It was a tough trial."

"Of course not. Clay, I'm sorry. I was so caught up in my discovery, I didn't think. Please relax for a minute." I took a good look at him, and he did seem tired. The worry lines across his forehead seemed more pronounced.

"Would you like a drink, too?"

"Sure. I'll have what you're having. Light, please." I moved to his sofa and sat down with my laptop bag. I saw that a leatherbound collection of Shakespeare's histories was on his coffee table, along with a yellow legal tablet covered in notes. I glanced through the book, seeing it had annotated notes in the margins; it was better reference material than mine. I was reading the introduction when he sat down beside me.

"Here, Miss Enthusiasm," he said, handing me my drink.

"Thanks. I think I'm becoming a scotch fancier." I took a sip. "Remember when Josie told us about the book that was turned into her library that referenced Psalm forty-six and the words *shake* and *spear*?" He nodded. "Well, I never got around to researching the translator, John Overall. That prompted me to look closely at the chapter." I handed him the copy of the 46th chapter.

He read the chapter out loud:

'God is our refuge and strength, a very present help in trouble.

Therefore will not we fear, though the earth be removed, and though the mountains be carried into the midst of the sea;

Though the waters thereof roar and be troubled, though the mountains shake with the swelling thereof. Selah.

There is a river, the streams whereof shall make glad the city of God, the holy place of the tabernacles of the most High.

God is in the midst of her; she shall not be moved: God shall help her, and that right early.

The heathen raged, the kingdoms were moved: he uttered his voice, the earth melted.

The Lord of hosts is with us; the God of Jacob is our refuge. Selah.

Come, behold the works of the Lord, what desolations he hath made in the earth.

He maketh wars to cease unto the end of the earth; he breaketh the bow, and cutteth the spear in sunder; he burneth the chariot in the fire.

Be still, and know that I am God: I will be exalted among the heathen, I will be exalted in the earth.

The Lord of hosts is with us; the God of Jacob is our refuge. Selah.'

"Okay. Now what?" he asked.

"When I read 'cutteth the spear,' it jogged something in my memory." I then handed him the copy of the Oxford crest.

"Note the spear. It looks like it is cut—not broken as it says in the notation at the bottom. The lion was used as a symbolism of God, or perhaps king. This crest fits directly into what the ninth verse says. Also, the notation that it is the Earl of Oxford's crest. But he died before the translations took place!"

"Hold on a minute. You're going too fast." I wiggled around while he thought about it and looked at the verse, and then again at the crest. "So, if this chapter is a tribute to Shakespeare, and the crest is an Oxford crest, then you're thinking the crest was designed after he died...Wait a damn minute. Look at that lion. It's a female!"

"You're right! I never noticed it. I was so excited to tell you about the correlation between the chapter and cut spear in the crest, I didn't take the time to study it further."

"Let's do it now. Maybe there are other clues to find."

Two hours later, and between the two of us, we figured out other clues in the crest. The tail in the shape of an S. The mouth biting the tongue. The lion's hair looking more like a woman's long hair. Then in verse five the repeated mention of "she" and "her."

"*Right early*, in verse five, must mean something," Clay said. "Strange phrase. *Early* is easy, same letters for Earl."

"Also Ely!" I said. "Is this further proof she was known as Ely?"

"Perhaps," he said. "Let's look at *Right*." When he said it, we looked at each other. "Right and Write!" He laughed. "Holy shit. I think we have it!"

Sitting next to him, I felt cold, like someone had just opened a window. Looking around, I saw the same shimmery substance I had seen in Sudie's attic. No—there were two mists, and they appeared to be vibrating. "Clay! Look. Do you see that?"

He lifted his head. "See what?"

"Over there by the kitchen." But they had vanished.

"I don't see anything."

Forty-one

I must be one of these same dumb wise men,
For Gratiano never lets me speak.
—*The Merchant of Venice*, Act 1, Scene 1

Ely raised her arms as Marie helped remove her sweaty nightgown. After slipping on a fresh gown, along with a warm woolen robe and slippers, Marie said, "May I brush your hair, milady?"

"Please Marie. I must look presentable for my guests."

The maid gently unbraided her mistress' long hair, now nearly white. "When will they arrive?"

"Anon—" Ely's response was cut short as she began to cough. Marie stopped brushing and placed her hands upon Ely's shoulders until the coughing subsided.

"Perhaps I should return to my bed. A little more rest until they arrive." After the countess was back in bed, she asked Marie to leave. She did as she was bid, but never strayed far from the door.

Ely had never been bothered with more than an occasional head cold, but when the cold settled in her lungs, the coughing became worse, along with weight loss and nightly sweats. She knew enough about consumption to know she would not recover.

Why now? Didn't I escape the pox that took Dorothy's life? Wasn't I at my queen's side for days on end until she died of the strange malady? Wasn't I able to nurse my husband when he lay dying of the plague? She gave a small shake of her head. *Self-pity is something you've never engaged in before, so why do so now? You have been blessed to have enjoyed fifty-three years of good health. Why should you question God's almighty wisdom?*

She lifted her newly published King James Bible and turned to Psalm 51. She closed her eyes and prayed with words written by King David centuries before and transcribed by her four years earlier:

"Have mercy upon me, O God, according to thy loving kindness: according unto the multitude of thy tender mercies blot out my transgressions. Wash me thoroughly from mine iniquity, and cleanse me from my sin. For I acknowledge my transgressions, and my sin is ever before me..."

As she continued reciting the complete chapter, it brought forth the comfort she sought. Her thoughts turned to a poem written by Thomas Campion. The ending seemed so fitting now:

When timely death my life and fortune ends,
Let not my hearse be vexed with mourning friends,
But let all lovers, rich in triumph, come
And with sweet pastimes grace my happy tomb.

She would instruct her family to celebrate her life, not mourn her death. Having dwelt too long on her dying, she brought her attention back to the unfinished task of writing her will. There were a few remaining objects that needed to be included.

Trying to rise from her bed brought on another coughing spasm. "Frailty, thy name is woman," she thought ruefully, quoting Edward's phrase from Hamlet. After a few minutes, she was able to struggle to her feet and walk the few short steps to her writing table. She rang a bell and Marie quickly came back into the room.

"More wood for the fire, please." Marie bobbed a curtsy and completed her chore. "Tell the cook to prepare a tray. Make certain there is something hot to drink. My guests will be chilled from their journey."

"Yes, milady." Marie bobbed again and left the room.

The canopied bed occupied the rear of the large room with Elizabeth's writing table nearby. A tapestry covered one stone wall, depicting woodland creatures and fairies cavorting about a forested area. On the opposite wall, three narrow, unadorned windows let in the weak winter sun. A portrait of Queen Elizabeth hung on the left side of the fireplace and a portrait of Edward hung on the right. Four wooden chairs of various sizes and a small settee had been placed near the crackling fire.

Ely gazed at the small gilt bell she still held in her fingers. Setting it aside, she picked up her quill pen and listed the bell alongside her mother's name. Jane, a widow now for nearly twenty-five years, had survived not only her husband, but three of her children's deaths—soon to be four. She thought of her mother living her solitary life in the North Midlands, happy with her grandchildren and her garden. *It's the clean northern air that has kept her well. So different from the soot-laden streets of London— the city with its reoccurring plague that came to haunt each house regardless of circumstance.* Ely turned her attention to her will and carefully documented the few remaining possessions and their chosen recipients.

She glanced at the inconspicuous oak chest at the foot of her bed. Anyone looking inside would see bed linens, but underneath was Edward's and her life's work. Since she valued her good name above all else, she dared not list the manuscripts in her will. Beth would be coming soon to collect them. Her stepdaughter wanted to see them published and Ely agreed, providing afterward they be buried with her and Edward in their tomb at St. John-at-Hackney Church.

Ely had just written the final entry in her will when she heard a knock at the door. Lady Katherine Stanhope let herself in without waiting for a response. Ely looked up, laid the quill aside, and with difficulty, pushed herself up from the chair.

"Oh, sweet Kate—you've finally arrived." The two sisters hugged each other. Kate's smile faded.

"Ely, let me look at you," she said and backed away. "You're much worse. Tell me..."

"I'm as well as can be expected, but 'tis the cough that plagues me night and day. The wretched weather is partially to blame, I am sure."

Kate took her sister's hand. "Your fingers are like ice. Come to the fire and warm yourself."

Ely leaned heavily on Kate as they slowly moved closer to the fireplace. "I disliked having you come a far distance but feared to wait longer." Looking toward the door she asked, "Did Francis not travel with you? Where is he?"

"He's on horseback. We stayed at the same inn near Luton last evening. I expected him to be here by..." Kate stopped talking when Elizabeth doubled over with a racking cough. She held a kerchief to her mouth, and when the coughing had subsided, the cloth had rust-colored stains. Kate knew her sister suffered from consumption, but said nothing as she rubbed Ely's back. "Let me bring you a cup of ale."

"By my bedside." She looked at Kate. "My ministering angel shall my sister be."

"Do you suppose anyone would remember when you first used that phrase at Dorothy's grave?" Kate asked as she held the cup to Ely's mouth.

"Probably not." She wiped her mouth with the kerchief.

Ely rested on the settee as Kate covered her with a warm quilt. The women chatted comfortably, with Kate bringing news of the northern shires. They talked of Kate's life, their mother in Rocester, and Ely's numerous nieces and nephews still living in the area. They were interrupted when they heard a rap on the outer door.

"Enter," said Ely. Their brother Francis came in, followed by Margery carrying a tray of hot mulled wine, manchet and butter, prunes, and nuts, which she placed on a table near the fireplace while Francis greeted his sisters. Margery quietly left the room.

After they had exchanged pleasantries and Francis warmed his backside near the fire, sipping the hot wine and munching on a slice of the soft white bread, he inquired after Ely's son.

"Is Henry to be here?"

"Nay. He is not to know the terms of my will until after my death. Is that understood?" She looked first to Francis and then to Kate.

"Please explain. Is something amiss with the young man?" Francis gazed into his sister's pale face. Ely's eyes watered, and Francis moved across the room to sit on the divan next to her. He put her hand in his. "Tell me, dear sister. What may I do to help?"

"I have taken control of the situation." She pulled her hand away as she coughed. This spasm was less severe, but her voice was becoming raspier with each breath. "Please do not concern yourself. I wrote to Robert Cecil and he took the action I requested. John Hunt and his confederates have been banished from England." She paused to take another deep breath. "Henry is now nineteen years, and if he has access to his fortune, I feel certain he will rejoin Hunt and be influenced to return to his former lewd behavior."

"'Tis wise of you to withhold his estate until he is repentant of his rebellious years," Kate said.

"Is the will prepared?" Francis asked. "Shall I call in a lawyer?"

"Please do not insult me, Francis. You know I am quite capable of drafting my own legal document."

"It was not your ability I questioned, but your weakened state."

"'Tis prepared. It lies there." She clasped her hands together. "I did consult with my good friend John Wright of Gray's Inn. Did you receive word that I have asked him and Sir Edward More to join you as executors?"

"I approve of your choices, sister," Francis said. "It appears you have made it impossible should Henry want to dispute your wishes."

"Aye, 'twas necessary. John Wright will manage Henry's legal affairs after I am gone. I expect him to arrive on the hour to serve as a witness. Methinks he is bringing a friend, a Mr. Hawkridge, to witness—and my steward, William Thoroughgood, is standing by. I am sorry Sir Edward More is unable to join us. He has his own family matters to attend to this day."

She watched Francis and Katherine approach her desk. "Please read what I have prepared. I have private requests of you that have not been included in the will. One concerns the transfer of my papers to Edward's daughter, Elizabeth." She looked toward the chest. "The other concern is the amount of the quarterly payments to Will." Kate sat at the desk with Francis looking over her shoulder. "You will take note I have substantial debts, thanks to my dear son."

After a few minutes, Kate spoke. "You are including payments to a 'dumb' man—why not call him by name? And you have omitted the amount. Have you not paid him enough over the years? Why should he receive more after you are gone?"

"I am happy you now know my secret activities, Kate. Only a very few of you are left who know, and I beg of you to continue to keep my confidence. My good reputation means more than any small amount of recognition I might have received. Perhaps someday, someone may be able to discern the truth."

"All the same, it does not seem right you were forced to hide..."

"Hush, Kate," Francis said. "It would not only besmirch her and Edward's name, but ours as well. Even the queen did not divulge—"

"I do not have the strength to argue, Kate. I feel I must continue to pay the man lest he divulge my secret. Now, mum's the word. Is that understood?" Kate shrugged but finally agreed.

Ely knew her sister well and she wasn't at all sure she could trust her to keep silent. But not wishing to belabor the issue, she turned toward Francis.

"To avoid curiosity about including him in my will, I did not write the amount. Let others assume I have befriended a mute. Francis, as we have in the past, please see to it he is paid on the four feast days. Whether you want to continue advising him on investments, I will leave to your better judgment."

"Yes, I understand. I for one am happy he was forced to retire," Francis replied. "Shall the amount be the same as in past years?"

"Whatever amount will ensure his silence."

Forty-two

Clay and I were on our way home from our first weekend at his cabin. We'd taken up more of the supplies I would need to begin my writer's retreat. Clay purchased a solar generator, which would allow me to keep my laptop charged. Even though I wouldn't have access to the internet, I had so many notes and reference materials, I didn't think I'd need it. Enjoying our first weekend together, we made plans for our future and continued to talk about it on our drive back to Portland.

"How long do you think it will take to have the first draft of your book finished?" Clay asked as we passed the campground and headed up the road toward the main highway.

"Let's see. I've already made an outline of what I want included. This is the first of May. I think I could have a very rough draft done by early July—or maybe sooner," I said.

"Judge Andrew Hunter is the man who convinced me to run for circuit judge. When I told him I was getting married, he said he'd love to marry us. What do you think, or would you prefer a church service?" Clay asked.

"I had hoped for a small wedding, just a few close friends. I plan to ask Josie to stand up with me. A wedding before a judge would be perfect."

"Good, I hoped you'd say that. I think we should host a party afterward, though. It would be my way of saying goodbye to all my co-workers and fellow attorneys. You include whomever you'd like as well." Just then, my cell phone rang.

"Hi Josie. We're driving—on our way back from Clay's cabin. What's going on?" I put her on speaker.

"Cynthia. You'll never guess what I found on the UK government website."

"What's that?" I looked at Clay.

"I don't want to tell you—I want to show you." She paused and we could hear her talking to Frank. "I've prepared a large lasagna today and would love you both to come for dinner."

I wasn't keen on seeing Frank, but knew Josie would want him to meet Clay.

Clay answered her. "That would be great, Josie. Thanks for the invitation."

"Clay?" Josie said. "Could—or would you mind bringing the *Midsummer* page? I've, I mean, we've never seen it and..."

"I don't mind a bit, Josie. You're part of our research team and deserve to see it."

~ * ~

We stopped at Clay's condo so he could change and pick up Sudie's strongbox from his safe. Then, we stopped off at my condo so I could change. Next, we picked up a bottle of wine from a grocery store. It was about six when we arrived at Josie's house. Frank opened the door.

"Hello, Frank. This is my friend, Clayton Darnell. Clay, this is—" Before I could finish, Frank interrupted.

"I'm Frank Hacker." He shook hands with Clay. "Let me take your coats." Clay set the strongbox on a small table near the door and helped me take off my coat. Just then Josie came in through the dining room.

"Hi, you two. We're so happy you could come."

"Our pleasure," Clay bent over to give her a hug, then took off his coat. I handed her the bottle of chianti.

"Thanks," she said. "Perfect choice to go with the lasagna. Would you like to come into the kitchen? I want to show you what I found."

"You've really piqued our curiosity." I turned to look at Frank. He had picked up the strongbox and was holding it in his hands. *He's such a jerk.* "Why don't you put that down. Clay will show you and Josie the page later."

Going through the dining room toward the kitchen, I saw Josie had her fine china on the table along with gleaming silverware and crystal wine glasses. A bit fancy for lasagna, I thought. Either this was to honor Clay, or Frank had insisted, which I think was the latter.

"It smells terrific in here," Clay said. "I'm especially fond of Italian."

Josie smiled. "It's nearly ready. We should eat in about half an hour." She walked over to the kitchen table and pulled out some papers from a manila envelope. "Let me show you what I've found. It's Elizabeth Trentham's will!" She looked like the cat who just lapped up cream.

"Her will? You mean, she actually had a will?" I took the pages from her hand. "You've got to be kidding. Wherever did you find it?"

"It's from the UK's archive website. I think it must be a recent entry; otherwise, one of us would have found it before this. I was looking for any documents related to the Earl of Oxford and found this—plus a lot of other stuff." Clay was looking over my shoulder.

"That's amazing," Clay said. We continued to stand in her kitchen.

She pulled out more paper. "Here's Katherine Stanhope's will, too. These women were very wealthy. And here is a letter Elizabeth wrote to Robert Cecil about her son."

I held the page so Clay and I could read it together.

"For Christ's sake, Josie. Have them sit," Frank said.

Clay and I sat, but Josie and Frank continued to stand.

"She sure was religious," I commented after I read the first lines. "Look at all these men she names in her will. More names to research. She was truly wealthy in her own right."

Josie nodded. "Keep reading."

"Dumb man! She left money to a dumb man...Clay, look!" I looked at Josie and she was smiling ear to ear. "This could be proof she was in fact paying Shakespeare to keep quiet."

"I thought the same thing, but then wondered what dumb meant four hundred years ago. I searched to see if dumb was mentioned in any of the plays. Look what I found." Josie picked up her volume of Shakespeare plays from the table and turned to *The Merchant of Venice*. "Here, look." She pointed to act 1, scene 1 and read aloud, "'I must be one of these same dumb wise men, for Gratiano never lets me speak.'"

"This is proof, four hundred years ago, dumb meant to keep silent."

"Oh, I wish Sudie were here to see this!" I stood up, pulled Josie close in a hug and we jumped up and down like teenage girls. Clay grinned but continued to read the document. Frank looked disgusted.

"How about something to drink?" Clay was too engrossed in reading and must not have heard him. Frank tapped his shoulder.

"Want a drink?"

Clay looked up. "Sure, thanks."

"I have a bottle of scotch in my office. Come with me?" Frank turned to Josie. "My ice bucket is empty."

Josie stepped back from me as Frank and Clay walked down the hallway. This was another way to get from the kitchen to other rooms in the house, ending back in the living room. "I need to take the lasagna from the oven."

"I'll do it," I said. When Josie returned with the ice bucket, I tried to pin her down. "Why do you let him order you around like you're his servant?" I whispered.

"It's no big deal," Josie said as she filled the bucket. "There's white wine in the refrigerator. Help yourself. I'll be right back."

I saw a loaf of French bread on the counter and decided I'd help.

After she returned, I said, "I'll be going to Clay's cabin for a few days. I'm hoping to leave tomorrow or the next day." I went on to tell her about the cabin and where it was located. "It's a perfect place for a writer's retreat."

"What kind of report do you plan to write?" She took a small dish of melted butter and garlic from the microwave and handed it to me.

"Actually, I've decided there's enough material we've accumulated to write a book of Ely's life. You finding her will, plus Clay and I solving the riddle of Psalm forty-six, puts the icing on the cake."

"You didn't tell me. You solved...?"

I explained how Psalm 46 had a direct correlation with the Oxford crest. I briefly told her where to look for the other clues we'd uncovered. "When I get back, let's get together and I'll show you. It's really exciting. I think we've accomplished what Sudie wanted...and even more."

"There's something I want to tell you, too. I'm glad we're alone," Josie whispered. I hoped she was about to tell me she was kicking Frank out of the house, but it was just the opposite. "I'm pregnant."

"Josie! My goodness—that's a surprise." I looked closely at her, trying to see how she felt about it. "You don't know for sure?"

"Yes. It's due this fall."

"What does Frank think about it?"

"I haven't told him. I know I need to tell him, but I'm afraid." Josie grabbed my arm. "He'll tell me to get another abortion. That's what happened a month after he moved in here." Her eyes started to cloud over. "I want this baby, Cynthia, and don't know what I'll do when Frank..." She quickly dried her eyes. "Before, I was just a week overdue and...I went to the clinic. I felt so miserable about doing it. Guilty, too." I put my arms about her. "Oh, Cynthia. I really want a child."

"I know you do. You're great with children. I know you'll be fine even if Frank...We'll figure something out."

"I know you don't like Frank. Now I know how right you are. I went off the pill thinking having a baby would cement our relationship and we'd be married. I know now how naive I was."

"You'll need to decide what you want most. Frank or the baby." She sniffled and backed away from me. "You've got time to figure this out. I'll help in any way I can...Clay too," I said. I had planned to tell her about being engaged, but today wasn't a good day either. "Why don't we have our dinner and Clay will show you the *Midsummer* page. Can you put your mind off it? Until I get back anyway?"

"Yes. I will," she said. "Let's finish getting our meal on the table."

When it was ready, I went down the hall to tell the men. I was surprised, then angry, to see Clay had the strongbox open. Frank must have convinced him...Oh God. I hope he didn't give him the page to have tested. This too was not the right time to say anything...

After dinner, when Clay and I were on our way home, I told him about Josie's pregnancy. "She's wanted a child for as long as I've known her. She sure as heck picked the wrong father, though," I said.

"I'm happy for her, but I can certainly understand why you have misgivings about the man. He tried to convince me to give him the page to have it tested. I told him that I wanted to be present when the testing was done." He looked at me. "Which, by the way, I think we need a reputable firm to do, not Frank."

"I so agree. Do you want it done right away, or should we wait until the book is published?"

"Later—I think." He turned the corner into his parking garage. We continued to sit in the car after he turned off the engine. "I did give Frank one of the blank pages to have tested—just to get him to shut up about it."

"Blank pages? Oh, that's right. Sudie said they used them to stiffen the binding in the prayer book," I said. "I wondered why you had opened the strongbox for him."

"When I showed him the Shakespeare page, he was more impressed as to how much it would be worth, rather than the historical significance. Sure a lot different than when Josie looked it over. She was so much in awe, she nearly cried."

"I know. She always had a deep reverence for literature and reading—which is why she's a librarian," I said. "Before I drive this to the cabin, is there anything special I should know?"

"Not really. Everything is automatic, no matter the weather. Just drive it like any other car." He handed me the keys.

We had already discussed my taking his four-wheel drive to the cabin. Even though it would be nice to spend the night with him, it made more sense for me to go on home so I could get ready for my retreat.

"I want to give you my pistol to take, too. It's in the glove compartment. Don't leave it in the car, though. Better take it out and put it in your suitcase."

"Pistol. What do I need it for?"

"Probably won't, but just as a precaution. You'll be taking walks and you never know when you could meet a wild animal. There have been cougar sightings in the area over the years. It's doubtful you'll see anything, but just in case. Don't try to hit it, just shoot to scare it off."

"Will you be coming up over the weekend?"

"Yes, I plan to—Friday night, I hope. Howard McCall is loaning me his pickup. You haven't met him yet. Another attorney in our firm."

I left him waving goodbye to me from the parking garage.

Forty-three

Tomorrow, and tomorrow, and tomorrow,
Creeps in this petty pace from day to day
To the last syllable of recorded time.
And all our yesterdays have lighted fools
The way to dusty death. Out, out, brief candle!
Life's but a walking shadow, a poor player
That struts and frets his hour upon the stage
And then is heard no more. It is a tale
Told by an idiot, full of sound and fury,
Signifying nothing.
                                        —*Macbeth*, Act 5, Scene 5

June 1613
Elvaston, Derbyshire

An apple blossom branch snagged Kate's headscarf, pulling it away from her hair. She stuffed it in the pocket of the long muslin overcoat she wore on this warm spring afternoon, the coat only needed to protect her white and green cotton lawn dress. Brandishing her small blade, she cut more of the fragrant blossoms. Nothing is more like heaven on earth than a spring day in rural England, she thought, as she set about filling her basket with lavender, wild roses, daisies, and violets—every now and again pulling grasses away from the roots of her prized flowers. Her basket full, she walked across the yard and entered through the back door into the scullery.

"Mary."

A servant dressed in a long gray dress came from the hallway wiping her hands on a soiled rag. "Yes, ma'am. What is it?"

"Fetch me two containers. I'll arrange these myself." The maid gave the lady a quick curtsy and disappeared down a dark hall. Kate set the flowers on a scrubbed wooden table in the middle of the cavernous room. She breathed in the wonderful aromas created by the smoked meats and cheeses hanging from the low ceiling. Marsh and lavender rushes scattered the dirt floor, and stewing chickens bubbling in an iron pot hung on a spit over a fire in the open fireplace. Barrels and kegs filled with staples and ale were stacked on racks against one wall, and water pots and wash pans were piled on a bench near the rear door that led to the gardens.

Kate hummed as she sorted the flowers according to length. Holding a sprig of lavender to her nose, she breathed in its soothing fragrance. It reminded her of Ely, who had given her the lavender starts from her own garden. Kate's thoughts often returned to her sister, dead now these past six months. *So much unfairness in this world, and my sister's life the best example.* She pulled unwanted leaves from the prickly roses. Her sister's advanced intellect and talent far surpassed that of any man she'd ever known. Mary returned carrying two brass urns.

"Will these serve, or should they be smaller?"

"No—'tis good. I'll arrange the violets in a nosegay and pin them to my frock." She set the violet stems into a cup of water. "Did cook tell you we're twenty for dinner tonight?" Kate was now a widow, having lost her husband, Sir John Stanhope, two years earlier. She had remained on in the Stanhope ancestral home in Elvaston even though her stepson, Philip Stanhope, had inherited the manor and lands. The baby boy born after John's death was playing with his toys in the nursery, watched over by his nanny.

"Yes'm. Cook told me Sir Philip will be having business associates here after eventide. She's gone to the fishmonger and is having me polish the silver." Kate secretly dreaded the day she would be relegated to a more subservient role when Philip married. In the meantime, she accepted her role as housekeeper, though she missed her position as John's wife. Fortunately, John also owned a small house nearby, which he had left her in his will along with a sizeable yearly allowance, but this was the only home her children knew, and she would stay on as long as her youngest children needed her.

"Fetch a pitcher of water and fill the urns. You may then return to your other duties." After the flowers were arranged, Kate called again to Mary. "I desire a cup of broth. Come join me, Mary."

Her favorite servant came back into the scullery and gave her mistress a grin, showing several missing teeth. Taking two earthenware mugs to the fireplace, Mary took a piece of cloth to protect her hand from the heat, swung the iron pot forward, and dipped out ladles of broth from the stewing chickens. The women sat on stools in front of the fire, visiting as they dipped hunks of bread into the broth, enjoying their repast together.

"It's nearly midsummer. Do you remember telling us fairy stories when you first came to serve my mother in the kitchen?"

"Very well, ma'am. Children love to hear the stories."

"I know we did. After Ely saw the fairies, we all wanted to go in the fields on Midsummer's Eve, but only Ely was brave enough. I for one was too afraid of being captured by the pixies."

They laughed as they spoke of the lives of their respective families who lived in Rocester, where Katherine's brother Francis and mother still lived. Her mind wandered again toward her sister, which led to their discussion of Ely's son.

"How is the young lord now? Missing his mum, I should imagine," Mary said.

"That rogue. He was such a trial to my sister. I have no idea where he is. Traveling abroad, last I heard. Now he's of age, I suppose he's spending his inheritance as fast as his father did afore him." Kate took a sip of broth and continued, "Ely had just the one son and I have eleven children, counting Philip, all of whom are better behaved than he." It wasn't as though Kate made a practice of gossiping with the servants, but Mary was more like one of the family, having been with her for nearly forty years, serving as both nurse and maid.

"Oh, my lands. I nearly forgot. Whilst we were givin' the library a good cleanin' this morning, I found a scrap of paper. I thought it best not to throw it away until I showed it to you." Mary stood from her stool. "I'll fetch it." When she returned, she handed the page to Kate. "I don't know if it fell from a book, or what. I wish I could read, but..."

"No. It's Ely's handwriting—a poem, I think." After she had read it, she smiled and held the page close to her breast. "It's not just a poem, but methinks it's a page from a play. Come, show me where you found it."

Kate followed Mary as she led her down the hall. They crossed the dining room and entered through another door that led to the library.

"It had lodged itself right behind that desk, stickin' between the paneling and a sliver of wood. I don't think that heavy thing's been moved in ages. It took Harris, Botchkin, and me all shovin' and pushin' to budge it."

"It must have been lost the fortnight Ely stayed here. That would have been when young Henry was a baby." She turned toward Mary. "Remember when we all traveled to Rocester to visit my mother?" Mary nodded. "My sister came here for solitude whilst she finished a play. She wanted to have it completed before the wedding of her stepdaughter. I'm sure this is one of the pages." Kate looked at the large desk. "I wonder how it came to be behind the desk—mayhap a gust of wind." She paused as if deep in thought, then smiled and said, "Thank you for finding this. You may go now." Mary curtsied and left the room.

Kate sat at the desk and smoothed the paper with her hand. She sharpened a quill, dunked it into a pot of ink and started to write her sister's name on the bottom of the page, but she stopped herself and left only the name Ely. She realized that no one would believe this was a piece of her sister's work, even if she wrote her sister's full Christian name on the document. She needed more proof, something more significant. No one would ever admit a mere country woman was capable of writing poetry and plays...but maybe someday. Kate at least hoped there would come a time when women would be accepted on an equal level with men—even if it took a hundred years.

A plan began to germinate in her mind...a plan to help Ely receive the credit she deserved. She stood and began to pace, trying to think of a way she could use this page to prove Ely wrote it. She casually picked up her book of prayers that was lying nearby and noticed the leather cover had become loose. She then had her answer.

She took several blank pieces of parchment and a pair of scissors from the desk drawer, and using her prayer book as a guide, she cut the paper slightly smaller than the book. She pulled open a drawer and removed a pot of glue. She then uncorked a different bottle of ink, a special ink her husband had used to write secret dispatches. With a smile lurking about her lips, she began to write a letter to no one in particular.

Forty-four

It was Friday, my fourth day at the cabin. I had made progress with my writing, finishing with the argument that it was not logical for Shakespeare to have been the true author of his works. It was easy to pull together Edward de Vere's background from books and articles I had read that postulated he was the logical playwright, but I needed to show how it was also logical for his second wife to have been his collaborator, who carried on after his death. Sudie's page and the solved riddle of Psalm 46, along with the de Vere crest, allowed for proof of my work. Now that I had Elizabeth's will, I felt even more confident. What I lacked was the ability to prove she had the innate genius to be the writer. Even with the historical facts I had of the Trentham family from Emma's journal, how Ely received an education was still an unknown. Coming to an impasse, I decided to take a break and walk to the campground on the other side of the lake.

The sun had come out and I wanted to take pictures of the area to send to Mark. Our correspondence was done entirely through email. I did miss the written letters, but there was no holding back progress. I went into the bedroom to change into warmer clothes and my snow boots. I reached into the side pocket of my suitcase for my woolen scarf when I felt Clay's pistol; I remembered putting it there after taking it out of the car.

Since I would be on at least a six-mile walk and the area was deserted, I decided it would probably be a good idea to carry it. I pushed the clip into the handle and made sure the safety was on before slipping it into my jacket pocket. Deciding to take a small backpack, I packed a lunch and put in my writer's journal in case I received divine inspiration on how to continue with my story. My cell phone was in another pocket to take pictures and hopefully get a signal. It would be nice to know if Clay was coming for sure.

Thus armed and with the door locked, I began my walk down the road with the majestic, snow-covered Mount Hood as my companion. I took a multitude of pictures across the lake toward the mountain. I challenged myself with trying to identify the different types of evergreen trees surrounding me. It was over an hour later before I reached the campground. Pine needles, cones, and leaves covered a picnic table, and after I brushed off a place to eat my lunch, I sat down with my tuna sandwich. Still no signal on my phone. A little chipmunk jumped on the table and gave me a bright-eyed look. I laughed and tossed it a bit of crust. It scurried off with the bread in its mouth.

I pulled out my journal and had started to write about the scenery when I noticed the wind pick up and clouds start to form, hiding the mountain from my view. Deciding I'd better head back to the cabin, I repacked my backpack and took off at a much faster pace.

Light snow began to fall just as I reached the cabin. I hung the backpack on a row of hooks to the left of the doorway along with my coat and scarf. After I freshened the fire with a few small pieces of wood, I went into the kitchen to heat the coffee.

It had got much darker outside, so I lit the lantern in the center of the table. The heat from the lamp felt good to my icy fingers. Sitting with coffee and a cookie, I opened my laptop and read what I had written that morning, still feeling no closer to knowing how to proceed with my story of Ely. Thinking I still needed inspiration, I opened the strongbox on the floor next to my feet. Rereading the *Midsummer* page, I remembered this is what had started my journey with Sudie. It never ceased to give me a thrill, knowing it had been written over four hundred years ago.

Perhaps what I needed was to read Emma's journal again; maybe that would help point me in the right direction. I took out everything from the box including the blank pages. Fingering one of the pages, I wondered if they were really used to stiffen the binding. I held it in front of the lantern to examine it more closely and much to my surprise, writing began to appear.

"Oh, my God. What is this?" I moved the page around the heat, and more writing came into view. I picked up another page and did the same thing. This page was signed, Lady Katherine Stanhope, Wife of John Stanhope, Knight. My hands were shaking by the time all four pages had been held to the heat.

"What have I found?" I stared at all the pages. The writing was tiny, but neat. I couldn't make much sense of what she had written other than to realize one page was addressed to "Whoever is reading this letter." Realizing I had identified the first and last pages of a letter, I needed to find out where the other two fit in. My heart was beating so fast I almost felt faint. I took several deep breaths. I took a sip of my now-cold coffee and decided what I needed was a glass of wine to settle my nerves. If only Clay or Josie were here to help me decipher what I had just uncovered! I picked up the pages and set them on the coffee table in front of the fire. Putting on another log, I went to the pantry to pour myself a glass of red wine. I sat on the sofa to read what Katherine Stanhope had written.

The style of writing four hundred years ago required some deciphering. This would be challenging because some of the words seemed to be missing or faded. I assumed writing with invisible ink would have been difficult. I went back to the table to get my laptop. I opened a blank document and began to type my translation.

5 June 1613

My sister is Elizabeth Trentham Vere, a royal lady to Queen Elizabeth for ten years and second wife of Edward Vere, the seventeenth Earl of Oxenford. She died six months ago, keeping secrets I will reveal. My brother, Francis Trentham, and I promised we would continue to keep her secrets, and by using invisible ink I am honoring my promise until such a time as it no longer matters. This information must not die with her.

Countess Elizabeth was known as Ely by her family, and they called me Kate.

It was fitting I found a page from a play my sister wrote titled A Midsummer Night's Dream. I will hide the page with this letter in my book of prayers with the hope a kinsman will find it first. She wrote this play for her stepdaughter, Elizabeth Vere, for her wedding celebration. Ely resided in my home that summer to escape from the black plague in London.

My sister is not a blood relative of my parents. My brother told me this after Ely's death. She was raised as their own child from the time of her birth. Ely's birth mother, Ann Sneyd, was the bastard of Queen Elizabeth, born when the princess was fourteen years of age. My kinswoman, Dorothy Sneyd, was a lady-in-waiting to Catherine Parr and a friend to Princess Elizabeth. Dorothy took Ann as her own child. Dorothy and baby Ann came to live in Chester with Dorothy's brother, William Sneyd, a lawyer and knight—our grandfather. Ann married a seaman. She died after giving birth to Elizabeth. On her deathbed, Ann asked her cousin, Jane, and her husband, Thomas Trentham, to raise her baby.

No one knew the truth of Ely's birth until it was revealed after she became a maid for our queen. Ely was loyal to the queen and promised never to reveal the truth of Ann's birth.

Ely excelled as a student of our tutor, Master Anton Regiers. We all learned French from him as well as Latin, Hebrew, and Greek, but Ely learned other languages after she became a maid to the queen. Her memory was remarkable, and she could recite long poems and Bible verses. Her passion was writing poetry and plays. She loved the theatre, and that is what she and Edward had in common. It was through him that she began to write plays that were performed in London."

At this point I had read three pages. It was then I remembered Clay had given a page to Frank to have tested. I hoped he had not discovered the writing before I had a chance to tell Clay, and that we could get the page back. That page must tell of her marriage and having a son.

I continued to read the final page:

...forced to write anonymously or use the name Edward used: Shake-spear. Lord Oxenford allowed a man from Stratford-upon-Avon by the name of William Shaksper to take credit as the playwright. Ely and my brother paid this man to keep the identity of my sister unknown. That is the secret my sister took to her grave.

Some of the plays were based on experiences she had growing up in Rocester. One experience was so profound that plays were produced telling of how she was dressed as a boy. She ran away from home in our brother's clothes to escape a marriage my father had arranged. She ended up in Chester in the home of our kinswoman, Dorothy Sneyd. She continued to dress as a boy as she worked in Grandfather Sneyd's law office. My brother also told me Ely was asked to work with King James' translators of the Bible. I am not sure if she transcribed all of the Psalms, or just the verses of King David. These were her secrets. You may reveal them as is appropriate to your time.

—Lady Katherine Stanhope, Wife of Sir John Stanhope, Knight

I had wanted to tell Ely's story, and here I had it in front of me. The page Frank had must cover the ten years with the queen, her marriage to Edward, and the writing of the plays. I felt the urge to get in the car and take what I'd found to Clay—or at least go somewhere I could get cell phone service.

While I was trying to decipher Katherine's archaic writing, it had become very dark outside. I opened one of the sliding doors to the deck. A thin layer of snow covered the ground. It was after eight and the fire had died down, and I was hungry. Going somewhere tonight would be out of the question. Even with four-wheel drive, I didn't relish driving in the snow after dark. Resigned to another night here, I laid the letter and the *Midsummer* page out on the table close to the lantern and took careful pictures of each of the pages with my phone.

When I stirred the embers in the fire, I put on a few sticks of kindling and the last piece of wood in the box. Needing to fill the wood box again, I pulled on my jacket and picked up a flashlight to go to the shed. It had stopped snowing. I saw headlights headed my way.

Oh, Clay's here! I waved and stepped down onto the driveway. He parked next to me—but wait. This wasn't the pickup Clay was going to borrow. A man stepped out of the passenger side. I pointed my flashlight into his face. It was Frank. He wasn't alone. Thinking the driver must be Josie, I turned the light toward the face, but it wasn't she. It was a man I had never seen.

"Hello, Cynthia. Surprised to see me?" Frank walked toward me.

"To say the least. I'm expecting Clay. Why are you here—and who's that man?" The driver remained in the car.

Frank turned around. "Him? You don't want to know. Let's go into the house and I'll tell you why I'm here."

Why doesn't he want me to know? I was instinctively afraid. I didn't want Frank in the house. "I was just on my way to get more wood for the fire."

"It's good I came. I'll help you."

"I don't really need any help, but if you want to, it's in the shed." I pointed to the back of the house.

He turned toward the shed, but I remained standing. "If you don't mind, I need some light."

He acted friendly, but I still didn't trust him. The last thing I should do was to go into that dark shed with him. "Here, take this." I handed him my flashlight and turned to go back into the house.

I looked back toward the car, but the man hadn't moved. I let myself in through the side door and considered locking it, but decided it would be futile. I stood by the stove waiting for Frank to come in. I shoved my hand into my pocket and touched the pistol. Would I need it? I hoped not, but took the precaution of releasing the safety. After a few minutes, I saw the flashlight come toward me. Frank was on the deck, and I could see him standing in front of the sliding door with his arms laden with firewood. He must not have noticed the side door in the dark. He smiled at me. I slid it open.

"It's slippery out here; damned near fell down." I stepped away from him, pointing toward the wood box. He dumped the wood into the box, took out two pieces, and put them onto the fire. The mesh screen sat off to the side where I had put it earlier.

"There, that does it," he said as he brushed the sawdust off his black leather jacket. He took off his gloves and put them into a pocket. I backed up toward the side door, watching his every move. He turned toward the table. Sudie's page and the pages from the prayer book with the revealed writing were obvious.

"Ho, ho. I see you found out those pages weren't blank after all." He started to laugh. He looked back at me. "That's one of the reasons I came. I wanted you to know how to reveal the writing." He moved to the table and picked up one of the pages. "I wondered what they said. The page I have does offer proof that woman was actually..." He started to read.

"Put it down, Frank. It's about time you told me why you're here...and who is that man?" I backed up further toward the door, thinking I could run if I needed to.

He turned toward me, still holding the page. "That guy? You'll need to be careful. He's a bad man."

"What do you mean? What did you...? You're gambling again."

"Again? Josie opened her big mouth, didn't she? The bitch." He started to snicker. "What an idiot."

"You're the idiot. She loves you, and you've done nothing but use her from the beginning. I don't like you, Frank. I never did. I want you to leave—now."

"I'm taking these with me," he said as he started to gather the pages together. "Ah, and here is the famous Shakespeare page. I didn't expect it to be here." He had a huge smile on his face.

"Put them down, Frank. I'm not kidding." I pulled the pistol out of my pocket.

"What the hell?" He continued to hold the page. "Put down the gun, Cynthia. You don't know what you're doing. You won't have a chance against that guy."

"I mean it. I'm not afraid to shoot. Down—now!"

"You don't understand. He said he'd kill me if I didn't..."

The door suddenly flew open, crashing into my back. The gun went off, an explosion. I was falling toward the fireplace; then, only darkness.

Forty-five

Smoke...I coughed. I felt icy grass against my face.

"Cynthia! Where are you?"

Piercing pain—couldn't hold my head up. "Here." My voice only came out as a whisper. I cracked an eye open. Blue lights flashing in circles. People wandering around in a haze. Am I dreaming? Feeling nauseous, I closed my eyes again. "Cynthia!" The voice was closer—I forced my eyes open once more.

"Here." I could barely talk, my throat dry and sore. I tried to swallow. "Here!"

"She's over here! Oh, thank God." Clay's voice. He came? I felt tears streaming down my face and my shoulders being lifted onto his knees. A flashlight beamed in my face. I had to squint. Everything so blurry. I retched, trying to throw up.

"Let me see her." A police officer leaned over me, his light in my eyes. "Concussion, I think." I could feel him checking my arms and legs. "Her jacket sleeve is burned. Her wrist will need to be tended to." He stood up. "It would be faster if we drove her to Government Camp. I'll call for an ambulance to meet us there." He looked around. "Whose SUV is this?"

"It's mine," Clay said.

I must have passed out again because when I awoke, I was reclined in the back seat of Clay's SUV, a blanket wrapped around me. Someone was holding my hand. "Josie. Clay? Where's Frank and...that man?"

"I'm taking you to Government Camp. An ambulance will take you to a hospital," Clay said from the front seat."

"We couldn't find Frank," Josie said. "Can you tell me what happened?"

"My head hurts. Throat's so dry."

"You must have breathed in a lot of smoke before you escaped from the house," Clay said from the front seat.

"Don't remember. How did I get outside? Who...?

"You must have been conscious enough to get yourself out of the fire," Josie said. "Can you tell us what happened?"

"Don't make her talk now," Clay said. "The police will want to question her, too. Let's get her to the hospital first."

"I think I shot Frank."

"What! You shot him?" Josie yelped, dropping my hand.

"Josie, stop. We don't know what happened. He may be fine. Maybe hiding out somewhere."

"Cynthia, the police stopped a car racing down the road near the campground. The man was alone. They're taking him in for questioning." Josie squeezed my hand. "The police will search for Frank when it's light," Clay said.

"The man hit me in the back..."

"We're here now." They moved me onto a stretcher and then into the back of an ambulance. They put something in my nose. Then everything faded to black once more.

~ * ~

The next morning, I discovered I was in a small hospital in Gresham. I had a concussion and a nasty burn on my right wrist. I had just finished a light lunch when Clay came in.

He leaned over and kissed me. "How do you feel?"

"Better. Do you know when I can go home?"

"No, I don't. Haven't seen the doctor yet." He sat by my bed and reached for my hand. "Josie's here—the police, too. They have her in a room taking her statement."

"Statement, why should she need...?"

"It's about Frank. The police will be here shortly to take your statement, too. They gave me time to talk to you first. I'd like to act as your attorney while they're in here. Is that all right with you?"

"Lawyer? Why do I need a lawyer?"

"I don't think you do, but my gun was involved and..." He kissed my hand.

"What? Clay, what are you trying to tell me?"

"They found Frank's body this morning."

"Oh my God! I killed him? Clay, did I...?"

We heard a knock at the door and two men came in. One was in a uniform and the other was in plain clothes. They introduced themselves as detectives from Clackamas County.

"Do you feel well enough to tell us what happened last night in Mr. Darnell's cabin?"

"It's okay, Cynthia. You had a severe bump on your head. We can postpone this if you still feel unwell."

"I'm okay, Clay. I want to know what happened. I have a lot of questions, too."

"What do you remember, Ms. Parsons?" one of the men asked. "And why were you in his cabin by yourself?"

"I was working on a book—sort of a writer's retreat. I had valuable historical documents and had been trying to transcribe some writing. Around eight—I remember looking at my cell phone. I had been so engrossed in my work I'd lost track of time." I looked at Clay. "Should I tell them about our project?"

"Mr. Darnell already gave us a statement. Just tell us what occurred when Mr. Hacker and Mr. Mendoza drove up."

"Was that the name of the other man? He never got out of the car until...Frank said he was a bad man. Gangster, I guess." I reached for the glass of water on my bedstand. Clay handed it to me. "I had on my jacket to go to the shed for more firewood when I saw headlights. I waved, thinking it was Clay." I went on to tell them about how friendly Frank was, bringing in firewood, then telling me he needed to take the pages. "He told me he'd be killed if he didn't take them. I assume he intended to sell them so he could pay off gambling debts to that man. I had Clay's gun in my jacket pocket and—"

The detective interrupted. "Why did you have a gun?'

"Just as a precaution, since I'd be by myself. I took a long walk yesterday. Clay said I might need protection against wild animals... that's why it was in my coat pocket."

"Was there any other reason you wanted her to have a gun?"

"Not really," Clay said. "I doubted anyone knew where she'd be, but gave it to her just in case someone showed up. If I'd known, I would never have allowed her to go to a remote area alone. The gun was just an afterthought. When I found out from Josie Jenson that Frank knew where Cynthia was—that was when I called the police."

"We'll need to get more information about that later, but for now, please continue, Ms. Parsons."

"I did tell Josie where I was going."

"You must have given her the location of the cabin, too," Clay said. "Don't worry about that now. Just tell them what happened."

"Frank saw the documents on the table, and got excited. He picked them up and was ready to take them. That's when I held the gun on him and told him to put them down. He said the man with him was dangerous. I was standing by a doorway, thinking I could run if I needed to, when the door opened suddenly and hit me in the back. I remember hearing an explosion and getting pushed toward the stove. I'm not sure, but it felt like someone was pulling me from the fire. That's all I remember—except when I woke up, I was lying on the ground outside the house and someone was calling my name. Who pulled me out of the house?"

"We have no idea. One officer said he thought he saw two women in the yard before they got there."

"That seems impossible," Clay said. "You were alone, and all the other houses were empty. You somehow managed to get to safety by yourself."

I thought about it for a second, trying to remember. Was I being pulled? The ghosts of Ely and Kate came to mind. *Could it have been...?* I shook my head, deciding I was being too fanciful. But what if...?

The detective closed his note pad. "Thank you, Ms. Parsons. That should be enough for now."

"What about Frank? Did I shoot him?"

Clay started to answer when the policeman interrupted. "No. You shot the propane lantern. It exploded. It appears you either fell or were pushed into the stove, hitting your head, knocking it away from its chimney. Burning wood rolled onto the floor which is how you burned your wrist. It's good you managed to get away." He paused. "That portion of the house had the worst of the fire damage."

I looked at the bandage on my right arm.

"What about Frank? Where...?"

"When the lantern exploded, it must have sent a fireball and shrapnel his way and set the papers on the table on fire. From the tracks on the deck, it appears he ran or slid from the house, but... well, as you know there's a steep drop off at the edge of the deck. Even though he landed in a lot of brush, his head hit a boulder. The brush hid his body, which is why we had trouble finding him. His face showed burns."

"Does Josie know?"

"Yes, the police called her this morning," Clay said. "If it hadn't been for Josie, we would never have known Frank was headed your way."

"We have what we need from you. You'll need to testify at the inquest and against Mr. Mendoza. Please don't leave town." They shook hands with Clay and me before they left. "We'll be in touch."

My nurse came in as they were leaving to check my vitals. "Would you like to get out of bed?"

"Yes, I would."

"I'll bring in a wheelchair," she said as she released the blood pressure cuff from my arm.

As Clay pushed me toward a sitting room at the end of the hall, we spotted Josie headed our way. "Josie, what happened to you?" She had a black eye and her right arm was in a sling, something I hadn't noticed last night.

We were both looking at Josie when she started to cry. "Oh, Josie. I'm so sorry—I know you loved him." I started to get out of the chair so I could comfort her but I was so dizzy, I had to sit back down. I reached out for her, but Clay had already put his arms around her.

"It's okay, honey. You don't have to talk—I can explain everything if you'd like," Clay said. She nodded against his shoulder. "If I get anything wrong, you just speak up. Okay?" She nodded again as she pulled a Kleenex from her pocket and wiped her eyes.

Clay cleared his throat. "Josie was home doing chores. Frank was out and she didn't know where. When she was cleaning Frank's office, she happened to see a page with handwriting in the Old English style. It put her in mind of the Shakespeare page you had shown her. When she picked it up and started to read, she couldn't understand where Frank had got it. She felt it was related to your research and wanted to question Frank—so she called him. He hung up on her and a few minutes later he came home alone." Clay stopped talking and looked at Josie. "Do you want me to tell her about...?" Josie shook her head no and started to speak.

"He came home, and we had the biggest fight we'd ever had. He was so angry and accused me of spying on him. He finally told me when he started to test the page, invisible writing appeared. He said it was a page from a bigger letter. If he could get his hands on the other blank pages you had, he could sell them and get his gambling debts paid off." Josie paused for a minute, taking a couple of deep breaths, before continuing. "I made the mistake of telling him I was glad you were out of town so he couldn't get them. That's when he started to hit me, trying to force me to tell him where you were..." She paused again.

I was afraid for her to continue. "That's okay. I think I can figure out what happened next."

"No, let me finish," she said. "When he hit me in the chest, I sat down on the floor so I could protect my baby. I blurted out that he needed to stop because I was pregnant. That's when he really got mad. He hit me in the face and grabbed my arm and twisted it behind my back." She grimaced as she lifted the arm with the sling. "Dislocated my shoulder." She started to cry again. "I'm so sorry, Cynthia. I had to tell him where you were."

"Oh, honey. Don't talk about it. You've been through so much—so much more than me."

"She called me," Clay said. "I left immediately and drove to her house. It's a wonder I didn't get a ticket." He swallowed. "When I saw Josie, I knew I had to take her to the ER. Fortunately, we got there fast. They took her right in. I immediately called the police. I knew they needed to get to you before Frank did. I convinced them you were in danger." He paused. "Have I forgotten anything?" He looked at Josie.

"Other than I insisted you wait for me to go with you," she said. She looked at me. "I'm sorry I did." Josie started to cry again. "Waiting for the doctors to finish took a long time. If I hadn't insisted, maybe Clay could have got there before Frank."

"Please, don't think about it," I said. "What happened, happened. What about the cabin? Did it burn down?"

"No," Clay said. "The police were able to use fire extinguishers to put out the fire. Only the area around the table and fireplace were damaged." He paused again. "But honey, I hate to tell you. Sudie's page and Ely's sister's letter were destroyed."

Epilogue

Armed with flowers and gifts, Clay rang the bell to Josie's house. When she came to the door, I couldn't believe the change in her. Besides beaming with happiness and good health, she looked twenty pounds lighter.

"You're finally back," she squealed. After hugs all around, she asked, "How was England? I can't wait till you tell me everything."

"You'd better let us see the baby before I tell you a thing," I said.

Clay handed her a bouquet of carnations arranged inside a vase. "We purchased this in Staffordshire for you."

"It's a beautiful vase. Thanks so much. The baby's sleeping in the kitchen. I was making a batch of cookies. Come on back."

Josie put the flowers on the dining room table and we entered the kitchen. The wonderful odor of baking assailed us.

"What a little sweetie. Clay, isn't she beautiful?" She wasn't sleeping, her blue eyes taking us in. She was fastened in a little bouncy chair Josie had sitting on the table." I sat on a chair near the baby. "Look how she's grown. Do I dare pick her up?" I asked. Clay softly scratched her little belly and she gave him a big smile. "She's smiling."

"She's been doing that for a long time now." I unhooked the strap around her middle and picked her up. Josie took another batch of cookies from the oven and slid them onto a wire rack on the counter, then turned off the oven. "There. That's finished. How about a cup of coffee?"

"I thought you'd never ask," Clay said as he stole a cookie. "Chocolate chip. My favorite." Josie poured a cup of coffee and handed it to him.

"Why do you think I made them?" She grinned, giving him a sideways glance. "By the way, congratulations on the election. Do I call you 'judge' now?"

"Please don't—at least until I hear a few cases." He laughed. "But thanks. No big accomplishment since I was unopposed."

"Let's go into the living room and visit." She put two more cups of coffee on a tray along with a plate of cookies. I happily carried her baby. Josie named her Cynthia Ely but I insisted she call her Elly.

I sat on the sofa with Clay alongside of me. I couldn't take my eyes off the baby, trying to get her to smile for me. Josie set the tray onto the coffee table and sat in a padded rocking chair.

"Okay, you two. Tell me about the trip."

"Clay, where shall we begin?" He put his arm around me.

"While we were in London, we stayed at The Savoy." He winked at Josie. "That was our official honeymoon."

"My, how grand," she said. "So you did all the touristy things?"

"Yes, and we saw two plays at The Globe. You know they restored it just like it was originally. We splurged and rented cushions and sat on the top tier," I said. "We saw *A Midsummer Night's Dream* and *Hamlet*. So amazing."

We both chimed in, telling her all that we had seen and done while in London. "I couldn't convince her to go on the London Eye, though," Clay said.

"Heights are one thing I'm not so good at. He had to do that alone. Besides, to me, a huge Ferris wheel in the heart of an ancient city seems out of place."

"You have to admit, I did get some amazing photos," Clay said. "We learned how to use the Tube and buses. Didn't need a car until we left the city."

I chimed in. "Our first stop was Windsor Castle, and you won't believe what I saw. I don't know if it was a painting of Ely, but think it might have been."

"Tell me," Josie said.

"In the queen's bedroom—Queen Elizabeth the first, that is—there's a painting of her, and on the opposite side of the fireplace is a painting of a woman. The docent said it was an unknown woman, and what I noticed was she had the same color of hair as the queen, and the artist had included faint blue veins in the side of her forehead. Of course, there are dozens of paintings throughout the castle, but why one so prominent in her bedroom? I'd like to think it was Ely."

The baby began to cry. Josie said she needed to change her diaper, and I followed her into the hallway and then her bedroom. The doorbell rang about that time and I offered to change Elly so Josie could answer the door. I heard her and Clay talking to someone. After the baby had on a dry diaper, I went back into the living room where Josie and Clay were talking to a young man in his mid-thirties. He was fairly short, about my height, with brown hair that had begun to thin out on top, and clean shaven. I remembered meeting him briefly at the hospital when Elly was born.

"Cynthia, this is Brian Jamison." Josie took the baby from my arms so I could shake hands with him.

"I saw you at the hospital, but don't believe you met my husband, Clay Darnell."

"Josie just introduced us," Clay said.

"Josie and I went to high school together." Brian blushed a bit and I thought, what an endearing quality. The baby was crying in earnest.

"I'm going to need to feed her." Josie looked at Clay. "Would you please get Brian a cup of coffee in the kitchen?"

After she and I were back in the bedroom, Josie settled down in a wooden rocking chair. "I wouldn't have been embarrassed to feed her in front of you and Clay, especially with a blanket over my shoulder, but Brian is a bit shy."

After she was settled with the baby nursing, I asked, "So tell me, how did you and Brian reconnect?"

"We met again at a class reunion picnic in August. I was eight months along and as big as a house. We ended up sitting at the same table and got to visiting. Found out neither one of us was married, but I did tell him about Frank and the accident. He asked if he could call me sometimes, and I agreed." She shifted the baby into a more comfortable position. "He came to see me at the hospital when Elly was born, and we started seeing each other regularly about the time you left on your honeymoon."

"I'm so happy for you, Josie. So, developing into something serious, you think?"

"I think so. He's a good person—a hundred and eighty degrees different from Frank. And he loves Elly." Josie kissed her baby on her fuzzy hair.

"Where does he work?"

"In Salem, as a claims adjuster for the State Insurance Fund. A good future, I think." The baby was sound asleep and had stopped nursing. "And he doesn't believe in gambling." She put the sleeping baby into the crib near her bed, fixed her bra, and buttoned her blouse back up.

When we rejoined the men, I could tell they were getting along famously. We spent the next hour telling them about our trip. "After London, we rented a car," Clay said. "An experience never to be forgotten. Not only driving on the wrong side of the road, but those roundabouts took a lot of getting used to. We drove all over England."

"Where did you go?"

"After Windsor Castle, then Stonehenge, and a couple of days in Bath. Then to Cambridge and then Oxford," I said.

"We got lost in Oxford looking for the B&B we had booked," Clay said. "She needed to find a restroom so bad, I had to park the car by a hedge. Then I needed to dig through the suitcase to find a change of slacks for her."

"You didn't have to tell them that!" I said as we all laughed. "We then stopped in Stratford-upon-Avon and spent the night there. Then we drove to Staffordshire and stayed in another B&B in Derby. We spent about a week in the area. The highlight of the trip, though, was when we went to Rocester. Coincidently, we met a woman who was carrying flowers into St. Michael's church. We introduced ourselves and before I remembered I was married, I said Cynthia Parsons. She said there was a Parsons family that had lived there for generations."

"She was great," Clay said. "I mentioned the name Trentham, and she was familiar with that name, too." Clay put his arm around my shoulder. "We may be long—long, long ago cousins. Anyway, she took us on a tour of St. Michael's church. It's the third one built on that site. She showed us a painting of the old abbey tower and gave us a history of the town."

"We roamed through the entire graveyard surrounding the church. The earliest tombstone I could find was in the 1700s and she thought there were probably older graves beneath. There was a stone wall around the graveyard and she thought the stones were from the original Roman fort on this same site."

"Next stop was in Chester, then in the Lake District."

"Speaking of that," I said. "While we were there, we visited the Beatrix Potter museum and I bought a Peter Rabbit book for Elly." I picked up a sack and removed the book.

"We ended up in Scotland and spent a week there," Clay

continued. "By then, I was so tired of driving, I turned the car in and we took the train back to London."

"We went to Paris for a few days. Spent time with Colleen. Then to Germany so Clay could meet Mark. He was kind of in the dumps, as he and his fiancée had broken up."

"I showed him a picture of Colleen, and he said he'd call on her next time he's in Paris," Clay said. "You never know what may happen."

"What a great trip," Josie said. "I'd love to go someday—when Elly is old enough to appreciate it." Brian acted like he wanted to say something, but kept quiet. "Did you gather enough information to finish the book?"

"Yes, I think so. I feel terrible about Sudie's page and Kate's letter being destroyed. It would have added so much to the book."

"But you have copies, don't you?" Josie asked.

"They were on my phone." The feeling of guilt swamped me. "I should have downloaded the pictures onto my laptop, but never got around to it."

"The phone is lost," Clay said.

"Oh no," Josie said. "Where...?"

"I don't know. We inquired everywhere I may have left it. I suspect someone found it and..."

"Cynthia. Don't keep beating yourself up about it. You have more than enough evidence to prove Shakespeare was in fact Ely and Edward," Clay said.

"He's right, Cynthia. Your book will be convincing even without the *Midsummer* page and Kate's letter."

Clay and Josie's trying to cheer me was comforting. But I knew in my heart it wasn't just finding the page, or our research. It was the chain of events, both normal and paranormal, and the many coincidences that occurred along the way that led me to the woman who was Shakespeare. Sudie was right...it all had to do with timing.

The time is finally right for the woman to reveal herself. And why I was chosen to be the messenger—is anyone's guess.

Author's Notes

To keep as close as possible to facts, the reader may note the transition from the historical reference to Edward Vere, the Earl of Oxenford, to de Vere and Oxford.

Elizabeth using the nickname, Ely, is found at the bottom of an untitled poem the author believes to be written by her. It begins: "When I was fair and young then favor graced me."

The question of what is true and what is imagined in the life of Elizabeth Trentham may need clarification.

What's true:

* She was born circa 1560.

* She grew up in Rocester, Staffordshire as the eldest child of Thomas Trentham III and Jane Sneyd.

*The history of the townships of Rocester and Chester.

*At the age of nineteen or twenty, she became a maid of honor in Queen Elizabeth I's court and remained unmarried for ten more years.

*She served as executrix of Thomas Trentham III's will.

*She married Edward de Vere, the Seventeenth Earl of Oxford in 1591 or 1592, and had a son, Henry.

*Edward de Vere died in 1604.

*She died in December 1612—the same year William Shakespeare retired.

*In her will, she leaves money to her "dumb" man.

Other accuracies of all historical characters may be found by exploring the internet.

What is speculated is Elizabeth's relationship to Queen Elizabeth I. Was she the queen's granddaughter? Research reveals that all the Trentham children's births are noted in the Staffordshire records, but Elizabeth's is not. Also, researchers have found that she may have been the queen's goddaughter. The author questioned both, and came up with an imagined explanation. This may be why the resemblance between Elizabeth and the queen is similar. Also, this may be the reason Elizabeth Trentham Vere was purposely kept in the shadows and why a portrait has never been found, even though she was countess to the Earl of Oxford. Unless, because of their close resemblance, perhaps one of Queen Elizabeth's many portraits is actually that of Elizabeth Trentham.

With regard to Elizabeth's translating the Psalms for King James, the author has no proof, only speculation on how else the words "shake" and "spear" appear in the 46th chapter at exactly the 46th word from the beginning and the 46th word from the end of the chapter. Also speculated is Chapter 46, 3rd verse...why add an extra "her" to the verse and add the words: "right early?" The correlation between Chapter 46, 9th verse, "cuttteth the spear" and other clues in the Oxford crest of the female lion is indeed compelling evidence Elizabeth Trentham de Vere was also Shakespeare.

Meet Deena Lindstedt

Deena is a widow living in Tigard, Oregon. She has three sons, nine grandchildren, and six great-grandchildren. Following her twenty-five-year career in the field of workers' compensation claims administration, besides going back to college, she devoted herself to a second marriage to Donald Lindstedt and living in Cannon Beach, Oregon. Her first novel, *Deception Cove,* was published by Wings ePress in 2010. Following Don's death in 2014, she moved to Tigard, Oregon to be closer to family. She is kept busy with writing and meetings with writers' groups. She is a member of P.E.O. and plays bridge once a week.

Besides her novel, *Deception Cove,* other fiction honors include third place winner for a poem: "Two Ladies of Chedigny" for Willamette Writers, Portland, Finalist for short story: *Simply to Fly* for NW Writers Association contest in Seattle. She presented a paper at the Virginia Woolf Conference, Lewis and Clark University and was a guest speaker at the 2011 Shakespeare Authorship Symposium delivering her paper, "Shakespeare, Perhaps a Woman."

Other Works From The Pen Of

Deena Lindstedt

Deception Cove - An insurance investigator discovers she has married a drug smuggler. While investigating his death, she gains insight into herself, finding love and peril in the process.

Book Club Discussion Questions

1. How did you feel about the interwoven modern and historical stories?

2. Was there a smooth transition between the two stories?

3. Who was your favorite modern character—and why?

4. Did you find you wanted to do your own research into historical characters and events?

5. Other than the Shakespeare quotes at the beginning of each historical chapter, did you find other quotes?

6. Were the fictional use of finding an original page from *A Midsummer Night's Dream,* and Katherine Stanhope's letter written in invisible ink believable?

7. Did appearances of the ghostly apparitions add to the story, or were they too farfetched?

8. What is your opinion about the ending of the modern story? How would you have changed it?

9. What changes/decisions would you hope for if the book were turned into a movie?

10. Do you have a new perspective as to who actually was Shakespeare?

Letter to Our Readers

Enjoy this book?

You can make a difference.

As an independent publisher, Wings ePress, Inc. does not have the financial clout of the large New York publishers. We can't afford large magazine spreads or subway posters to tell people about our quality books.

But we do have something much more effective and powerful than ads. We have a large base of loyal readers.

Honest reviews help bring the attention of new readers to our books.

If you enjoyed this book, we would appreciate it if you would spend a few minutes posting a review on the site where you purchased this book or on the Wings ePress, Inc. webpages at: https://wingsepress.com/

Thank You